P9-AFU-798

RANDOM HOUSE
LARGE
PRINT

ALSO BY MARTHA HALL KELLY
AVAILABLE FROM
RANDOM HOUSE LARGE PRINT

Sunflower Sisters
Lost Roses

THE GOLDEN DOVES

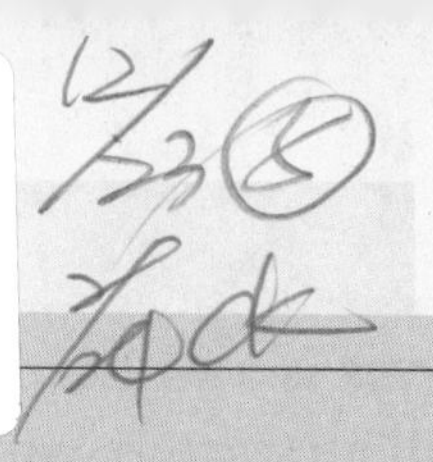

THE GOLDEN DOVES

A NOVEL

MARTHA HALL KELLY

The Golden Doves is a work of fiction. All incidents and dialogue, and all characters with the exception of some well-known historical figures, are products of the author's imagination and are not to be construed as real. Where real-life historical persons appear, the situations, incidents, and dialogues concerning those persons are entirely fictional and are not intended to depict actual events or to change the entirely fictional nature of the work. In all other respects, any resemblance to persons living or dead is entirely coincidental.

Published in the United States of America by Random House Large Print in association with Ballantine Books, an imprint of Random House, a division of Penguin Random House LLC, New York.

Cover design: Laura Klynstra
Cover images: Ildiko Neer/Trevillion Images (women); Brzozowska/Getty Images (Paris view)
Title-page art from dreamtime and stock.adobe.com

The Library of Congress has established a Cataloging-in-Publication record for this title.

ISBN: 978-0-593-67836-7

www.penguinrandomhouse.com/large-print-format-books

FIRST LARGE PRINT EDITION

Printed in the United States of America

1st Printing

For all the women who survived Ravensbrück.

And those who never came home.

THE GOLDEN DOVES

CHAPTER 1

JOSIE

FORT BLISS, TEXAS
1952

I WAKE AT DAWN, FACEDOWN ON THE SOFA, thinking I'm back in Block Ten. The living room window's open a crack, and another Texas dust storm blows like hell outside, pummeling the room with more sand than dust. I swing my feet to the floor, head pounding. Sixty-five dossier photos taped above the sofa flutter in the wind, and the men look down on me.

Mengele. Von Braun. Speer.

I stand, head for the window, and kick over a half-full beer can. "Shit."

A gust hits my little shrine on the coffee table, the votive still flickering under my mother's picture and the photo of Arlette and me, arms linked at liberation. The wind catches my mother's photo and sails it into the air. I lunge to catch it before it falls, and then set it back in its spot.

I shuffle to the window, sand swirling in the air outside, so thick that the Franklin Mountains in the distance are just blurry mounds. A pigeon sits outside on the sill waiting out the storm. I wave her away and thump the window closed.

The kitchen wall clock reads 6:30 A.M. I'm already late.

Can't wait to get this over with. Hopefully a routine job. By my rules this time.

I pull on my regulation pinkish skirt, green blouse, and drab field jacket, then slide my silver PPK into my shoulder holster. That simple act calms me, the brown grip the perfect size for my hand. It's the Nazi police gun I confiscated from the suitcase of an incoming scientist, who swore he didn't know how it got there.

I stuff a pair of hospital gloves into one pocket, grab the welcome basket, and drive a government-issued jeep past the massive rocket at the entrance that reads WELCOME TO FORT BLISS: YOUR ARMY ANTI-AIRCRAFT AND GUIDED MISSILE CENTER.

I read the latest dossier as I drive. They all had quirks from their intake forms. One bathes obsessively. One masturbates too much. Krupp's quirk is that he's fastidious about his clothes and insisted he and his wife, Irma, buy all new luggage for the trip, specifying the exact models of the suitcases. Each new scientist was bound by their contract to declare the contents of each bag, but he'd written a missive on the packed items, down to his ten pairs of undershorts and his wife's cosmetic collection.

I find 210 Canyon Road, on the outskirts of a Fort Bliss residential neighborhood, a basic El Paso two-bedroom ranch house trying its best to be nondescript. It's the kind of place where military families come to forget the war and forge blindly into the 1950s with the help of bourbon and barbecue.

Only this is no average family.

I press the doorbell and stand in the stinging wind listening to the Westminster chimes, my palms wet on the cellophane of the basket. I survey the olive branch of a gift the Intake Group has assembled; a cheap woven bowl filled with someone's idea of foods representing American and German cultures. A can of Spam. Some stollen one of the secretaries baked. Oreo cookies, a bottle of Riesling wine, and a six-pack of Pearl beer.

I go to press the bell again and he opens the door a crack. **"Jah?"**

Just hearing that accent, my skin tries to crawl off my body. "Open up, Mr. Krupp. It's Lieutenant Anderson."

He swings the door wider to reveal Mrs. Krupp and two male children bathed in the yellow light of the foyer.

I consider getting back in the jeep and telling

Tony P. to do his own intake from now on. Not that he can ever tell if these criminals are hiding anything. He usually ends up knocking back beers with them after a cursory look in their bags.

"I'm here to do your intake briefing, Mr. Krupp."

The mother holds her children closer.

He beckons me in. **"Guten morgen."**

What would Krupp do if I took my gun and waved it in his face like the Ravensbrück guards used to do to us for fun?

"English only, Mr. Krupp."

"Please enter," he says and reaches to guide me in.

I step back. "Don't touch me, sir."

It's the same interior all these houses have, low popcorn ceiling, black iron handrails leading to a sunken living room, the carpet still wearing its vacuum marks. It smells like Pine-Sol and pancakes, and the only object in the room is a low oak cabinet, inset with a television, the green screen like one unblinking eye.

Herr Krupp steps back, wringing his hands. "We haven't much furniture yet, though we were promised it."

He looks nothing like his photo from the dossier. He's at least ten years older, a bit stooped, and has lost the cocky grin of the old Reich days. A flat worm of a saber scar shines along his left cheek. The aristocratic badge of honor, proof he can take the pain. It's the fashionable accessory that every German fencer longed to collect in great numbers, but Herr Krupp was happy with only one.

Without the SS uniform he's smaller somehow, but my hands sweat just the same.

Mrs. Krupp is more attractive in person, brunette, and gets points for wearing faux pearls and a petticoated dress at this hour of the morning, after traveling all night. For my benefit? She wears no makeup and looks worried, but she'll shortly bond with the wives of the other Nazis brought here for the rocket program and will soon be bringing tuna casserole to the potlucks at the pool as they reminisce about how handsome Hitler was.

"What is the purpose of this meeting?" she asks.

"To officially welcome you." **And make sure you haven't smuggled in half the Reich's treasury.** "You two meet me in the kitchen."

She clutches the boys closer. "But the children."

"Do I have to ask you again?"

The two shuffle off, casting back looks, and I pull the Oreos from the welcome basket, take the children to the television, turn it on, and motion for them to sit in front of it.

Crisscross applesauce. They're becoming American already. I wait for the tube to warm up, and soon the game show **Winner Take All** appears with Bill Cullen wearing a striped tie.

"Do you want to be a **winner**?" the announcer shouts, and the audience claps.

A chiropractor from Grand Rapids has just won a generous supply of Prom home permanent and a $250 U.S. defense bond.

The younger boy looks up at me, tears in his blue eyes.

They're so young and scared. It's not their fault their father is a murderer.

I hand him the package. "Go ahead," I say in German. "Open the cookies."

Welcome basket in hand, I head for the kitchen, where the Krupps wait under bright fluorescent lights, giving them both a hollowed-out look as they sit at their new cherry-red table and pleather upholstered chairs. Their luggage is stacked against the wall, and on the refrigerator someone has trapped a postcard under a grinning sun face magnet that reads **Welcome to El Paso!** A plate of pancakes the cafeteria must have sent over sits on the counter, untouched. Mr. Krupp crosses his legs, arms folded across his chest.

I lob the beer into the fridge, lean against the counter, and read his folder. "Ah, I see. One of the good Nazis. So, they've made you a glowing résumé. This is what you call a **Persilscheine,** isn't it, Mr. Krupp?"

He looks out the window. They're always astonished they've been accused of doing anything wrong.

"What's that word mean, Mr. Krupp?"

"Detergent."

"That's right. It's cleaned you up well. Says here you worked on a farm. Were pressed against your will to support Hitler. I think your past needed a good bit of cleaning, didn't it? Luckily, we have some additional reports on you."

"I am the victim here."

I take up my clipboard. "Name?"

"Please, can we do this another time?" Krupp asks. "We've only just arrived, and my wife is tired from the long journey. She is not happy with the degrading medical examination she was forced to have upon arrival last night. And she thinks the milk is not fresh."

"Name."

"Herbert Krupp."

"Born?"

"Munich."

"List any medals you have received in the service to your country."

"None."

"Not even the War Merit Cross? No Art and Science award?"

He runs his fingers through his hair. "Absolutely not."

"Last place of employment?"

He hesitates and glances about the kitchen.

I hover my pen above the space. "Let's just say the Reich." I fill in the blank with a swastika. "And where were you employed by the Reich, Mr. Krupp?"

"Outside of Bonn. At IG Farben."

"In what capacity?"

"In the household products division. Soaps for the housewife."

"Did you visit any concentration camps?"

"Very infrequently. And only when ordered."

"Says here you often visited the IG Farben facility named IG Auschwitz. Buchenwald, too."

"I called upon certain places as a salesman."

"I see. And your visits to the camps had nothing to do with distributing Zyklon-B? Demonstrating its use?"

He frowns. "Oh, no."

I turn to Mrs. Krupp. "Do you know what that is, Mrs. Krupp? Zyklon-B?"

She shakes her head.

"It is a cyanide-based pesticide used at Nazi concentration camps to murder prisoners. It says here, your husband was second-in-command to the guy who ran that part of the company."

She looks away.

"But here you are, Mr. Krupp. On Canyon Road in your new kitchen. Last question. Have you in your possession any cash, securities, or valuables not declared on form twenty-one ten?"

"There are so many forms." Sweat appears on his upper lip.

"Have you in your possession—"

"Nein."

"English, Mr. Krupp."

He reaches toward me. "Can't you—"

I step back. "Do not touch me. I won't say it again."

I toss the clipboard onto the table. It lands with a clatter that startles them both, and then I step to the pile of suitcases. Each piece of brand-new Samsonite navy blue luggage wears a red paper tag, BAGGAGE INSPECTED printed in black.

I snap on the gloves. "Nice new suitcases. No traveling light for you."

Krupp sits a little straighter. "They've already searched our luggage."

I reach behind the pile, pull out an untagged cosmetic case, and heave it onto the table. "What about this one?"

The fluorescent lights overhead shine on the sweat beaded on Krupp's forehead. "It contains my wife's personal items."

I turn to her. "Well, you don't mind if a fellow female takes a look, do you?"

She meets my gaze, remarkably composed.

I try to lift it from the table. "This seems much too heavy, Mrs. Krupp. A naturally pretty lady like you doesn't need so many cosmetics. What would the Führer say?"

I open the case, flip open my penknife, and Mrs. Krupp gasps.

Mr. Krupp stands. "Is this necessary? I've been brought here by the U.S. Army. I demand to see your superior."

"Sit down, Mr. Krupp."

He sits as I shove aside the jars and bottles and slit the satin bottom of the case. I reach in, a thrum of pleasure running through me, as my fingers breach a layer of cotton and find the unmistakable feeling of pebbled cowhide. I pull out a red leather box, a Nazi swastika and eagle embossed on the cover in gold. Inside, nestled in the purple velvet, rests a silver starburst with an inner band of good-sized diamonds at the center, and a red-enameled plaque superimposed with the golden head of Athena.

The Art and Science award.

I'm at once overwhelmed with the beauty and repulsed to see it in the flesh. No wonder Albert Speer wanted this one.

I hold it, heavy in my palm. "They say the recipient had to wear a special mount to support the weight."

Mrs. Krupp speaks up. "We wouldn't know."

"Platinum, am I right? This could have gotten you all the way to South America."

It gleams in the light, reflecting my face in the gold of Athena's helmet.

I turn to Krupp. "Why did Hitler institute this award?"

He looks away.

"It was meant to replace the Nobel Prize, was it not? And what did Hitler call the Nobel?"

"I don't—"

"Say it."

Krupp lifts his chin but keeps his eyes averted. "He called it a Jew prize."

"There you go. And he was so thin-skinned, when a German pacifist won it, he threw him in a concentration camp and declared no German could accept the Nobel again. Only this prize. Am I right?"

Krupp stares at me, unblinking.

"Were you awarded this, or just pick it off some dead friend?"

"I don't know where it came from. My wife borrowed that case."

I set the award back in the box. "You can quit the act. I know you supervised the delivery of Zyklon-B to every one of Hitler's concentration camps personally. Demonstrated its use with human subjects. I have the paper trail."

The wife makes a choking sound and clutches her pearls.

"If I were in charge you'd be hanging at the end of a rope. But you're here now, and starting today, when you report to Area C, you'd better start coughing up whatever sciencey state secrets you allegedly have, and more info on your scientist pals, or it's back to the fatherland you go to stand trial."

I stash the box in my bag and start off toward the door but turn back.

"Before I go, I'm curious, Mr. Krupp. When you were at Buchenwald, did you see what was written on the gates there, at the entrance? The German phrase facing inside the camp so the prisoners could read it?"

He shakes his head.

"**Jedem das Seine.** Can you tell me what that means?"

"We are very tired—"

"Tell me, Mr. Krupp."

In the living room Bill Cullen laughs, and the audience applauds.

"One might say it means, 'Everyone gets what they deserve.' "

"That's right, Mr. Krupp. Do you think that's what you got? What you deserve? Mrs. Krupp?"

They both stare back at me, unblinking.

I head out. "No need to see me to the door. And by the way, the milk is fresh. Army personnel just stocked it last night."

"Jüdischer Hund," the wife says, under her breath.

I turn to her. "What did you say?"

She looks away.

I go back and snatch the six-pack from the fridge. "I was going to recommend they go easy on you for smuggling that award in here, on account of your children. But those kids are better off without you murderers, and I'll make sure my boss knows what you tried here."

I need air and hurry out the way I came, past the boys still watching television, Oreos unopened, and head out the door. Would Karl punish these two? Probably not. He'd looked past much worse to get scientists for this program. But at least someone has held them accountable.

En route to my office in the jeep, sand collecting on the windshield wipers, I crack open a Pearl, down it, and then a second. Just another Texas breakfast.

CHAPTER 2

ARLETTE

PARIS, FRANCE
1952

DAWN BREAKS AS I PICK MY WAY ALONG THE icy Île de la Cité streets, toward the café. I cut through the Flower and Bird Market, the stalls shielding me from the wind whipping off the Seine. My thoughts veer toward finding Willie, and I stuff them down. Too much pain to think about this early.

It's been seven years since the war ended, and the market has come a long way, with new concrete floors and flower stalls. No more Germans in SS uniforms. And every vendor now has a transistor radio in their stall emitting a scratchy aria or weather report.

I'm envious, for I've not come that far or improved in any way. I hug the purse at my side, the one I made from my old green camp dress after Josie and I were liberated, as I pass a perfect little nosegay of white tuberose. They symbolize innocence, something long gone for me. I continue walking. I have little money for food, never mind flowers, and besides, all-white flowers are too weddingish anyway.

I stop and then turn back. I'll probably never have a wedding of my own, so why not splurge? I hand the flower seller my last few francs and tuck the flowers inside the V of my dress, the blossoms cool against my skin. Just the scent says hope.

And I have something to celebrate, after all.

It still hurts to walk, even so many years later, but I focus on the letter in my pocket, for I'm about to burst with curiosity.

I pull it out and check the return address one more time.

Wagner. 10 Ox Herd Road, Berlin.

I make it to the café, its windows lit amber in the darkness, and take in the place, **Le Joyeux Oiseau Café** written in black script above the door. A former cobbler's shop, it's stuck along a row of shops down a side street near Notre-Dame, like a bad molar in a perfectly good row of teeth. It's not much to look at, but it's a life raft for me and the two other waitresses, Ravensbrück survivors all, cocooned away from the world.

I turn the brass knob and enter, the scent of bacon tartine and arabica beans in the air. There are only six tables inside, their veined marble tops pocked with decades of coffee drips, and a worn, claret red velvet-cushioned banquette along one wall.

The owner, Marianne, keeps us open mostly to fuel the flower merchants, a colorful mix of men from all over France. They live on caffeine and cigarettes, running back and forth in their cobalt smocks to the steamy greenhouses of Les Halles, keeping chilly Paris in tulips and ranunculus.

We're throwing a little benefit this morning, proceeds going to an organization that supports Ravensbrück survivors. Being a survivor is Marianne's one requirement for employment, and Bep, Riekie, and I are still like a camp family, having lost only Josie to America. Though Bep and Riekie are both from Holland, they've been here since Ravensbrück was liberated seven years ago and now seem just as French as the rest of us.

Marianne, a former sardine woman at Les Halles, stands at the counter rolling out short-crust pastry as Bep hurries by with a tray of glasses. "Who washed those?" Marianne calls out.

Curvy and frizzle-haired, Marianne, rather than wear a yellow star, spent the war in hiding, in a coffin-sized attic space, while her mother died at Ravensbrück. This place is her life, but she's growing weary of the job, as the bruise-purple rings under her eyes attest. She is up at four each morning to grind beans and scrub the tile floor.

She steps to the tray and holds up a water glass. "This one still has lipstick on the rim."

Her nephew Raphael rushes by with a tray of coffee cups. “Not my shade.”

Blond Raphael, with his strong arms and dark-lashed green eyes, looks to me and waits for the laugh he knows will come since he’s the funniest person I know.

I arrange my nosegay in a water glass and remind myself it’s important to look happy.

Marianne pulls me to her, one arm around my waist, releasing a wave of lavender soap.

“Why are you here, Arlette? It’s your day off.”

I shrug out of my coat. “Is it?” **One day is the same as the next.**

“You need to keep a calendar. And look at you, sketch pencil still tucked in your hair. You should be home designing dresses, not here trying to make this place chic. You could be a very good businesswoman.”

“Men distrust ambitious women.”

“Who needs men? You take care of you.”

I smile. “I only do this for the coffee.” **And because this is the only real family I’ve ever had.**

“Look at you, so thin. Have you forgotten to eat again?”

Had I? Some old chardonnay for dinner last night.

“Did you get your cat?”

Why had I mentioned my most fervent wish to her, of having an orange cat named Saffron someday? I wave that thought away. “No. I’m waiting for the right one to come along. But I can barely afford my own food.”

Bep rushes by. "Everyone will arrive at once as we open." She pours boiling water into a French press, lets the grounds steep, and pushes down the stopper. "Not one of them understands fashionably late."

We don't talk about the camp, about her baby Thea and the **Kinderzimmer,** but Bep has healed well, at least on the outside. Still waiflike, with skin the color of unripe cantaloupe, she has grown her hair long enough to wear in a thick braid down her back and married a cheesemonger from Lyon who keeps us all in free, perfectly ripe Saint-Marcellin. They have one son named Remi, and Bep is finally putting on some weight. Marianne has been trying to feed us like foie gras geese for years.

Dear Riekie hurries by carrying a stack of chairs, her hair white and as fine as milkweed silk. She's still so quick to smile, and has married a Frenchman as well, a flower merchant named Paul, with beautiful pansy-brown eyes, the perfect man for her, since he keeps their apartment filled with roses. A living testament to the axiom that women become more beautiful under men's desire, Riekie has never looked more radiant. We all know that Paul wants a family, but she can't bring herself to attempt another child.

Even Marianne has a beau, which leaves me the only unattached one.

I tie on my apron and wave the letter. "The return address says Wagner."

The room grows quiet.

Marianne comes closer. "Well? Open it."

Riekie sets down her chairs. "Your Gunther?"

I nod, fingers trembling.

Raphael is the only one who doesn't wear a look of breathless anticipation.

I slice the envelope top with a bread knife, open the page, and read aloud.

Dear Miss LaRue,

Regarding your third letter here, we must ask you to stop writing to us. If you choose to continue, you are hereby notified our next action will be a legal one.

Sincerely,

Mr. and Mrs. Werner Wagner

I grip the sink edge. "Oh, dear."

Bep pulls the note from my hand. "Let me see that. Gunther's parents? How dare they treat you so?"

Riekie rubs my back. "Did you ever meet them?"

I retrieve the note and slide it into my apron pocket. "No."

At least this letter is something new for my grief box, something they'd had us make in the Mothers with Loss class I attended once at Marianne's church. I decorated a child's shoebox a parishioner had donated, glued paper lace to the sides and wrote **Willie** on the top in script. It's the perfect place to keep the few things I still have that connect me to my son. A feather that belonged to our camp daughter Fleur.

A cloth version of **Puss and Boots.** A rubber teething ring. And a lock of blond hair, close to my shade, tied with an apricot-colored ribbon. I carry my little cardboard coffin of love with me everywhere I go.

Marianne leans in. "Well, they didn't say their son is dead. Gunther could be wounded. With amnesia."

"For seven years?" I ask.

"Did you ever tell them about Willie? Their grandchild, after all."

"No. Couldn't bring myself to. What if they'd taken him from me?" I straighten up. "But never mind this. We have work to do."

The wall clock strikes six and the chaos begins as the flower merchants stream in from the cold, huffing breath on their hands, coat pockets bulging with twine and stem nippers, their berets and stocking caps little defense against the cold.

They jockey for the best seats at the café tables. We bring them their French presses of coffee, and they discuss the problems of the flower business, which are many, and smoke and express their ongoing dissatisfaction with the world. More patrons enter, until there's no more space, and some wait outside.

"How can you operate a café without serving café crème, Marianne?" one patron calls out. "When are you going to get an espresso machine?"

"When you pay for it," Marianne shouts back. "Costs more than this whole shack is worth."

Each one shuffles to the donation jar Marianne

has placed atop the bar, to deposit a bill or jingle in some coins.

"Happy to help the best I can," says Guillaume, a gentle ape of a man with an opium habit, who pines for Marianne.

The jar fills quickly as Raphael joins me at the deep porcelain sink, which faces out at the room. We wash coffee cups, sleeves rolled, arms up to the elbows in scalding water and suds. I pull cup number ten thousand and seven from the water, the water stinging my hands. But it almost feels good. Penance.

Raphael leans closer to me, our shoulders touching. "So, tell me. Will I ever have a chance with you, Arlette? I know many men admire you, but please tell me I'm the frontrunner."

I smile and shove him with my shoulder.

One flower seller enters, carrying what must be his granddaughter on his hip. She's about a year old and dressed in a sweet lilac wool coat with white velvet trim.

"Look at that child," I say. Would I ever stop comparing children to my Willie?

"Beautiful," Raphael says with a certain sadness. "Remind you of your boy?"

I nod.

He clasps my hand for a moment under the water, warm and strong.

What would Willie look like today? A grown up nine-year-old. No longer a baby, of course. Still blond? Gunther was blond and I am too, so yes.

Not as light and baby fine as his hair was back then, probably darker by now. Would Willie still have that same sweet, expectant look he always did, as if just waiting to laugh at something? I conjure the feeling of holding him in my arms—

Raphael shakes my arm. "**Arlette.** Did you hear a word I said?"

"I'm sorry." I return to my washing.

"I said, 'Would you ever start another search?' "

I shake my head. "I lost everything looking for him."

"Maybe this time use someone more reputable. A real private detective. I have a little money saved up."

"That's kind of you, but I have to move on. I don't have an extra centime to pay a detective. As it is, I can only go to the Louvre on free days. The crowds . . ."

"I'm happy to take you. Even on full-price day."

"I have to become self-sufficient. Besides, I already owe all of you a king's ransom."

"Would you consider adopting?"

I keep my gaze on the cup in my hands, scrub a coffee stain off the rim, and rinse the smooth white china, purifying it.

Adopt? How many times had well-intentioned people suggested that? It would only be a dreadful reminder my son was gone. I'd visited the orphanage in Montparnasse, but could barely look at their expectant faces, so tragic.

If Gunther were here, he'd help me find Willie. I try to recall an image of Gunther, back before he marched off with Hitler's army, but I can barely summon him. He would have been a good father.

Riekie hurries over and bumps her hip into mine. **"Arlette."** She leans in, her head practically on my shoulder. "Don't look, but the gentleman in the corner in the camel hair overcoat keeps looking at you."

"Don't engage in craziness."

"It's true."

I bite my lips to make them pink and regret that my toilette, once my masterpiece, has been reduced to brushing my teeth. "Who wouldn't stare at a tall girl with messy hair and dressed like a rag picker?"

Bep approaches and leans in between us, her hair perfumed with cocoa from stirring the morning chocolate. "We both know you could model those clothes you design. You're the closest thing to stunning this place has ever seen."

Maybe once.

I slide the pencil from my hair and toss it on the counter.

Riekie cranes her neck for a better view. "He looks like the type who buys expensive presents."

I shrug one shoulder. "Dangling jewels don't suit me."

Riekie smiles. "I guess you're used to the male gaze. But it's usually only Raphael who stares at you."

Raphael wipes something off my cheek with his damp thumb. "Me, attentive? She often has marmalade stuck on her face. Trying to keep the help clean for the customers."

"Don't look," Bep says, "but he's coming this way."

The man in the camel hair overcoat works his way through the crowd. I glance at him as he approaches. Some might find him attractive, in a rich way, with his dark hair and pink scarf folded at his throat. Hard to place him age-wise. Early forties, maybe? He carries a wood-handled umbrella, too prepared for my taste. How does one do the most romantic thing in Paris, stand in the middle of the street in the rain and kiss, wet to the core, if one brings an umbrella?

He leans across the counter to me. "The coffee was very good."

I keep my gaze on my work.

He takes a folded stack of bills from his coat pocket and slides it into the jar.

Bep slumps into me, and I hold her up by the arm.

Marianne comes by and considers our new friend.

"Thank you for donating, sir," I say, rinsing a cup.

He nods. "I'm Luc Minau."

I glance in his direction.

"Are you Arlette Dagmar LaRue?" he asks.

I set the cup in the drainer. "And if I am?"

"I have some important information for you." He holds out an ecru card. Bep takes it and holds it up for me to read. It's nicely engraved.

MAÎTRE LUC MINAU

PRATICIEN DU DROIT

10 RUE DES ROSIERS, FRANCE

I try to look casual, pull the dishcloth from my shoulder, and dry the cup. "What is this about?"

"Happy to explain. Kindly meet me at my office tomorrow at noon."

I continue drying as he walks toward the door and steps out.

Bep rushes to the jar, extracts the bills, and thumbs through them. "There must be one thousand francs here, Arlette. You weren't very friendly."

Riekie watches over her shoulder. "I do admire a man confident enough to wear pink. And I know you like your men on the scruffier side, but he's not bad looking."

"Tall, too," Bep says, pointedly at me, as if he's the only man my height in Paris.

I sling the dishcloth over my shoulder. "If he's indeed a lawyer as the card says, I doubt he's interested in me. Plus, he's at least fifteen years older."

Bep takes the cup from my hand. "Mature men can be very sexy."

"He looks shifty," Raphael says and walks off.

Marianne comes to my side. "It's good to be careful, my dear. You were smart not to be too nice."

"What's this information he has?" Bep asks. "With an office on rue des Rosiers he must be legit."

I examine the card. "Could be a fake. I attract lowlifes."

Marianne slides her arm around my waist. "Don't be ashamed you were taken in by a charlatan. I've gotten calls myself, about my mother mysteriously being alive. Don't you think I wanted to believe it?"

I watch Mr. Minau as he stands just outside the door buttoning his coat. "I suppose it's possible he knows something about Willie."

"Why not do your own investigation? You were a Dove, after all, one of our—"

I hold up one hand. "**No.** I'm done with all that. It leads to nothing but trouble. I just want a normal life. No espionage."

Marianne rubs my back. "Well then, meet with this man. Shall I come with you?"

Her concerned look makes me smile. "I'll be fine. It's a good address."

"Just don't hand over any money."

I link arms with her. "That's easy. I have none to give."

Bep slides the bills back into the jar. "Or maybe he's here to tell you your aunt has left you a fortune."

Just the mention of Auntie sends my stomach churning. I'd kept that so secret.

"The question is how did he find me?"

I watch Luc Minau walk across the street.

"I'm afraid my past is about to catch up with me."

CHAPTER 3

JOSIE

FORT BLISS, TEXAS
1952

I WAKE UP IN SYSTEMS AND PROCEDURES CLASS to my boss, Karl Crowell, shaking my shoulder. Rows of agents turn at their desks and stare at us. Tony P. stands at the overhead projector in the dark room, a page from the **U.S. Army Field Manual** projected on the wall: "How to Tell a Harmless Former German Wehrmacht Soldier from a Committed Nazi."

"Anderson," Karl says. "Your office. Now."

"Way to go, Anderson," Tony calls to me as we leave and the others snicker.

Clutching a folder in one hand, Karl follows me into my office, deep in the bowels of the building basement, the muffled boom of Skysweeper guns coming from the training field above.

It's my low-ceilinged, air-conditioned cube of calm, a whiff of cafeteria pork chop in the air, dossier headshots of Nazis taped on every inch of the walls. I have everything I need for tracking them. Telex, when it works. Typewriter. And the massive bulletin board I'd rigged, on which hung a map of the world, crisscrossed with thumbtacks and colored yarn.

"Come in, Karl."

"Wow. Is this an actual office?"

He seems overwhelmed by all the Nazi faces on the walls and glances at me with a look of alarm.

I wave him toward my chair. "I'd live here if they let me."

"Do you always sleep through class, Anderson? You only need ten more credits to be eligible for promotion."

"Only when Tony P. is teaching. He turns the lights off. Besides, I'm good right here. I don't want a promotion."

"You probably already know it all," Karl says.

Six days a week I track them. Examine photos, culling ordinary German soldiers from hardcore believers, helping to decide which of Hitler's scientists to bring to our program, looking for the so-called repentant ones, "minor offenders." I analyze their postures, SS blood-group tattoos, the dueling scars of the more privileged ones, and patches ripped from their uniforms, the cloth beneath unfaded. I listen to Nazis on tape as well, sorting lies from truth.

The Telex comes to life, and I step to it as a message comes through. CIC CLASSIFIED. ASSET CLAIMED IN LUXEMBOURG. EINSTEIN TO BRIEF HEMINGWAY.

Karl reads it over my shoulder. "Who's Einstein?"

"Me. Tony P. assigned code names. Gave me Einstein since I can add."

"Smart-aleck."

"And gave himself Hemingway since he thinks he can write. Narcissist."

Karl steps to the bulletin board. "What's with the yarn?"

"Indicates our Operation Paperclip scientists either expected here or being actively recruited. Green means 'Asset in transit.' Red is 'Asset pending contract approval.' "

"And the black thumbtacks?"

"Cyanide. They won't be joining us."

"Hope you're not encouraging them."

"Would that be so bad, Karl?"

"And the yellow yarn is the ratline from Spain to South America?"

"Yes. Yellow for Nazi cowards."

"And the red thumbtacks? There must be—"

"Six hundred and twenty-three. Those are the uncategorized Nazis 'at large.' Just the ones recently missing. Three and a half **million** Nazis were indictable, Karl, and we've still tried only a tiny fraction of that. Half of them are coming here through legit immigration every day."

"Got any on your radar from that camp you were in?"

"Ravensbrück?" I look away. "Perhaps."

"You do realize you report to me, right?"

"There's one named Snow I'm interested in. Behind some of the worst things at the camp. Disappeared after liberation, never tried, but I've been picking up some chatter."

"Useful to the weapons program?"

"Not sure. Specialist in infectious diseases, I think. He selected my mother—"

"I know it's hard, Josie, but you gotta stick to scientists we need. Chemists. Aerospace engineers. Keep this strictly business."

"I'm sure there are files about Snow in the system. If I just had a higher security clearance . . ."

"Focus on your job you do so well, which is bringing the useful ones here. Like Krupp. He knows a lot from working at IG Farben."

"I bet."

"But we got a complaint from them. You need to schmooze these former Nazis more."

" 'Former,' Karl? Krupp lied the whole interview."

"That's a serious accusation."

"He rubbed the tip of his nose, a grooming gesture. When liars get nervous, the blood vessels at the tips of their fingers, earlobes, and noses shrink and they itch."

Karl starts to touch his ear, then stops himself.

I step to the wall safe. "Krupp also displayed at least twenty-six other deceptive indicators. Aggression. Anchor-point movements like toe tapping. He's definitely guilty of a lot more than he admits."

Karl gives me his concerned look. "Don't get me wrong. You do a great job investigating these guys, Anderson. But you gotta follow the rules. On the intake forms write **National Socialist Party** not just a swastika."

I open the safe and slide out the red leather box, remove Krupp's medal, and toss it to Karl.

He catches it. "Jesus, Anderson. Careful."

"That's enough platinum to live in South America for the rest of their lives. You need to do something this time. Hold them accountable."

Karl sets the award on his palm and inspects it. "Wow, this is nuts."

I pluck it from him and nestle it back into the velvet. "We spend a fortune getting guys like Krupp here for a cushy life of Lawrence Welk and Fritos, and if they have the money, they disappear to Argentina? It's un-American."

"Don't waste your time fighting it. Their kind of technical expertise could give us a ten-year jump on Russia."

"Some of these criminals have been here five years already, and what have they contributed?"

"Run-proof stockings," Karl says, like that should

be meaningful to me. "And now yeast can be made in unlimited quantities."

"Hitler's wizards."

Karl steps to the headshot taped to the wall, of Nazi cover boy Wernher von Braun, the aerospace engineer the army brought to Fort Bliss after the war. "This one's been very helpful."

"He complained about the cafeteria chicken, Karl. You know what the Nazis fed us at Ravensbrück? Nothing. And we just ignore the almost three thousand London casualties from the V-2 rockets von Braun designed? The 561 moviegoers who died in Antwerp when a V-2 fell on the theater?"

"He says he's sorry about all that. And claims he was forced to join the party."

"You know he's just lying to save his skin. Like they all do."

Karl leans against my desk. "I hear you, Anderson, but in future intakes you need to tone it down. You're a woman. You must have motherly instincts. The Krupps have **kids.**"

"Nazis don't understand mercy. Or kindness. And do you know what they did to kids at Ravensbrück? The ones they didn't kill outright, they starved."

He jams his hands into his pockets and looks at the floor.

"These very guys, Karl. Just seven years ago. Not like the Dark Ages. You don't know what it's like to see them here, so comfortable." I hand Karl the case. "And the wife called me a **Jewish dog.**"

"How'd she know? You don't look all that Jewish."

"Do you know how wrong it is to say that, Karl?"

"Hey, I need a favor. You know the girl coming in. Nina Iwanska?" Karl holds out a photo, a Polish girl well known at the camp.

"Another face-to-face? That's Tony P.'s job, Karl. I need to stay here—"

"You know her?"

"Everyone did."

"She was a victim of the sulfa experiments—"

"I know, Karl."

"Thought you might like to see her. Reconnect."

"It wasn't sleepaway camp."

"Turns out our Dr. Schreiber may have done some things he didn't report on his intake form."

"Shocking. Former surgeon general of the Third Reich? Bet he left out a lot."

"They're sending him here from Randolph Field so Iwanska can ID him, so now we've inherited it. She says he was more involved in those sulfa experiments than he admitted as a witness at the Nuremberg trials. All we need is a positive ID from her and she can go."

"I never saw Schreiber at Ravensbrück. Most of the doctors were pretty good at hiding their identities."

"**The Boston Globe** got wind of it, and now it's a shitstorm. A group of Boston physicians wrote to Truman to expel Schreiber." Karl lobs the folder onto my desk. "JIOA is up my ass, too, now."

"I don't get it."

Karl looks at me like I'm twelve. "The JIOA is the subcommittee of the president's Joint Chiefs of Staff from each military service branch and—"

"Please, Karl. I know what JIOA is. I just don't get why they're holding on to Schreiber so tightly. He's not that valuable. Just send him back to Germany."

"And let Russia get him? No way. And we can't fight JIOA. They tell Truman what to do."

"But it's cruel making Nina look at this guy."

"They want an in-person ID. Sending him over today."

"Do I get a higher security clearance?"

"Are you in or not?"

"Know what it's like for survivors to come within five feet of these men? It's terrifying. He chopped her up without anesthe—"

He holds up one hand. "If it turns out Schreiber's contract will not be renewed, you'll order an unmarked transport to meet you outside of town, since reporters are waiting at the gate to follow every army truck that leaves here these days. Arrange for them to get Schreiber to Baton Rouge to meet his family and then on a ship to Buenos Aires. He has a daughter there, and I'm sure Perón will welcome him."

"Maybe we can fly him first class."

"JIOA has asked that you treat him well. Don't give him the bum's rush if it comes to that. If you make it all go away, there may be a new assignment in your future."

"Fieldwork? No, Karl."

"I already put you in for authentication. Gotta liberate you from this spider hole. Come see me when Schreiber's done, and we'll talk. It's a big assignment, Josie. Not easy, but it'll be worth coming out into the sun."

I CHEW DOWN A whole sleeve of Tums on my drive to the Schreiber ID. I slow as I pass the tennis court, where four German scientists play doubles in their sweatpants. I tamp down the rage as one lobs a winning shot, and the winners erupt in cheers.

But at least there's one bright spot. Though I didn't know her well, the prospect of seeing Nina Iwanska again is weirdly comforting, not that I'd tell Karl that. She and her physician sister had led the fight against the doctors experimenting on them. The whole camp rallied around those girls when the Nazis tried to get rid of them.

I hurry to the interrogation area, two bland rooms connected by a one-way mirror, a blue polyester curtain closed across it. Someone has placed a government-issued chair the regulation six feet from the viewing window. Hopefully this will be a quick ID without dredging up the past and I can get back to my office without a lot of chat about my mother.

I open Nina's dossier, flipping past the photos of the gruesome disfigurements resulting from the experiments done to her legs. Though we'd been in different barracks at Ravensbrück, I'd known about it. We all had. How she and seventy-three other "Rabbits" had been experimented on to test sulfa drugs. Nina currently lives in Paris, working as a journalist for Radio Free Europe, and is in the United States for two months. Her visa was sponsored by a New Yorker named Caroline Ferriday who has connections in high places. She'd arranged a stay for Nina at Beth Israel Hospital in Boston for corrective and plastic surgeries.

A secretary ushers Nina in, and I get surprisingly teary as she walks toward me, a limp still in her step. She looks very much the same, a pretty brunette, clutching her purse in one hand and the neck of her hand-knit sweater with the other. But she's more filled out, liberated from our diet of watery soup and a crust of bread. She wears thick socks, possibly to hide her scars, and is remarkably good-natured for having been the victim of such terrible abuse.

I take her two hands in mine. "Good to see you again, Nina. Sorry about the cold hands."

She gives me a nervous smile. "Mine are cold, too. Last time I saw you it was on Camp Road with Arlette. Right before they let you out. We were all so envious."

"Oh, Camp Road. Where the lovely Ravensbrück **Revier** could be found. Made lovelier by Dr. Oberheuser."

"Herta." She shivers. "At least she's still locked up. More than we can say for Schreiber."

"Thanks for taking time out of your trip and coming all the way from Boston. You live in Paris now, lucky you?"

"How did you—" She eyes the dossier folder. "Oh, I see. You know everything. Who do you work for here? Army Intelligence?"

"The Counter Intelligence Corps. What your file doesn't say is how you found out Schreiber was here."

"After my surgery, Dr. Alexander came to visit me at the hospital. I knew him from the doctors' trial. He told me he saw Schreiber in a medical journal. In a very high position at Randolph Field."

"So, he called the FBI?"

"I asked him to, after I read in **The Globe** that the program is called Operation Paperclip. They bring Nazi scientists here to work on government projects?"

"I can't comment, Nina."

She leans in. "I hear they call it that because the army puts a paperclip on the folders of the Nazis they want to bring here. All done quietly, so the world won't know they're escaping justice."

"It's a classified program."

"So, you pay these monsters to come here to live safe and sound, and they escape trial for killing innocent people? Girls you knew at the camp. Held down kicking and screaming while they cut us."

"We just need you to ID him, Nina."

"I already picked him out of fifty photos the FBI showed me."

"Schreiber says he doesn't remember you. Has never been to a concentration camp."

She pushes down her sock to reveal her withered calf, a fat scar running knee to ankle. "Perhaps he'll remember the number of the experiment he performed on me? It is tattooed here. **TKM III.**"

I avert my gaze, and she pulls up her sock.

"We just need a live ID for official purposes."

Nina wraps her sweater closer. "Is he here?"

I nod. "In the next room. But he won't see us. Just a mirror from his side."

I wave one hand toward the chair and Nina sits, purse in her lap.

"Before we start, can you tell us anything more about Schreiber and what you knew to be his role at the camp? I never knew about him when I was there."

"Well, they tried very hard to hide their identities, but I spent so much time in the **Revier** after my operations I saw him more than once when they thought we were asleep." She inhales a big breath. "He often came with Dr. Gebhardt to inspect our casts. Gebhardt reported to Schreiber, I think, since he seemed to defer to him."

"Did Schreiber wear a white doctor's coat?"

"Most times but not always. I also saw Schreiber when Himmler brought high-ranking Nazis up from Berlin for a conference about our surgeries, and he led them around explaining what they'd done. We called it 'the great marveling,' for they always seemed very impressed with Gebhardt's cutting of us. That's all I know. It makes it hard to breathe just thinking of it, really."

"As surgeon general of the Reich, Schreiber was an expert in gangrene."

"Me too, thanks to him," Nina says with a wry smile.

"How did you know the doctors' names?"

"They often spoke as though we, being Poles, didn't understand what they were saying, but most of us spoke German well. Here and there a doctor or nurse would slip and say a name."

I rub my hands together trying to warm them before taking Nina's hand in mine.

"I'll open the curtain now, Nina. All I need is a simple yes or no."

She nods.

I step to the window, pull the drapery cord, and the curtain opens. Walter Schreiber stands there, dressed in a dark gray flannel suit, white shirt, and burgundy tie. He straightens his horn-rim glasses and brushes a speck of lint off his sleeve.

He's an interesting one. I know from his dossier he is the fifty-nine-year-old son of a postal worker and rose quickly to the top of the Nazi medical hierarchy. He has some flimsy story about how the Russians kept him against his will after the war and how he escaped them when his daughter happened to come upon him on a train. Of course, the army is willing to believe anything as long as this Nazi expert in biological and chemical weapons works on our side now.

He stands five foot six, weighs 156 pounds, and while his face is free of dueling scars, he bears one on his right forearm. From fending off the blows? Surely his Nazi pals will notice that at the swimming pool and consider it a sign of cowardice.

I press the talk button. "Look straight ahead, please. And remove the glasses." He looks confused so I press the button again. **"Schauen sie bitte geradeaus. Und nehmen Sie die Brille ab."**

He removes and folds his glasses and stands straighter, eyes forward.

Nina leans over, elbows on her purse, and presses her face into her hands.

"I'm sorry, Nina, but I must hear verbal confirmation. Is that the Dr. Walter Schreiber you knew from Ravensbrück concentration camp, approximately 1943 to 1945?"

"I can't look again."

"Nina—"

"It is. Yes, yes. It's him."

There's no doubt she's telling the truth from her physical cues alone. I close the curtain, fast as I can, happy to not look at him anymore.

Nina stands, face blotchy, and sets her purse on the chair. "How did he even escape being tried at Nuremberg?"

"It's complicated. I'm not supposed to share this, but he claims he was held against his will by the

Russians and barely escaped with his life. Somehow, he fell through the cracks at the doctors' trial."

She paces the room. "What will you do with him?"

"He can't stay here now that you've made it public what he's done."

"Then he should go back and stand trial."

"Of course. But I really shouldn't discuss this with you."

"Do you know how many girls died because of him? What it's like to die from gangrene? Do they just not **matter**?"

"I know this is—"

"They executed Dr. Gebhardt. Schreiber was his boss. Shouldn't he at least go to jail?"

"That's not **up** to me, Nina."

She takes a step back. "I see. They'll just let him go, won't they?" Tears well in her eyes. "How can you do this? Help them all escape punishment for what they did?"

"Now that Russia's got the bomb, they're a huge threat. And if we don't hire these scientists, they will. We need the intelligence."

"**Shame** on you."

"I'm just doing my job."

"You sound just like them." She snatches her purse from the chair. "How can you do this? After your mother—"

"Don't talk about her." I blink away the start of tears.

"You need to do what's right, Josie. Send him back to Germany for a proper trial. She'd want that."

"Our time's up." I step toward the door. "Thank you for coming. The guard will see you out."

SCHREIBER CROUCHES LOW IN the passenger seat covered with an army blanket as we drive past the press waiting at the gate and make it to the road unrecognized. I squash the self-loathing I feel as I drive this criminal to freedom. I just want it over without having to think about the camp. Mother. The bad part.

"You can sit up now," I say as I slide the blanket off, releasing a wave of his cologne. Leather and spice notes. I'm sickened by my own complicity in his escape. How satisfying it would have been to dump him with the press.

I allow myself a glance at Schreiber, his expression hovering between content and cocky, probably pretty pleased with himself since he got the U.S. government to finance his family's trip to Argentina to live with his daughter.

We bump along in the jeep, not speaking, scratchy country songs on the radio, en route to the meeting spot, far enough outside of town to avoid any lurking reporters. Rain patters the windshield as he combs his hair in the visor vanity mirror, a brown suitcase on his lap, a camera hung around his neck by a leather strap. I turn the music louder to drown out the panic welling up from sharing that small space with him.

The DJ cuts in with a hailstorm alert just as pea-sized hail starts battering the windshield, and then "Your Cheatin' Heart" resumes. Hail was a major topic in our basic training, including the various sizes of ice precipitation, pea, marble, and egg, and their corresponding diameters. At least one thing in our six-month instruction has come in handy.

As we reach the meeting spot, a highway sign outside of town reading EL PASO, the hail grows to marble sized.

He peers out the windshield and speaks the first words addressed to me since we met.

"We experienced hail like this once in Germany. Ten-centimeter diameter. Killed three zoo animals."

That accent sends my skin clammy.

He looks about the jeep. "Have you brought an umbrella for my use? This camera must not get wet. It is a Leica. Very valuable. I was forced to leave the case in Germany when I left."

I stop the jeep, the windshield wipers straining to fight the hail, now mixed with rain. It's close to egg sized now.

A flash of Ravensbrück comes to me, standing at roll call in the sleeting rain, and I tamp it down.

A large hailstone hits the glass and startles us both, leaving a spidery crack along the top. How satisfying it would be to shoot him right here.

"End of the road," I say, motor running.

Schreiber clears his throat. "You no doubt disapprove of all this." He shrugs his shoulders and brushes off his pant legs. "But you must remember, the system was criminal, and I was part of it, but I am not criminal. I've done nothing wrong. Never even been to Ravensbrück."

He's a terrible liar. Three blatant deception indicators in one response.

"Out."

He looks at me directly, as if seeing me for the first time. "You don't expect me to go out there? Without even a rain jacket?"

"I do."

He hugs his suitcase tighter.

I rest my hand on the gun at my hip. "I won't ask again."

Schreiber hesitates, looks at me for a long second, and grabs his suitcase by the handle. He yanks open the jeep door and slides out, making his way through the hail, one hand shielding his camera. He stands at the side of the road, posture erect, and rests his suitcase atop his head, sending hail bouncing off it, a move I grudgingly applaud as resourceful.

I wait. The rain is coming sideways at him, and he and his camera are drenched in seconds. His arms must be tiring since he rests the valise at his feet for a moment and is pelted with hail before returning the case to rest on his head.

All too soon the unmarked army-type truck I'd

ordered appears in the distance, making its way toward us. After a few more satisfying minutes of Schreiber trying to shield his camera from the elements, the truck pulls in front of me and stops near him. He opens the rear door and, as he steps up to enter, a particularly large hailstone catches him in the back of the head.

The truck idles and I stare at the open back of it, tailgate closed, canvas top blowing in the wind, so like the ones at Ravensbrück. The sickening smell of gas exhaust floods in through my jeep's air vents, and panic swells in me again as the memory surfaces. Why does it always come at the worst times?

I shift into reverse and screech out of there.

That was not the time to revisit losing my mother. There were so many other monsters to catch. And so little time.

CHAPTER 4

ARLETTE

PARIS, FRANCE
1952

THE DAY AFTER LUC MINAU'S VISIT TO THE CAFÉ, I stand outside the door of his office, rainy wind biting through my thin trench coat, regretting somewhat my decision to choose it over a down parka as my one coat. I wear the cross-body shoulder bag I'd made from what was left of the dress I'd worn every day at the camp, a signature piece so many people admired. It holds my cardboard grief box and little else.

I steel myself to the possibility he's a huckster. The last man seemed so legit, with his file of documents, kindly urging me to share the story of losing my son, until he vanished once I paid his fee. Hopefully this will be over quickly before Mr. Minau can draw me into yet another pit of longing for Willie.

The place seems legitimate, behind the national bank of France off an appealing cobblestone courtyard. I knock, and Mr. Minau opens the door. I step in, a thick gray wool carpet cushioning my steps to a modern desk, two very nice Roland Rainer chairs opposite it. A fire in the fireplace warms the room, and a potted gardenia plant sits on the sideboard along the opposite wall.

That flower has so many meanings. It symbolizes gentleness. And trust. And the secret love between two people.

I try not to stare at the painting behind the desk, of an open window looking out over a tropical harbor, done in vivid emerald and pinks. Could it be a real Matisse?

I take a deep breath and steel myself. This whole fancy office could be a façade. Marianne might be right. He could easily be some sort of swindler.

I sit down and take in the framed photos arranged on the sideboard, of what look like happy parents and children posing after being reunited.

I nod toward the painting. "Is that a Matisse?"

He turns and looks as if he's forgotten it's there. "Oh, yes. It was my father's. I inherited my love of art from him."

"Aren't you afraid it will get stolen, here in your office?"

"Oh, no. It's wired with an alarm. Coffee?"

He looks more approachable today, suit jacket draped over the back of his chair.

"No, thank you. I can't stay long."

I slide off the gloves and lay them on my lap.

He smiles. "What handsome gloves."

"Thank you. My father's. They're a bit too big for me, but I love them."

"How does he do without them himself?"

"He's been dead for years, so they're of no use to him now."

"I'm sorry."

"Don't be, Mr. Minau. I barely remember my mother or my father."

"So, you know firsthand the difficulties of not having parents."

I keep my chin high. "You asked me here for a reason, I suspect?"

"I represent Hope Home, which my grandmother Danae Minau runs. We take orphans from the war and place them with families, from our home base in French Guiana."

"And how does this relate to me, Mr. Minau?"

"We have reason to believe your child may be among the war orphans."

My whole body grows cold. "Who's to say I even have a child, Mr. Minau?" I sit back in my chair. "And I've never heard of your foundation."

"That's why we're planning a public awareness campaign for the spring. But our donors are high-level families. The fundraising is private."

"I think I made a mistake coming here." I gather my bag and prepare to leave. "There are many dishonest people preying on the bereaved—"

"Please let me tell you our story, Miss LaRue. After the war ended, German orphans went through terrible trauma. They were often called 'Kraut kids,' and no one wanted them. But it wasn't just German children. Orphans came from all over Europe, from Hitler's Lebensborn homes, or were simply abandoned on the streets of every major city. Norway had a particularly desperate situation. The government had collaborated with the Nazis, and at the many homes there, hundreds of children needed help, for their mothers were persecuted, often tossed into insane asylums."

"I know all this. Where do you come in?"

"My grandmother established a charity to help them. Set up a boys' camp called Camp Hope in French Guiana on her property there, so the children can escape the cold. She lives nearby in a little place near the water called Cove House.

"Here's the kids' camp." He unfolds a lovely brochure with photos of suntanned children in shorts and uniform shirts attending classes in grass huts and playing on the beach. How lovely and warm it all looks, but brochures are easily faked.

"We seek good adoptive homes for these kids, but most of them are older now and not always the first choice for parents who want infants. So, we teach them to be good members of society. Work with the local Maroon community, tribal descendants of fugitive slaves that have been in French Guiana for over a century. We provide vaccinations and healthcare to their children. And soon some of our Hope Home kids will even go out into the world as our first goodwill ambassadors, a wonderful outreach program. But our greatest joy is to match a biological parent to one of our orphans."

"Why South America?"

"The weather, for one thing. French Guiana's climate is close to perfect. My family home is there for another. The French government keeps the taxes low, so a nonprofit foundation is viable for us."

"They say many Nazis went to South America after the war."

"Yes, regrettably, some Nazis escaped justice and took refuge there, but Europeans have been in South America for years. Starting in the 1820s, German-speaking peasants came as farmers and now constitute a large part of the population. German Swiss. Mennonites. Especially in Argentina. And there's nothing nefarious going on three thousand miles to the north of there in French Guiana. I am inviting you to be our guest."

I try to avoid looking at his kind smile. "What leads you to believe my child is among your orphans?"

"We have in our ranks several children rescued from a German Lebensborn home in Steinhoering once the Allies liberated Europe."

"And how did you connect me to all this?"

"I cannot take credit. My grandmother does the research. Since Grandfather died, she's become quite the amateur detective. Works with the International Tracing Service. German Red Cross. She found your name connected with the Association to Support Mothers of German Children. You are a member?"

I glance out the window. "I am. Only one of a handful. The world has little sympathy for us now."

"Grandmother also found you on some Nazi records from a French Lebensborn home in Chantilly. As a birth mother. So, here we are." He leans in. "You are the only Arlette Dagmar LaRue in Paris, by the way. When was the last time you saw your son?"

"His name was . . . Willie." I wrap my arms across my belly. "It's too hard—"

"I understand, Miss LaRue, but I can't help you if you don't tell me."

"At Ravensbrück." I hold back the tears. "I'm sorry. It's excruciating to think about."

"Bien sûr." He hands me his nicely ironed handkerchief.

How many times had he done that with other mothers?

"What a terrible place for such innocents," he says.

"I was part of a small group of mothers allowed to keep our children. Before that the babies were . . . done away with upon arrival."

"Was it a special barracks?"

"Yes. Set up just for mothers and children. Called

the **Kinderzimmer.** An experiment of sorts, no one really knew."

"You must have felt very lucky."

"That is not a word any of us would have used, monsieur. They barely fed us and all we mothers thought about was getting back there to our babies at the end of our shifts. And then one day . . ."

"I'm so sorry, Miss LaRue."

I dab my eyes with the handkerchief. "My friends from the café, Bep and Riekie, also lost their babies there."

"I'm sorry to have to ask this, but is there any way your son may have survived?"

"The camp staff, a guard named Dorothea Binz in particular, took a liking to him, perhaps because he was three quarters German. I've often thought she might have taken him."

"What year did this happen?"

"Spring of forty-five. My friend Josie and I were liberated soon after."

"It's possible your son somehow made it to that Lebensborn home in Steinhoering. Many camp guards traveled south in Germany to escape the Allies. It's a long shot but possible."

"Did your grandmother find no child named Willie?"

"Unfortunately, no. Most were too young to know their own names, so we've had to assign them random German names. Your Willie could be any one of them." He pauses. "If you don't mind me asking, how old are you now?"

I brush a lingering raindrop off my coat sleeve. "I'd rather not share such intimate information, monsieur."

"I understand. But if you are now, say, twenty-five, that would have put you around seventeen when you had a child. He would be eight now?"

I shift in my seat. "He would be nine."

"Do you have any articles of his from that time?"

"Not many." I hold my bag closer and feel for my grief box, the corner of it jutting out against the fabric.

"I would be skeptical in your shoes, Miss LaRue. But I'll have a list of references sent over to the café for you to contact. I also have some items that may shed light on the match, if you'd like to see them."

I push my hair back, fingers shaking. "What kind of things?"

He steps to a bar. "Tea? Water? Something stronger? Sometimes parents need a little reinforcement."

I decline his offer, folding my arms across my chest to keep my hands from shaking. "How did you acquire these items?"

"Hope Home has become a clearinghouse of sorts. The German government funnels all child assets found at the Lebensborn homes our way to help facilitate reunions."

How kind of them. After ruining our lives.

Luc steps to a standard wall safe, turns the dial

twice, and draws out a cardboard box the size of a small toaster. As he does, the light catches a stack of silver cups at the front of the safe. The Himmler cups? The ones he gifted special children. Perhaps the one he intended for Willie is among them.

"You keep such things in a safe, Mr. Minau?"

"We're committed to the privacy of our adopting families and biological parents. I hope this won't be hard for you." He slides the box toward me across his desk, the top flaps closed. "These are some of the personal items on site the day the children were found at the home. The staff had abandoned the kids, poor things. Perhaps you can see if anything seems familiar?"

I press the box with two shaking hands, barely able to open it. How terrible it was, losing him. Why open myself up to that again?

"Perhaps I can come back another time, monsieur?"

"You don't want to take a look?" He comes out from behind the desk and sits in the chair next to me. "It's not uncommon for mothers and fathers to feel nervous as they take such an important step."

I breathe in deeply and exhale. I just want it to be Willie so badly. To keep the hope alive as long as I can.

"You take all the time you need."

I sit up a little straighter and open the flaps to find two manila envelopes.

"Is this all you have?" I ask. "There are other things in the safe. Are those silver cups? I know the staff at the time had prepared one for Willie's German adopted family."

"This is actually considered a good amount of adoptee assets. Often children have nothing."

I lift one manila envelope from the box, unclasp it, and pull out a celadon green receiving blanket with satin edging. "My God. I had one like this."

"It took some skillful detective work, but my grandmother saw that the monogram on the blanket is **JA** and matched the Ravensbrück records of the woman you were released with. Josie Anderson."

Time stands still as I run one finger along the monogram. I hold it to my face and inhale the scent. Just laundry soap.

I hug the blanket to my chest, tears pricking my eyes. "How is it even possible you have this? It was Willie's. Josie's mother gave it to him."

Luc smiles. "It's a good sign that you remember it. Take your time. This must be overwhelming."

"He loved that blanket. They let him keep it at Ravensbrück."

I set the blanket on my lap and open the second envelope.

"This one was easier for my grandmother," Luc says. "It's personalized."

I slide a photo from the envelope of Gunther staring off into the distance.

"My God."

"Do you know him?"

I nod, more tears filling my eyes. “Willie’s father. Gunther Wagner.”

“Was he present at the birth?”

“No. He was at the Russian front. He had no idea what he’d left me with.”

CHAPTER 5

ARLETTE

KRAUTERGERSHEIM, FRANCE
1943

Before.

THE DAY GUNTHER WAGNER CAME TO FETCH ME at school he wore his new Wehrmacht uniform, deep bottle green, the silver buckle of his black leather belt polished bright. I wore the best outfit I had, my uniform from the BDM, Hitler's youth group for girls—a welcome change from my scratchy black wool school uniform pinafore.

It was the only new ensemble Auntie ever bought for me, with its flared, ocean blue skirt and ochre jacket, and the crisp white blouse I ironed last each night, only after I'd finished Auntie's dresses and nighties. I'd pinned my new BDM badge to my breast, over my heart, so proud of that red and white ribbon woven through the gold letters. At sixteen I had only a vague idea of the terrible things it stood for.

Gunther walked right into our six-room village school, where I was busy studying for my diploma the next year, strode into mathematics class, and caused all to turn to him, there at the door. He was due to report to the front, clean and fresh, cheeks flushed from the walk.

The teacher waved me out and I hurried to Gunther, happy to be liberated from algebra.

Ordinarily I would not be allowed to leave with him during school hours, but these were unusual times and a soldier of the Reich visiting our little French village of Krautergersheim, from just across the border in Offenburg, Germany, was afforded every consideration.

My Gunther had just finished cadet school and at seventeen was on a high, the Reich having won the latest battle, or so we thought. He'd traded in his schoolboy's kepi for a soldier's cap and believed Hitler was a mythical being, like Odin, who'd sent him his uniform from his place in the sky.

Little did we know the war was not going well for Germany, with many of their major cities heavily bombed, since the radio my aunt listened to said Hitler was winning. Nearby Strasbourg was a torn place, half supporting the Reich, half condemning Hitler, however silently.

"You leave tomorrow?" Tears pricked my eyes.

"The Twelfth SS Panzer Division. Rumor is we're going east."

"So many French oppose the war. Do you feel bad to fight for Hitler?"

"Not at all. The French will someday be our subjects, and we'll show compassion. It's all for the good of Germany, Arl. And you may call yourself French, but admit it, you're mostly German."

"Just my mother."

He slid one arm around my shoulders. "But your father was half German, am I right? I'm required to form partnerships only with girls of untainted blood, but I will forgive the French part."

"Thank you."

"Besides, you look more German than most pure German girls."

He pulled me closer. "And you know it's our duty to do our part for the Reich in other ways, too." He leaned in and whispered, so close I could smell the scent of pine and woodsmoke on him.

"I want ten children," I said.

"It may take a few tries. It doesn't happen on the first time."

He was right about that, according to my BDM leader. She also told us we needed to do our part for the Reich. She said, "In view of the prevailing shortage of men, not every girl can expect to get a husband in the future," and that we girls should "at least fulfill our task as German women."

As we passed other girls in the hallway, they lowered

their eyes and snuck envious glances at Gunther and at me, my black uniform tie loosened, white-blond braids tied off with white scraps. I may've been poor, but I had the ultimate prize.

Gunther signed me out at the school office, the secretaries wishing us well, and we walked from the building inhaling fresh air.

I pirouetted as we walked. "I'm happy to miss mathematics class."

"You won't need it as a mother. School is more important for boys."

I shrugged. "I like art class, though. I'd miss that terribly. We're sculpting in metal this week."

He linked one arm with mine. "I like you, Arlette. Even the art part."

I thanked God every morning and night that Gunther's Hitler Youth group had come to stay near our village, to "hamster," forage for food in the rural farm areas. He'd looked so handsome in his uniform of white shirt, khaki shorts, and neckerchief. Auntie had given him six of her precious potatoes for the cause, and Gunther and I became instant friends.

"Where are we going?" I asked as we walked the road toward my aunt's rented shack on the outskirts of town. "I hope not straight home. Auntie will have a stroke if she knows I left school early, even with you."

We walked through the town in minutes, and into the outskirts, past more widely spaced farm properties. Gunther and his group visiting was the most exciting thing that had ever happened there.

He took me by the hand and pulled me toward a barn near the road. "Come with me."

I knew where all this was going and didn't resist, just happy someone wanted me. As the BDM handbook counseled us, racially pure girls that were modest, neat, and frugal could count on a German boy choosing them as a worthy partner.

"We don't have much time. School will be out soon, and your aunt will miss you."

"Auntie will only miss the dinner I cook every night while she's pasted to the phonograph listening to Hitler's speeches."

"She's not so bad. She sacrificed a lot for you."

"If you call daily beatings with the stick sacrificing. Or sleeping in the bedroom near the fire while I sleep in the cold basement. Plus, she burned my sketchbook. Two years of drawings in there. Before she left, Miss Fouchere saw them and said I would be a famous designer someday."

"Miss Fouchere was a Jew and didn't know the first thing about it. They just sow the seeds of materialism and greed. It's better to not be thinking of our own glorification. Just what benefits the Reich."

We entered the barn, swallows playing up in the rafters, and Gunther pulled me down onto a heap of warm hay. He reached into his rucksack. "I've brought you an early birthday gift." He pulled out a black-and-white photograph. "It's my class picture from cadet school. I signed it here on the back, **To Arlette, with fondest wishes,** and listed the division I'm reporting to."

"Oh, Gunther." It was a good likeness of him, in his cadet uniform shirt, his best-in-class ribbon pinned at his chest. He was looking off somewhere with a serious expression. "I'll cherish it."

He brushed his hair from his forehead, an endearing habit I would miss. "And my field number is 02498/L, if you would write to me?"

I nodded, lost in the beauty of him. Even more handsome up close, he was somewhere between a man and a boy, with a strong, proud chin and blue eyes. I ran my fingers through his hair. It was as fine as corn silk and what an artist might call wheat, just a touch yellower than mine.

"Are you happy, Arl?" He stood and adopted his serious face as he unbuttoned his uniform coat and removed the rest of his clothes down to his uniform undershorts. He folded them in perfect squares and settled down in the hay. I sat near him.

Having no father or brother or books to show me even a glimpse of male anatomy, his came as a surprise.

"Is it always so . . . straight up like that?"

He set his lips in a hard line. "No, Arlette."

"Does it hurt you?"

"It will feel good for both of us I think if you'd take your clothes off and stop talking."

"Yes. But you look cold." I grabbed handfuls of hay and covered his torso.

"Stop that." He sat up and brushed himself off. "Please be serious. You can be so immature."

"I suppose you want to kiss me again."

He glanced at my skirt. "If you let me touch you there, I promise I'll stop if you don't like it."

He leaned in and kissed me, and I pushed him back onto the hay, disregarding the BDM handbook, which instructed girls to relax and let the boy perform his duty. I kissed him back and then slipped out of my own uniform.

He lay there and watched, hands behind his head. "You're so beautiful," he said as if in a dream. "You could be on the cover of **NS Frauen-Warte** magazine."

I smiled, slid my skirt down, and removed my blouse. How often I'd fantasized about being a model, photographed and in the pages of that magazine Auntie loved so. Maybe then she'd be proud of me.

I turned to lay my clothes in the hay.

He sat up sharply. "How did you get those bruises on your back?"

"Auntie. I told you. She only hits me where it won't show."

He frowned. "It's not right to hit girls."

A warm hum vibrated through me. What a good man he was. How happy we'd be, living in a snug home of our own, far from Auntie. Someone to take care of me, love me. A real family.

"How did I get so lucky?" he asked, pulling me down to him.

After some initial fumbling, we fit together well, with little awkwardness, and after, we lay together as it grew dark, his arms warm around me, stroking my bare back and kissing the bruises there, as the birds prepared for bed.

Soon we helped each other dress, and he walked me home.

I brushed my skirt as we linked arms. "Do I have even a bit of hay on me anywhere? Auntie will have a heart spasm."

"I hope you like your birthday present," he said, pulling me closer as we walked.

"It's the best gift I've ever had."

We stopped at the fork in the road to Auntie's house.

"Will you come back for me?" I asked.

He bent and kissed me, long and slow as if neither of us wanted it to end. "Of course I will."

He walked off, whistling, leaving me hopelessly in love. And little did I know, with a different sort of gift.

CHAPTER 6

JOSIE

FORT BLISS, TEXAS
1952

I ARRIVE AT MY BOSS KARL'S HOUSE FOR HIS son's potluck birthday party somewhat hungover, and start up the bluestone walk, plate of bagels and lox in hand, which I had to drive an hour out of town to find, my feet already killing me in my new regulation pumps.

Construction trucks fill the lawn, and blinding rays of sunlight bounce off the chrome bumpers of the Fords and Chevys parked along the driveway.

The front door is open, and I walk in, hoping to make an appearance and slink off before cake, to the cool recesses of my office and a dinner of beer and soft-boiled eggs at my desk.

I enter into an open floor plan, a blue haze of cigarette smoke in the air, and crave a Scotch and soda to get me through this. I mosey into the living room area, which is decorated entirely in white, the sofa and chairs zipped into clear plastic slipcovers. A glass pitcher of orange drink sweats on the coffee table next to a neat stack of **CHARM** magazines. The scent of pigs in a blanket wafts in from the kitchen.

Karl's wife rushes to me, the petticoats of her turquoise dress rustling. "Leave shoes at the door, **merci**!"

I kick off my pumps and set them next to the rows of lace-up wing tips. Six pair. Five agents are there, plus Karl. The magician is probably not a wing-tip guy.

It's too bright and hot in that house, and I miss my dark apartment. The contractors are jackhammering, and someone has the Bob Wills and His Texas Playboys hit "Spanish Two Step" turned up on the stereo console to drown out the noise. One of the secretaries from travel is out on the screened-in porch wearing a red cowboy hat, teaching the typing pool to dance the "Texas Two Step."

In the kitchen, a magician in stocking feet scares a ring of kids seated on the linoleum floor by pulling fire from a hat and singeing the ceiling. At the far end of the place, in the dining room, Karl chats with his head intelligence officer, Tony P., a mushroom cloud of blue cigarette smoke forming above. Three dark-suited agent pals of Tony's cluster around the television nearby: his fellow intelligence officers

Captains Bobby Flynn and Tony G. and a skinny new recruit I don't recognize who will probably outrank me soon, too.

Karl's wife bends to arrange the shoes and then stands, patting her hairdo in place. "Well, Lieutenant Anderson. Look who finally crawled out to join the living."

I try to walk away, but she pulls me back by the arm. "Come sit."

She's Karl's second wife, attractive in a bland way, Fort Bliss's Debbie Reynolds. Karl's first wife, Sharon, the love of his life, died several years earlier in a gruesome car crash.

I hand her the bagels, which she stares at like they're moon rocks. She sets them on the white buffet table just outside the kitchen, which is already crowded with platters.

"You've become a hermit, Josie. Just like Karl, holed up with his ham radio all day talking about walruses in Antarctica."

"You have a beautiful home."

She leans forward, releasing a wall of Jean Naté perfume. "Orange drink? I wanted to serve a little champagne, but Karl nixed that."

"No, thank you, Mrs. Crowell."

She pours a glass and hands it to me.

"Please call me Debbine. This is what they call an **open** plan. No actual rooms, just areas. A dining area. A den area. A kitchen area. A—"

I try to smile. "Very Frank Lloyd Wright."

"Only the bedrooms way back there have walls, so everyone can see what's going on here at all times."

"The no-privacy plan."

Debbine rocks back and slaps her thighs through the petticoats. "You're funny, Josie. Betty Jo is teaching a quick class on Texas dancing. You can get in on it. The boys like a girl with some pep in her step."

"I'm okay, thank you."

"Do you do **any**thing for fun? Mahjong or book club? You lived in France for so many years with your ambassador daddy, right? Why not start a French club? The girls in the typing pool would sign up to learn a few words."

"I'll think about it, Mrs. Crowell."

"Karl says you hike those gypsum hills outside of town. Careful your legs don't get all muscley."

Just the thought of the vast gypsum dunes calms me, the towering white sands where I walk on my days off, the wind erasing my footsteps, my only companion a roadrunner or a prairie lizard.

I start to set my glass on a side table, and Debbine jumps to slide a coaster under it.

It's so different from my childhood home in Alexandria, a suburb of Washington, D.C., and my mother's comfy couch with the chenille cover you sank into like a hug, the dining room cabinets filled with tchotchkes from my father's diplomatic travels, her trophy case for his career. You could park a drink wherever you liked on her oak side tables. I sit up a little straighter and deep-breathe away a stab of longing for my mother.

Debbine leans in, eyes wide. "Heard Bobby Flynn took you off base to the diner."

Seems the whole world knows the details of that date with Tony P.'s studly best friend. Bobby wasn't exactly a Chaucer scholar, but the night had gone reasonably well until he'd pinned me to the front seat of his Buick Roadmaster, shoved his hand up my skirt, and tried to yank my underwear down. I walked five miles home, earning me the clever nickname "Frigid Frenchie" among the male staff.

An agent with the physique of a twelve-year-old, his pant cuffs dragging on the carpet, walks toward the buffet table and stops to watch the typing pool dance.

Debbine nods toward him. "That's Jeff Shapiro, a new hire. From Karl's alma motto, Texas Tech."

I consider correcting her Latin, but it's not worth the effort.

"I can introduce you." She whispers behind one manicured hand, "Jeff's Jewish, too."

Jeff heaps chicken wings on a sagging paper plate and scurries back to be with Tony P.'s guys, without even a look at my platter of bagels.

"It's not good to date co-workers," I say as I scan the TV area for Bobby Flynn and find him now sitting apart from the others, arms spread along the back of the sofa. As if sensing my gaze, he looks toward us, and I turn away. I'd made the mistake of being drawn to his all-American good looks. Am I doomed for life to be attracted to horrible men like my father?

Debbine flips me a dismissive wave. “Oh, you’re probably up to your eyeballs in boyfriends, pretty girl like you.”

I decide not to tell her that despite having been out on plenty of first dates, I haven’t kissed a man on the mouth since Tommy Kennefick in eighth grade.

She pats my hand. “Not easy meeting men at an all-female concentration camp, I imagine.”

“That’s right, Mrs. Crowell.” I lift the glass of orange drink to my lips, but the smell triggers a wave of nausea and I set it back on the coaster.

“But every girl needs companionship, Josie. I hear you play poker with the boys.”

“I won twice, and now they don’t invite me anymore.”

“Well, you don’t want to hang around Fort Bliss forever anyway, am I right? Once you get a husband and the baby shows, that’s a career ender.” She sips her drink. “What’s your actual job, anyway? What’s a research tech?”

“That’s classified, Mrs. Crowell.”

The truth is I’m lucky Karl created this position for me and promoted me to the rank of lieutenant when so many talented women here work in low-level jobs.

“There should be more women in high positions, don’t you think, Mrs. Crowell? Anna Paganini in the cafeteria has a foreign service degree from Georgetown.”

"The boys live for her lasagna. Anyways. Karl says you're one of his best. That you went from steno to systems in two months. That you **invented** that ranking system for the Nazis they bring here."

Though it's just from Debbine, the acknowledgment feels good, since the most concern my male colleagues have shown me is when one asked, "Hey, Anderson, why the wet pits?"

"If you **wanted** a bigger job, I bet you could get it, but you gotta gild the lily more." She studies my hair as if inspecting the fruit at the Piggly Wiggly. "Grow out that hair—bet it has a nice curl to it. Wear some rouge on that pretty olive skin of yours."

She pulls a magazine from the stack and opens it to a lingerie ad. "Every girl needs a push-up bra. I know you grew up in France, but this is Texas, honey. You gotta strut your stuff and get your nails done pretty."

She scoots along the plastic, closer to me. "I'm terribly sorry about what happened to you and your mother at that camp place." She blinks away tears. "Karl told me about that necklace the Nazis took from her—that you and your mom used to exchange, with little trinkets hidden inside? Just about broke my heart."

I look toward the dining area. "Is Karl ready for me?"

She slides a Kleenex from her sleeve and dabs her eyes. "My mother, may she rest in peace, used to put notes in my school lunch box she packed every day. So, you see, we had a similar rapporterie." She pats my hand. "I heard about you gettin' so sad you tried to—"

I stand. "I'll head over and see if Karl's ready for me."

She looks up, blinking. "Oh."

"I'd rather not talk about that, Mrs. Crowell."

"Well. Of course. You go. He's tête-à-tête with Tony."

I head for the dining area where Karl sits with Tony P. and get a closer look at the scrum of black-suited agents watching the Texas Longhorns football game, rocks glasses in hand. They look up as I pass, do the usual tits and ass evaluation, and return to their game. **What a bunch of skaters. Do they even work? Just sit around in each other's offices flipping paperclips into the trash?**

I approach the dining area, an overlit, bland little space separated from the rest by open teak shelving, and hear Tony P.'s Brooklyn accent.

"I'm telling you, Karl, she's too green."

Karl spots me and waves me toward him with two hands, like someone backing a truck into a delivery dock.

The construction pounding is louder on this side of the house.

Karl stubs out his cigarette. "I need the room, Tony."

Tony P. stands and passes me as I approach the table. He's at least ten years older than me, outranks me, and if not for the paunch and the Brylcreemed blue-black pompadour and overconfident walk, he might be mildly attractive.

He leans in as we pass, releasing a burst of garlic breath and In the Mood cologne. "We all know you're only considered for this because your dad's cozy with Karl."

I don't break stride.

"And just so you know, Anderson, I was first choice, but turned it down."

I step to Karl and salute. "Major Crowell."

Karl stands, returns the salute, and opens a nearby door. "Want to see my new baby?"

I peek in at the construction site in progress, the only furniture a folding table topped with a shortwave radio, a call sign tag taped to it: WEE-EL PASO.

"Wow. An SCR-299? WWII army trucks had those in the field."

Karl slides his hands into his pockets and jingles his change. "Carried the voice of victory to the world. Figured why go through the comm center when I can talk to the world from here?"

Karl closes the door and offers me a seat next to him at the polished mahogany table, the only stick of furniture not white in the whole place. His rocks glass of Scotch sits sweating next to a crystal ashtray bristling with butts.

I sit.

"Hey, smile, sport. You're a pretty girl. It's a party."

Once friendly with my parents, Karl and Sharon came to a few cocktail parties at our Alexandria house. I have fuzzy memories of them as a couple, mostly of

Sharon, a kind blonde with model-perfect features, and of coming down the morning after to scavenge leftover onion dip and potato chips from the coffee table while my parents slept off the alcohol.

Compared to my slick Ivy League father, who holds a higher position in the competing CIA, Karl has none of the J. Press no-socks-and-penny-loafers' edge. He wears his Fred MacMurray cardigan and fat paisley tie just as comfortably as his own father back in Bakersfield probably had, complete with brown socks. He's been at Fort Bliss eight months to my seven, and I'm proud to see he has resisted the cowboy hat every non-Texan buys the minute they move to town.

"I have a shitload of work to do at the office, Major."

He winces. "Could you take it easy on the cussing, Anderson? My kids are right over there."

I smile. "You bring it out in me."

He shakes a Lucky Strike from the green pack, lights it, then rests it on the edge of the crystal ashtray. "Good job with Schreiber."

I watch the ice in his glass melt into the Scotch. "He personifies scum."

"I don't see the man; I see the scientist."

"Karl."

In the living room, someone on the TV scores a touchdown and the agents cheer as one.

Karl slides a manila folder along the table toward me. "Got an EXORD."

Why does everything in the army have to be an acronym? It's Karl's favorite thing about the military.

"Can't we just call it an execute order, Karl?"

"Straight from JIOA."

"Geez."

"Obviously, Russia is the new threat now, and this guy, whom you're already familiar with, is top on their wish list."

He opens the folder to a thick dossier. The square at the top, usually reserved for a photo, is bare.

"No picture as you can see. Careful to stay out of the limelight. But we do know that he was widely known as your pal Dr. Snow."

Everything slows.

"You okay, Anderson? I know you've been tracking him. Thought you might like a shot."

I steady myself with one hand on the table. "You want Snow **here.** To be a paperclip scientist."

That sinks in as I page through the photos of Ravensbrück that must've been taken at liberation. The shooting wall. The crematoria. A black **mina** van, the tailgate open. All at once my stomach hurts.

"Why, Karl?"

Karl takes a drag of his cigarette. "I know this may be hard for you, after what he did to your mother, but the 'why' part is above your pay grade. Just get him here."

"He did more than experiment on my mother."

"Yes. Snow was a virologist and headed up every

sort of disease trial you can imagine, since they had free subjects to test on. Also, mustard gas testing at Sachsenhausen next door. Experimented on apes and cats. Men, too. Sixty of the ninety test subjects suffocated in agony."

I stare at the empty photo square. "Busy guy."

"He was a gynecologist as well, and as a hobby devised ways to increase the ranks of the German master race. Studied ways to encourage multiple births. Also led experiments to turn brown eyes blue. Sick stuff. Headed up a botched experimental children's ward at Ravensbrück called the **Kinderzimmer.**"

"My friend Arlette lost her son there. But why bring Snow here?"

"JIOA wants him. Mostly because the Russians do, and they have a jump on us. They have this guy's research." He slides a glossy photo toward me on the table, of a scared-looking middle-aged man wearing a pinstripe suit and a saber scar across his upper lip.

"Kurt Blome? He was on trial at Nuremberg. Can't believe he got off."

"Turns out the Red Army captured his research institute in Poland."

"I hate it when that happens."

"Well, he's on our team now. Says Snow is known as the most talented scientist working on infectious diseases and numero uno on the Russians' wish list. Won't give us a description of the guy, though. Claims he never saw him. Seems spooked."

"So?"

"All we know is Snow's continuing his work out of some secure location, and the Russians will do anything to get him."

I sit back in my chair. "What's the campaign? Candidate target list?"

"That's all I got. Wish we had more to go on, but I do know that if the Russians get Snow, we're in a bad spot."

"Why me? Tony P. jacks off to thoughts of being assigned to something like this."

"Jesus, Anderson. Keep it down. Do you want my kids to grow up perverts?"

"It's not like I know anyone who saw Snow at Ravensbrück. The smart doctors stayed incognito."

"You're a rare bird. An American that survived a Nazi concentration camp for starters. You know the territory, which will be a huge advantage for us. Plus, you've already been looking for him."

I shrug. "True."

"You're the best tracker we have. You have a freakish ability to spot liars, a useful skill in the circles you'll be traveling in, **and** you spend more time at the gun range than Tony P.'s group combined. And don't forget you literally wrote the book on SS blood-group tattoos." He reads from my bio: "**SS Blood-Group Tattoos and the Self-Inflicted Wounds Used to Eradicate Them.**"

"It's a pamphlet, Karl."

"The whole army uses it now. And the best thing about you? You're not on any covert radar. We barely even know you're here, ourselves."

"Thanks, Karl. But the only problem is I can't be in the same room with those murderers."

"No one **likes** it, Anderson. Also says here, 'accomplished photographer.' "

"Now you're just grasping for things."

"And some sort of fancy Columbia physics degree from the"—he checks his notes—"School of Engineering and Applied Science."

"Like that'll help in the field."

He continues scanning my biography. "Speaks French, German, and Slavic languages. Deep knowledge of Latin, comfortable in Greek."

"My Russian's not great."

Karl leans in. "Tony P. has barely mastered English."

I smile.

Karl stubs out his cigarette. "You just need to get over your mental health situation. The psych report said—"

"Major Vincent? The hostile Radcliffe grad who starts every conversation with, 'When I was at Cambridge . . .'?"

He checks the report. "She says you're still not sleeping well. Intrusive thoughts. Seeing her every month?"

"It's mandated, isn't it?"

"After your—"

"Leave it, Karl. I'm complying."

"Well, the good news is she just moved to the Paris office to head up all of Europe and has agreed to keep you on as a patient."

"Lovely."

"So, you can continue your mental health therapy if you accept the mission. Otherwise, no service weapon."

"I'm not **insane,** Karl."

The football watchers sense a disturbance, and a few look our way.

"I just need you **well.** No one can do this job like you. You've got scores of Nazi IDs cataloged in that beautiful brain of yours. Plus, you were a legit journalist."

The magician in the kitchen has moved on to balancing a chair upon his chin, as the mini guests jump up and down around him.

I shift in my seat. "I wrote for a propaganda rag in Paris for a few months. And worked for **The Daily American** for five minutes after the war."

"We'd like to give you a reporter cover."

I play with his cigarette package. "That's original. Do I get an alias?"

He grabs the package and tosses it aside. "No. You're not on anyone's radar. But you'll get a new security clearance."

As a peon I had a classified clearance. Next was secret and then the most coveted, top-secret, my dream.

I try to sound casual. "Bumped up to secret?"

He nods. "And you're lucky to get it with your, well, mental health situation, and all that French underground work in your past. **And** a non-American mother."

"Maybe you need someone heavier for this."

"I'm up to my armpits in feasibility studies. I need new eyes in the field, someone who can go in and get their own information. I've got six conflicting reports about what's happening out there. I want you to take your time, use your instincts, and follow every lead no matter how unlikely."

"But I just got my new map set up."

"Get Snow and you could write your own ticket back here in intelligence. That's how your dad climbed the ranks so fast."

"My dad's an asshole."

"Those Yale guys in the CIA think they're better than us. What is it they call him?"

"The Smartest Man in Washington."

"Only guy in foreign service history to ace his oral **and** written exams, and rumor was he didn't even study. We were all pea green with envy he and your mom got assigned Paris. Living at Hôtel de Pontalba."

"Didn't work out so well for us."

"Give him a break. No one realized how fast Hitler would grab Europe." Karl leans in. "That's ancient history now." He pauses and gathers strength. "So, what do you say? No more grunt work. You'll get to travel. The best hotels."

I try not to look at Karl's kind face, his raised eyebrows.

"The Grand Hotel Plaza if I go to Rome? The Ritz in Paris?"

He shrugs. “If the mission takes you there. You can retreat. Draw the shades and order room service.”

“Let me think about it.”

“I may be able to swing a promotion. How does Captain Anderson sound? There’s a pay bump.”

I sit up a little straighter. Equal rank to Tony P. and his acolytes. Would I get equal pay? Doubtful. I’d steamed open his pay envelope once when it came to my box by mistake. He makes four times what I do.

“How will I stay in contact?”

“No free mail, just regular status updates by encoded cable. Your case officer can help with that. And if you need to call long-distance, no names. We’ll just talk about the weather.”

“I don’t know, Karl.”

“You’d prefer the Russians get Snow? Why not bring him to justice?”

“It’s not exactly justice, tanning here at the pool, knocking back beers with the rest of Hitler’s friends.”

Karl leans back, fingers laced at his belly. “Y’know, I thought the world of your mother—got to know her well, back when Sharon and I visited Paris. Heard her sing in Montparnasse. Line around the block to get in to see her, ‘Lylou’ in lights on the marquee. ‘The Jewish Nightingale.’ I think she’d want you to do this.”

“I need to go.”

“And Johann would be your case officer. I know you two got on well when he was here for training.”

"I work best alone."

"You need an eye in the field, and Johann's it. That's the deal. What do you say? I can order activation now. You can leave tonight. Get your shots and briefing on board."

"Just don't know if this is right for me."

He sits forward, arms on the table. "Look, you can stay this way for the rest of your life, lock that soft part of yourself away and not give it to anyone. It feels good to wrap it carefully with routines and solitude in that basement office. Or you can take a chance." He looks down at his hands for a long second. "To really live is to be exposed."

Is this how caring, fatherly advice works? If it's a ploy to get me to commit, it's working.

"Plus, getting Snow would make JIOA very happy. I don't have to tell you what pleasing the president's most trusted military advisers means. They've got Korea to worry about. Now's not the time to start another war."

"Roger."

"You'll have every man in that living room jumping to your orders."

I smile. "Like that'd happen."

"Your country needs you."

"Give me twenty-four hours, Karl."

He nods. "I'm here."

I salute and leave the dining area, hurrying by Tony P. and his pals. They make little kissy sounds as I pass.

"Frigid Frenchie," one of them mutters with a snicker, and I vow to get off the base soon and have sex with the first tolerable human I see.

Bobby Flynn leans back and blows cigarette smoke in my path. "Gonna go chase some bad Nazis, Anderson?"

I raise my middle finger and keep walking.

"Oooooh, feisty," one says.

"Good luck, Anderson," Tony P. calls after me. "See you back here in a week."

I RETURN TO MY apartment, head pounding, and wish my mother were here to help me decide what to do. Though I hadn't told Karl, the thought of finally seeing Snow face-to-face torches my insides. How many times had I imagined that death? I could hunt him courtesy of the U.S. Army and then take things into my own hands. Maybe arrange an accident at the grab site or even back here at Fort Bliss. Justice would finally be done, after all that suffering at Ravensbrück. There would be no steak and BBQs for Snow.

But the thought of leaving the safety of my office is daunting. And where would I even start looking for him?

After draining a bottle of bad white burgundy, I'm still torn and drift off to sleep, hoping I'll think better in the morning. In the light of day, I'll weigh the choices and surely realize it's better to stay here. Status quo.

Soon my mother comes, as always, arm outstretched, hand reaching for me. It's all so **real,** and it's good to see her, so young and carefree, dark hair long to her shoulders. That look on her face, like she has some sort of delicious secret to share. She's so happy to see me, too, and I take a step toward her. Why haven't I seen her in so long? I try to reach my hand out, but my arm won't move, like it's pinned to my side.

"Where's Mimi?" I ask.

She doesn't hear me. Just starts receding into the darkness, as always.

The panic rises. "What's happening, Mother? Please stay."

She fades farther into the darkness.

I try to follow. "Don't leave me."

She smiles as she drifts away.

"Come back," I call after her.

I wake bathed in sweat, heart beating out of my chest, and sit up.

The clock on the dresser reads 4:00 A.M.

I hurry to my uniform on the floor where I left it, pull it on, throw some clothes in a suitcase, and arrive back at Karl's house in minutes, knocking on the door, as a black-windowed car idles in his driveway.

Karl answers dressed in khaki pants and a button-down shirt.

I salute him. "Major."

He returns the salute and tries to do the stoic military thing and hide his smile, but it's there. "Had a feeling you'd be here, Anderson. That's your ride. The plane's waiting. We'll get you out to the airstrip stat, airborne in one hour. You'll arrive in Paris at 1400 hours, lay over, and continue to Vienna to receive orders."

"Will do."

"And just make sure you take him alive. Only shoot to incapacitate. Got it?"

"Yes, sir."

I head down the gravel path toward the car, and he calls to me. "Bring back Snow, Anderson."

I turn to him there standing in the doorway and salute.

He returns the salute. "For Lylou."

CHAPTER 7

ARLETTE

PARIS, FRANCE
1952

THE BELL RINGS, AND I RUSH TO MEET JOSIE AT the door of my apartment. I can't wait to see her and get her help sorting through all the Luc Minau confusion. She'll be so happy to hear I may have found Willie.

Every part of me rejoices to see her standing there with that perfect caramel-smooth complexion and lovely gamine way. She looks chic in a black cashmere coat. Though she carries her old army-green backpack over her shoulder, her only fashion faux pas, I'm relieved to see she's holding a bottle of my favorite pinot noir, saving us from the day-old sauvignon blanc in the icebox. Her dark hair is cut a bit shorter, but her beautiful, expressive face still shows every thought and feeling.

We wrap our arms around each other, jump up and down, and share a happy little scream. It's not until I kiss her on both cold cheeks that I see the tears.

I hold her at arm's length. "Don't cry. You'll get me going."

"I'm just so happy to see you."

"How's my favorite female?" She laughs and I pull her in. "I long for you to move back here so desperately. It's like I'm missing an arm."

Josie surveys the room, and her eye falls on the bassinet, but she doesn't mention it. I know I should get rid of it, but somehow I can't.

"I've missed you, too." She hands me the wine bottle. "It's hard to have fun in Texas."

She doesn't mention our arrest, which happened on that very spot, or my aunt's unfortunate demise, but her gaze flashes to the place on the parquet floor where the blood stained the wood, still there, now under a suitcase-sized hooked rug. A wave of dread washes through me, and I tamp it down. What she doesn't see is the dresser drawers still holding the clothes Willie wore before we left here so abruptly that day.

And three stacks of never used cloth diapers.

She slips off her coat to reveal the blouse and Marlene Dietrich trousers I made her so long ago. It's the outfit she'd been arrested in and wore every day at the camp. The blouse has faded, except for the triangle-shaped area on the left sleeve where she'd worn her red prisoner badge, but the trousers have only a small patch along a side seam.

My tears return. "Your signature outfit." I run one hand down her sleeve. "It's a miracle it survived the camp."

"Best birthday gift ever. Took forever to get the white paint off the back."

"Willie loved that blouse. Remember?"

Josie smiles and brushes away a tear of her own. "He had good taste for a baby."

I place my hands over my face.

I blot my wet cheeks with the cuff of my shirt. "I'm sorry. This is supposed to be joyous."

Josie sits on the sofa. "I think about him every day."

I step to the kitchen and open the wine. "I have so much to tell you, Josie. I think I may have finally found Fleur, at Metropolitan Women's Hospital. A ward of the state. I tried to visit her there, but the staff is so hostile—they'll only allow family and doctors to visit."

"Last time I saw her she was going to break into the **Revier** and get Mother's necklace back. She could have written by now. Hope she's okay, sweet girl."

"She was taken a whole month before we were liberated. God knows what Snow did to her in that time. But I gave Metropolitan what money I had, to make sure she's treated well."

"And they still won't let you see her? Did you tell them she's an orphan?"

"Yes. But I thought they wanted more of a bribe, so I sold your radio."

"**What?** How could you?"

"I had to, Jos. To a memorabilia collector. I gave the money to the hospital. Not sure it will even go to Fleur. They keep saying they need more before I can see her."

"They're scamming you."

"I want Fleur to come live with me. First step is to get her out of there. I hear they beat the patients. We can move her right around the corner here—to Paris General. Maybe even visit her together while you're here? Try to figure out a way in? I overheard them saying the patients exercise in the yard at noon."

"Wish I could, but I'm just in Paris overnight. Only have time for a quick drink."

"I wish you'd stay here with me. Like the old days."

"Let me at least help you fund Fleur's care, though."

"I hate to have you—"

"I love her, too, Arl. The paper booked me at the Ritz. I'll ask them to wire funds."

"The Ritz?" I pour the wine into two glasses. "How is that possible? One night there costs more than I'd make in six lifetimes." I stop mid-pour. "Wait. Are you back into undercover work?"

She laughs. "No. Of course, I'd tell you. Just doing a story on hotels. They'll probably put me in the broom closet or something. Then I'm booked after that. My shrink moved here to Paris. Need to see her."

"Still seeing a psychiatrist? You know you can always call me if you feel sad."

Josie accepts a glass of wine. "I'm fine. Still have your grief box?" she asks in an offhand way.

In the early days after liberation, after we'd walked out the Ravensbrück front gates, physically free but crippled by loss, she'd become concerned about me. Once I came back to an empty apartment without my son, I obsessed over my little shoebox, endlessly examining the contents like a magpie. Sketching pictures of the items inside. Stroking the lock of Willie's hair against my cheek. I read **Puss and Boots** aloud, trying to remember the expressions he'd had when I'd read it to him as a baby. Had he smiled? I sit. "Oh, no. I'm well past all that. I'm so much better now."

"No more thoughts about . . ." She nods toward the fireplace. "You know."

"You can say it. Auntie? Perhaps I still think of it on occasion."

"You saved us from her. Protected yourself, and you have to keep doing that. How are Bep and Riekie?"

"Good. Both married. And you're not going to believe it." I pause. "I may have found Willie."

"What? No." Her eyes grow moist. "How is that even possible?"

I pour us both more wine. "Yes, a man who runs a foundation called Hope Home looked me up and said they think they may have my son."

"Have him where?"

"Down at their children's camp in French Guiana."

Josie sets down her glass. "Doesn't that sound strange to you? Who goes to French Guiana?"

"Many Parisians. It's warm and sunny there right now. But, yes, I'm skeptical."

"And what foundation is this?"

"It benefits underprivileged children. Run by Mr. Luc Minau. His grandmother matches the orphans to long-lost parents as a hobby."

"And they just happened to find your child."

I sit back. "Why do I feel like I'm on trial here?"

"I'm just worried he might be another scammer."

"You're right. That's entirely possible, so I'm being careful, but he really may have found my **son,** Josie. He's sending over references. Showed me some things at their office that may have been Willie's. His blanket."

"My God. The green one?"

"Incredible, right? Same monogram and everything."

"Where did they find it?"

"They have all these things found at the Lebensborn homes."

"How did they get them?"

"The German government uses them as a clearinghouse of sorts, where parents can go to find lost kids."

"Had you ever heard of them in all your charity work?"

"No, but there are hundreds of organizations doing this work." I sip my wine. "And I saw some silver cups in the safe. I need to sneak back in to look at those. He might have the one they intended for Willie."

"Why break in? Just ask—"

"I did, but Luc avoided answering me directly about it."

"Willie never got one of those cups."

"**No,** but they had one waiting for his adoptive SS family. It would be engraved with his birth date and the name of the family he was promised to. Perhaps they took Willie after all. I could at least track them down and inquire."

"If this guy is rich, he has an alarm system."

"Just his Matisse is wired."

"Matisse?"

"And I'm sure he's not there at night."

"You must be rusty."

"I've kept my hand in it. Broke into the American embassy and took two cartons of caviar for the Ravensbrück survivors. It was embarrassingly easy."

Josie smiles. "Old habits never die."

"If de Gaulle helped the female survivors I wouldn't have to do such things. It's a disgrace."

"Luc's office door isn't wired?"

"The front door isn't armed, simple pin-and-tumbler lock. And the safe is a common dial combination—ninety percent are the same pattern. Nothing I can't handle." I pour more wine. "**And** he invited me to come to French Guiana to meet some of the boys."

"Isn't it a bit hasty, flying off with someone you barely know? You need to be careful."

"Well, I did agree to go out with him for dinner."

"Arlette—"

"At Chez **Dauphine.**"

"Wow. No one can get in there. Is this . . . romantic?"

"No. But so what if it was?"

Josie evades my gaze. "Well, you know how you are."

I set down my glass. "So I like strong men."

"Controlling, more like. There was that bartender from Biarritz who had you working for him for nothing—"

I set down my glass. "Do we have to dredge up my romantic past? I do need to find out if Willie is down there, don't you agree?"

"This guy can send you photos of the children. You really shouldn't go running off—"

"I'm twenty-six, pretty much broke, and couldn't live with myself if I didn't pursue this."

Josie shakes her head. "Fine."

"If there's a shred of hope I might find Willie, I need to go. And is it so terrible it might be somewhere warm and pleasant? Don't I deserve a break? Do you know how many coffee cups I've washed as of yesterday? Ten thousand and seven."

"You're counting again?"

"I go on dates and hard as I try, they don't call. Who can blame them when they see my leg? It nauseates **me.**"

"Who needs a man? Be your own knight in shining armor."

"They pretend not to notice, and I never see them again. Why shouldn't I pursue this? If there's a shred of hope Willie is alive, I have to consider it."

"Then keep it strictly business."

"If I have to flirt with him a little to get my child back, so be it. You Americans are such prudes."

"Maybe just focus on your own happiness, not on pleasing a man. Your own countrywoman said it best. 'A girl should be two things. Who and what she wants.' "

I pour myself more wine. "Eh. Coco Chanel. Collaborator. She should stick to clothes. How's **your** man situation?"

"Nonexistent."

"Then perhaps focus on your own love life," I reply with cold formality. "Maybe find a good lover. Some sex would do you good."

Josie rubs my back. "Don't be cross with me, Arlette. You're right. If this really is Willie, it's a miracle. And if you want to encourage this Luc guy, that's your choice. But the French Guiana part is troubling. South America's crawling with Nazis. Mengele's running around scot-free down there somewhere."

I lock my fingers in my lap. "Luc told me some Nazis have escaped to Brazil and Argentina, but Germans have lived in South America for years. Besides, Luc's no Nazi sympathizer—he's French."

"There were plenty of French Nazis in German uniform, Arlette." Josie slides a sheath of contact sheets from her bag. "Look. If you do end up going down there, take these with you. If you recognize any of them, call me—"

"Journalist? Really? Carrying around contact sheets of fugitive Nazis?"

"I don't control what stories they assign."

I push the photos away. "I'm going there to see if I can reconnect with my **child,** Josie, in French Guiana, a colony of France, not some Argentine Nazi hideaway."

"Another way to ferret them out is to check under the left arm for a blood-type tattoo."

"That'll be a fun dinner activity. I assume Luc'll be wearing a shirt. And frankly, I don't have the stomach for espionage anymore."

"We've been through a lot together, Arlette. You survived Ravensbrück, got out of that Lebensborn home."

"I don't even know what I'll do if I find Willie. Might lose my mind with happiness. But I'm not sure how he'll feel about me. Plus, it'll be an expensive flight. At least three hundred dollars."

"I can help—"

"Thank you, but **no,** dear friend. I must do this myself. At least it will be a nice warm stay at Luc's grandmother's place, called Cove House. If it's terrible, there are flights back every Saturday."

"Just be careful, Arlette." Josie scribbles down an

address in Vienna. “I know you have great instincts, but unfamiliar places can cloud judgment. Money has a way of doing that, too.”

I sip my wine. “Might be nice to see how the other half lives.”

“Money can cause more problems than it solves.”

“Easy to say when you’ve had it your whole life.”

Josie leans closer. “I’m just trying to keep you safe. I hate being so far from you. If you need me, contact me here. If you’re compromised, remember the code phrase.”

“Toast with marmalade? Aren’t we being a bit dramatic, playing spy?”

“Just promise me you’ll think twice before you trust your happiness to a man.”

“It’s worth at least checking this lead, don’t you think? Sometimes I think if Gunther were here—”

“You don’t need him to find your son. Just be smart about it. I almost lost you once. Won’t let that happen again.”

CHAPTER 8

JOSIE

PARIS, FRANCE
1952

THE MORNING AFTER SEEING ARLETTE, I WAKE at the Ritz, in the most beautiful hotel room in Paris. Even in my travels with my diplomat father I've never seen such a room. True to his word, Karl has pulled out all the stops. The Belle Epoque décor. The canopied bed, soft creams, and whites. Robin's-egg blue suede upholstered French chairs. The impossibly perfect sheets, crisp and smooth and scented with lavender. It's easy to see why the Ritz demanded the respect of even Nazi military forces, who requisitioned the hotel during the war and agreed to lay down their arms at the door and not wear uniforms when in residence.

The only thing my room is missing is a view of **la tour Eiffel.**

I force myself out of bed to bathe, due at the therapist's office that morning and then on a flight to Austria to meet with my new field boss. But then, seeing it's a gray day, I slide back into bed. I'm not looking forward to the forty-five-minute session with the headshrinker, picking through my neuroses together like Alaskan cannery workers through crab bodies. I write in my notebook a list of places we might find more Snow information. Johann has an aunt who may have known Snow. Rome seems like a good prospect, too. The Vatican was involved in ferrying Nazis to South America. The ratline. But where to start?

When I finally dress and get underway, I'm late for the appointment. But it's for the best. Less time to get to the deeper questions. I've gotten good at providing the answers she needs to hear. Anything to not feel the worst part.

Dr. Marjorie Vincent's office is on the sixth floor of a fabulous old-world Paris sort of building, with a gray limestone façade. As I climb the worn marble steps, I have plenty of time to consider my own behavior from the previous night. Was it the wine? I'd been such a harsh critic, interrogating my best friend like that. Arlette was right; I should be happy for her. But I had to stick with my instincts. It was as if when she lost Willie she lost all self-sufficiency, too.

I make it to the sixth-floor office, located in

a residential apartment as so many doctors' offices are in France. There's no one in the reception area, so I wander back to what was once the dining room to find Dr. Vincent sitting at a small writing desk near the window working on paperwork. It smells like every Parisian's apartment, of strong coffee and something buttery warming in the oven. Croissants?

She's backlit by the window and basically just a silhouette, but I'd know that hunched posture anywhere. I step closer. She has new horn-rim glasses. And how confident of her to wear pants. Now that she lives here, she'll probably act like she invented Paris.

"Congratulations on the promotion," I say. "I like the new digs."

"Nice of you to show up." She sips her coffee. "Twenty minutes late."

The doctor is already settled in, thick, green felt stapled to the dining room door for patient privacy, and she has arranged on end tables the statues she had back at Fort Bliss, copies of what Freud kept in his consulting room back in the day. One of Eros, winged god of love, running, torso rippling, arms raised as if ready to ascend. And the other, Thanatos, god of death, who stares at the ground, sword raised. Freud thought everyone was driven by one or the other, love or death.

Pretty sure I'm on the Thanatos side.

The croissants smell good, like my mother's apartment the last time I saw her. The coffee smells good, too, but I hesitate to ask for a cup, wanting to get the session over with.

"My bed at the Ritz was too warm to leave."

"At least you're sleeping. Care for coffee?" Her gentle voice is so soothing. **Did they practice that in Radcliffe psychotherapy class?**

"No, thank you." I step to the window and look out. On the street below, a woman dressed in a pea green coat leans on her broom as she argues with two young boys.

Dr. Vincent moves to her official leather upholstered doctor chair near the sofa, and then waves me over.

"It's customary to sit for therapy sessions," she says.

"I like standing, thanks."

She stares at me for a moment and then nods as if replaying our last disastrous session in Texas. She lifts her pad and pen from the table.

"Have you made any progress on your treatment goals?"

"Refresh me."

"In touch with your father?"

"No, thank God. He's too busy with his ladylove."

My gaze wanders to her desk, invoices and letters strewn about on her blotter.

"How's the drinking?" she asks.

"Mine or his?"

She stares at the floor.

"No more Scotch for me, per your suggestion. A beer now and then." I look to her and smile. "Actually, come to think of it, I **would** like some coffee. Might get the memories flowing."

She stands and hurries off to the kitchen, and I step to her desk and rifle through her papers, looking for the shine of plastic. I hear the clack of her heels on the parquet hallway floor as she returns, slide open the pencil drawer, and find her identification badge there. I pocket it and return to stand at the window.

Dr. Vincent enters with my coffee, sets it on the windowsill, and takes her seat.

"Did you schedule the hydrotherapy?" she asks.

"I did. Just made my fingers pruney."

All at once freezing rain pelts the window, melting the Paris rooftops into a blur of grays and blues.

"Did you try the ceramics class? Leather making?"

"I'm not insane. Just having some thoughts. That ping-pong around in my head. Won't go away."

She smooths back her hair with one hand. "The Buddhists call that monkey brain."

Down on the street the freezing rain pelts the woman with the broom, and she hurries inside; pedestrians scatter.

"Eating again?" she asks.

"Some. I stopped taking the tranquilizers. They made me feel weird."

"It would help to know these things." She stares at me for a long second. "Are you willing to talk about . . . the incident?"

"You can say it."

"Your attempt at taking your own life? There's mounting evidence that talking about your issues may help you deal with them."

I toe the parquet floor. Like those in our Paris apartment. Such intricate work, just to get walked on.

She crosses her legs. "I can't certify you for duty this time without serious progress. So, you need to cooperate or hand in your service weapon."

"Fine," I say. "It was a garden-variety suicide attempt. After my dad got Arlette and me out of Ravensbrück, so-called liberation. We walked out of there, and Dad had sent a car for us. It was so strange being in a car again after so long."

"And the attempt?"

"Once I got home to Washington, the house was so quiet without my mother there."

"And?"

"I did it in my childhood bedroom in Alexandria. Would have succeeded if the cleaning lady hadn't come in and heard the chair tip over and cut me down."

"Says here you used an unusual method—"

"I suppose. I hung myself with my dog's leash. Former dog. We were inseparable before my father gave him away when we moved to France."

She nods as she writes.

I heave a sigh. "Talking about it just makes it worse."

"It's important to probe the trauma, Captain. Any more suicidal thoughts?"

"No. But I do keep replaying one scene in my head, from the last time I saw my mother. Like it's stuck. Comes back at the worst times. When I see a truck like those at Ravensbrück. Or just a whiff of gasoline exhaust can set me off."

"People with your type of hyperactive memory often suffer intense snapshots of certain traumatic moments." She holds up one splayed hand. "Normal memory is like a web." She holds up her pen in the other. "Yours is like a spike, and once a traumatic memory is impaled there it's very difficult to shake. Often recurs during stressful moments. Can be triggered by anything associated with the event."

"When I dream of her I always wake up before I get to the worst part."

"So, you've never allowed yourself to revisit it?"

"No." The thought makes my throat constrict.

"Can you describe it?"

"Drinking helped at first. Now, even that won't help. Can you just give me an injection or something?"

"It's not that easy. We've been having good results with electroshock therapy. But without extreme measures, you must confront the moment. Do everything you can to relax."

"I'm bad at relaxing."

"Try square breathing. Deep breath in. Hold. Deep breath out." She raises one eyebrow. "Or take a lover."

"You're not the first to suggest that."

"Why not consider it? When was the last time you were interested in getting intimate with someone?"

I watch the rain. "At Ravensbrück. My Italian bunkmate fellow prisoner."

The doctor looks at me over the tops of her glasses. "Freud considered lesbianism a gateway to mental illness. And you know how the army feels about that behavior. I won't put it in the official notes."

"Her name was Ariana," I say.

I still love the feel of her name on my tongue, even after all she did.

"She didn't exactly return my affection. Double-crossed me, in fact. Maybe it was just a crush, I don't know. I like men, in theory, but it's hard to find any worth the time."

"If you stay closed off like this, you may wait forever. Now that you've been promoted to captain, are you connecting better now? With co-workers? Friends?"

I shrug and look back out the window. "I'll be happy to see Johann Vitner again. My new case officer."

She checks her notes. "You met him when he was in Texas for orientation."

"He's not like the other agents."

"Meaning?"

"Assholes." I rub a smudge off the windowpane. "He's a homosexual, so the other guys berate him mercilessly."

"And you?"

"I think he should be able to do what he wants. It's stupid the army threatened to take his security clearance away just for having a boyfriend."

"How is your friend Arlette?"

"We had kind of a fight. Some man showed up telling her he thinks he has the son she lost at Ravensbrück. I told her she's making a mistake pursuing it."

"People have to make their own decisions."

"Lately she seems incapable of protecting herself. Can't get mad. Hold people accountable."

"Like you do?"

"Yes. I think if you do something wrong you should pay."

"Your new mission seems right up that alley."

"Dr. Snow."

"And how was he connected to your mother's death exactly?"

"It all came out at the Nuremberg trials, though Snow had already vanished, well before the trial even began. He headed up many of the worst things at Ravensbrück. And then selected half the camp for the gas chamber."

"How do you know that?"

"Evidence at the trial. Signed orders."

"Are you making progress?"

"I just got here."

"Can you tell me more about what happened to your mother?"

"Just that I was afraid to die and that my cowardice killed her."

She leans forward. "You could have saved her?"

"If I'd admitted I'm Jewish. She came to the camp

well after us, so no one knew we were related. She was adamant about me not revealing our connection. Thought I'd be in danger if they found out I was her daughter."

"It could have meant death for you as well."

"A good person would have done it regardless. At least I could have been with her. At the end." I cross my arms over my belly. "She must have been terrified."

"Did you get to say goodbye?"

My chest goes tight. "I really can't—"

"You need to confront it sometime, Captain."

I stare out the window.

She sits up straighter. "If you catch the elusive Dr. Snow, what then?"

I shrug. "He goes back to Texas."

"Then your job is done?"

"According to the mission plan."

"You clocked more than twice the number of gun-range hours than any other agent at Fort Bliss. Can you hand him over without killing him yourself?"

I look her in the eye and shorten my answer since liars tend to babble. "Yes."

She gazes back. "I'm not feeling confident you're being honest with me, Captain."

I clap my hands together. "Am I free to go now? I have to catch a plane."

She scribbles on her pad. "This was good work today. I'll file another extension. But I need to see you in a month." She hands me the paper. "Be careful out there."

Clearly, she's referring to more than the freezing rain.

She stands. "I know losing your mother was difficult, Captain, but killing an asset you've been ordered to catch and return won't solve the problem."

"Can I keep my firearm?"

"For now. But this is the last extension if you can't confront the crux of this. It may come at the most seemingly random moment, but let it come; don't repress it. Your life may depend on it."

I hurry down the stairs, my steps loud on the marble. The doctor is 100 percent onto me, as usual. I feel the photo of my mother I carry deep in my pocket, the one of her with her head turned as if looking over her shoulder. Just in case I do come face-to-face with Snow, I'll brandish the photo and ask, "Remember her? This is for Lylou," before I pull the trigger, aiming for the high A-zone. Lungs **and** heart.

I step out onto the street and walk back to the hotel, my mind a whirl of fragments and places. My mother. Mimi. It hurts to think of them, but I breathe, deep breath in, deep breath out.

I surprise a flock of pigeons on the sidewalk, and they flutter off in one hundred directions, taking me back to another time, to another glorious Parisian house. So many years ago.

CHAPTER 9

JOSIE

PARIS, FRANCE
1943
Before.

I SPRINTED THROUGH THE COBBLESTONE STREETS, back to our apartment behind the grand Hôtel de Pontalba, a gendarme close behind. I lost him and ducked into a side entrance, the sounds of German officers at the midday meal coming from the grand dining room in the main house, the scent of knockwurst wafting into the vestibule. How good it would be to eat something besides root vegetables.

I followed the scent of lye and cooked turnips up the stairs to the third floor of that glorious old place, the marble steps bowed from centuries of footfall. I entered and stepped through fresh laundry hung from the clotheslines that crisscrossed the front parlor, to my mother at the stove shaving turnips into a pan of boiling water, as Herr Bauer's underpants bubbled in lye next to it on the stove.

"Where have you been all morning?" Mother asked.

I shrugged. "How is a person supposed to enjoy April in Paris when the streets are clogged with Nazis?"

Mother stepped to me. "Keep your voice down, **ma chère.**"

I set my ugly little potato on the kitchen counter. "At least I got this."

"Oh, **Josie.** How wonderful."

"Do you ever get mad? You don't even blame the Nazis. Look at this place. What they've forced us to do."

We'd relocated from D.C. to Paris just months before the war, with my father, in his new position as deputy chief to the ambassador, carrying out directives from Washington. Along with some other embassy staff, we'd been staying temporarily at the magnificent Hôtel de Pontalba, once a grand private residence, and had expected Father home any moment from a trip to Rome, when the Nazis rolled into Paris. There was a short window when we could have left with the rest of the embassy staff, to the south where they relocated, but Mimi, my grandmother, was sick and could not be moved.

So, there we were, stranded in Paris without him.

The Nazis took the Louis XVII bronze clocks first. Then Mother was forced to sell most of her own furniture, in what she called her "Flea Market Phase."

First, the regency dining table. Then they rolled up Mimi's Hamadan carpet and dragged it down three flights. That's when Mother started doing paid singing engagements in cabarets again, what she called her "Rebirth Phase."

I headed for the door. "I'm going back out."

"Again? Have you finished your math work?"

"I've taught myself the whole course. I need to get out there and live."

Once it was clear Father was not coming back, the Nazis relocated us to the apartment of the former hotel manager, in the rear annex of the mansion, a separate three-story add-on. They slipped an envelope under the door, and Mimi opened it to read, as Mother and I gathered close, a black eagle at the letterhead. **"Warten auf eine diplomatische Lösung,"** Mimi read.

Awaiting diplomatic resolution.

That was the last thing we'd heard, but we knew we were watched, followed by a revolving band of Gestapo agents, at first robustly and now less so. Clearly, they wanted my father. To use as a negotiating tool with Roosevelt? And we were the bait. They must have wanted him badly, to keep Jews alive.

It had once been quite a nice apartment, the soaring windows overlooking emerald stretches of garden, the Eiffel Tower in the distance always a symbol of hope. It was so different from our stone-fronted bungalow in a suburb of Washington, D.C., back in the States, during Mother's "U.S. Diplomatic Wife Phase."

Gradually her clients' sheets and underpants and trousers filled the clotheslines, a window open to invite the spring air in to dry them. There was a breadbox-sized unpainted section of wall near the service entrance door, wires poking out like Medusa's snakes, from where the telephone company man had ripped out our phone.

"I'm very sorry," the man had said as he pulled the phone from the wall. He had kind eyes, and it wasn't his fault Jews could no longer have phones. But it was one less lifeline to my father.

At least Mother had managed to hold on to the original sign from LaPaix, her father's famous jewelry store, which stood on the opposite wall.

Mother brushed my bangs back, her fingers cold on my forehead. "Please wait for a bit, **ma petite.** They'll be arriving for lunch soon."

By "they" she meant Goebbels's soldiers who'd moved into Pontalba once Hitler occupied Paris. We could see them down there from the kitchen window, the dining room of the mansion crowded with them, as they sang German folk songs, the sweet scent of baking marzipan drifting upstairs.

"Best for you not to be out walking with them arriving. Especially when you refuse to wear your star. One wrong move and they'll have you for good."

I rubbed Mother's back. How thin she'd become, her famous curves now gone. But even three years after the Nazis rode into Paris and raised the swastika over the Arc de Triomphe and the Eiffel Tower, she still took great care of herself and Mimi. She wore her favorite green dress from her days as a performer, now baggy through the waist and threadbare at the elbows, a yellow star sewn at her chest. Every now and then the officers would get drunk and call up to her from the terrace below to come sing for them.

One night they offered her some bread and cheese if she came down to perform, and she didn't return until morning. She brought a whole chicken back with her, but my grandmother barely spoke to her for a week.

I hugged myself. "It's chilly in here."

"Keep your coat on. And must you wear those trousers?" She pulled me close. "**Résistance** fighters wear them. Are you working in the underground?"

"I wish. I'll go mad if I don't go out. You used to go out all the time and were fine."

As soon as I said it, I wished I could take it back. How gay Mother's life had once been, one of the most famous singers in Paris. But once we got stuck there with no money, she'd sold the Model O Steinway with the satinwood case, a gift from her father. Something died in her after the moving men opened the French windows and lifted it out by crane to the terrace below, but the proceeds got us through the worst of the war. Then she took in laundry, a new phase too degrading to name.

"Stay in for now." Mother leaned in closer.

"Imagine the conversation if you're caught. 'I don't wear my star since my father is Episcopalian and my mother is a Jew from Le Marais.' We'd all be carted off."

"Mimi's wasting to nothing. You as well. Once Father returns, he'll find our mummified corpses."

Mother threw back her head and laughed. The old Mother from what seemed like a faraway time. "Such drama. We'll make do."

"There's still hope Father's coming back, don't you think?" I held back tears for Mother's sake. She missed him more than anyone.

Mother smoothed one hand down my cheek. "It's impossible to get diplomatic families out now. I'm sure he's back in Washington lobbying for our release. We just need to wait."

"I don't understand why he hasn't written."

"Of course he has. But the Germans are probably just withholding the letters, so he'll come here, and they'll arrest him. He's too smart for that."

All at once something gray shot in through the window and flew under one of Mother's sheets. She let out a little yelp and ran to it. "Oh, Josie, help me. That bird will soil my laundry—"

The poor thing struggled, trapped under the linen, beating her wings, until Mother pulled the sheet from the line, shook it from the window, and off the bird flew.

We stood and watched it soar off above the rooftops.

"Just a pigeon," I said.

One hand to her forehead to shield the sun, Mother watched it go. "That's a dove."

I helped her pull the splotched sheet back in. "Same thing. You even think the best of pigeons."

Mother continued to watch as the bird became just a speck. "She's beautiful and strong and whatever we call her, she's free now."

"Look at your sheets. Ruined with pigeon tracks. And she didn't even pay for her crime."

Mother turned to me. "You're a funny girl, Josie. Always wanting justice. Forgiveness is better, **ma chère.**"

"I will never forgive them for this stupid curfew. How is a young person supposed to enjoy life stuck at home past nine o'clock? It's barbaric."

A sharp knock came at the door.

Mother pushed me toward the bedroom Mimi and I shared. "Quick. It may be one of the officers. Better if they don't see you."

"Why?"

"**Josephine.** Just go."

I stepped into the bedroom, and Mother closed the door behind me, just as my grandmother hid something under the covers.

I squinted one eye at her. "Were you listening to the BBC again, Mimi?"

Mimi, the product of a street sweeper and a cheesemonger, at just seventeen had married a talented young jewelry designer, Josel Charpak. The true brains of the business, Mimi helped him build a renowned Paris jewelry business, and at eighty years old, her bright eyes still caught everything. We'd sold most of our clothes, but she'd held on to the old chinchilla fur she wore like a bed jacket. I noted the framed photo of my father I kept by the bed now lay facedown on the bedside table again.

"Don't tell your mother. I can't listen to French news anymore. All that Nazi propaganda. They are now calling this the decade of lies. Is that not true? Truth and trust are gone. Replaced with fear, and hatred."

I stepped to the bed. "No more BBC, Mimi. Just read a novel."

She'd been known as quite a beauty back when she'd met Grandfather, evidenced in the photos from her younger days, with her glorious dark hair, now pure white and worn up in a topknot. They'd owned many Scottish terriers through the years, and her collection of glass Scotties, those we hadn't sold off, sat up and begged from the table next to her.

"I need this to all be over so I can find your grandfather."

Just the thought of my gentle grandfather roused a sob, and I turned from her to hide my eyes, glassed with tears. I was named after Josel and he'd always favored me, showing me off at the store to his customers. How could I even say the words that he was probably dead, for Nazis took him from his office in the jewelry store the very first day they rolled into Paris? Mother and I had watched from the end of the street as they ransacked the building, carrying off the three safes full of jewelry trays. They even took the employees.

"And you must be careful listening to the radio, Mimi. If they hear downstairs . . ."

She reached out one hand. "Give me a kiss, my **sheyna punim.**"

I bent to kiss her soft cheek and smiled. "I'm not a beautiful face."

I breathed in her scent, of sugar baked into her from years of making her raspberry crumb babka.

"Anyone can be pretty, but **your** face. Those high cheekbones and smart brown eyes. That is an **intriguing** face. Like me as a girl. Same dark hair, thick as a horse's tail."

"Father always says I look like him."

She waved that idea away. "**Ach.** Don't talk to me about him."

I lifted Father's photo and set it upright again. "You've never given him a chance."

"He married your mother for the money, not that she admits that. You'll see. He has no intention of coming back for us." She drew me closer. "He was always asking your mother for loans from her trust that we worked day and night for. And where is he now?"

"We need to be quiet. Someone's at the door. Let's sit you up."

I felt the bones of her spine through her fur jacket as I lifted her and slid a second pillow behind her head.

"Shall we play cards?" Mimi asked, eyes wide. Her most adorable hopeful look, impossible to resist. A stab of sadness wrenched me. Her life had been reduced to this.

"Mother wants me to study."

"I don't know how an old woman is expected to pass the time without some sort of hobby. Gin rummy? We could play for cigarettes."

The apartment door closed with a distant thud.

Mimi clutched the neck of her coat. "Is it one of them?"

"Maybe. Try to be quiet now."

I pressed my eye to a crack in the door and saw a man standing in our living room talking to Mother, holding a paper carton. He was on the older side and quite stout, dressed in the whole horrible black uniform of the SS. As they talked, she pulled sheets down off the lines and folded them.

"What's going on?" Mimi whispered.

"A soldier has brought a box," I whispered back.

I pressed my eye closer to the crack and took in the man smiling at my mother. I saw only part of a thick neck and face, his white-blond hair ruffling as he removed his cap.

The man waved toward the clotheslines. "Is my laundry ready?"

"Almost, Herr Bauer. I'm behind on my ironing."

He handed her the box. "Take this as early payment, since I'm sure your laundry skills are as good as you are pretty."

I turned and whispered to Mimi. "He's **flirting** with her." Disgusting.

Herr Bauer left, and I hurried out.

"What did he bring?" I stepped to the carton. "Two potatoes and a rotten onion?"

"And a little flour, can you believe it? We can make some fried apples for Mimi."

"He was flirting with you, and you smiled at him. How can you?"

She averted her gaze. "We just need a little help. We'll starve otherwise."

"He's at least ten years older than you, and you flirted back. What would Father think?"

"These days we must take kindness wherever we can." She drew me closer. "And remember, we can replace anything they take."

"But they'll never get this." I pulled the gold necklace by the chain from the throat of my dress, the eighteen-karat gold acorn, which her jeweler father had made for Mimi, so beautifully detailed down to the little fish-scale-like chevrons on the acorn cap. No one knew that just by pressing the right spot the cap popped open, offering the perfect little place to hide a treat.

Since we came to live in Paris, whoever had the necklace would give it to the other to wear, the secret compartment inside hiding a note or a special little thing to brighten the other's day.

I took off the necklace, lifting the chain over my head, and then slipped it over my mother's, as we'd done so many times before.

"What did you bring me this time?" she asked, holding the little acorn on her fingertips. She touched the spot on the base and the acorn cap sprang open and she pulled out the prize. "Oh, Josie! Where did you find this?"

She dangled the tiny oval charm, an enameled sprig of lily of the valley pictured on it, one of the white bells rubbed clean of enamel.

"I cannot reveal my sources."

It had been a lucky find on the floor of Les Halles, the vast wholesale market where all the food in Paris came from. My favorite hunting ground. Perhaps it had been dropped there by a German woman, so fond of their edelweiss, but I preferred to think of it as French muguet.

Mother dropped the charm into the faded pink satin box with the rest of our little treasures, and then slipped the gold acorn down her dress front and patted it. "At least we still have this."

She took my hand and led me to the kitchen. "Please stay and help me make the apples. We will see your father soon but for now we must just lie low. And not do anything that ruins our chance to see that happen."

CHAPTER 10

ARLETTE

PARIS, FRANCE
1952

I WEAR MY LONG BLACK A-LINE DRESS, THE thrift shop find with the moth hole in the hem, to dinner with Luc Minau at Chez Dauphine. It's my signature piece that makes me feel invincible, and with its scoop neck and long sleeves shows just the right amount of skin. I smooth my hair back into a neat chignon at my nape. No use in being frumpy even if it is strictly business.

My stomach growls as I stand in front of the famous eatery, for the place emits scents of caramelizing sugar and roast duck. On this last day before payday, my bank account is dangerously close to zero and I'm down to eating the stale croissants from the café for dinner, reluctant to dip into the money Josie sent to pay for Fleur's transfer to the new hospital.

I fall somewhere between nervous and eager to see Luc Minau again, but my goal is to enjoy some delicious free food, hear any actual proof that Mr. Minau may have my son, and get home before he talks me into anything rash. After all, I have a life to lead and can't be distracted by any more wild-goose chases. I need to keep my mind on work and earning enough to stay afloat in case I do find my son, and to continue my quest to see Fleur. She'd practically been our adopted child at Ravensbrück, and I owe her my best efforts.

The restaurant is an unassuming place from the outside, just a black-painted door, a brass plaque on the wall next to it, **Chez Dauphine** written there in script. I enter the vestibule, which is draped in claret-colored velvet, the maître d's podium a work of modern art.

"Miss LaRue?" A trim man dressed in a suit appears and ushers me to a heavily draped private room, which contains only one table, where Mr. Minau sits in the near darkness, enjoying what looks like Scotch in a rocks glass.

Though my leg aches with every step, I try to keep my gait even as I step across the carpeted floor to the table. It is beautifully set, with handblown wineglasses and gleaming silver on the white tablecloth. A single white rose stands in a silver cup next to a candle flickering in the near darkness.

He rises to his feet and seems taken aback. "You look perfectly stunning tonight. But I'm sure you get tired of hearing that when you wear clothes as well as you do."

I nod and sit. "Thank you, monsieur."

"Have you considered modeling? I've met Bronwen Pugh **and** Praline and you are much prettier than they are, in a more delicate way. Grandmother says wearing black makes most women look sallow, but it suits you—brings out your eyes."

Though I am not averse to flattery, it feels gauche to discuss the details of my exterior with a perfect stranger. "You flatter me, monsieur. But I'm afraid my moment to join the fashion world has passed."

I had indeed wanted to model clothing once, as my mother had. How many nights lately had I stood on the sidewalk across from the House of Balmain? I watched, every floor ablaze with lights, as model girls readied for a collection debut, stripped to pants and brassieres, trying on the incredible hats.

But after the events at Ravensbrück a fashion career could never happen.

"I love dressing well, too," he says, running one hand along his sleeve.

Fishing for compliments. It takes him less than a minute to violate one of my five date faux pas. Not that this is a date.

"A white rose," I say as I lean in and breathe the scent. "The symbol of purity."

"Is that appropriate for you, Miss LaRue? Purity?"

I open my menu. Such an odd question it doesn't deserve an answer.

"You know a lot about flowers," he says.

"My grandfather was a flower seller, Mr. Minau. But I'm really just making conversation."

He reaches across the table and plucks the menu from my hands. "I hope you don't mind that I chose our menu tonight. I ordered the squab and the fish soup."

My stomach growls again. Can he hear?

"Fine," I say. **I like strong men, but I also like choosing my own food.**

"And a pinot nero from Alto Adige, if that's all right. Nineteen thirty-five, a pretty good year, though we already know that from the price."

Faux pas number two: Flaunting money.

"Of course, very good," I say, as if I know.

"So, have you thought about coming down to French Guiana? The sooner I know the better."

Again, with the overbearing way.

"I think about a lot of things, Mr. Minau. I'm afraid I can't afford to just fly off and leave my job. Not to mention the cost of a plane ticket."

"We don't expect our parents to carry the costs, Miss LaRue. Part of Hope Home's mission is to make the whole experience of reuniting families seamless and stress free. And prospective families stay at one of the many cottages on the Cove House property. The children's camp is just a short walk away."

"It's a bit overwhelming to think about."

I consider his face in the light of the flickering candle. He seems a typical rich French man. A good nose. Receding dark hair. But his eyes are perhaps a little too close-set. And his chin has a habit of collecting a fine layer of sweat so it looks like he's dribbled melted butter there.

"Well, let's talk about something less . . . intense, Miss LaRue. I know you work at the café, but what else do you do for a living?"

Faux pas number three: Asking what someone does for a living. Would four and five be far behind?

"Just a waitress, Monsieur Minau."

"Where did you grow up?"

I avoid his gaze. "Krautergersheim."

He sits back with a smile. "Of course, the sauerkraut capital of France. There's a festival—"

"Last Sunday in September every year. The whole town reeks."

He sips his Scotch. "You must be quite a connoisseur."

"Of sauerkraut? No. Even the smell of cabbage cooking makes me ill."

Luc squints one eye. "There's a famous German war hero from there. Perhaps you knew him?"

"Hans Wietholter? He was my uncle. My mother's older brother."

Luc smiles, the kind the rich have perfected, just familiar enough. "Are you serious?"

"He was a wonderful man. Ran his family locksmith business between wars."

"Every German looks up to him. Not only a World War I hero but World War II as well—didn't he die in service to Hitler?"

"Just happened to be riding with Reinhard Heydrich when Czech dissidents blew them up, that's all."

"But Hitler laid a laurel wreath—"

"At his grave, yes. But we've talked so much about me. Where are you from?"

"South of Krautergersheim, actually. Ribeauvillé."

"Lucky you. The perfect French town."

A waiter brings us each a bowl of soup, saffron crumbled on the top. I taste one bite and hold back from picking up the bowl and drinking it.

"What school did you go to, monsieur?"

"Boarding school. Saint Stephen's in Switzerland."

The sommelier arrives with the wine.

I hold up one hand. "Just a taste, please."

Mr. Minau accepts a full pour. "I sat out the war in Zurich, at a hospital there. Recurrence of a childhood bout with rheumatic fever. My parents had died by then, so my grandmother stayed with me. It was hard just lying there, not joining in the fight. So many of my friends from school died fighting the Nazis. I guess doing what we do at the foundation helps me feel like I'm making up for that, at least a little."

I try the wine and instantly regret asking for just a taste. "Maybe it was better you spent the war in that hospital."

"Was it hard being in Paris during the war? Having missed it all, I have a bottomless curiosity about that period." He pours me more wine. "I will shamelessly ply you with alcohol to get you to tell me."

I smile and sip the wine, noting that his blue shirt suits him, but he's just not my type. As Josie says, I like my men blond, pretty, and looking like they just rolled out of bed.

"In some ways Paris during the war was fine. Having the Nazis squatting here, a constant ominous presence in the cafés and shops, was horrible. But we didn't know what horrible was until we were arrested."

Two waiters appear, each carrying a white plate with a silver dome on top. They serve the plates, lift the domes, and release a cloud of tarragon and butter. I taste the squab, so tender and intensely flavored it's hard to say it's a relative of any chicken I've ever tried.

Luc frowns, a little furrow between his brows. "What was the charge?"

What's the harm in telling him? It was widely known at the time.

"I was living at my parents' apartment with a friend, and a Hungarian urchin girl we called Fleur ran into our place to escape the police, and they followed her in."

"Were you working then?"

I pause, certainly not willing to divulge my underground past.

I go with the usual story I use for public consumption. "Odd jobs. The Gestapo found some underground newspapers we'd been reading and sent us all off to Ravensbrück."

I ask Luc to pass the salt, and in a flagrant display of bad manners he hands it to me directly instead of placing it on the table. But why am I suddenly the etiquette police? My manners are seldom perfect.

"You kept your son with you the whole time?" he asks.

I nod, my eyes welling at the thought of my son, such a good boy throughout it all, unaware what was about to happen to him. "Fleur became very dear to me, a big help with the baby at the camp."

Just the thought of Fleur holding Willie takes me back to his sweet scent, his soft weight against me as he lay his dear head against my shoulder, the two of us almost as one.

A waiter sets a serving of crème brûlée in front of each of us, and I crack the sugar crust of mine, releasing the vanilla scent.

"What became of the Hungarian girl?" Luc asks.

"At Ravensbrück she lived with me and the other mothers and babies in the **Kinderzimmer** at first, and then she just disappeared. My friend Josie and I were liberated early, but we couldn't find Fleur to get her out. I've been trying to find her and finally located her here in Paris."

"I know this has been a difficult journey for you. And it all started at a Lebensborn home. You were such a young girl to find yourself in that place."

"It was both a supremely happy time and just the beginning of my troubles."

CHAPTER 11

ARLETTE

KRAUTERGERSHEIM, FRANCE
1943

Before.

BY APRIL, I'D KEPT MY PREGNANCY FROM Auntie for almost nine months. All it took was wearing my blouses untucked and timing my baths well, since she barely noticed me most days. I felt confident about the birth since I'd arranged to have my baby at the home of the village midwife, Frau Dressler, in her snug bedroom with the lace curtains. She said it was a small baby, promised an easy delivery, and offered me a place to stay after the birth in exchange for housework. Once Gunther came back from the war, we could raise the child together.

Saturday afternoons I took a cold bath in the kitchen washtub, while Auntie sat in the front parlor near the fire and listened to Hitler's speeches on her phonograph. She buffed the records with a special chamois cloth and sat in her old pink chenille robe and drank Riesling wine, trained on the sound of his voice.

Auntie was not my blood relative but was once married to my mother's much older brother, my gentle uncle Hans Wietholter. With her fleshy arms and anthracite eyes, Auntie was born of big-boned barrel makers from nearby Mulhouse. Raised on sausage and fried carp, she liked to boast she once killed a runty piglet with her bare hands. Though French by birth, Auntie tried to be German in every way, lacing her girth into a sky blue dirndl dress on holidays, her figure long since lost to gobbled chocolates.

One Saturday, Auntie surprised me, just as I stepped out of the tub, by entering the kitchen to pour herself more of the milk I was not allowed to touch.

She set her glass on the sink, mouth agape. "My God, what's happened?"

I stood, my swollen belly dripping. "A baby, Auntie. Frau Dressler says it will be an easy birth."

I braced for the blow.

She stepped closer. "Whose is it?"

"Gunther's, of course."

Though I barely knew Gunther, I felt like I'd been with him my whole life.

She yanked me out of the tub by one arm. "Get dressed, stupid girl, and pack a suitcase. You're not staying here any longer."

I hurried to my bedroom in the basement, the former utility closet, the planked walls stuffed with newspapers to keep out the wind. I slid my mother's old suitcase from the closet, set it on the bed, and stroked the wheat-brown side to which I'd applied a vivid **Scenic Krautergersheim!** travel sticker. I clicked open the locks, ran my fingers down the sagging, silken lining, and breathed in what must have been her scent, of Arpege and cedar.

My nightdress went in first, and then my uniform from the BDM, which was the best outfit I had, and then the dress I'd made over from Auntie's old gingham one. I laid Gunther's picture atop the pile and shut the case.

I yanked on my coat, the front nowhere near buttoning. How could my own aunt boot me out of the house? Where would I have my baby? I'd done everything she'd ever asked of me. Had I said a peep after Uncle died and she'd made me break into the houses of those who'd been arrested by the Nazis, to get her the brandy and stale bread they left? I washed and ironed all the laundry. Put up jams and pressed cheeses.

As we ran to the car my wet hair froze into icicles, and as we drove to the outskirts of town, I finally gathered the nerve to speak. "I know you are disappointed in me, Auntie. I—"

"You have somehow done something smart for once in your stupid life. You are carrying a precious life. Your mother was a Wietholter, an ancient

German family almost extinct now, your uncle a famous war hero, and with Gunther as the father, the Reich will see this as a great triumph."

She pulled onto the highway, the engine of her big old car thrumming through the darkening forest.

"Will we come back soon?" I pressed my palm to the cold window. "Where are we going?"

"To a place called the spring of life. My sister, Hermione, told me about it."

Auntie worshipped her sister, who had married well and moved to Austria long ago.

I tried to recall the last time I ate. "I'm very hungry."

"You are **just** like your mother was, always talking. My husband was a slave to his sister, the great beauty. She could have married well but insisted on marrying for love. I tried to tell him. 'Hans Wietholter,' I said. 'You're a hero of the Great War. Don't waste your time. Let her marry some poor artist.' "

Outside my window the spruce and hemlock loomed.

"I miss Uncle Hans." Tall and sandy-haired, with his infinitely patient way and the famous Wietholter ice-blue eyes we had in common, Hans was the closest thing I'd had to a father.

Auntie turned to me as she drove. "I told him, 'Hans, who cares what happens to your stupid sister?' She had been offered model contracts at every great house but did she take the money? No. She was an **artiste.** Work was beneath her. But did he listen to me? No. Tried to help her till the day of his heroic death."

Auntie had always been so secretive about her past, but, sensing a new openness, I probed deeper.

"So, she had to give up the Wietholter name to marry my father?"

"Yes, genius. The woman takes the man's name. Her rich parents didn't think he was good enough, of course. Cut her off with nothing. Hans was always handing her money."

"Did my parents leave me anything?"

"Your mother died, run over by a horse on the Champs-Élysées while **painting** no less. The driver didn't see her there in the street, skinny as a willow, no bigger than a twig around the waist. Your father died the very next year. They said it was a broken heart, but it was the drink that got him. They died penniless, aside from their apartment, and didn't leave a will. Artists. Never thought ahead."

"What happened to Uncle Hans's money?"

"His family hated Hitler and disappeared when the war started, took it all with them. He ran that locksmith company they left behind, which got us by for a time. In the war he served as a secretary to Reinhard Heydrich, a very good friend of Hitler's. Got blown up with him riding in his car. Hitler himself laid a laurel wreath at the grave."

"Where is my parents' apartment?"

"Who knows? Somewhere in Paris. Probably a dump of a place. Where your father thought he could make a living as a painter. He always had some stupid fantasy."

"I'd like to see it someday."

"Well, you won't. First of all, there's no deed. Without that, it will go into probate. Then, if they left it to you, I'll make myself your official guardian, sell it, and make back all the money I've wasted on you."

I closed my eyes, cradled my belly, and pictured my parents in love, Mother pregnant with me and living in a Paris apartment, Father bringing home lily of the valley for her.

Suddenly I felt the baby move. I smiled and pressed my belly. "He's kicking."

"You had better hope it's a boy. Then Himmler **himself** will give you one of his pure silver godfather cups."

Pure silver? I had a vague idea Himmler was Hitler's friend, but clearly, he was very rich. "I want one for my baby. Are these cups to drink from?"

"No, stupid, just for show. A gift from one of Hitler's most trusted men. A thing like that is a treasure."

Auntie smiled as she drove, her face glowing in the lights of the dashboard. She brought to mind a donkey I'd seen in a book, wearing a flowered hat, with a long face and upper teeth jutting out.

Auntie pinched my arm.

"Ouch," I said, rubbing the spot.

"Are you even listening to me, Arlette? I said you've finally done something good. After all that wasteful drawing pictures of skirts and dresses."

It seemed like we drove forever and finally arrived at a stone-pillared entrance to an estate in the Chantilly Forest.

"Lamorlaye," I read from the bronze plaque on the pillar.

We drove on, past dark barns and outbuildings, a brightly lit main house looming in the darkness.

I pressed my face so close to the window my breath fogged the glass. "Is this the spring of life? Is there a fountain here? Will they feed us?"

"Your job is to hold your tongue and deliver a healthy child. Get out and keep that big mouth shut, hear me?"

I took my suitcase from the back seat and followed Auntie to the door, and she rang the bell. We stood shivering there until a woman with a placid expression answered. She wore a brown and white seersucker wrap dress with a white apron over it and a white nurse's cap.

"Yes?"

"Heil Hitler!" Auntie said, back straight, as she lifted her arm and gave a most ardent German salute. "This is Arlette LaRue. I am her aunt Henriette. I phoned earlier."

Auntie wrapped her arm around my shoulders, startling me, for she'd never willingly touched me in any sort of caring way before.

The woman nodded. "Nurse Knoll."

She stepped aside, and we followed her through the first floor of the house, quite a splendid place, with a grand staircase and tall windows hung with velvet drapes. In what looked like a living room, girls about as pregnant as me sat in rows of folding chairs listening to a different nurse, uniformed in blue, read aloud from a book in German.

Nurse Knoll waved toward the furnishings. "This place was once called Lamorlaye, the manor of a wealthy French family, Bois-Larris. They were persuaded to donate it to the Reich for such a worthy cause as this. Now it is called Westwald."

How sad it was the Germans stole someone's house for their venture. Like a cuckoo bird I saw once that took the nest of a songbird, rolled the eggs to the forest floor, and moved her own family in.

She led us to an office, the library of the former home, and we sat in the cushiony chairs facing her at the desk. I set down my suitcase, the brown of it blending nicely against the soft maroons and creams of the room.

There were two sorts of nurses at Westwald, and right away I could tell there was a great deal of tension between them. The Brown Nurses, like Nurse Knoll, seemed to be exclusively German, wore brown and white striped dresses, and were the majority. They were stricter and cared only about the rules. The Blue Nurses, all French women, wore long baby blue dresses topped with white aprons. They were much kinder and were often given orders by the Browns.

Nurse Knoll sat behind the big desk and put on her glasses. "Full name, please?"

"I am Arlette Dagmar LaRue. Dagmar for my mother. She died when I was four. My father, William LaRue, died the next year. We lived in Paris."

"Your mother was German?"

"On both sides, yes." I handed her my papers, and she read.

"It says here her maiden name was Wietholter?"

"Yes."

She removed her glasses. "As in Hans Wietholter?"

Auntie raised her chin. "My husband, rest in peace."

"That's a very old Teutonic name," Nurse Knoll said.

All at once my back hurt and my belly grew oddly hard. "Oh," I said, clutching my middle. "Something is happening."

Nurse Knoll smiled. "Probably just a contraction."

My breath came faster. **The baby? Now?**

She rang the bell on her desk, and another nurse entered, a Blue Nurse, who smiled at me so kindly I liked her right away. She looked about twenty-five years old, had a gentle, calm way, and a lovely round face and deep dimples around her mouth when she smiled.

"Thérèse, please fetch Dr. Ebner."

Thérèse hurried off, and soon a tall man entered, wearing a white doctor's coat over his blue shirt and dark trousers. Just one look at him made my blood run cold, with his parchment-white skin and big, bald head, like the vampire in the German movie **Nosferatu,** the only movie I'd seen.

Nurse Knoll stood. "Doctor, Arlette LaRue and her aunt are here from Strasbourg."

He glanced at me. "How many months?"

The nurse handed him my papers. "Nine, Herr Doctor. Contractions already started."

My whole body shook. **Please don't let him touch me,** I prayed.

Auntie sat up straighter. "She has been eating well. Meat and milk, always first before I have a thing. And may I inquire if there is to be compensation for the family for all this?"

Nurse Knoll kept her focus on Dr. Ebner. "The girl presents well, racially. And her mother was a Wietholter."

"**Very** old German family," Auntie said. "Her uncle was **Hans** Wietholter. She has the famous Wietholter blue eyes."

The doctor glanced at her and continued reading. "The father of the child?"

"Gunther Wagner from Offenburg," I said.

"Pure German?"

I nodded. "Yes. He's gone to join the military."

"Which unit?"

What number had Gunther told me that day in the barn? "Well, I don't remember exactly."

The doctor fixed his gaze upon me, his watery eyes magnified four times their size by his lenses. "Did you not bring a copy of his papers?"

"No. He left so suddenly." Tears stung my eyes.

"He told me his field number. Asked me to write to him. It's zero, two . . . oh dear. It has an L at the end."

"I see," the doctor said and tossed my papers on the desk, a greenish branch of veins bulging at his temple. "We are building something very special here, Miss LaRue. Some French women as yourself are just now being considered suitable to procreate Aryans but only on a select basis and not without some verifiable evidence as to the sire."

Dr. Ebner turned to leave.

I stood. "Wait." I stepped to my suitcase, popped the locks with both thumbs, and held out the photo. "Here, Herr Doctor. Gunther gave this to me before he left. His school picture in his cadet uniform. He's seventeen as I am. Told me we should do our duty for the Reich before he left to join his fellow soldiers."

Nurse Knoll joined Dr. Ebner and considered the picture. "That is a German boy if I've ever seen one."

The doctor flipped the photo over and read the back. "Gunther Wagner. First Panzer Division." Dr. Ebner looked at me, his eyes shining in the lamplight. "The future of our country, boys like this. Will you take an oath you did not have relations with any other man at the time?"

I sat up straighter. "Of course."

He handed the photo to Nurse Knoll. "She may stay while we verify this."

Dr. Ebner told Auntie she had to go, and she

lumbered out of the house in a fit of ill humor and sped off, more upset to be going away empty-handed than sad to leave me there.

I was assigned the Blue Nurse Thérèse, a French nurse-midwife, tasked with preparing me for the birth, who took me to join the others in the dining room, the scent of roast chicken in the air. It was an elegant room, a crystal chandelier hanging over ten round tables, most of them full with women of all ages, their pregnant bellies pressed to the tabletops.

Thérèse pulled out the last empty dining room chair at one table. "Sit here. I'll fix you a plate."

How fancy I felt sitting there, while someone else fetched my food, like I always did for Auntie. As I waited, Nurse Knoll approached the table, wearing hospital gloves and holding a silver cup in her hands gently as one holds a baby bird.

"I promised you I'd show you the cup, ladies."

One woman twice my age set down her fork. "It's beautiful. May we hold it?"

Nurse Knoll smiled. "Oh, no. This will be presented tonight to the family of a new baby. Must be pristine."

"The family?" I asked the girl to my left, but she was too busy looking at the cup.

Nurse Knoll walked solemnly around the table, crouching low, so we could marvel at the ultimate prize. As she passed me, she slowed and I admired the little cup, no bigger than my fist, chandelier lights bouncing off the polished silver. It was etched with the new baby's name and birth date and was the most beautiful thing I'd ever seen.

But before Nurse Knoll could make it all the way around the table, the contractions grew stronger and Thérèse walked me down a hallway to a birthing room, settled me in a bed, and held my hand.

We talked about all sorts of things to keep my mind off the impending birth. How to breathe during labor. My parents and the apartment they owned. How I wanted to get away from Auntie and her Nazi ways and go back to Paris. **This is what it's like to have a mother,** I thought, as Thérèse and I talked through the night.

Soon two nurses joined us, both Brown. The head nurse, Pauline, a particularly strict one, busied herself filling a basin with water, as she chatted in low tones with a nurse in training.

"What happened with this morning's birth?" the trainee asked.

"Deaf, poor dear," Nurse Pauline said.

"Did Dr. Ebner do . . ."

"The right thing of course. Best to get it done quickly. But at least there's some good news today. This will be a healthy baby and is going to . . ." Nurse Pauline leaned close to the trainee and whispered, but I distinctly heard the name "Reichman."

The trainee stood up taller, eyes wide. "**Such** a high-up family. Lucky child."

Sweat prickled the back of my neck. **Someone is taking my child?**

Thérèse wiped my forehead with a cool towel. "Stop saying such things, Pauline. Can't you see Arlette is trying to do an important job here?"

"We should all be supportive of the Reich," Pauline shot back.

While I huffed my labor breathing, panicked thoughts plagued me. **Will they really take my baby? What if there is a problem? Will they end his life if he isn't perfect?**

I sat up as best I could and checked the window. I could climb out. Hitch a ride on the highway. But it was cold, and I would be weak from delivering. And wouldn't get far.

All at once, the nurses turned as Dr. Ebner entered and came to loom over me at the bedside. He smelled of rubbing alcohol and onions, and I tried not to look at him as he wrapped his long fingers around my wrist.

He pulled back the sheet and my nightie, and my cheeks burned. No man but Gunther had ever seen me naked like that. He felt my belly, his hands cold on my skin.

"It's a boy," he pronounced.

Nurse Pauline smiled. "We'll engrave the cup, Herr Doctor."

He can tell just from feeling?

Dr. Ebner left as suddenly as he came. "Call me

when she crowns," he said over his shoulder to Thérèse as he departed, the Brown Nurses in his wake.

I turned to Thérèse. "Is it true? They are giving my child to a German family?"

She looked about. "Quiet. They'll hear you."

"I'd rather die. Please send word to Gunther—he'll help me."

She leaned in close. "You must play along so they don't suspect a thing. You're too young to raise the child alone. They will take the child as soon as the cord is cut, so you don't form an attachment."

A stab clenched my belly. "I can't do this." Tears filled my eyes. I yearned for Frau Dressler's little bedroom.

"You can and you will. And no crying. You must appear to be a loyal subject, happily contributing your child to the Reich."

"But I'm not."

She considered me for a long moment and then looked about. "Listen closely, for I cannot repeat this, and do not tell a soul. After the birth, I will say the child has a breathing problem and needs to be watched for the night in the nursery. I will then get you two out of here."

I imagined two white wings sprouting out of her back, smooth and white, like those of a swan. Thérèse was my angel sent from God to fly me away from that place.

"To where?"

"Let me worry about that. I work with a group of incredible patriots."

"But what if my auntie finds me? She'll be mad if I leave here."

"Let's deal with that if we have to."

"But they'll know you helped me."

"I won't be coming back here. I'll get you settled in your new home, then rejoin my group."

"How can I ever repay you?" A contraction gripped me, and I called out.

Thérèse smoothed back my hair from my forehead. "I'll tell you more soon. But for now, when I tell you, just push."

WILLIE WAS FINALLY BORN at ten o'clock that evening and Nurse Thérèse got me out of there two hours later in the back seat of her car. We stayed in the basement of a building in Le Marais for two days before Thérèse came to me one morning, smiling a wide grin. "We've hit the jackpot, Arlette. We are moving you in to a place of your own."

As we hurried through the back streets of Île de la Cité, past Notre-Dame, Willie in my arms, pressed to my chest, a balloon of joy swelled in me at the thought of finally having a home. Gunther could come see Willie and me there once the war ended and France was back to normal. But if he could find me, couldn't Auntie as well?

"We're almost there," Thérèse said, as I followed her through the streets, a satchel of Willie's few baby things hanging over my shoulder. A light perfume of tuberose and lily filled the air as we approached a market where porters pushed wooden carts filled with potted plants and tubs of cut flowers.

Thérèse turned and guided me by the arm along a rabbit warren of hardpacked earth paths lined with fragrant lemon trees and potted ferns, dappled sunlight slanting in through breaks in the ribbed tin roof.

"This is the Flowers and Birds Market. This is where many Parisians come to buy their flowers. And birds on Sundays. I see the vendors are here early as usual."

"There are so many flowers. How can that be, with the war on?"

"Hitler has ordered that Paris stay full of flowers. To show how good Germany is for France. All the flowers come from Les Halles, the wholesale market, and from the greenhouses there in the winter."

I slowed. "But how—"

"Stay close. It quickly gets very crowded, and there are many Germans here shopping."

Part of the market was housed in art nouveau glass pavilions. And part was outdoors, rows of booths, each the size of Auntie's little kitchen, their bouquets artfully arranged with ferns and moss and periwinkle leaves.

As the crowds grew, housewives and merchants flooded the narrow paths bartering for roses and camellias, even hothouse lilacs, which lay in cardboard boxes on beds of emerald moss. Flower sellers trimmed leaves into a pile on the dirt floor and pounded lilac stems with wooden mallets, as the lady primrose sellers wandered the paths with their wicker baskets, loud as any fishwives, shouting out, "Five sous a bunch!" Willie slept through it all in my arms, sweet boy.

Thérèse stopped, her eyes trained on something behind me. "Come. **Now.**"

As I hurried on, I turned and saw the cause of her alarm, Nazi officers strolling three abreast behind me, hands clasped behind their backs, enjoying their promenade. My breath caught in my throat as I dodged the other patrons to follow Thérèse.

At last, we arrived at a salmon pink door at the far end of the market, the din of the crowds a distant roar, the stone façade of the little place overgrown with ivy.

Thérèse unlocked the door, and we entered to a lovely scent of turpentine and Marseille soap. She waved one arm toward the tidy living room with a white wicker bassinet set up in front of a brick fireplace. "It's small, but it's all yours."

She lifted the baby from my arms and rested him in the bassinet. "Make sure you sleep when he sleeps."

"How did you learn so much about babies?"

She looked down on Willie. "I had one of my own once upon a time. I lost him too soon."

"I'm so sorry."

She stood up straighter. "But that won't happen to Willie."

I took in the living room with its chintz slipcovered

sofa flanked by end tables, each bearing a lovely lamp. "I have no money to rent such a place."

She smiled and rested one hand on my arm. "It already belongs to you."

"I'm sorry. I don't understand."

"This is your parents' apartment. And your grandfather's before them." She opened the kitchen window a crack, turned the squeaky taps, and ran water at the sink. "It's been empty since your parents died."

I shook my head. "This cannot be. How did you find it?"

"The group I work with found that your parents were well liked in the merchant community here. Got a tip the couple banked with Banque de France. This deed was located, which proved your parents left the place to you, and we paid some back taxes . . ."

Thérèse handed me an envelope, **Arlette** written there in a delicate hand. My mother's script? I slid out a single-leaf bifold sheet covered in ancient handwritten legalese, Marianne the French symbol of liberty stamped in the upper corner, her torch aloft.

"Your parents left it to you as the sole heir."

I held the deed to my chest and inspected the room. "It's all so unreal. And how is it there's not a speck of dust?"

"A team was sent here to clean and fitted it with the necessary things for Willie."

I stepped back from her. "Who do you work for? Is this a trap to set me up?"

Thérèse took my hand. "No, Arlette."

I wrested my hand away. "Then why will you not tell me who supports you?"

"I work for a group of people who risk their lives to fight the Nazis. You are the beneficiary of that group, but I cannot tell you more about them."

"Why?"

"I know only a limited amount myself, for safety's sake."

"No one does anything for no reason."

"If you want to know the truth, I'm what's known as a recruiter."

"So, you want me to work for this group, too?"

She stepped to the window. "We like to have options."

I followed her. "Why did you choose me to help? Have there been others?"

"You're the only one from Westwald. I'd been working there for a while. Waiting for the right person, and there you were. Smart. Resourceful. You don't like Hitler."

"Where do you live?"

"I really can't—"

"**Tell** me."

"Nowhere. I don't sleep two nights in the same place. The Germans have a sophisticated network of agents working to find people like me."

I stepped to the fireplace and admired the fine plates, hand-painted with violets, leaning on the mantel wall. How many fires had my parents enjoyed here? "I feel like I'm in a wonderful dream."

She smiled. "Of course. But it is rightfully yours. I've been told there's an old photo on the hallway wall of a flower seller, believed to be your grandfather. And a whole set of flower books in the studio." She handed me a key. "This came with the deed."

I turned it over in my fingers; the brass was warm from waiting in her pocket. How many times had my parents held that key?

"Enjoy this place as your parents would have wanted. You've been through a lot. Your job now is to rest, recover, and enjoy your baby."

I wandered the place, which I didn't consider small at all, after living in Auntie's one-room basement my whole life. The apartment had two bedrooms and a living room, with high ceilings and good light. I admired the lovely Chinese screen painted with emerald birds and pale flowers that stood against one wall in the living room.

I found the sepia photo of my father's father, a tall, bereted man posing at his flower stall under one of the glass pavilions we'd just walked past. He stood in his apron and dark jacket, one fist on his hip, in front of five tiers of cut roses, and rolls of moss bound with twine.

I stepped into one bedroom, a snug room just big enough for a bed and a small desk, the velvet drapes drawn across the window. I drifted into the little kitchen, ran two fingers along the oilcloth cover on the table for two, and pictured my parents cooking shoulder to shoulder at the wooden counter.

I hurried into the second bedroom, which my parents had used as a studio, a turpentine-scented shrine, filled to the ceiling with sculptures and paintings. I ran one hand along a dusty green leather flower encyclopedia, **Les saisons des fleurs illustrées de A à Z,** chose a volume, and opened to random pages. A lovely botanical painting of the common daisy with its symbolic meaning printed below: **Innocence.** A cobalt columbine: **Endurance.** A purple hyacinth: **Forgiveness.**

I passed an easel, which held an unfinished painting of a woman, painted from behind, dressing in front of a mirror. She wore a gold dress with a low-cut back, the fabric painted so realistically it shimmered. I stepped closer to discover the woman looked very much like me. Slighter in frame, but with my same mouth and our Wietholter pale blue eyes.

I stood there many minutes as a deep calm settled over me, for I'd met my mother at long last.

Deeper in the studio I found a metalwork corner, complete with all the tools required for sculpting in bronze and brass.

"You can go out but stay close to home. Just to the park and back." She walked to the bedroom and peeped out the side of the closed drape.

"Is something wrong?"

She came back to the living room. "A highly ranked SS family had very much looked forward to adopting your child. You are now officially what they call a 'vanished mother.' They will search all of Paris for us. Every hospital."

I held Willie closer. "What will we do?"

"Nothing. Little do they know you're right here under their noses. Your bedroom window backs up to the rear of the Police Prefecture—and an office some high-up Nazis are using. So keep that curtain drawn."

Willie fussed and I rubbed his back. "I hate them so much for what they've done. Took Gunther away to the front, tried to steal my child."

"Soon there may be an opportunity for you to fight them."

"How?"

"I can't give more details."

"I wouldn't want to do anything dangerous. Or illegal."

"You wouldn't want to go back to Westwald, either, **n'est pas**?"

I held Willie closer. "What does that mean?"

"For now, just rest and gather strength in this lovely little place with your sweet boy. When it's time, you will lend a hand."

CHAPTER 12

JOSIE

PARIS, FRANCE
1952

AFTER MY SHRINK APPOINTMENT, I WALK BACK to the Ritz, check out, and stop by the hotel dining room looking for a quick breakfast and limited interaction. It's a grand room, with a perfect fire blazing in the marble-manteled fireplace and the soaring Palladian window at the far end encased in a layer of ice.

Every table is occupied, and the line to be seated is several people deep. I join it and wait, inching forward, the air perfumed with coffee and **oeufs en cocotte,** punctuated by murmured French conversations and the clink of butter knives on Limoges porcelain.

Soon, I leave the line to inquire, drawing cool looks from the other patrons, and step to the maître d', a silver-haired gentleman with an efficient way. His name tag identifies him as Alfred.

"Pardon me, monsieur. I am very sorry, but I have a flight to catch. Will the wait be terribly long?"

"My deepest apologies, madame, but we are unexpectedly busy this morning, due to the ice storm. I have been offering patrons the opportunity to dine with a guest already seated if that is amenable to you. I have one gentleman who might be open to sharing his table. Especially with a breakfast companion, if I may say, as appealing as you are, Mrs. . . . ?"

"Miss. Anderson."

"Hotel guest?"

"Yes, Alfred. Room twelve."

He turns and makes his way through the tables to a gentleman reading a book at a small table for two by the window, confers with him, and hurries back. "Mr. Salinger is perfectly amenable to a companion this morning." He slides a leather-trimmed menu from a pile. "This way, please."

I follow Alfred to the table, the boxwoods outside the window coated in ice. My dining companion sets down his book, **The Caine Mutiny,** and stands as I'm seated. It's hard not to notice how attractive he is. Dark hair. Late thirties. Gray flannel suit and tie.

He's drinking tea, which is unfortunate since it means he has no pot of coffee to share.

He nods. "Aaron Salinger."

I set my purse under the table as Alfred unfolds an enormous white napkin across my lap.

"Josie Anderson." I remove my gloves. "Thank you for sharing your table."

"My pleasure," he says in good French. "I was just finishing."

I suddenly wish I'd done more than run a comb through my hair.

"Do you stay here often?" I ask, scanning the room for a waiter with a coffeepot.

"When I can. I'm in insurance. Here for a meeting."

I watch his nonverbal responses for deceptive indicators and find none. No evasiveness or hands to the face.

I glance at the menu. "I need coffee. And something quick. My flight leaves at eleven."

"Hmmm. Everything is good here, but quick . . ."

He takes my menu and considers it as I consider him, the way basic training taught us to note a suspect. Brown eyes, medium build. Just under six feet. No distinguishing marks. No wedding ring. Skin golden peach-tan. Ballet pink lips.

"The eggs Florentine are probably the quickest. But I'm afraid you're not going anywhere today, Miss Anderson. Flights are grounded."

His glance meets mine, and I look away. "We'll see about that."

I order the eggs and a pot of coffee. It's been so long since I've been within three feet of a man I was attracted to, my fingers shake as I smooth my hair back.

"A snow day they'd call this in the States," I say. "Children live for them."

"Not a thing in Israel."

"Well, I need to be somewhere. So, no snow day for me."

"A warm destination, I hope."

"Even colder. Austria." I sip water. **Where's the coffee?**

"Ah, the birthplace of Hitler. I was sent to Bergen-Belsen with my parents. I won't be going back to Germany or Austria anytime soon."

"You survived. And your parents?"

He looks out the window.

I set down my water glass. "I'm sorry. I was at Ravensbrück. Where I lost my mother."

"How did you end up there?"

I reach for the book. "Have you finished this?" He reaches at the same time, and his warm fingers brush mine.

"Just finished. Best book I've read in a while. Got to live vicariously since I was never allowed in combat." He places one hand over the left side of his chest. "Heart condition."

I try to enact the advice Arlette gave me back in our Doves days, to not be **too** interested in what a man has to say.

I flip through the book's pages. "Hated the ending."

"When he asks May to marry him?"

"It felt like a dodge to leave that unresolved. Not fair to the reader."

He leans back in his chair. "My guess is she turned him down. Attractive women often do that to men."

"I wouldn't know."

He levels his gaze at mine. "Then you haven't met enough men, Miss Anderson."

I set my napkin on the table. "Sorry, but I have to go."

He sits up straighter. "I hope I'm not running you off. It's not like me to suddenly be so forward. Guess I'm just defenseless, here in lovely Paris."

A hot flush creeps up my neck. "I don't know why I thought I had time for breakfast. I overslept. The bed was so comfortable."

He sips his tea. "It **was** hard leaving that bed this morning. I request the same room every time I stay here, the little penthouse with the skylights. This morning I woke to the sound of icy rain on the glass above."

I cast my gaze about the dining room. "How nice. I was hoping for room service this morning, but they were too busy."

"You can see the whole city from up there, glittering with ice. It's magical."

"Is there a view of **la tour Eiffel**? My room doesn't have one. Overlooks Place Vendôme."

"Yes, I'm on the other side of the hotel so there's

a nice view. You see the dome of Church of Notre-Dame-de-l'Assomption and then the tower beyond, rising up as if it's there just for you."

"I know it's a cliché to love it, but I lived here during the war, and it came to mean something important to me."

"You should see it covered in ice, one ray of light hitting it this morning."

I push back my chair and stand. "I'm sure it's beautiful."

"You're welcome to come see it. It won't take long."

Karl would have a heart attack if he found out I'd slept with some stranger while on assignment.

"I don't think so, Mr. Salinger."

"I have a plane to catch as well. If the airport opens again, we can share a car, since they may be hard to find."

I hesitate. It's doubtful this guy is an agent. He shows no deceptive behaviors, and I was the one who sat at his table, after all. Plus, haven't I vowed to lose my virginity first chance I got? Mr. Aaron Salinger seems a promising candidate. We're stranded anyway, and it **was** Dr. Marjorie Vincent's orders to relax.

I gather my purse and gloves. "Perhaps I can have my breakfast sent up? Maybe then I can get some coffee."

"Smart." Aaron waves the maître d' over. "Could Miss Anderson have her order sent up to my room? With extra coffee?"

"Of course, monsieur."

"Yes. And quickly, please? Hopefully we'll have planes to catch."

He nods. "Right away, monsieur."

Aaron stands and offers his hand. "Shall we? You won't be disappointed."

CHAPTER 13

ARLETTE

PARIS, FRANCE
1952

THE NIGHT AFTER MY DINNER WITH LUC MINAU at Chez Dauphine I barely sleep, thinking about those silver cups in his office safe. **What if the one that had been intended for Willie was sitting in that safe? I could break in and just look at the name of the German family he'd been promised to. Not to steal anything. Then I could track the family down. See if they knew anything about his whereabouts.**

It would be an easy job from the look of the door lock.

I leave my bed, dress, and head for Luc Minau's office ready to help myself to the contents of his safe. Am I rusty as Josie suggested? We'll see. Will Luc even notice one silver cup is missing? If I'm caught somehow, I can simply plead a desire to revisit the objects that might be my son's and be on my way.

The place is dark when I arrive, at half past four in the morning—the perfect break-in time every Parisian thief knows, when security guards are asleep at their desks, and police not yet en route from their warm beds.

I slide my tension wrench into the office door keyhole, turn it clockwise, and I'm in. It's almost too easy, and I step across the room in near darkness to the safe, one ray of light streaming in from a streetlamp. I brush the fingertips of my right hand on my jacket, press the left flat on the safe door, and set my fingertips on the dial lock. **Light as a butterfly,** Uncle Hans would say. I was right about the combination. Before long the fence drops, engages, and the door releases with the lovely little motion that says, **I surrender.**

I bask in my prize, the gush of warmth that rushes down my arms after every successful crack, and revel in the idea I'm not the least bit rusty. I then slide the box of mementos out and lift the clusters of silver baby cups from the safe, leaving stacks of francs filling the dark recesses. I count the cups, twenty in all, as I line them up on Luc's desk.

Training the flashlight on one, I read the three lines engraved upon one side:

OCTOBER 2, 1943
VON PATENONKEL
H. HIMMLER

Von Patenonkel. "From Godfather."

How strange that Hitler's brutal lieutenant Heinrich Himmler had gifted the boy children born at his Lebensborn homes with such a personal gift. How I'd yearned so deeply for this odd little love token.

I turn the cup to reveal the name engraved on the opposite side. **Albert Jorgenson.** I shine the light on the next to see **Otto Weber** engraved there. Then **Paul Becker. Franz Meyer.**

I shine my light along the rest of the cups and come to one with Willie's birth date.

APRIL 7, 1943
VON PATENONKEL
H. HIMMLER

My heart thumps harder as I lift the cup from the desk and turn it to reveal a name engraved there. **Klaus Reichman.**

A shiver shoots through me. **Reichman. The family Willie was meant to go to. They really had been ready to take my child home with them. They'd already named him Klaus.**

I click off the flashlight and stand there in the dark. **Am I not the rightful owner of this cup? Himmler,**

the monster, had meant it for Willie. Luc would surely not give it to me. Would they even miss it?

I slip it into my pocket and set the other cups back, careful not to make a sound, arranging them as found. I resist the impulse to grab a fat stack of francs, gently close the safe door, and return the dial to the original number.

Job well done, girl, I imagine my uncle Hans saying, as I move quietly to the front door. He would have applauded my use of the tension wrench to get in, **the queen of wrenches,** he called it.

I step outside into the cold Paris night and close the door behind me. I walk on feeling happier than I've been in a long time, the sweet rush of adrenaline singing through me.

"What are you doing here?"

I jump at the sound of a man's voice, and turn. "Luc. My God. You startled me."

He steps toward me in the darkness. "I'll ask you one more time. What are you doing here?"

"I—"

"If it's money you're looking for, we're a charitable organization. I thought you understood that. A woman who lives across the way called me and said she saw strange lights in my office, and I came straight over."

"It was open—"

"I locked it when I left."

"I swear it was open. I was out walking—"

"At this hour?"

"I couldn't sleep. With all the new information about Willie. So, when I saw the door open, I just went in."

"That is obviously a lie and a serious affront to the important work we do here."

He's certainly more attractive when he's angry, unshaven, and right out of bed.

"I'm sorry, Luc. To be honest, I had two reasons. One was to see the mementos again. I can't stop thinking about them."

"You could have just **asked** me. Have I not been completely generous with my time?"

"I know. It's stupid really. I hope this doesn't ruin my chances of working with you and your grandmother."

Real tears come to my eyes.

He looks off into the distance. "We'll have to reassess, certainly. We've never had this happen before, one of our mothers breaking and entering. Did you take anything?"

I step back and the silver cup in my pocket swings against my leg. "Of course not. I just wanted to see the blanket again. I can't believe you've found it."

He shakes his head. "This is highly irregular."

"Why did I do this?" I wipe a tear. "It'll ruin my chances of ever seeing my son."

He runs his fingers through his hair. "Please don't cry. It will all be fine. But of course, I'll have to report this to the police."

I pace the cobblestones. "**Police?** But I'll lose my

job at the café. I'll never see my son." **Would they find out about Auntie?**

"Please, you must calm down, Arlette." He takes me by the upper arms and shakes me. "You'll wake the whole neighborhood."

I hang my head. "I'm sorry. You're right. I should be arrested. I'll wait here while you call the police."

He places two cold fingers under my chin and lifts my face. "And what was the second reason?"

"Well . . ." I have to come up with something. "I came to see **you.** I thought you might be here."

He looks away. "Please. You expect me to believe that?"

I embroider the story as I go.

"Talking to you the other day was the first time I thought my life might actually get better. I just wanted to see you again and continue that." I check his face to see if he's buying it, but he's in shadow. "For me at least, there was a real connection there." I wipe my wet cheek with my coat sleeve. "Maybe it's just that thing that happens when someone you look up to does something wonderful and you suddenly have a crush on them. Like . . . a favorite teacher. I'm so sorry."

He pushes the hair back off my forehead. "I had no idea."

I start to believe the story myself, run my fingers down the lapel of his coat, the cashmere soft under my fingers. "I haven't felt that way about someone in so long."

"So, you think you can seduce me into forgetting about the fact you broke into my office?"

"No. I mean, I just felt like we had a special something." I shrug one shoulder. "Thought maybe you felt it, too."

He folds his arms across his chest. "I can't say I didn't."

"But don't get the wrong idea. I don't go around propositioning men like this."

He gazes at me for a long moment. "I suppose we can wait on alerting the authorities."

"Thank you." I exhale a long breath. "I'm so grateful."

He checks the door to make sure it's locked, turns back to me, and extends one hand.

"And since you're so interested in me, come along then. My apartment is just around the corner."

CHAPTER 14

JOSIE

VIENNA, AUSTRIA
1952

I MISS MY FLIGHT FROM PARIS TO AUSTRIA AND blame it on the ice storm, which is good cover, since it has ended everything in Paris, including my sexual dry spell.

The flight I eventually take is diverted to Berlin and I arrive in Vienna two days late, but more relaxed than I'd been in a long time, thanks to Aaron Salinger, but still a bit hungover from the Scotch he'd ordered at our second room service. Dinner this time, steak au poivre in bed. What would Debbine think about that delicious encounter at the Ritz? **Every girl needs companionship, Josie.**

And what companionship it was, the handsome

Mr. Salinger, as close to Eros as I'd ever come, his torso smooth and taut. And somehow, he doesn't even know how attractive he is and would probably treat it like an amusing sidebar, confronted with the idea that women have probably been hurt on the street after wandering into traffic, unable to stop staring at all that attractiveness. To him, it seems to be immaterial how he looks, the perk reserved for the truly attractive who walk among us, perfectly secure that no one would ever tell him his body could be a nine if his ass was rounder.

My new boss, Johann Vitner, has invited me to stay with him at his apartment in the heart of Vienna, tucked above a sweet-smelling bakery with one skimpy chocolate torte displayed in the window. My plan is to get the mission details, reconnect with my old friend, and focus on work and his life, not mine. No need for us to dredge up past stuff about my mother. Ravensbrück.

Food is still scarce, eight years after Austria's surrender, and the capital remains occupied by the Allies, though Vienna itself is an international zone. According to my briefing doc, the denazification of Austria's more than half a million registered Nazis is complete, which seems optimistic, since this is Hitler's home country, the birthplace of bullying.

Having stayed up most of the night with Aaron, my eyes feel filled with sand, and I press the buzzer. As I wait, I take a closer look at the lone torte and hope Johann is planning on serving one tonight, the only way I may get through dinner.

The door buzzes and I haul my suitcase up the steps. He'd insisted I stay at his place, not my favorite idea, since it means I miss one of the best perks of the job, a fabulous hotel, but there was no persuading him.

Johann meets me at the door, looking good in his Nordic sweater. I'd missed that face, the blue eyes that crinkle when he smiles, always giving the impression he's about to share something amusing.

"Come in, Josie. So very good to see you." He wraps his arms around me in an uncharacteristically warm Austrian welcome. "I've missed our late-night chats."

It's a charming place, snug. Besides the two small bedrooms it's just a kitchen and living room with a fireplace, where a fire dances in the hearth. Vivaldi plays on the stereo and a print of Gustav Klimt's **Kiss** hangs above the fireplace, which conjures an image of my night at the Ritz and sends a warm flush up my neck.

Johann carries my suitcase down the hall. "Hope you don't mind staying here. I know how you like your hotel time."

I follow him to a high-ceilinged guest room, complete with half-timber walls, right out of **Heidi.** I admire a Chinese brush painting of a koi, hung near the bed, and check out his collection of spoons, gathered from around the world, set into an oak spoon rack. **Cairo. Kyoto. Nairobi.**

He sets the suitcase on a wooden luggage rack.

"I took the liberty of making the bed with down pillows. Is that your preference? The right pillows are critical to a good sleep, aren't they?"

"Yes, and thank you for hosting me, Johann. This is lovely. You expect Heidi's grandfather to emerge any minute."

"I adored that book as a child. First sign to my parents I was not going to have babies with Gretta Shuman."

I smile. Texas would have been so much more fun if he'd stayed.

We walk back to the kitchen on worn tribal rugs.

"Thank you for coming all the way here to Vienna. I've been caring for a sick friend and haven't had a chance to move into the London office."

I inhale. "Is that lemongrass?"

"I made that chicken soup you liked. How are things in El Paso? Gotten any livelier?"

"Not exactly on the international party circuit. Before I forget, can you get me a dossier on an Israeli citizen?"

"Happy to, my love."

"Name is Aaron Salinger. Israeli."

He nods, posture perfect.

"And a Luc Minau? French."

"You'll have them soon."

He lobs me an oversized wallet. "And before I forget—this is compliments of Karl." I open it to find a stack of bills in various currencies, and Karl's business card in the plastic ID sleeve. "Turn in your receipts, or Jim in accounting will ding you for car fare."

Glamorous espionage.

"Care for a beer?" Johann asks. "Austrian brands are very good."

He pulls a bottle from the refrigerator. "If I remember correctly, you like it straight from the bottle like they do in Texas?"

As he hands it to me, I see his fingernails, and am startled for a moment. How had I forgotten? His right fingers bear the evidence of torture, the nails rippled from a brutal technique called de-nailing, according to the **U.S. Army Field Manual.** He'd been arrested and interned at Buchenwald after a neighbor denounced him as homosexual.

He catches me looking at his nails and smiles. "I hope the other agents didn't give you too much of a hard time about working with me. Heard they've been tossing around the word 'indecent.' "

"I don't care what they think. I did hear Washington tried to yank your security clearance."

"I had to promise I'd forgo my unhealthy lifestyle, or they'd pursue chemical castration." Johann steps into the living room and sets a covered dish on a low coffee table. "Sit. You must be tired. It's off to bed with you when we're done. We have a big day tomorrow."

I wander to the mantel, to a framed photo of a handsome young dark-haired man. Reginald, his lover, who was sent to Buchenwald with him.

"Reginald? You were right about him being good-looking."

He smiles, and the fire catches a glint of a tear in his eye. "Yes, I don't know what he was doing with me. You remember me talking about him."

"You only told me you were arrested together right before the war. Please forgive me if I'm overstepping."

"Oh no, it's fine." He dabs his eye with his napkin. "Though it feels like a million years ago now. Berlin was fun in those days."

"You didn't know it was dangerous?"

"Had no idea Himmler was having the police draw up 'pink lists' of suspected homosexuals. So many arrests followed. They came to my home for me first. Then took Reggie and his mother and sister, too, since they tried to hide him. All part of Hitler's grand plan to purify Germany."

"But I thought German blood was so precious."

"To him, homosexuality was just another deviance. What good is a German man who won't procreate? They tried experimenting with ways to fix us."

"At Buchenwald?"

"At night we could barely sleep, hearing the cries from the row of tall poles on which condemned men were hung. They called it 'the singing forest,' where everyone who was sentenced to death would be lifted onto a hook and held head down until they died. You cannot imagine the howls. Otherworldly."

"How long were you there?"

"No more than a month. I knew it was a matter

of time before Reggie and I would die that way, so I managed to pull a scheme and get us out, by masquerading as Hitler Youths."

He was quiet for a moment, and we watched the fire.

"You escaped?"

"Both of us, right out the front gates. But Reggie turned back. Couldn't leave his mother and sister behind."

"Oh, Johann."

"I begged him to come with me, but he said he had to go back to them."

He stands and ladles chicken soup into bowls and then sets a plate of dumplings down. "But you're not here to listen to my life story. What about Ravensbrück? You so rarely mention it."

"Perhaps it's best to discuss the mission?"

He nods. Survivors understand the reluctance to share.

"The way I see it, the objective is to get Snow, so the Russians don't. Ever since the Soviets got the A-bomb it's like JIOA lost their minds, welcoming the worst criminals with open arms."

I try the soup and it's even better than I remember. "At Fort Bliss the paperclip scientists have their own bowling league now. With exclusive use of the army lanes on Sundays."

"It's sickening but the threat must be real, I'm afraid. The Russians don't go after something unless it's important, and they've been all over this thing."

"How do we know that?"

"Karl's one of the top surveillance experts in the army, didn't you know?"

"Must be above my security clearance."

"He came up through special ops. Knows his stuff, and they've picked up increased Russian chatter featuring Snow's name. Only good news is, they don't seem to have a clear handle on where he is. But we still have the advantage."

"Which is?"

"You."

"Oh, great."

"The Russians may have top-notch assassins, but no one who can put all the pieces together like you can."

"It's hard to know where to begin. My briefing doc suggests Poland to start. Blome's lab there."

"That seems like a waste of time to me. That lab's been picked clean."

"There's nothing in the doc about the ratline. From Italy or the Vatican's part in it."

"Worth looking at, but first, I've arranged for us to go to Salzburg in a few days, once Karl authorizes our game plan. My great-aunt Bertha lives there, in the family castle. It belongs to her brother Bertie, a devoted Nazi, who long since high-tailed off on the ratline. Probably living deep in the Argentine jungle."

"Really think she'll have much for us?"

"I do. My uncle served as a camp accountant for a year at Sachsenhausen, Ravensbrück's brother camp.

Quite the party boy. Knew everyone there, so it's the perfect place to start. She has miles of the home movies he took, and he may have known Snow."

"Fun." I tip back my beer. "What will you tell her about me?"

"She knows what I was arrested for, but still prays every night for me to marry. Might help your cover, if you agree to this, to have her tell half of Austria that we're a couple. She'll be more inclined to talk with my fiancée."

"Hope I can keep it together there."

"She still holds a candle for Hitler and the place abounds with Nazi memorabilia so, yes, it may be hard after all you and your family've been through. But I think we'll learn a lot. And we'll be there together—so come now. Let's get you to bed."

I repair to the guest room and slip into that heavenly bed, the sheets cool and smooth, and put out the light. I try to turn my thoughts from Aaron Salinger, but every touch of the tongue to my puffed bottom lip, my lovely souvenir, brings it all back. He'd barely tossed the room key onto the demilune table in his room when he came to me with no pretense.

Turns out I am pretty good at the sex part of things. Seems it's all about stamina and a willingness to experiment with the crème fraîche and **sauce au chocolat** from the room service tray, and in places other than beds, Widor's Piano Quartet in A Minor playing softly on the phonograph, arguably the world's sexiest classical piece.

The next morning, I woke to find his lovely bare arm splayed across me, half of him uncovered. His back was bronzed, lighter where his swim trunks had been. A sun worshipper. Where had he been to the beach? I drew the tip of my index finger down his side, and he woke, ready, and kissed me harder, the heft of him on me, my bruised lip happily sacrificed to the cause.

I wonder what my mother would have thought about my little affair. And about her half-Jewish daughter from Washington, D.C., going on some wild-goose chase to a Nazi castle to chat with a Hitler-loving baroness. Just the thought of being face-to-face with Nazi Aunt Bertha makes me queasy, but it's necessary to get the asset. What would Mother have said about my hunt for Dr. Snow?

I try to turn my mind to other things, but I spiral into sleep thinking of a time when I still had my mother and how lovely it had been to live in her orbit, even in occupied Paris. Why had I not told her what I was getting into?

She could have saved us all.

CHAPTER 15

JOSIE

PARIS, FRANCE
MAY 1944

Before.

I LEFT HÔTEL DE PONTALBA, LOOKING TO STAY out of trouble and steal a few scraps to contribute to dinner that night. Another fish head maybe? It had been over a year since my mother advised me to lie low and just get to liberation so we could see Father again, but it seemed like it would never come. I resented the chestnut trees happily blooming everywhere in the city, while Parisians suffered the same horrible grind. At least there were rumors floating everywhere that an Allied invasion would come soon and free us all.

I hurried to Les Halles, the massive wholesale market not far from our apartment, where all the smaller markets in Paris bought their produce, meat and seafood, and flowers. Even during the war, Les Halles—always crowded and thrumming with action and some sort of fight between sellers—was my favorite place to steal food. I passed one produce man shouting at another and was about to grab a small turnip and slip it into my pocket, when a woman looped her arm in mine and guided me toward the fish stalls.

"Walk naturally," she said. "We are old friends."

Her French was good with just a trace of a British accent.

I snuck a look at her. With her nicely patched navy blue jacket, wooden platform shoes, and net grocery sack, she seemed the typical Frenchwoman, late twenties.

"I know you," I said.

"Yes, it was me behind you when you pocketed that fish head yesterday."

"You've been following me?"

"For a while now."

She worked for **la résistance,** of course. With her placid expression and mass of curls, I never would have taken her for an agent.

"Do you hate the Nazis?" she asked, as if inquiring about the weather.

I paused to consider the possibility of a trap. "I better get home."

She pulled me closer. "This is not a trap, if that's what you're thinking."

I met her gaze. There was something very trustworthy about her. Perhaps British intelligence? "Of course, I hate them, after what they've done to my family."

"Yes, I know about your mother and grandmother being separated from your father. That must be difficult."

"How do you know?"

She shrugged. "We are skilled at what we do."

How good it felt to share our plight with someone who understood. "They took everything from us. I watch the officers feast while my mother and grandmother waste away. They've made the exchange rate so favorable it's like organized stealing for them. It's disgusting seeing them buy up all the meat and vegetables with children and the elderly so malnourished—"

She scanned the crowd as we walked. "I agree. But are you brave enough to act on those principles?"

"Depends."

"We need you to do something for us."

Every part of me rejoiced. "This is terribly exciting."

"Americans. Always so excited about everything. But thank God, they assigned me a female. My male agents are driving me crazy. Always in need of bailing out. One bounced checks at a brothel. Another lost his briefcase on the Metro. **Much** worse than children. Whatever you do as an agent, never trust your happiness to a man. Embroider that on a pillow, for it's the best piece of advice you will ever hear."

"Will I carry a gun?"

She shook her head. "No. If they find one on you, they will have you shot on the spot."

She pulled a softcover book from her jacket pocket and slid it into mine. It was the size of a greeting card and had **Liaison and Intelligence in France** printed on the cover. "You need to know how to operate in the field, the critical nature of acting as an ordinary French citizen."

I waved it away. "I don't need that. I've lived here for several years now. I don't stand out."

"I knew you were an American the second I started following you from Hôtel de Pontalba. The easy gait, hands in your pockets. You once sat in a café alone. Only prostitutes do that here."

"But I—"

"And look—the buttons on your blouse are sewn in cross-stitch, not straight across in the French way."

"Such small details."

"Details that will risk your life. As you get deeper into fieldwork you, too, will notice these things in others and learn to never attract attention as a foreigner."

"My papers say I'm American."

"You'll be getting new papers that say you're a French Gentile, last name Porter. And out in the field, it's safer to blend in as French. So, learn to move like a European. And don't call attention to yourself by acting in any non-French way, by perming your hair or forgetting that cafés sell alcohol only on alternate days, or by, God forbid, chewing gum. Even in the privacy of your own home, practice eating in the French way, sopping up soup with your bread and finish everything on your plate. And above all, be sure not to appear overly cordial."

"No danger there."

"Be aware of your surroundings at all times and if you suspect a tail, double back and then lose him. Trust that little tingle of instinct."

"Who would want to follow me?"

"There are plainclothes German agents everywhere. This place is full of them. Not to mention Parisians looking for people to turn in for the reward. And we female agents are at much greater risk. You'll be tortured even more vigorously by our friends the Gestapo if caught. So, study the manual well."

"Why do—"

"You will tell your mother you have a new job, as a journalist, writing for **Pariser Zeitung.**"

"That's a propaganda rag."

"It is and the Nazis' favorite pet project right now, and they will hire you since no one else will write for them."

"Will it endanger my mother? Mimi?"

"Not if you keep your distance from them. Plus, the job includes a stipend and some black-market food."

"We need the help."

"Good, then. In the manual you will find a slip of paper with an address. You will come to that apartment each day. There you will find a radio under the bed in a leather case. Set it up and listen only. No transmitting. You understand German, I hear."

I nodded.

"You need to listen for German chatter. Transcribe on paper what you hear and deliver what you learn to the tailor shop, your **boîtes aux lettres.**"

"My mailbox?"

"Your place to drop messages. They will be sent on to London via Bern. When you monitor the airwaves, listen for high-level conversations and city-specific phrases. 'It is raining in Lyon,' for example. Report that immediately. It means the RAF has dropped supplies in that town and we must fetch them. Do you understand? I must warn you, this is a complex and exhausting job, not to mention a dangerous one. The survival rate for our radio operators is less than two months."

"Why can I not just send a coded message directly to London?"

"It is very dangerous. The Nazi **Funkabwehr** drive around in vans listening. Any message transmitted they can track within minutes. So this method is better, trust me."

"May I ask who I'll be working for?"

"The British underground, but it's best you don't know the details. I can tell you our leader is called Sandman and everything we do helps France rise again. We're expecting an Allied invasion in the coming weeks."

"That's no secret."

"True, but you must listen for any German mention of code name 'Jour J.' Or you may hear the words 'D-Day.' What you pick up will be sent to the highest ranks of our allies."

"You do realize I'm seventeen years old? Why me?"

"Frankly, we are desperate, with few other options here in occupied France. But you are half French, and we know your politics. That is the most important. You will be visited by trainers and then your partner who shall be assigned soon. At that time, you will move in to an apartment together."

"I don't need—"

"Yes, you do. You have much to learn."

I shrugged. "I guess."

"I know you are young, but you need to lose the sullen attitude and grow up. When you're given an order, you will take it and understand it is for your safety and those around you. Yes?"

I nodded.

"So, take care. Rest assured, I have cyanide with me at all times in case I'm caught and will use it before I give up my recruits. I also carry a vial of sleeping draught that one finds a number of uses for, including helping yourself to a good night's sleep. You will be given both and I suggest you keep them on you at all times."

Questions flooded my mind. "Can you tell me your name?"

"You will receive communication from me under the name Thérèse and remember in the field there are only two alternatives: Learn quickly or get arrested. I hope for your sake you are in the former category."

I HURRIED TO THE address, found the worn leather case under the bed, and opened it to find a tangle of wires sprouting from a toaster-sized radio. Who had operated that radio before me? They were probably in a work camp somewhere. A chill shivered through me. Or dead.

I learned quickly. My "trainers" turned out to be the plumber one day, a flower merchant the next, each taking me through the equipment and giving me tests to complete. After that crash course, I was on my own and set up the radio on my desk, taped the aerial to the wall, and started listening for German chatter in my headphones. Before lunch I'd picked up two mentions of the phrase "The rain has stopped" and came upon a promising conversation between two Germans. The transcribing took the longest, since my written German was not the best, and then I took them to the tailor shop and slipped them to the woman at the counter.

Two days after my first delivery of radio reconnaissance I received a note back from Thérèse.

VERY GOOD WORK. THE SANDMAN IS PLEASED WITH WHAT HE CALLS HIS GOLDEN DOVE.

CHAPTER 16

ARLETTE

PARIS, FRANCE
1952

UNDER A BLANKET OF LOW, SLATE-GRAY clouds I arrive at Metropolitan Women's Hospital, a state-run asylum located on a former estate on the outskirts of Paris, minutes before noon, eager to see Fleur.

After Luc had caught me breaking into his office and I feigned affection for him to make my break-in story believable, we'd ended up having an impromptu liaison at his apartment. It was not completely unpleasant but left me feeling awkward. But it had all been worth it, to be able to carefully set that silver cup into my grief box. Another piece of Willie I would have forever.

I step around to the back of the hospital in search of the exercise yard. For now, I just want to tell Fleur she hasn't been forgotten and that I'm trying to get her out of this terrible place. A security officer in a dark blue suit holds a dog by the leash in the distance, as they stroll the grounds.

The asylum has fallen on hard times, the yard overgrown, and I find the exercise area, a rusted chain-link fence surrounding a dirt yard. It's packed with women wandering about in varying stages of undress. I stand behind some ivy that had grown up the fence and watch one attendant dressed in a pale blue jacket smoke a cigarette as patients shuffle around him.

I move my toes in my thin boots to warm them and suddenly my attention is drawn to a figure sitting on a folding chair, head down, rocking gently. As I hurry along the fence, I already know it's her just from the curve of her cheek.

The sight of her stops me in my tracks. She wears only a sweater in this cold, and shackles on her ankles. I swallow hard to find my voice. "Fleur."

She looks about, mouth agape.

"It's me," I say. "Here."

She turns and stands. How thin she is. **She's been living like this for all these years? Here in the same city. Why had I not found out sooner?**

I step closer, hands cold on the metal fence. "I love you, darling girl. I haven't forgotten you. Just didn't know where you were."

Fleur tries to walk to me, but the shackles allow only short steps. She reaches out both arms toward me.

My tears blur her image as she shuffles closer. "Yes, it's me," I say.

She tries to run and falls, drawing the guard's attention.

Fleur makes it to her feet, hobbles closer to the fence, and threads her fingers through the chain-link. I place my fingers over hers. "You're so cold. I've missed you."

Fleur hands me something smooth and white through the fence and I pocket it as the attendant comes toward us.

He blows his whistle. "Get away from there!"

I turn as I run and see the guard with the dog rounding the building corner and Fleur standing where I left her at the fence. The attendant yanks her away as she lifts one hand to wave goodbye.

"I'll be back," I say and hurry off the best I can. "I'll never leave you."

I return to my apartment and take my mail from the box, determined to find a way to get Fleur out of that place. Why did she not speak a single word? I settle in with a cup of tea and slide the sculpture she gave me from my pocket. I turn it in my fingers. It's cool and smooth, carved from ordinary white bath soap. Some sort of animal with a long snout. She's such a good little sculptor, and my thoughts return to the flower she made for me that Christmas at the camp. Was this some sort of symbol of the terrible things she'd suffered? Josie's right. I can't go to French Guiana with Luc Minau. I have things to attend to here. He can send me photos of the boys. And if I stay here I can research Willie's intended family, the Reichmans. Maybe the guard Dorothea Binz allowed Willie to live after all. Brought him to his intended SS family.

I sort through my mail and find a letter from the Association to Support Mothers of German Children listing German Lebensborn families who'd adopted, and their status, so helpful in reuniting children with their birth mothers. Why had I not thought of requesting this before?

I read down the column. Reichart. Reichenbach. Reichenberg. **Reichman. Alpenstrasse, Ebersberg.**

Ebersberg. A very nice town and so close to the Lebensborn home in Steinhoering, which ended up as an orphanage, a ten-minute drive at most.

I run one shaking finger across to their status.

Deceased.

I sit back and sink into the sofa cushions. **Perhaps the Reichmans really did have Willie, both died, and my boy ended up at the orphanage there after the war?**

A knock comes at the door and startles me. I stay still and listen, hoping the visitor has the wrong apartment.

The rap comes again, and I stand.

"Who is it?" I ask at the door.

A woman's voice. "Hermione Marchand."

My whole body goes cold. Auntie's sister?

I scoop up the list and tuck it into a drawer. "Please come back another day!"

"Arlette LaRue? Is that you?"

My heart thumps my ribs. "She no longer lives here."

"Let me in, Arlette. Promise I won't bite."

I pause. If she's anything like Auntie was, she'll find a way in anyway.

I open the door and a woman hurries in wearing white gloves, a good leather handbag looped over the crook of one arm, and a Jean Patou coat nipped at the waist, the liver gray color of it doing nothing for her complexion.

"Do you know how long it took me to track this place down?" she asks.

"Who are you?"

She removes her gloves, snaps them in her purse, and lights a cigarette. "Your aunt Henriette's sister. I live in Linz."

Her beloved Hermione. A slightly more attractive version of Auntie, Hermione has the money to blur her flaws with powder and lipstick, but all the money in the world cannot hide the unfortunate family resemblance.

"Please don't smoke in here."

"Well, that's a fine welcome." She takes a drag of her cigarette and I barely breathe as she steps to the little hooked rug in front of the fireplace. My stomach contracts as I picture the bloodstained boards beneath it.

She picks up one of my mother's violet plates from the mantel, examines it, and places it back. "I haven't heard from my sister since the middle of the war. We were terribly close, and she just stopped writing."

"The war was hard on families," I say.

An ash from her cigarette drops on the rug, and she rubs it away with her shoe.

"Well, in case you haven't seen the newsreels, the war's long since over. I just came from Krautergersheim, and my sister's nowhere to be found."

"Of course." My hand shakes as I brush a phantom speck off my sleeve. "I often wonder myself."

"Really? Then why have you not searched? Did you file a formal missing-person claim?"

"Yes."

"Where?"

"Krautergersheim, I believe."

She tilts her head. "Funny. They told me at the town office that no such claim had been opened."

"The war must have disrupted it."

"Why did you not follow up?"

"I was arrested toward the end of the war and taken to a camp."

"Released when?"

"Spring of forty-five—and I did look for her when I got back."

"The last letter I have from her says she was coming to find you. That you'd stolen a child from a Lebensborn home."

As if a switch turns on, my fear turns to rage. "He was my child. They were stealing him from **me.**"

"She also implied she may have an ownership claim to this apartment." She brandishes a page of airmail stationery. "I have her letter right here if you'd like to read it."

Just a glimpse of Auntie's spidery handwriting roils my stomach.

I wave it away. "No, thank you."

Hermione slips the letter into her purse. "So, you were the last to see her?"

"She never made it here."

Hermione steps across the little rug and a corner of it flips up. I barely breathe as she stops and smooths it back with the toe of her shoe.

"Did she ever stay here with you?" Hermione flounces to the bedroom and peeks in.

I hurry to the rug and stand on it. "I told you. She's never been here. Many things happened to people back then—"

"Like **what**?"

Suddenly she looks so like Auntie standing there and it all returns. That horrible crack. The thud of her falling right there.

I open the window and breathe cool air. "You need to leave now. I'm expecting guests."

"Company? Really? With an inch of dust on

everything? You need a maid, I must say." She heads for the door.

"If I hear anything—"

She tosses her card onto the table. "Contact me here. In the meantime, it's convenient we're right here at the police station. The war may have disrupted the investigation, but I'm stopping there today to lodge a formal complaint and reopen it."

I try to appear casual. "Is that really necessary after all these years?"

Hermione looks me up and down. "Expect them to come see you soon. They'll do a thorough check for fingerprints. Just standard procedure, of course."

"It's been eight years. I doubt—"

She leans in. "You don't know me, Miss LaRue, but you'll see. I will not rest until my sister is found."

I close the door behind her and head for the kitchen. Hands shaking, I grab a rag from the counter and go about cleaning every doorknob. **Why had we not wiped the whole place down right after it happened? How long do fingerprints last?**

I step to the fireplace and pull back the hooked rug, the stain seeped there like spilled burgundy. There had been no scrubbing that out.

I can't stay here. The police will come. Find the blood. But what about Fleur? I can help her from afar. I close the window and sit. **I can send Josie's money to Paris General to get her transferred. Fleur wouldn't want me to stay here,**

a sitting duck for the French police and Auntie's greedy sister.

I step to the telephone and dial Luc Minau's number. I'll be accompanying him to French Guiana after all. And the sooner we leave, the better.

CHAPTER 17

JOSIE

EN ROUTE TO SALZBURG
1952

As Johann's Opel Kadett strains up the mountain road toward the castle, I question my decision to make this trip to see his aunt and tamp down my impatience to find Snow. It took us almost a week to depart from Vienna, waiting on clearance from Karl and the background checks I'd ordered. And would visiting Johann's aunt even produce any sort of actionable information? What secondhand info from her brother could Aunt Bertha possibly have to justify staying overnight in Château Third Reich? I just have to keep it together, play the part, and hope to extract some clue about where to go next.

To quell my nerves, I flip through the pages of the background check I asked for.

"Aaron Salinger,' " Johann says, eyes on the road. "Also known as Adam Green. Aaron Grossman. Alexander Meisner."

Every part of me wilts. "Oh, no." **Mossad.**

"Temporarily expelled from school at thirteen for some sort of insubordination. Made it to captain in the Israeli army, but that's not uncommon. Do note the reconnaissance background. Started out making surveillance electronics for them and quickly moved on to wet work."

An assassin.

"Now leads a guerilla splinter group dedicated to sensitive jobs. Has a daughter with his Russian national ex-wife. The child is currently at boarding school in Lucerne."

I lift the black-and-white photo from the stack, of Aaron maybe five years younger. How did I not see that one coming?

"I think the picture says it all," Johann says. "Damaged and waiting for you. To blow up your life or at least tempt one of us to jump into bed with him."

"May have already happened."

Johann glances at me. "You do realize you're doing critical covert undercover work here?"

"It won't happen again."

"It's not like you to make such a rookie mistake.

The Israelis are after Snow, too, you know. **And** this guy targeted you in Paris."

"**What?** No. It was just breakfast—"

"The Ritz dining room?"

"Yes."

"Alfred the maître d'hôtel? Sat you two together?"

"Perhaps."

"Let me guess. There was mysteriously no coffee, and your breakfast order was delayed, and Alfred had it sent up. It's an old play. Alfred knows all the agents. But it's unlike you not to see it."

I slump down into the leather seat. "I checked him for deceptive indicators."

"Seems he's **multi**talented."

"I actually thought we had a connection. I suppose the Bergen-Belsen story was fake?"

"No. Read on. His parents never made it out, but he did."

Of course, Aaron was too good to be true. But perhaps I'd seen only what I wanted to see? Clearly, he was too vigorously healthy for someone claiming to have a heart condition. But part of me is excited by it all. His con was a smart one. And what of the assassin part? The dossier could be wrong. If he'd wanted to kill me, wouldn't he have done it already?

I watch the countryside glide by. "Not that he learned much of consequence from me."

"It's his Russian connection I'm concerned about."

"Only his ex . . ."

"The Russians pose the biggest threat. Their agents are subtle and patient."

"Better than ours?"

"By far. Been doing it longer. Masters at exerting leverage, they exploit any character flaw. Greed. Ego. Stupidity. I'm assuming you had no written information with you."

"Just my notebook with some travel info—"

"Now he knows where you might be headed. So, steer clear if he shows up again."

"Can you leave my little rendezvous off the status update to Karl?"

"If you promise it won't happen again."

"No problem there. And what did you find on Luc Minau?"

"Less on him. The Minau family is well-heeled but never been much for the limelight. They kept a low profile during the war. Nazis seized their Paris apartment, but the Minaus have since reclaimed it. Seems the foundation his grandmother Danae founded helps war orphans and native kids in French Guiana. Somewhat too clean, I think."

We wind our way through the quaint Salzach Valley, past snow-dusted towns dotted with chalet-style homes. Soon we turn a bend and Johann points to a castle sitting perched on a rocky outcrop, snow-capped mountains behind it.

"That's where we're headed. The castle's been in my family for six generations. Built in the twelfth century."

My stomach tightens as I take in all three stories of battlements and turrets.

"That's a serious castle." I shift in my seat. "People live there?"

"It's not a particularly famous one—technically a fortress, and now only Aunt Bertha lives here with a few servants. I grew up coming here for Christmases. My uncle invited his Nazi pals here quite a bit during the war."

We climb toward the fortress, and it's hard not to imagine Hitler arriving on this same road, SS men on the running boards, swastika flags fluttering.

My heart beats harder against my rib cage. "Not sure about this, Johann. Do we have to stay overnight?"

"Actually two nights. Sorry. She planned a small reception for the second night and I couldn't say no."

"Really? Just let me out here."

"Almost there," Johann says, like we're rounding the bend to the Grand Canyon. "Remember, when you meet Bertha, you and I have been dating for only a few months. But we are very much in love. You're a reporter doing a puff piece on this town. And I met you at church."

"What? I haven't been in a church since I was twelve. Spent more time with my mother at her synagogue."

"I wouldn't mention that. I'll steer the conversation to my uncle. Just express interest in the family lineage. She's a roaring anti-Semite so my apologies in advance, but you have to stay cool."

"I can do the whole Gentile thing pretty well.

My father's mother practically lived at Columbia Country Club. He wasn't allowed in, married to a Jew, but she'd sneak me in there, tell her friends I was a cousin they'd never met."

"And I may have told my aunt you're Canadian. Sorry, just better that way."

We drive across a long stone bridge, tires bumping over cobblestones, and approach the castle courtyard. "Himmler and his mistress spent long weekends here. They called her 'the Little Hare.' "

I breathe deep. "This is more troubling than I thought, Johann."

He swings the car around to the massive oak front door. "Hitler and his lieutenants met here many times at the start of the war. Göring slept in that front bedroom with the stained-glass windows, the only room with a bed big enough for him. I give Auntie two minutes before she tells you."

I make a silent prayer to sleep anywhere but the Göring bedroom.

The castle is even more imposing viewed from the front courtyard and looms over us as twilight falls. A butler greets us and leads us into a three-story-high entryway with a wide staircase, its crimson carpet in need of a shampoo.

An elderly butler takes our coats. "Good evening, Master Johann."

I stand and wonder where they once hung the Nazi flag and then get a little nauseous picturing fat Hermann Göring preening in the entryway mirror.

A small woman makes her way down the stairway. She wears a gray topknot, a high-necked black dress, and a hand-knitted red sweater, the elbows worn through.

"Welcome, both of you."

I force myself to shake her cold and papery claw of a hand and tamp down an image of the witch from **Hansel and Gretel.**

"I had Cook save you some dinner. Not much beef, only chicken, I'm afraid, since your uncle took off with all the money. Had to sell the porcelain to buy bread. After that, the Americans came, and I almost lost this place just for being a party member."

Johann speaks into her right ear. "I guess Hitler wasn't the great savior after all, Aunt."

She swats Johann away. "Then concentration camp criminals took the whole place over."

"It was a survivors association, Aunt."

"Well, they used it as an office. Without even asking. Rifled through my unmentionables. All worse than under Hitler, a regime they condemn."

Aunt Bertha looks me up and down. "So skinny, poor girl. Wish we had some maple syrup for you."

"I beg your pardon?" I ask.

"Isn't that what Canadians eat?"

"Oh . . . of course, yes. But I'm not hungry."

Aunt Bertha draws me close. "It's nice to see my nephew's recovered his sanity and finally realized he likes girls."

"Auntie—"

"I knew it would happen one day if he just set his mind to it. And not only did he find a girl, but a **thrifty** one **and** a Canadian. So far superior to Americans."

I smile and lean in. "Yes, far."

"Did you tell her all about the castle history, Johann?" Aunt Bertha tips her head toward me. "He may have told you about the room at the front corner, where we put **Göring** when he was here?"

Aunt Bertha walks on, as Johann mouths "One minute" to me.

"So, you're a reporter?" she asks. "I'm happy we'll finally get a story in the papers about the truth. All this bad press about Hitler doing the devil's work. So one-sided."

She walks ahead of us down a stone-floored hallway. "The staterooms here on the first floor were built in 1570 for receiving royalty. Note the Swiss pine paneling and pear wood rosettes on the ceiling."

I peek my head into one stateroom. "Just like our library at the club. Divine."

Johann forges right in. "Tell us about Uncle Bertie, Aunt. He knew the infamous Dr. Snow?"

"They ran in the same circles. Snow had an incredible reputation . . . very private person, of course."

I slide a notebook from my pocket. "Do you have any of Uncle Bertie's photos?"

"Mostly home movies. My brother was crazy about his movie camera. Have good ones of the Winter Olympics. The Adolf Hitler ski jump."

"Did Uncle Bertie take any movies at the camps?" Johann asks. "We're looking for anything concerning Ravensbrück. The concentration camp for women?"

"Why didn't you say so? I have the projector all set up. Got some footage of that place." She waves us toward the castle library. "You're in for a treat. And I have a whole box of film of Göring doing his morning exercises. Such a charismatic man. And surprisingly muscular under all that fat."

"You said you had some of Ravensbrück?" Johann asks. "The staff there?"

"Some. That's where the lady guards were, so of course your uncle was interested. The officers' canteen there was staffed by the prettiest Polish girls, too. He said there were a great many Poles at the camp."

"Really?" I ask. "Were there Jews?"

"Oh **yes,** at certain times. Of course, not serving in the canteen. Bertie said all the prisoners were treated well. He asked them and none of them ever complained. But Himmler didn't want Jews there at all. He chose Ravensbrück as **his** special place to visit. Saw to the women's punishments personally."

We stop in the hall, and I scribble it all down. "Impressive."

"Yes. Raised the number of beats with the stick from twenty-five to forty. The women were terrible criminals. All prostitutes and murderers. Hitler showed great mercy not killing them all."

"What did Uncle say they did with the Jews?" Johann asked.

"He said at first they sent them to other camps to be dealt with. Couldn't have them there at Ravensbrück since it was a show camp. The **Japanese** toured there. Then, later, many Jews came from Auschwitz when the Russians advanced, so they dealt with them."

"Better to kill them, then," I say.

Johann sends me a glance.

Aunt Bertha shrugs one shoulder. "It was war and they started it."

"The Jews started it?" I ask. "How exactly?"

"By taking all the jobs in Germany. Infecting society with their Jewish science."

I fan myself with my pad. "How do you know so much about it all?"

"Hitler's radio addresses. He was an **orator.** Spelled it right out, directly to the people. He told us that Jews were the whole problem."

"And you believed him," Johann said.

"Of course. Why would he lie?"

Suddenly I can't breathe, and I turn to Johann. "I need to rest, darling. It's been a long day."

Aunt Bertha folds her arms across her chest. "What? You must see the home movies."

Johann slips his arm through mine and walks me close. "Of course, we'll watch, Aunt."

We enter a library, which is bigger than the footprint of my entire childhood home in Washington, D.C. In the center of the room a projector sits upon a card table, a white sheet thumbtacked to one paneled wall.

"Hang in there," Johann whispers to me as I sit on the sofa.

He brings me a glass of brandy from the bar as Aunt Bertha plucks a silver film canister from a box on the table.

She shuts off the lights, the projector starts its ticking whir, and she aims the lens at the white sheet. First up, a rotund man, well known as Hermann Göring, one of Hitler's most trusted lieutenants, soundlessly walks a long hallway lined with artwork and tapestries on the walls, oriental carpets on the stone floor.

"Ah, Göring. At his beautiful Carinhall. **What** an estate."

The camera pans framed paintings.

"That one is a Van **Gogh,**" Bertha says. "Some bridge he painted in the south of France. They say it was Göring's favorite one."

Johann sits up a little straighter. "Langlois Bridge at Arles. Van Gogh painted it many times. It wasn't **his,** Auntie. It was stolen from a Paris museum by the Reich."

Next on the reel, a flickering black-and-white scene of a woman in a white bathing cap doing a handstand on a diving board.

Aunt Bertha leans forward, squinting. "Eva Braun at the pool here. What a body on her, am I right? No wonder Hitler adored her so."

"Lovely," I say as Johann holds my hand.

"Your uncle Bertie had that pool filled in. Too

costly to maintain. And look, here's the grand dinner, remember those silver candelabra, Johann? We served six pheasants and a whole pig. I took a picture of it and won a photo contest in **NS Frauen-Warte** magazine."

"Mazel tov," I mutter, and Johann squeezes my hand tighter.

"Was Dr. Snow in that picture?" Johann asks.

"No. I've never met the man. Rarely left Ravensbrück and camera shy, too. One of the smart ones. He knew if the war ended badly one photo could mean death."

Bertha waves toward the screen. "Here's one of Bertie skiing up in the Austrian Alps." The camera catches Johann's uncle, on skis, head upturned, capturing the sun on his face.

The reel ends and Johann steps to the projector. "Aunt, do you mind if I find some of those reels you talked about? Taken at the camps? Would love to show Josie the work side of Uncle's life."

She waves toward the canister stack. "Be my guest, but it's all quite boring."

Johann replaces the projector reel and soon the screen flickers with three women in a boat rowing on a lake, chatting and laughing with one another.

Aunt Bertha leans back. "That's Ravensbrück. The camp was built on a lake."

I recognize one of them as a guard at the warehouses and take a sharp breath in.

"How can they be so happy?" Johann asks.

"Why not? They're young people. At Lake Schwendt. Good fishing."

Johann returns to me on the sofa. "But, Auntie, these female guards spent their days abusing and often murdering women at the camp. It's a strange contrast to see them out for enjoyment."

I lean forward, a sharp pain in my belly. "Some of the women imprisoned there for years never saw that lake once. They were kept within those walls and died never even knowing it existed. And it's been said that they dumped the ashes from the camp crematoria into that lake."

Aunt Bertha shrugs. "People died. The remains had to go somewhere. It's all a part of war."

The camera finds a line of female guards, a good-looking young man standing in the middle, clearly Johann's uncle from the resemblance.

Aunt Bertha smiles. "And there's your uncle Bertie. He did love the ladies."

The camera pans along the women's faces and lingers on a familiar one.

I sit up and huff a little gasp.

Aunt Bertha smiles. "Yes, she's quite a beauty, isn't she? Dorothea Binz. Bertie was quite taken with her. Now there was a patriot."

How strange it is to see Binz laughing.

"She was found guilty at the Ravensbrück trial," Johann says.

"They hung her, poor thing. While others go scot-free. I hope someone adopted her beautiful dog."

The camera pans to Dr. Herta Oberheuser casting an admiring look at handsome young surgeon Fritz Fischer. I recognize him from his dossier, though I never saw him at the camp. He had operated on the Rabbits and became famous in the Nazi medical community for his work using prisoners' limbs for transplantation experiments onto healthy German soldiers.

Johann stands to change the reel as Aunt Bertha hovers her magnifying glass over another silver film case. "This one says, '**Neige.** Hitler's birthday party in Snow's office.' "

I clench my hands in my lap. "That might be worth seeing."

"It is labeled **Neige,** Aunt, 'Snow.' Why?"

She shrugs. "I assume Dr. Snow shot that roll. Bertie had guests take turns filming. Probably so Bertie could be in them all, the show-off."

The film starts in the Ravensbrück **Revier.** The camera pans down a hallway and into an office, past a tourist poster tacked to the wall of palm trees on a beach, and on to a desk that holds a birthday cake lit by one candle.

"So that was Snow's office?" I ask. The camera pans up to a group gathered around the desk gazing at the cake.

"Looks like a birthday celebration," Johann says.

Herta steps to a closet, pulls out a stack of Red Cross care packages, and sets them on the desk. My breath comes hard and shallow, as the group crowds around the boxes, pulling out tins and packets, eating and mugging for the camera.

I can barely keep my voice steady. "Looks like they're eating the food sent for the prisoners."

"It was war, Miss Anderson. Germans were starving."

"They were eating birthday cake, Aunt," Johann says.

In the film, Herta sits in Snow's chair, puts her feet up on the desk, and leans back, smiling.

"Were Herta and Snow close?" I ask.

"I believe so. She was just an aspiring surgeon. Low-level. But I've heard she happily did Snow's bidding."

The reel comes to an end, Bertha flicks on the lights, and we all walk out toward the entryway.

"Do you know anyone else we can interview for this story?" I ask.

Aunt Bertha waves that thought away. "They're all dead or off to Argentina." She grabs my arm and jerks me so close I can feel her stubbly chin whiskers on my ear. "But the good news is you two don't have to worry about making bedtime fun together. I turn my hearing aid off at ten."

I try to pull away, but she holds me fast.

"And I don't usually put an unmarried couple in the same bedroom, but you two shall have the best one." She bites her lower lip to suppress a smile. "The very bed Göring slept in."

CHAPTER 18

ARLETTE

SOMEWHERE OVER THE CANARY ISLANDS 1952

A WEEK AFTER OUR CHEZ DAUPHINE DINNER and just two days after Auntie's sister and I spoke, Luc and I take off for South America. The president-class Pan Am flight to French Guiana is mostly smooth, there in the wood-paneled cabin, the green leather seats more comfortable than any recliner. The airline is famous for luxe service, and we sit side by side dining on rack of lamb served on bone china plates, an unspoken awkwardness in the air after our unplanned late-night tryst.

I vow to keep it businesslike, to focus on finding my son and getting back to Paris with him. No strings attached. Nothing will distract me from that.

"I've told my boss I'll be gone for two weeks only," I say with crisp formality.

"Did you call the references?"

"Yes. Spoke to a nice woman who found her son. She gushed about your grandmother. Could barely get her off the phone."

"Sorry about all the vaccinations you had to get. French Guiana's a poor country, and we need to keep you safe."

"Thank you for having the nurse do them in your office."

The perks of being rich.

I sip my champagne as the stewardesses glide by. They bend close to Luc to offer mint jelly, slide a newspaper into the seat pocket in front of him, or top off his drink.

Somehow the attention these beauties pay him makes me feel like flirting with Luc, a skill I haven't used in so long. Though I'd had a few brief relationships with men, most of them domineering brutes, I'd always felt a loyalty to Gunther. It felt like I was cheating on him to show affection to another man, though Gunther had been assumed dead for almost a decade.

Luc slices his meat, and I wonder why the stewardesses aren't jumping to cut it for him; they've done everything else.

"These seats fully recline so we can get some sleep," he says. "After a stop in Lisbon we'll refuel in the Azores, and an hour before landing they'll serve us coffee and croissants. I hope you're not scandalized we're having breakfast in bed together."

"It's a bit late for that," I say.

He smiles. "I want to clear the air. I hope our . . . time together the other night doesn't—"

"Make me think you're somehow committed to me? Don't worry. I'm just here to find my son. If I could erase—"

"That wasn't my intention at all. I was going to say I hope it doesn't make you feel awkward with me, since I enjoyed it very much. If you didn't notice."

"Oh," I say, not sure how to respond. "Please don't tell your grandmother."

"My grandmother is a lot less easily shocked than many people think, but of course. A gentleman never kisses and tells."

Another stewardess removes our trays with crisp efficiency.

"All done here?" she asks with a trace of a German accent, and suddenly her mouse-gray uniform and pillbox hat take me back to Ravensbrück and the guards there.

I gulp down the rest of my champagne.

The pilot comes on the intercom and warns of choppy air.

I must look alarmed because Luc takes my hand in his. "Don't be afraid. It's always bumpy right about here."

Maybe I'm not the first mother of an orphan he's done this with.

"Have you never flown before?" he asks.

I shake my head. "A bit claustrophobic, I'm afraid."

Once things even out, he releases my hand as the stewardesses serve coffee, tea, and profiteroles.

"I hope I didn't uproot you from your friends," he says.

A stewardess offers me one of the sweet miniature cream puffs; I wave it away and sip my tea. "I'll be back to Paris soon enough. They're all the family I have."

"It's a charming little café but seems a bit sad to me. And a coffee shop that doesn't have an espresso machine? That's not a good business model."

It's not about the coffee, I think, but instead smile and say, "You are so right."

I must stay in his good graces, if I expect him to work to help me find my son.

He pulls a calendar from his briefcase. "Just so you know what's ahead, here's the plan. We'll let you get settled at Cove House. Then, the next morning, introduce you to the boys in the right age range, those we suspect might be included in what we call your match 'possibles.' "

"How do I narrow it down?"

"There's no substitute for instinct. Spend time with the boys. Saturdays are visiting days. Then, if you decide to stay and pursue a 'possible,' he becomes a 'potential.' If all four of us believe there is strong evidence of a match, we do the blood test."

"What do you mean 'If all four believe there's a match'?"

"My grandmother, myself, you, and Father Peter."

"A priest?"

"We're not a religious organization, but, yes, Father Peter is an ordained priest who found his calling at Hope Home. Couldn't run the place without him."

"And if the blood types match, he's my son?"

"Unfortunately, it's not that easy. There's no test that's proof positive of parenthood. But if your blood types match, we go to the next step."

"I don't need a blood-type test. My auntie said I was type O, the universal donor. Badgered me to sell my blood when I lived with her."

"We're required to officially test every possible pairing, I'm afraid. It will just confirm your O type, I expect."

"So, if I am O, my son would need to be O as well?"

"That would be a very likely indicator."

"Why not test all the boys?"

"We try not to expose them to unnecessary blood work and the possible letdown of a false potential match. We've had boys get their hopes up only to be disappointed. It's important to take things slowly and follow protocol."

"What if the blood types match?"

"If all other physical characteristics correspond—eye color, for example, is a helpful predictor since a brown-eyed child is not impossible but rare from a blue-eyed parent—we consider the pairing valid and order a birth certificate."

I slide my sketch pad and vine charcoal out of my carry-on bag and begin drawing the clouds outside the window. A few sketches I'd tucked away in the back of my pad slip down.

Luc pulls out two, the first, a yellow Dior, the model surrounded with white blossoms. He reads the caption. "A Dior-inspired day dress and bolero jacket for an afternoon lunch in Le Marais."

My cheeks burn. "I'm just an amateur."

He considers the second, a wedding sketch, and reads. "The bridal suit. Who says it must be snow white or even a dress at all for that matter? Ecru is au courant." He points to the sketch. "Wedding trousers? That's a bit déclassé, don't you think?"

"Not at all. It's just a dress with narrow trousers worn underneath. I try not to be chained to fashion."

"I just realized why you'd want the trousers," he says with a look of genuine concern. "Your leg. It's terrible what they did to you."

I pluck the sketches from his hand, with a bit too much force. "Just a silly hobby. But I've dreamed of being a designer someday."

"They look chic to me."

I shrug. "The most personal is always the most creative."

He stares at me for a long moment. "You're an interesting person, Arlette."

I slide the sketches back into the pad. "I like drawing."

"And white flowers, clearly. What about writing?"

"Do I like it? Somewhat."

"You know, a thought occurred to me . . ." He turns away with a little wave. "No, never mind."

"What is it?"

"You might hate this idea, but we need a public relations person badly and it's been impossible to find someone we like. Would you consider the position? Until you become a famous designer?"

"Me? Oh, no."

"The job requires creative energy, people skills, and a discerning eye. I haven't known you long, but you seem to have all three in spades."

"I don't think so."

"Perhaps you could do a few things for us while you're down here? We're shorthanded and in terrible need of a new brochure for fundraising. And I have a commercial shoot planned that just needs supervision. Perhaps you'll change your mind?"

"No, thank you. I've come on this trip to find my son. And I'll be in French Guiana only until that question is settled."

Luc slides a Paris newspaper from the seat pocket, snaps it open, and reads. "Most of the job takes place in Paris, actually. Dealing with donors and the media. So just think it over. It pays well."

"Fine."

I sit back. **Why is he so insistent? And why is it so hard to say no to him? The sex was tolerable, but is he that starved for female companionship? He's clearly used to getting his way. Maybe he just wants a convenient sexual companion for his tropical getaway.**

"We should sleep now." I settle back into my seat and watch the clouds sail by. **I need to be rested when I arrive, so I can start my search for Willie.**

THE SUN IS BEGINNING to set as Luc and I land in French Guiana at the Cayenne airport and I breathe in the sweet, humid air. It's been two long days en route and seven thousand kilometers from Paris, I've left the past behind. If Auntie's sister does contact the police about her disappearance, it will take them a long time to find me here. The Minaus may know a bit of my early life, but not about Auntie. Or about my secret life with Josie as a Golden Dove. How we got to Ravensbrück. I want to forget those parts myself and just focus on the search.

Luc smiles. "You're a trooper, Arlette. Just one more flight. Chopper to Cove House."

A helicopter? I've never set foot in a helicopter or, before this trip, a plane for that matter. "I'm not the best with enclosed spaces. Can we drive?"

"It'll be fine." He takes me by the arm. "You'll love the ride."

The balmy breezes play under my linen blouse as we board the helicopter. A tawny-skinned young man wearing headphones sits in the pilot's seat and turns to wave as we enter.

"How old is the pilot?" I whisper to Luc. "He doesn't look very experienced."

Luc smiles and guides me to my seat next to the window. "Claudio? He's not that much older than you but he's clocked a lot of hours. Don't worry."

"As a pilot for an airline?"

"No. Private clients—his father taught him. Been flying since he was twelve. I met him here in town, a bit down on his luck. Gave him some decent clothes and a steady salary, and now he'd take a bullet for me. You can feel safe with him."

Luc seats me next to the window, and right away I feel the panic rise. I tamp it down as we take off straight up and fly low over the coast, and I huff short, calming breaths. The pilot maneuvers the chopper out over the ocean, and I force myself to take in the turquoise water lapping the shore, the jungle stretching back to the horizon.

Luc leans across me and points out the window. "See that island offshore? That's the famous Devil's Island. Been open one hundred years."

I try not to look down. "Uh-huh."

"Terrible conditions. Started as a leper colony. When Europeans came here in the sixteen hundreds, they were looking for the lost city of gold. But mostly found just fights with the local Arawak people. After some time, the French founded Cayenne and made it the capital."

I try to appear interested. "Are the Arawak tribes still here?"

"Yes. Mixed with Maroons, descendants of Africans who formed settlements once they escaped slavery. They still have villages in the jungle upriver. So hidden you can walk right by one and never know it's there. Their lives depended on staying concealed once they escaped the slave traders years ago, and they remain isolated and fortified."

I hold on to the seat with a death grip as the pilot banks, heads back toward land.

"There's Cayenne below. About fifteen thousand people. That big white building in the middle of town, over by the beach?"

I take a quick glance down.

"That's Hotel Lotus. Cayenne is a pretty unsophisticated place, but now we have our own fire department. And even a little television station next to it . . . see?"

On the outskirts of town, long rows of some sort of crop grow next to a metal-roofed barn. "What's growing in those fields?"

"Cayenne peppers. That's where the name of the city comes from. They're dried and ground for spice."

I breathe deep to quell the panic and start to relax.

We fly low over a peak-roofed shack, a colossal antenna planted next to it. It's an odd sort of building, not in keeping with the other architecture, and something about it sends a shiver up my back.

I lean closer to Luc. "What's that little house on the hill—with the giant antenna?"

"Father Peter's ham hut."

"My uncle had a ham radio. Is that how you stay in touch with the world down here?"

"Sometimes. The telephone service is almost nonexistent. We can barely call the drugstore and then it's a party line, every person in Cayenne on it."

"Surely you can send a telegram."

"If the moon and stars align maybe, from Hotel Lotus, but they're always having line trouble. Letters are the way to go. My grandmother's in charge of that."

"I've never been out of France, so I must say I'm a bit overwhelmed. What's happening down there in the streets?" I ask, my voice raised over the whir of the blades.

"Carnival. The pre-Lenten festival. Started by slaves to celebrate fertility, and look what it's become. We have the longest celebration of Carnival in the world."

"Mostly French people?"

"Mixed population—Creole and French, German and Brazilian. You should see the colors. Groups of men bare-chested and coated with molasses, celebrating their fugitive slave ancestors. Chinese dragons. Zombies. And the **food.** Fish chowder. Fried bread. They sell **galette de rois** at every corner."

"The cake of kings. We make it at the café."

He smiles, teeth white in the low light. "The Creole version's nothing like the one in Paris. I hope I'm not being a bore. I do love the food and the drama of it all. But stop me if it's tedious."

"I can't wait to see it."

"You must be careful there at night if I'm not with you. A great many homeless folks, sadly. The foundation does what we can for them, especially the children, but you should stay to the main streets."

We fly north of the city, along the water, and Luc moves closer to me. "Look straight down."

"Must I?"

"It's what you've come all this way to see."

Below us twin peninsulas jut out, like two arms wrapping themselves around a wide inlet.

"There's the kids' camp—Camp Hope. See the tower peeking out of the jungle? You can see the roofs of sleeping huts through the trees, built in concentric circles around the dining hall."

I press one hand to the cold window. Willie could be down there right now.

"There's the landing strip for the mail plane—see it just outside of town?

"And there's Grandmother's house on the cove."

The house is much grander than I pictured it, a terra-cotta-tiled patio extending out toward the ocean, over a wide canyon of trees.

We descend toward the helipad, an oval of

hard-packed dirt a short walk down a path from a grassy area along the cliff top edge where a long black car waits.

Young boys below gather at the cliff edge and jump off into the churning water.

I turn to Luc. "They must be very brave."

"Foolish, actually. That's a fifty-meter drop. Can't get too mad at them. When we were kids, we did the same thing. Only at high tide."

"Lucky you're alive."

"Must hit the water just right though or be crushed by the impact."

We set down ever so lightly on the helipad, and the chopper blades come to rest.

"Great flight, Claudio," Luc says as we disembark.

"My pleasure, sir," he answers as he takes my hand to guide me down the stairs.

I'm happy to be on solid ground again and it's hard not to notice how good looking Claudio is, dark-haired, his tawny skin a lovely contrast to his white uniform shirt. He's a bit broader in the shoulders than Luc and seems the type whose role might include bodyguard as well.

Luc leads me along the path to a grassy area overlooking the ocean and we step to the cliff edge.

"It's getting dark now, but during the day the view from here is incredible. Highest point around. Otherwise, a pretty flat place."

Even in the twilight, one can see the most incredible

panorama, from the revelers in Cayenne all the way to craggy Devil's Island rising out of the sea. Below us, the boys swim and splash one another in the water.

Luc smiles. "It really is like heaven, isn't it?"

I step closer to the cliff edge.

"Careful. The clay's been eroding. Claudio will take your luggage."

Apparently, Claudio is the driver as well, and he helps me into the back seat of the waiting car. It is so like the one my uncle Hans's family drove, a Citroën Traction Avant, the windows tinted dark and the finish so shiny black I can see myself in it. I run one hand down the smooth taupe tweed of the leather-trimmed seat. Such a beautiful French car.

We head off down a steep incline, and I catch Claudio looking at me in the rearview mirror and look away. How flattering it is for such an attractive man to openly admire me. I glance over at Luc. But how would his boss feel about it?

We take a coastal road, and I glimpse the beach through the palm trees now and then, waves lapping the sand.

Luc rolls down his window and lets the warm breeze run about the car.

"You've seen many families reunited?" I ask.

"Going on twenty-two. To be honest, we've been wrong twice. But I have a good feeling about this one. Usually, you just know. Even without the blood test and the background check."

My throat constricts. "Background check?"

"Did I not mention that? We do a thorough check on each parent we reunite."

"Who does it?"

"We use an expert company. They look under every rock." He looks at me coolly. "Why? Do you have some sort of nefarious secret you're not telling us?"

"It just seems silly, if the blood types match."

"Simply a precaution." He leans closer, and smiles. "But if you've got some shady past, you need to come clean."

I turn and look out the window.

He waves the thought away. "Sorry I even mentioned it. I'm sure you'll pass with flying colors. But now you need to pass with my grandmother. She's the toughest hurdle here. Though you have a lot in common. She grew up in Alsace, too."

"Does she spend much time with the boys at the camp?"

"She's slowing down these days. Takes care of the bills mostly, though not particularly well. Tried to force a personal secretary on her but she had a fit. Fiercely independent. When she ran the jeep into a palm trunk, and I had to take away her keys, she didn't speak to me for a week."

Claudio turns down a dirt drive in the near darkness and stops at a gate in a fence twice my height. The guards wave us through and after a longer drive through dense jungle we pull up to a low-slung, modern-style home, the interior aglow, cicadas and frogs calling in the night.

Luc helps me from the car.

He's right about his grandmother. She waits at the front entrance, leaning on a bamboo cane, a bit stooped but surprisingly youthful, silver hair drawn back in a low chignon, her French blue silk caftan fluttering behind her as she comes to greet us.

"Miss LaRue, at long last. You're just what we need right about now, with all this heat. A breath of beautiful, cool air."

I kiss her on both cheeks and breathe in the heavenly scent of gardenia. In classic French style, she no doubt claimed her signature scent long ago and has worn it for the past thirty years. She's a stunning woman, with wide-spaced eyes and full lips, in her youth probably often mistaken for my favorite French actress, Simone Signoret.

"Thank you for doing all this. For finding me and getting me back together, possibly, with Willie."

We step in the front door, and it's perhaps the most breathtaking home I've ever seen outside of magazine spreads. The sunken living room is long, beautifully underlit, and completely open to the dark night as the waves crash in the distance. Low sofas and upholstered chairs flank a chestnut sideboard topped with a bar tray of crystal decanters, and what looks like a sleek kitchen stands at the far end of the room.

"It's my pleasure, dear. This won't be easy, I'm afraid. You'll meet all twenty-two of the possible matches tomorrow. Get a good night's sleep. The first day is always the hardest for the mothers."

"I've been through worse, Madame Minau."

"Yes, I know from my research that you were at the infamous Ravensbrück. Such a terrible, lonely place to be as such a young girl."

"I had Willie. And my friend Josie Anderson. She's a reporter now. American."

"An American in Paris during the war?"

"Her father was a diplomat."

"How did you know her?"

"Just as one meets friends anytime. But it was not an instant friendship—in fact, she was the last person I thought I could ever be friends with."

CHAPTER 19

ARLETTE

PARIS, FRANCE
1944

Before.

THÉRÈSE VISITED ME AT MY PARENTS' APARTMENT on the April day Willie turned one year old. He was getting a tooth and fussed every now and then, but I'd finally settled into a routine of sorts and savored our solitary life, having surrendered to the tides of motherhood. I wanted it to stay that way forever, just the two of us, waking to Willie's warmth next to me each morning. But the specter of Thérèse's cryptic words about repaying her haunted me. I knew she was part of a resistance group and every day wondered when she'd come to request her favor.

It was good to see Thérèse. She kissed me on each cheek and tickled Willie under his chin. "Look what

I brought for the birthday boy," she said holding out a lovely, ripe peach.

I took the peach. How strange to hold the fuzzy little fruit, a rare delicacy. "Where did you get such a prize this time of year?"

Thérèse smiled. "Himmler's private stock at the Les Halles greenhouse."

I set the peach on the kitchen counter. "Thank you. I will cut it up for him and he'll devour it, no doubt."

Thérèse handed me a waxed paper packet of tea bags. "I hope you've been happy here. I can't believe a year has passed."

I bounced Willie on my hip. "Da-da," Willie said, his first word, a stab to the chest every time he said it, making me all too aware of Gunther's absence.

"Every day I'm grateful you saved me from that place. Willie's first words would have been German."

"You've often said you'd like to pay me back for all we've done for you and contribute to the resistance. Well, today that can happen. I have a partner for you."

I stepped back. "Now?"

"An American girl. You're both about the same age. Have much in common."

"I'm happy to help, but please not some perky Yank?" **Who most likely dresses worse than a German.**

"She's half French and we're shorthanded."

"She's probably always snacking and does calisthenics or some horrid exercise that will wake the baby."

Thérèse stepped closer. "Please behave reasonably."

The coded rap came at the door, and Thérèse opened it to reveal a young woman.

"Thérèse?" she asked as she stepped in.

Thérèse closed the door, kissed her on each cheek, and spoke in hushed tones. "Josie, may I introduce you to Arlette and little Willie? Arlette, Josie here is known in the organization as the Dove."

"You know each other?" I asked.

"Yes," Thérèse said. "I do have other agents working for me."

I looked her up and down, this partner foisted upon me, with her petite frame and dark hair cut in a French bob that flattered her face. Certainly, better than pin curls or a hideous pompadour. She wore a good wool suit, possibly Lanvin, which had been cut down. It made her look older than her age, as she dragged in two lovely Moynat suitcases. She was clearly rich or had been at some point. Had she brought all her worldly possessions?

Thérèse reached for one of the suitcases. "May I help?"

"Careful, that's my radio," Josie said.

I turned to Thérèse. "A **radio** operator? Here? With Nazis right out the bedroom window? My God, this is upsetting."

"Get ahold of yourself," Thérèse said. "We've lost many of our radio operators. This is critical to our mission."

I paced, craving fresh air. "I have a child to

consider. Nazis smoke all day right there at my bedroom window. And she'll be operating a radio here?"

"Only listening, not transmitting, and she needs help. You would simply be asked to copy over what she transcribes and deliver it."

"I'm very good at it," Josie said, in surprisingly good French.

"Why can she not deliver it herself?"

"It's riskier for her since she is an American. Her French is accented. Plus, she's Jewish. If she is caught, well . . . Let's just say you would have a better chance of surviving. And we can't afford to lose a radio operator as talented as she is."

"But you can afford to lose me?" Willie fussed, and I smoothed one hand down his back. "You planned this all along, didn't you, Thérèse? That's why you helped me get out of Westwald. You needed cover for your radio operator here, and the baby helps, doesn't he? Who would suspect two women out with a child?"

Thérèse stood straighter. "I won't deny that was my initial motivation, but I truly wanted to help you keep your child. I will do my very best to protect you."

I held back a sob. "You don't care about us."

She ran one hand down my arm. "Of course I do. But you knew this day was coming. And I honestly think you and Josie will like each other."

I eyed the girl's green khaki backpack that swung down from her shoulder. She'd become prey to the fashion of substituting army gear for a proper handbag. That would have to change. And her olive-green blouse didn't suit her at all.

"You're probably used to better, but you must sleep out here on the sofa."

She shrugged. "Fine."

Thérèse stepped to the door. "Good, then. It's settled. You'll receive further instructions about your drop-offs at the tailor shop. Make your visits there brief and don't share anything personal. It's the little things that get one caught."

She stepped out, and the baby, watching her go, arched his back and cried.

I stroked his downy hair. "He loves Thérèse. And as you can see, it isn't restful living with a baby."

Josie handed me a pale green baby blanket, edged in matching satin. "My mother had me bring this when she heard my new roommate has a baby. It was mine as a child. My mother monogrammed every item I owned. Even the diapers."

Though Josie first came off as proud, there was something very caring about her way. And though it would be a project, she could look good in the right clothes.

I ran one finger along the monogram, **JA** embroidered in navy blue script. Hot tears filled my eyes. "It's very pretty, thank you. I have so few baby things."

Josie lifted Willie from my arms and bounced him on her hip. She opened her eyes wide at him, and he smiled his sweetest gummy grin at her and flapped one pink hand against her cheek.

"Oh, look at your four little teeth," Josie said to him.

"He's already fond of you," I said, holding back tears. How few people he'd been allowed to meet.

"And I'm smitten myself. But you must be desperate for a bath. I'll keep him while you soak. Perhaps we'll have a cup of tea when you're done?"

In the wake of her kindness a gush of emotion and exhaustion crashed over me. "I said terrible things. I'm sorry. I'm just so tired."

"I hope you'll take your time and enjoy it. It can't be easy taking a new person into your home, but perhaps we can make the best of all this. It's crazy, isn't it, us working against the Nazis?"

"I want to beat them so badly."

"Welcome to **la résistance,** Arlette. That's exactly what we're going to do."

AS SPRING UNFOLDED, WE took to our new roles quickly and spent most of our days with me sitting as bait, smoking at the open bedroom window. In the metalsmithing station of my parents' studio I made a key for the lock at the German-owned **tabac** on the corner. It was an easy, common lock, and we came away with pockets full of French and Indian cigarettes to use in our open-window smoking sessions.

From our new bedroom window setup, Josie was able to listen in on conversations between what sounded like Nazi higher-ups, especially when both our window and theirs were open, and the signal came in perfectly clear. We found that if I sat at our open window, this invariably caused the Germans in the office opposite to open theirs and flirt with me, giving Josie longer periods of surveillance time. The space of one of Willie's nap times usually produced at least six pages of conversation for me to transcribe from German and deliver to the tailor shop once Willie woke.

I enjoyed my trips to the shop, which was tucked away on a quiet side street. The owner, the widowed and very serious Monsieur Laurent, was a supremely gifted master tailor, once employed by the best couture houses in Paris. His handsome son, Theo, who'd inherited his talent, had died fighting at Dunkirk, and his remaining child, a daughter named Magdeleine, was a perpetually happy young woman with auburn hair who worked the counter. The Laurents had devised a simple drop-off system with Josie, and once I joined the team we continued it. Magdeleine would hang one brown sock on the clothesline in the shop window if it was safe to enter. Once I saw that sock was there, I would come in to the counter with my market basket and drop off the yellow skirt with the transcribed notes tucked in the pocket.

Our conversation was always the same. "Can you take in the waist?" I would ask.

"Certainly, mademoiselle," Magdeleine said. "It will be ready next week."

One day I came to make a drop and from the

room beyond, which was curtained off with a velvet drape, came a baby's cry. Monsieur Laurent emerged, an infant at his chest, patting the child's back in a soothing way. How well Magdeleine had hidden her pregnancy, behind the counter all day.

"Boy or girl?" I asked.

The time had gone quickly, since Willie was that small. How nice it would be to go back to when he was an infant. Though I did not want to revisit the sleepless nights.

"A boy. Theo after my brother." Magdeleine leaned in. "Papa won't put him down. The child will never sleep on his own."

"I have a boy as well. A little over a year old. Willie."

What harm could it do to share a little with a fellow mother?

"How did you get him to sleep at night?" Magdeleine asked.

"We live near the flower market. At first, the sound of it woke him every morning before dawn. But now he's used to it and a year older and sleeps through anything. Just make sure he is burped before you put him to bed. One bubble can keep them up all night."

She smiled. "Thank you. We mothers need to stick together."

I left that day happy to know the Laurents better but with the uneasy feeling that I had better not share any more information with my new friend.

It was the little things that got one caught.

—

ONCE OUR MESSAGES STARTED being delivered regularly, our superiors in London became so pleased with our work they'd amended Josie's code name and came to refer to us both as the Golden Doves in their correspondence.

One of the first things we did together as Doves was intercept a conversation about a new factory in Bergerac that was making bullets and guns. Once we relayed the information, we read in the paper a few days later that RAF planes had then bombed the factory, and Josie and I celebrated with stolen champagne.

The following week, Josie scored an even bigger coup when she overheard a German radio exchange saying Himmler was planning a secret trip to visit Paris. We sent this conversation in our usual way, and thought nothing of it until two days later when we were out at twilight, coming home from a stop in our favorite park, Place Dauphine. We often took Willie there, the leafy historic square on the western tip of the Île de la Cité, lined with historic buildings with their warm beige stone façades, the Eiffel Tower rising beyond. The Germans also admired the place, with its lovely trees and cobblestone streets, but we kept to ourselves on a bench in the park, as they swarmed the street-level outdoor cafés and restaurants.

We were getting ready to head home when all at

once we heard planes overhead, RAF cubs that often flew at night, and seconds later a blizzard of paper floated down over the park, through the trees, and drifted onto the café tables and cobblestone streets.

A paper glided down onto Willie's carriage. I picked it up, and we read the words printed in lino-typed French:

TO THE GOOD PEOPLE OF FRANCE. BEWARE.
HEINRICH HIMMLER, *REICHSFÜHRER*
OF THE SCHUTZSTAFFEL,
IS SECRETLY PLANNING TO VISIT PARIS.

An SS man at a café table stood, picked up a leaflet, and read. "Shit. Now he won't come at all." He turned and shouted to his men. "Get these picked up—every one!"

We watched the German soldiers scurry about the park scooping up handfuls of leaflets, some of the men snatching them in midair.

Josie and I exchanged glances. How good it was to be us. We'd stopped Heinrich Himmler himself from visiting France. And we couldn't wait to do more.

CHAPTER 20

JOSIE

SALZBURG, AUSTRIA
1952

JOHANN AND I MAKE IT TO OUR CASTLE BEDROOM, which looks like something out of a **King Arthur** novel, tapestries gently swaying on the walls. Aunt Bertha has staged the room like the newlywed suite at a hotel, with rose petals scattered on the duvet, slippers on white mats beside our bed, and an ice bucket with a chilled bottle of local sparkling wine on a bedside table.

But at least the walls are covered in photographs. Maybe one of Snow? I try to keep the conversation away from next steps, secretly hoping Johann doesn't suggest visiting Herta at Landsberg Prison to ask about Snow. Just the thought of being in the same room with her knocks the wind out of me.

In the bathroom Johann squeaks open the tub taps as I step to the wall of framed photos next to the fireplace.

"No way am I sleeping in that Göring bed," I call to him over the sound of running water. "Hopefully they've changed the sheets."

As Johann bathes, I browse the wall of photos, searching the faces for someone who might be Snow. But most of the photos feature Johann's uncle with women, many taken on the terrace of Hitler's Eagle's Nest retreat, including one of him embracing a grinning Eva Braun, snow-peaked Alps in the background.

I move in for a closer look at a group shot taken in Dr. Snow's office, featuring Binz and Herta and several men and women I don't recognize.

Johann emerges from the bathroom wrapped in a white robe.

"Can we borrow one of these photos?" I ask.

He pulls the camera from his bag. "I'll just snap a pic." He focuses on the Snow office photo and shoots. "If there's one you want a hard copy of, just take it out of the frame. She'll never notice."

I slide out a picture of three men posing outside the Ravensbrück gates.

"You do realize the packages the happy camp staff opened in Bertha's movie were Red Cross?" I ask.

"Sent for the prisoners. Children died from lack of food while the camp staff gorged."

"It's revolting, the whole lot of them. I wish Bertha had a photo of Snow. It's like trying to trace a ghost. Interesting to see Herta Oberheuser in those films. She might be worth visiting."

I slip the photo into my bag. "I don't know, Johann. I saw her at the doctors' trial. There was no way she'd talk. Not sure I'll get anything new out of her."

"You can play off the fact you were both at Ravensbrück at the same time. Ever meet her?"

"No. I never had much contact with the doctors. Just saw her at the camp here and there. Heard a lot about her, but pretty sure my mother met her. Arlette as well."

"Did Herta know you and Arlette worked in the underground?"

"No one at the camp did until the Gestapo came there looking for us on a tip."

"But the Golden Doves were known throughout France. How did you become so famous?"

"I'd rather not—"

He smiles. "Remember, you report to me, Captain."

I sigh. "It isn't easy to go back there. But we were just two stupid teenage girls having the time of our lives trying to bring down the Reich."

CHAPTER 21

JOSIE

PARIS, FRANCE
1944

Before.

OUR SPY GAMES CAUSED AN UPROAR AT German High Command. And once Himmler canceled his visit to France, gendarmes and Gestapo swarmed Paris in an extraordinary manhunt to find those responsible for the security breach. All roads, bridges, and railway stations were either closed or put under twenty-four-hour watch, and a new fleet of gray-green **Funkabwehr** listening vans roamed the streets. Anyone even suspected of resistance activity was summarily executed.

We had to be extra careful because the Germans had a new way to pick up radio workers, what the French called stork planes, because their wheels hung down like bird legs as they flew. They could pick up radio transmitters **and** receivers and pinpoint a location within meters.

I hurried along the Seine to Arlette's apartment, breeze in my hair, my cyanide pill and the tiny vial of sleeping draught tucked in my hem, high on the success of my radio work, eager to do more. Delivering those conversations felt wonderfully dangerous and was addictive, knowing every word we sent to London got us closer to liberation.

How satisfying it was to be secretly fighting the Germans, who strolled in packs all over Paris, buying up everything at ridiculously low prices. Since March, it was clear they were losing the war, after they'd retreated from the advancing Russian army, though on the Nazi conversations I monitored, the men remained oddly confident.

Having memorized the maze of paths that led to the apartment hidden deep in the Flower and Bird Market, it was a fun game seeing how quickly I could get there. As the war dragged on, many of the little flower kiosks were shuttered due to arrests or merchants fleeing south to unoccupied France. But peony season had just begun, and scant bunches lay in some of the stalls, their legs bound, pink heads still balled tight.

The blue-jacketed flower men argued with their neighbors and smoked cigarettes as they snipped stems and slid skinny bunches into zinc buckets. How many of them worked in the resistance as we did? Every now and then Thérèse brought a downed RAF pilot there, helped him into a blue smock, and hid him in plain sight. He was always gone the next day.

On Sundays came the bird merchants as well, the cages stacked, cups of birdseed scooped and sold from the burlap bags. But I would never own a bird. There was something terribly sad about those poor things huddled on their perches; they would never fly free.

But of course every German in Paris was there, shopping the canaries, lovebirds, and gold finches, carrying home their prizes in little paper boxes, as always, devotees of trapping innocent creatures for their own benefit.

Arlette's apartment provided a front row seat to spy on the Nazis, since it backed up to the massive Police Prefecture, the six-story mansard-roofed building where Gestapo, uniformed German intelligence agents, and plainclothes officers mixed in with the French police in their kepis and blue jackets.

I hurried on. Though beautiful and sweet-smelling, the flower mart was a dangerous place, mostly shopped by Germans those days, always enthralled by Paris's most decadent pleasures, and I could not risk blowing our mission.

I arrived at Arlette's apartment, rapped our arranged knock on the door, two knocks, a pause, and two more, and she let me in. She was in a good mood that day and wore one of the many beautiful pieces her mother had left behind after her death, a silver silk kimono, which fluttered after her as she walked.

"I'm almost done with the windows," she said. "Isn't the scent just glorious wafting in? One more benefit of living in a flower market."

What a lovely place to come home to, Willie resting on the sofa, light filtering in the living room window as Arlette cleaned the panes with vinegar, hair tied up in a scarf. How beautiful she was, skin practically translucent. So gentle and kind, she embodied the French word **soigné.** Well groomed and elegantly done.

She was perhaps my complete opposite and living with her had been a master class in dressing as a young French woman should. While my French mother was more bohemian in her taste, Arlette understood haute couture.

I stepped toward the bedroom.

"I'll be in to help transcribe when Willie naps," Arlette said. "Our German friends should be ready for a cig break by then."

I hurried to my radio, the aerial snaked up and taped to the wall. Most times we closed the drapes in there, keeping it permanently dark, since the Nazi office staff often stood smoking at their window, a stone's throw from my radio.

After she put Willie down, Arlette took her place on the window ledge and lit the stub of a cigarette. She was careful not to smoke full cigarettes, which would have marked her as a fraud, since women were not allowed to purchase tobacco and most scrounged the streets for butts.

Sometimes it took a while for our German marks across the way to note Arlette's presence there and open the window. How nice it was, just the two of us. We took in the scent of lilac and bacon frying somewhere, wafting on the warm breeze, just talking about anything we liked, as the baby napped.

Arlette nodded toward the headquarters building. "I'm afraid these are the only eligible men left in Paris."

"Who needs a man anyway?" I asked.

"You say that now, but I don't want to end up alone like my auntie, old and hunched, my stomach bigger than my breasts."

I smiled. "Oh, Arlette."

"It can happen, you know."

"That's your biggest fear?"

She waved a fly away. "One of many. The other is that no one comes to my funeral."

"Please."

"Oh, and not having anyone to hand down my parents' precious things to. And after my lonely, unnoticed death, our paintings end up in the dusty corner of some sad **brocante.**"

I shook my head. "A perfectly stunning girl like you has nothing to worry about. Men stop and stare in the street."

"A marriage proposal is quite another thing." She brushed away an ash from her skirt. "But at least

I can make clothes. Love fades, but good fashion lasts forever."

A window scraped open across the alley from us, and Arlette turned, in her perfectly casual way.

"Hello there," a man said in German-accented French.

I peeked out at him, as he stood by the window, a typical German man, not unattractive. Medium build, with a receding hairline and wire-rimmed spectacles. He carried a little German-French dictionary with him, which he frequently referenced.

Arlette smiled, toked her cigarette stub, and tipped her head. "Nice weather, finally." She was perfect for this job, born, as French women are, with a whole quiver of skills meant for captivating the opposite sex, and the innate genius for deploying them.

"I anticipate your beautiful appearance each day here at this window," he said, pausing to look up the French word for window. "You are my favorite female."

Arlette and I both stifled a laugh at his awkward phrase.

"What a fine compliment," she said.

I slipped on my headphones, hoping to pick up chatter about the much anticipated Allied invasion Thérèse had spoken of. All of Paris buzzed with talk of it, and the Germans had fortified the western coast of France, focusing on the ports. Hitler had installed massive gun batteries in Calais, the closest point to England, their cannons pointed twenty short miles across the English Channel at Dover. But every day the question loomed: Where exactly would the invasion happen and when? Stepping through the Flower and Bird Market one heard the merchants whispering. "The troops will land down in Normandy to save us." "My cousin who works at the dock in Le Havre says it will be there for sure." "Clearly Hitler thinks the Allies will land up in Calais."

But for once it was not up to Hitler. The command would come from General Eisenhower and the other Allied heads. And it could be anywhere along the western coast.

I listened in to a few different conversations taking place in various parts of that enormous building, adjusting my crystal to find the frequencies. Soon I picked up a phone conversation so startlingly clear it sounded like the two men were right there in the bedroom.

"Is this a secure line?" a man asked.

"Do you think I'm stupid?"

The other one laughed. "Yes, actually."

"Coming up to Ravensbrück?"

"Not sure."

"Snow's arranged a new playhouse."

"I don't need syphilis, thank you."

"Suit yourself. Everyone's clamoring for it."

They spoke at length of some old-school stories and then turned to work. "So, when is the big event happening?"

"Soon we think."

"You cannot be more precise?"

"We know it will be Calais."

"How can you be sure?"

"They've moved tanks to Dover. Planes. Camouflaged, of course."

"Is Göring going to be awake for the big invasion?"

The other one chuckled. "Who knows?"

Static scratched the line.

Arlette closed the window, and my connection ended. How lucky I'd heard such a high-level conversation. My whole body hummed with the satisfaction of it.

Arlette closed the drapes.

"How is your German friend?" I asked.

"I think he must be an accountant or something. Very boring. But isn't he funny with his broken French?" She folded her arms across her waist. "He suggested a visit. So, I had to end it." She stubbed out her cigarette in the ashtray. "I hate cigarettes."

"We've done enough for one day. I have plenty to deliver once you transcribe it. Let's go when Willie wakes up."

"Maybe we should stop listening every day, Josie. Cool things just a bit?"

"Whatever you like," I said with a smile. "After all, you're my favorite female."

WE RODE OUR BICYCLES to the tailor shop so Arlette could make her delivery of the Calais conversation transcription, Willie in the pack at her chest. A spring day like that could make a person almost feel like the war would be over someday. There was much to be optimistic about. Due to our covert work, I was now able to provide my mother with increased rations. Thérèse even slipped us my favorite bergamot tea and teething biscuits for Willie.

After rooming with Arlette, I knew I would live in Paris forever. She'd not only taught me how to dress and how to appear nonchalant at all costs but taught me so many things my mother had not. Such as how to celebrate my imperfections, like the little gap in my smile.

"But don't laugh **too** hard, Josie," she'd say. "No one should ever see your gums."

I tried to follow her advice, for she was a fair, yet vigilant tutor.

We rode on, soon heard a familiar voice, and braked our bikes.

"Stop, stop!" It was a street urchin we'd seen before, here and there, an elfin girl with skin the color of a chestnut husk, who might be a shade lighter if washed.

She came to Arlette and handed her a daisy. "For you."

"What a darling girl."

"Hold on to your valuables," I muttered.

"The daisy symbolizes innocence," Arlette said to the girl, which seemed wasted on her.

She handed Arlette a little waxed paper bag of what looked to be cigarette butts.

Arlette took the bag and looked inside. "How did you know I collect these?"

"I saw you."

The girl skipped a few paces away.

Arlette followed. "What's your name?"

The girl shrugged.

Arlette stood and tucked the flower behind her ear. "May I call you Fleur? I think it suits you."

The girl just stepped to the baby, tickled him under the chin, and made him laugh.

"Where is your mother?" Arlette asked.

The girl kept her eyes on the baby and shook her head.

"Me too," Arlette said.

"His name?" the girl asked.

"Willie," Arlette said.

The girl ran off, and we watched her go.

"What a charming child," Arlette said. "I think she sleeps under the Pont Neuf bridge with a whole pack of others, poor dear."

"Steer clear of her," I said.

Arlette turned to me. "My God, Josie, she's an orphan. Can you not show some compassion?"

"I care only about us. She can bring us nothing but trouble."

I DIDN'T WANT TO stop at the newspaper kiosk on the way home from the tailor. I'd been feeling overexposed, watched somehow, with all the new security, and something told me we'd be better off going straight home. But I gave in when Arlette insisted, and we stopped so she could look at the fashion magazines.

I held Willie and browsed the advertisements and posters, which covered the kiosk, while Arlette stepped to the magazine rack.

Suddenly, three men in German uniforms rounded the kiosk, one with a chatty, dark-haired French girl on his arm. As they read the chalkboard menu, one of the men stepped to Arlette, hands in his pockets. "Hello there. It's you."

It was Arlette's "favorite female" guy from the window. If she was caught off guard, she didn't show it.

She smiled. "What a funny thing to see you here."

He beckoned to her as a person coaxes a reluctant stray dog. "Would you like to come to the park with us?"

She shook her head and flashed me a glance. "My friend is waiting."

"My treat. What is the complication?"

"I'm sorry."

"Your friend is welcome, too. What do you say? I'm Ernst, by the way."

He stepped to the kiosk window and ordered two ginger ales.

Arlette caught my eye and nodded toward a poster on the kiosk, at least three feet high, WANTED FOR CRIMES AGAINST OUR STATE printed in French across the top. I stepped to the poster and my whole body went cold to see two women photographed from behind, walking their bikes along the street near the Flower and Bird Market, one with blond, shoulder-length hair, the other dark-haired. The blond was clearly carrying a baby at her chest, a wisp of yellow baby hair visible. Just under the headline I read, 2,000 FRANCS EACH FOR INFORMATION.

I held Willie closer. Who had taken that photo? I was not recognizable, for it showed just the back of my head, but Arlette's face was turned slightly to reveal the curve of her cheek.

The French girl left the soldier and stepped toward us. We'd seen her around town many times, and it was always impossible not to notice her new clothes and especially her fashionable shoes, for there'd been so few new styles in Paris. This time she wore burgundy Salamander leather pumps, and Arlette and I couldn't help but stare at the beauty of them.

She sidled up to Arlette. "I'm Louise. You should come with us to the park and bring your friend with her baby. These guys are surprisingly good company." She leaned in and murmured, "If you like champagne."

I tried to stand in front of the poster, but Louise's gaze locked in on it. It took her only a second to know it was us, a stunned look of recognition in her eyes.

Ernst hurried back toward Arlette carrying two ginger ale bottles in one hand. "Last chance."

"Not today," Arlette said, in that wonderful way

French women have of simultaneously treating men with scorn and sexual allure. “We’re taking care of our friend’s baby.”

Ernst grabbed Arlette by the arm. “Bring the child along. No need to be shy.”

With a knowing look at Arlette, Louise pulled Ernst away. “We’ll see them another time, won’t we? Best not to have a crying baby spoil our fun, don’t you boys agree?”

Ernst set off with his friends, and Louise looked back over her shoulder. Her quick look said it all. **You are in terrible trouble. We are all French women first and I wish you bonne chance.**

Once they’d left, Arlette exhaled. **“Merde.”**

We stepped to the wanted poster and I took Arlette’s hand, as we read the last line printed there. **Les Colombes Dorées.**

The Golden Doves.

CHAPTER 22

ARLETTE

FRENCH GUIANA 1952

MY FIRST MORNING IN FRENCH GUIANA I wake early to the clang of a bell, think I'm back at Ravensbrück, and reach next to me on the bed for Willie. Not finding him, I realize he's been gone for years and the familiar dread sets in, mixed with longing for my boy.

I sit up in a gauzy haze, waves crashing in the distance. Will it happen today? Finding him? How will I even know it's Willie? If all goes well, we could be on the plane back to Paris next Saturday. Luc's words about the background check haunt me. The quicker I find my child and get on my way the better.

I consider my new temporary home. The furnishings

are old-world lovely, some probably there since the place was built. The fabulous bamboo canopy bed complete with mosquito netting. A cornflower blue Swedish desk in one corner stocked with Cove House stationery. A lovely full-length mirror and a bronze sunflower clock on the fireplace mantel. I even have my own mirrored wet bar, stocked with rum and crystal rocks glasses.

Out of habit I check the picture frames and usual places for listening devices, and then throw on my mother's sleeveless white poplin shirt and a pair of capri pants I'd made from some wonderful old curtain fabric I'd found at a Paris **brocante.** I hurry to the main house, the warm breeze on my skin.

Why does anyone even live in Paris in the winter?

I enter the main house vestibule and stop, for in the light of day one can see the terrace outside and the azure ocean beyond, which stretches to the horizon. The beauty floors me, joy welling in my chest, the windowless living room open to the air, the painting above the sleek white sofa, a tornado of pastels. This place is proof, as if anyone needs it, that money can indeed buy happiness.

Luc's driver, Claudio, stands near the terrace doorway and stares straight ahead as I enter. **What is Luc so worried about that he needs a bodyguard?**

Luc stands and comes to me. "Hope you don't mind we started without you."

"Oh, no. I'm just a bit overwhelmed by this place." I point to the painting. "Is that a de Kooning?"

"It is. Untitled."

Luc ushers me out to a glass-topped table on the terrace where his grandmother sits reading the morning papers. She beckons me, and I try not to limp as I walk.

A white-uniformed maid pulls out a chair for me and I sit.

"Good morning, Madame Minau."

"Call me Danae, please. Welcome to Paradise."

I take in the view. "It's spectacular. You know, when Luc and I first met in Paris, he told me this was 'a little place near the water.' "

Danae smiles. "I hope you didn't expect a chickee hut with a petrol-tin gong calling you for dinner?"

"I never expected this."

She looks about the terrace. "We do enjoy our slice of heaven. My husband, rest his soul, said he always slept best here. It's designed in the style of Mies van der Rohe. The windows on the seaward side of the house retract into the lower level."

The sea air is perfumed with jasmine, and I bask in the warmth and the tingle of expectation. If I find Willie I might explode with happiness.

I wave off a maid who offers a plate of croissants. "Just coffee, please."

The table is exquisitely set with Limoges plates, Christofle salt and pepper shakers, and what might be a Baccarat vase, which bears a single lavender orchid. If Auntie had been here, surely she would have already snuck those salt and pepper shakers in her purse by now.

Danae pats my hand. "Must be overwhelming for you, dear."

Luc sits opposite me. "We have several children here who might be matches for you—the right age, physical characteristics."

Danae sips her tea. "If you feel good about one or two, we'll move on to the next step, a 'getting to know you' period. You may want to hang back a bit in the first days. It has backfired on us before when a prospective parent comes on too strong."

"What will they be told about me?" I ask.

Danae butters her toast. "As you can imagine, the boys are eager to find their birth parents as well, so we're very careful about raising their expectations. Usually, we tell them the visitors are just here on foundation business."

Luc waves a maid over, and she hands me the green blanket Luc had shown me in his office.

"I thought you might like to have this. Perhaps it will spark a memory in one of the boys."

"Thank you, Luc." I set the baby blanket on my lap and turn to Danae. "And thank you for finding it through your superb detective work."

"My pleasure, dear. It's one of my great joys as I get older, making those long-lost connections. Your son was how old when you last saw him?"

My eyes sting with tears. "Twenty months, seven days."

Danae leans in. "If one of these boys is indeed him, I doubt very much he would remember anything from that age, but mothers have a sixth sense about these things." She pats my hand, hers warm and soft. "And it's best to try to remain composed."

Luc stands. "No crying. It scares the children. Ready?"

I take a deep breath and join him.

Danae sets her napkin next to her plate. "Good luck, my dear. Just use your instincts. You'll know when it's him."

LUC AND I STEP along a path through the hazy jungle, the humidity starting to rise, and we get peeks now and then at the milky blue sky. It's like walking through an emerald basilica, dense parasols of trees soaring above us, their great trunks fuzzed with moss.

Luc takes my hand and helps me over a fallen tree in the path. His palm's a bit moist, and I'm eager to release it.

"I'll escort you today, but Claudio will accompany you on future trips."

"I don't need—"

"While you are here, allow me to decide what you need. The entire interior of the peninsula is cordoned off and make sure you mind the fence. This is no place for the uninitiated to roam freely. There are big cats in this jungle."

A crimson bird with turquoise wing feathers lights on a vine above us.

"How beautiful—"

"Just keep walking. There's a six-meter anaconda that likes to rest in the sun along here."

Luc acts rather formally toward me, but deferential, as if my little break-in never happened. He and his grandmother seem terribly close. Had he told her about our liaison?

"This Father Peter sounds like an interesting man."

"He's an orphan himself, so he can relate to the boys. Bakes them stollen on Christmas Day."

We approach the camp, and everything quickens.

Luc points up above the canopy of trees. "See the tower? Father Peter built that. The whole camp is oriented around it. The dining hut is in the center, the sleep cabins are built around that, with Father Peter's office hut beyond those, then the soccer field and the beach on the far point."

I breathe deep to stem the excitement. My son could be playing on that soccer field right now.

We hear the voices of children, and I press my fists into balls so hard my nails dig into my palms. **The boys.**

We come to a wide clearing with low bunk houses scattered throughout the property and a tall watchtower made of concrete blocks rising out of the center. A man in black trousers and shirt stands atop the watchtower peering toward the ocean with binoculars.

Everywhere we look, children are crisscrossing the camp. They span a wide age range, the oldest around twelve or so, the youngest five or six. Is my son here this very minute? One of these boys walking about in little groups headed to the thatched hut?

"What a charming place, Luc."

As we walk into the camp proper, uniformed children mill about, lining up for the dining hall. I try to check faces. There are many boys with the same pale skin color as mine, but a sprinkling of darker-skinned children as well.

The man in the watchtower hurries down the steps and into the dining hut.

"Everyone looks so happy," I say to Luc.

"The Maroon kids and German kids mix well together. Brought up as color-blind. Some deep friendships form. And you should see how they eat. The freshest vegetables and fruits."

"That's lovely."

"Come with me. Need to introduce you to Father Peter. He's overseeing breakfast no doubt. The boys do everything here, but he's their North Star."

I follow Luc into the shade of the hut, through the crowd of boys finding their morning tables.

A man steps to us wearing wire-rimmed glasses, black trousers, and a short-sleeved shirt, with clerical collar. He's flanked by two massive dogs, which cause me to step back, my hands shaking.

"This is our visitor?" Father Peter asks.

Luc presents me, palm up. "Arlette LaRue, I'd

like you to meet Father Peter. Friend of ours from Switzerland. He built this entire camp with his own two hands. Hope Home couldn't run without him."

The priest nods a welcome. He's a trim man in his sixties, at least, with white hair combed back, his cheekbones flushed geranium pink.

"Pleased to meet you, Father," I say. "Would you mind if we step away from your dogs?"

"They are entirely under my control at all times."

I feel a bit dizzy. "I'm sorry, but—"

Luc steps forward. "Let's have the dogs take a rest, shall we?"

Father Peter whistles a command, and the dogs retreat to the dirt just outside the dining hut. I exhale.

"Miss La Rue is here for an initial 'possibles' meeting at ten o'clock. She'd like to meet boys in the nine-year-old range."

Father Peter consults a list, and it's hard to miss the fine, leather-banded gold watch at his wrist.

"I would never have made such an appointment on a Tuesday. You know we only allow visitors on Saturdays. The boys would have to miss soccer practice today."

We speak in French, of course. I'm no linguistics expert but Father Peter's French is heavily German accented. I try not to jump to the conclusion he's using the priesthood as a cover for a shady Nazi past, but it's hard to shake this first impression.

"Sorry about the mix-up but can you be flexible

today?" Luc asks with a smile. "Our guest has come a long way."

Father Peter scans the crowd of boys eating their bread and **chocolat chaud.** "The boys don't look at it that way. Practice is the highlight of their week."

Luc turns to me. "We love our sports, we males."

"Then why don't I just observe practice?" I ask. "It might be a good way to get to know the boys without being disruptive."

Father Peter waves my comment away. "You just being there will be disruptive. They all understand what visitors are here for. They all hope you're here for them."

I've never met a priest like Father Peter, not that I've met a great many men of the cloth. He has none of the quiet humility of our priest at Auntie's church, Father Renault, with his cowlick and slow smile, incapable of a harsh word. With his brusque way, Father Peter has more in common with the guards at Ravensbrück.

"Let's try Arlette's idea." Luc turns to me. "I have a meeting at the office in town. Are you all right on your own? Go right back to Cove House when you're done."

"I thought I might—"

"Back to Cove House."

I nod, as Father Peter calls his dogs and they leap up and gallop to his side.

"I'll do my best to stay out of the way," I say.

Father Peter strides out of the hut. "Practice starts

after breakfast over at the field. The nine-year-olds wear a red shirt. Observe from afar, and if you would be so kind, keep to yourself."

I FOLLOW THE STREAM of boys of all ages toward the soccer field in the distance, a wide expanse of browned-out turf set back from the ocean. Is it my imagination or has Luc become more demanding now that we're on his home turf? I just want to find my son and get back to Paris.

We arrive at the field. Each player wears a primary-colored shirt indicating their age level, and they run in packs according to jersey color, kicking soccer balls. The Maroon children mix in with the rest of the boys.

Father Peter stands observing the action. He seems so devoted to the children, the white ones at least. The Maroon kids seem to be at his beck and call, fetching him errant soccer balls and cups of water. Why is he so unpleasant to me? Because I'm a woman? Perhaps I just need to give him back that attitude.

My pulse quickens as I survey the faces of the boys on the red team; so many of them have blond or light brown hair. Would Willie still have light hair? Maybe it darkened as he grew older? If only I had a photo of him as a baby. My eyes grow moist. Is it the sun? Or just realizing I don't have a clear recollection of my son's face? Not since the last day I saw him at the camp, when—

"Can you play with us?" a boy asks. I consider his sweet face, such a typical German-looking boy, but with brown eyes. There's a low probability he could have been born to blue-eyed Gunther and me.

"I really shouldn't, thank you."

Soon, my head starts to pound and my eyes ache. After all, it's bedtime in Paris.

A rogue ball rolls toward me, I catch it, and a boy wearing a red shirt runs to fetch it.

"Sorry!" he says and comes closer. This boy is blond, close to my golden color, but looks nothing like me and with none of Gunther's delicate features.

Another child runs up and holds out his hands for me to throw the ball, but I hold it to my chest.

The boy approaches and his flaxen hair catches the sun.

"I'm afraid this ball needs some air," I call out to him.

He steps closer. His eyes are a color similar to mine, the same Wietholter pale blue.

"What's your name?" I ask.

"Thomas," he says, running one hand through his hair just as Gunther did so many times. I step back, a bit light-headed, and consider the boy closer.

I show Thomas the ball. "See? There's a leak just here? But I guess it's still okay." I twirl it on my index finger. "Want to try it?"

He steps back. "I couldn't do that."

"I bet you could if you tried."

He calls to a dark-skinned boy in a red shirt. "Hey, Obi! Come see."

Obi hurries to stand next to Thomas, watching with a wide smile.

Two more red-shirted boys join us.

"You should see her spin the ball," Thomas says to his friends.

I repeat my trick but this time my hand shakes. The boy looks so much like Gunther. Same mouth, strong jawline.

"Can you teach us?" Thomas asks.

I glance toward Father Peter, who stands on the sidelines looking in our direction.

"Quickly, since I don't want to interrupt practice. It's all in getting the ball to spin very fast."

Thomas tries without success as more boys from their team join us. What a sweet boy Thomas is and so like Gunther in his attitude, so positive, ready to learn.

A pair of blond twins join us, wearing blue kerchiefs tied about their necks. They are no more than five or six years old, a charming little matched set.

I hold the ball for him and turn his wrist. "Build up the force in your hand. And then the ball actually spins on your fingernail."

More boys gather and we are overrun as Thomas tries a few times and finally spins the ball for a few seconds. The boys cheer.

"Can Obi try now?"

"Of course," I say.

As Obi spins the ball, I search the crowd for a glimmer of similar familiarity in the faces, but they all seem like such generic nine-year-olds compared to Thomas.

A dark-haired boy steps up. "Are you here to make a match with a boy?"

"Well, I . . ."

"You are, I can tell." He takes my hand.

An olive-skinned boy, smaller than the others, takes my other hand. "Come closer and watch our game."

I smile. "I need to stay back here."

"You should come tomorrow and see our swim meet. The red team is the best. Father Peter says back in the day we would have been the pride of Germany."

"Does he?"

"And this will be a short practice anyway," Thomas says and makes a tragic face. "We need to all get haircuts today."

"You don't like it?" I ask, the world standing still.

"It's the worst thing in the world," he says. "I hate it more than anything."

CHAPTER 23

ARLETTE

PARIS, FRANCE
1944

Before.

SEEING OUR WANTED POSTER AND REALIZING we'd become known as the Golden Doves scared Josie and me into changing our appearances the next day. If we looked different enough from our wanted photo, the Nazis would not recognize us, and neither would Auntie, who I pictured prowling the streets of Paris hunting for me and Willie. I was happy to do anything to keep her out of our lives and was preoccupied with preparations for Josie's surprise birthday celebration I'd planned, low-key as it would be.

That morning at the kitchen table, Willie had the first trim, for his hair had grown quite long and prettily curled. His first haircut was a momentous occasion and I sat him on my lap as Josie snipped a good-sized lock from his nape and tied it with the yellow ribbon from the marmalade jar.

"Voilà!" She held it up to mine. "It's the exact golden color of yours."

"Guess that proves I'm his mother."

She then began snipping the front of his hair and Willie erupted in a fit of wailing so intense she had to stop cutting.

"He knows I'm not a registered hairdresser," Josie said with a smile.

I rubbed his back to calm him and once I got him down for a nap I cut and colored Josie's hair a dull red with stolen hair dye. She then wrapped the bath towel around my shoulders, and I held my breath as she bobbed my hair.

What would Gunther think of my new look? I longed to write to him, but knew it was safer to wait. Surely by now he'd seen the error of his ways following Hitler. Still, no one could know that a German soldier had fathered my child.

Josie handed me a mirror so I could admire her progress, and it was clear she'd cut my bangs ridiculously short.

"No wonder Willie was terrified of your shears. How could you do that? After the perfect cut I gave you."

"They'll grow quickly," she said.

I sipped coffee and spread marmalade on my toast as she finished. She was right, they would grow. I had much to be thankful for. How good it was to be away from Auntie, free and finally able to do things like taste marmalade for the first time, which Josie so cleverly kept us stocked with.

"We must agree on a secret word that signals danger," I said. "So, if we're caught . . ."

Josie snipped a lock at my nape and showed it to me for length. "Caught? We have a foolproof system. But I suppose it's good to have. How about 'My bangs are too short'?"

I smiled. "How about a painter's name? Picasso? Or a phrase, like, 'Is that a new hat?' "

Josie pursed her lips. "Sounds forced."

I watched with longing for my lost bangs as Josie brushed the last of them from the towel. "How about 'I'll have toast with marmalade'?"

"I like it. It's pretty much all you and Willie eat, after all."

I nodded. "Toast with marmalade it is."

Despite the short bangs, I liked the new me, hair cropped. With this cut I was no longer the child trapped with Auntie or a captive in the Lebensborn home, but an independent adult, a true member of the resistance. After so many years of having nothing but chores to do, I had an apartment, a child, and a mission.

We chatted for a while and when Willie woke I lifted him from his bassinet, stepped to the cupboard, and pulled out two packages wrapped in newspaper.

"You remembered my birthday," Josie said.

With my free hand I pulled a plated cake the size of a coffee cup from the icebox. "Your mother dropped this off yesterday. Said she and Mimi made it together, and Mimi made the icing with the sugar you brought, and she asks that you please don't judge the quality of the icing too harshly because she did not have a proper double boiler in which to cook it."

Josie smiled and opened the first package, with delighted cries, as she found a burgundy and white printed utility blouse I'd copied from a Jean Patou and a pair of navy blue wide-leg, high-waisted Marlene Dietrich trousers. I held my breath as she slipped on the trousers and tucked in the blouse.

"Perfect fit," she said. "How did you do this in secret?"

Every part of me relaxed. "I took your measurements while you slept. Thérèse got me the fabrics, but just enough, so there was no room for error. Hopefully they will be your signature pieces. Wear them when you want to feel strong."

I pulled another package from the cabinet. "And here's the best part. Thérèse found these. Your size and everything."

She opened the newspaper to reveal a lovely pair of leather shoes—black Oxford lace-ups with a Cuban heel.

"She's positively occult," Josie said.

Willie raised his arms toward her, and I set him in her lap. He loved the pattern on the blouse and patted the fabric at her shoulder.

I folded the newsprint and tucked it away. "With this new look I'll be surprised if every man in Paris is not in love with you."

Josie rubbed a spot off Willie's cheek. "Then maybe I'll have a proper kiss one day."

I turned, stunned. "Tell me you've never been kissed?"

"It's true. Unless you count Tommy Kennefick in eighth grade in Alexandria. I'm a late bloomer."

"We must find you a boyfriend right away. But you must **listen** to me this time."

"I promise."

"First, whatever you do, don't obsess over your faults."

"I don't—"

"You **do.** And that is not attractive to anyone." I mussed up her hair a bit. "Also, always leave one thing undone. Nothing too perfect."

"Got it."

"And when eating, keep both hands on the table, one on either side of your plate. **Not** in your lap. However, women may rest their elbows on the table."

"Why is that?"

"To show off their rings, of course."

I handed Josie the next package.

"Another gift?" she asked.

I shrugged. "Don't you rich girls expect it?"

This was another handmade gift, in a medium I'd tried for the first time. To commemorate our infamy, I'd taken to my parents' studio and melted down an old brass spittoon and sculpted a stylized dove, the size of a small grapefruit. She was a pretty thing, with her pointed beak and upturned tail.

Josie opened the package. "It's the most beautiful gift, Arlette. You are so talented. How did you get it to shine so?"

"Buffed it on my parents' jeweler's wheel."

Josie held up the brass bird, turning it in the light. "I'll treasure it."

She carried Willie with her as she set it in a place of honor on our fireplace mantel. "It's the perfect souvenir of our work as Doves. We're so lucky to be living this perfect life." She kissed Willie on his cheek. "Nothing can stop us now."

THE NEXT MORNING WHILE Willie slept before a planned walk to the park, I straightened up the bedroom as Josie sat at the desk, headphones on, listening.

She waved me to the second pair of headphones; I sat next to her and slipped them on. At first the conversation seemed like so many that took place next door. Though they could not hear me on the other end, I still held my breath.

"Just this one favor?" came a familiar voice.

"You have to let this go," the other said. "It's not helping that career you care so much about."

"But I know I'm right."

"Just keep your nose clean and take that girl you like so much out for a Weihenstephaner."

Josie and I exchanged glances.

"French girls don't drink beer."

"Do you know how lucky you are there in Paris? Enjoy it and forget all this."

"But my best source there says it doesn't add up."

"What source? In London?"

"Says there's proof the landing will not be in Calais."

"But they've amassed their firepower just across in Dover."

"He says it's all fake."

The other man laughed. "They call that paranoia."

"I have a feeling about this . . ."

"**You** tell the Führer about your **feeling.** His mind is made up; they will invade at Calais."

"I'm going to hitch a ride on a plane to get my own shots this week."

"You must be buried in recon photos. What more do you need?"

"A better camera. Lower angle. If I get proof, can you get me in with Jodl?"

All was quiet on the other end.

"If you get anything new, I will be very surprised, and yes, I will get you in with him. And you had better be prepared to speak with the Führer himself, as well."

"Thank you, my friend."

"Keep me apprised, Ernst."

The line went dead, and Josie and I exchanged a solemn look.

We removed our headphones. How strange it was to hear this man I'd assumed was so harmless speak of such critical high-level things. It made me feel oddly important to be the object of his affection. And terrified too.

"Your window friend isn't an accountant after all. He's an intelligence officer. High up, too."

"Yes. Clearly." I slid a sheet of paper from the desk drawer. "I'll transcribe it."

"Do you know who Ernst was talking to? Alfred Jodl's chief of staff. **General** Jodl. Hitler's chief of operations of Armed Forces High Command."

"I will do it right away."

"I can deliver it for you."

"You know that's not allowed. I'll be fine."

Josie leaned closer. "You've gotten to know Ernst. This may be hard for you—"

"Don't be ridiculous. Just because we've shared some cigarette breaks doesn't mean I want to marry him."

"We can't let him take those photos."

"Of course. Get the basket. I'll deliver it to the tailor right away."

LATER THAT MORNING I transcribed the conversation and was ready to take it to the tailor, the paper tucked in the pocket of the yellow skirt I'd folded into a neat square and set at the bottom of my market basket. Flashes of guilt nipped at me as I donned my disguise of cotton headscarf and sunglasses Thérèse had provided. How strange it was that my window friend Ernst was one of the key players. Surely Thérèse's underground contacts would want him killed.

I shivered and pushed that thought away. I just wanted to get the delivery over with and take Willie to the park. I was exhausted, up twice the night before, since he had been napping more during the day, and I hoped the fresh air would help him sleep longer at night. I was beginning to believe motherhood and espionage did not mix well.

As I stepped to the door, ready to head out, Willie in my arms, changed and fed, I swept one hand down his cheek. "You be good for Josie while I'm gone. See you soon and we'll go to the park."

IT WAS THE BUSIEST Saturday I'd seen in so long, the spring day warm under the ironwork canopies of the Flower and Bird Market. I had to take the most direct route, through the market, for the tailor shop closed at noon. I wove my way through the crowd, bumped and jostled by merchants pushing their boxy, blue-painted flower carts and patrons gawking at the jonquils and flats of lily of the valley.

I felt so conspicuous, taller than many of the patrons there. Despite Thérèse's optimism and the flower merchants' much appreciated whitewashing efforts, those wanted posters were still everywhere in the city. I kept my head down, my basket close, and barely breathed as I passed the flower stalls.

I allowed myself a glance now and then at the patrons milling about, a great stew of Parisians dominated by strolling uniformed Nazis. French women dressed up in the best they had, in their cork-soled shoes and patched dresses, strolled together as well, arms linked. A wave of citrusy perfume wafted to me, prompting thoughts of an exotic isle. Some women still had their fragrance. This was France, after all.

I hurried on toward the end of the market, my hand wet on my basket handle, when a male voice rang out. "You there. **Stop.** I know what you're doing!"

I kept walking, as others turned from their flower transactions and watched with guarded expressions.

All at once I felt a hard grip on my upper arm.

I turned, dizzy with fear.

Ernst.

"How can you run from me, Arlette?" he asked with a smile.

"I didn't see you—"

He reached for my basket. "Where are you going? Let me help."

I gripped the basket handle harder. "Oh, no. Please. I'm just going to the tailor."

He pulled at the basket. How could I insist on keeping it when that would only draw more attention? I let him take it from my hand, my gaze fixed on the yellow skirt that held the transcript of his own words.

"Don't worry, I'll guard it well. You French women take your clothes seriously, don't you?"

"I have to get to the shop. They will close for lunch soon."

He looped the basket over his arm. "Speaking of lunch. Why not come join me?"

Just what I needed. To be even more conspicuous, not to mention seen as a collaborator.

"No. I really must go." I reached for my basket. "Please give it to me."

He held it just outside my reach. "Only if you promise to have dinner with me tonight. Eight o'clock. Café de Cité."

I glanced about the market. How could I refuse? He knew where I lived.

"All right. Yes. I will join you."

"Shall I fetch you at your place? Say—"

"No," I say just a bit too forcefully. "I will meet you there."

He handed me the basket. "Eight o'clock."

"But curfew—"

He reached into his pocket, pulled out a pink coupon, and handed it to me. What a precious thing that was. I took it and walked on, happy to be free of him.

"If you are not there by eight, I will come and find you," he called after me.

I practically ran toward the tailor shop, down a

side cobblestone street, relieved to finally see that lovely little shop on the square in the distance. Local people milled about doing their shopping, and I found Josie waiting there, standing on the corner across the street from the shop, Willie in her arms.

As I approached, Willie reached out for me and cried. As much as I loved my boy, I suddenly craved a desert island somewhere, far from so many people needing me, free to just read a book or sleep.

"Where were you?" Josie asked, bouncing Willie on her hip to distract him.

"Guess who ambushed me in the market? Ernst."

Josie huffed a little gasp. "No."

"He made me promise to have dinner with him. At Café de Cité. **Tonight.**"

Her eyes grew wide. "You have to go. Otherwise he'll come poking around the apartment."

"I'm well aware." I switched the basket to my other hand. "But for now I need to deliver this." I stroked Willie's cheek. "I will be back, sweet boy, and we will go to the park."

I stepped down off the sidewalk to cross the street, and Josie held me back. "Wait. Look at the window."

The clothesline sagged there, empty. No brown sock pinned to it.

I stepped back onto the sidewalk. Monsieur Laurent was fastidious about the details of our drop-offs. It was an enormous risk to go in, assuming it was an oversight. But this was an especially important message to deliver.

All at once, cars came from all directions, six black Citroëns that screeched to a stop in front of the shop. I held the basket behind my back as Gestapo agents jumped out of the cars and sprinted in through the front door.

Many of the shoppers hurried away, while a small crowd remained, clustered near the shop. Even standing nearby was risky, but the Laurents were beloved.

Two men soon emerged carrying baskets similar to mine and cardboard boxes, some brimming with clothes, others with papers.

"We should go," Josie said.

But I was too transfixed by the scene to move, frozen as one might be by the sight of a train whose cars have jumped the track, incapacitated by the fear of what would happen to Monsieur Laurent and his daughter and grandson. I said a silent prayer that they had escaped. They must have known they were in trouble. Why else would they take the sock out of the window?

I was ashamed to think it, but did they have cyanide capsules? If tortured, would they give us up? Magdeleine knew I lived near the Flower and Bird Market. Were some of our transcriptions in those boxes?

The men soon drove two people from the open door, Monsieur Laurent and Magdeleine. The onlookers watched, many with hands to their faces, stirred to see their beloved tailor and his daughter pulled so violently from the place. The men shoved the two to the middle of the square and forced them to kneel. It was only then that I saw Magdeleine carried little Theo at her chest, inside her open sweater.

"The baby," I whispered, and started off toward them.

Josie held me back. "You can't help them."

They did not plead for their lives but stared ahead as Monsieur Laurent removed his overcoat and placed it around his daughter's shoulders.

Josie pulled me close. "Come away, Arl. Willie musn't see."

She dragged me along the side road toward home. I stumbled on the cobblestones, tears blurring my way.

We were not twenty steps away when we heard the two shots.

And seconds later, one more.

CHAPTER 24

ARLETTE

PARIS, FRANCE
1944

Before.

JOSIE AND I CAME HOME AFTER THE LAURENTS were shot, locked the door, and sat together on the sofa in shock. Willie slept on my chest as evening fell. A film reel of the Laurents being marched to the square replayed in my mind. **The baby.** With a shaking hand I stroked Willie's hair. Would the Gestapo find us?

"We cannot just stay here like this," Josie said.

I startled at the sound of two sets of knocks at the door, but Josie and I remained still, listening.

We heard the scrape of a key turning in the lock, and Thérèse entered.

"It's so dark in here," she said.

"Did you hear about the tailor?" I asked.

Thérèse shut the door softly and turned on a light. "Yes. It is a great loss."

Willie stirred and I sat up straighter. " 'A great loss'? How can you be so nonchalant? They were murdered in the square. An infant. The Gestapo got boxes of things from the shop."

"No physical evidence linked to you," Thérèse said. "Monsieur Laurent followed instructions to the letter."

"You don't know that for sure."

Thérèse pulled up a kitchen chair to sit near me. "They understood the need for sacrifice."

I held Willie closer. "I don't want to do this anymore."

Thérèse leaned in. "It must have been terrible to see. But that is why we fight."

"We picked up an important conversation about D-Day," Josie said. "That's what Arlette was delivering to the shop."

"And Ernst Weber my window friend was on the call," I said. "He says he knows the truth about the invasion from a double agent of his in London. Is going to take new photos."

Josie took Willie from me and set him in his bassinet. "We need to get out of the city."

"First we must find another way to deliver that conversation to London," Thérèse said.

"I could transmit," Josie said. "I've been practicing Morse code."

Thérèse smiled. "Of course you have. Where did you get a telegraph key?"

"A trash can in Luxembourg Gardens. I'm up to twenty-four words per—"

I stood in front of her, hands atop my head. "Are you both insane?"

Thérèse shook her head. "Of course. It's too dangerous. And sending the correct codes is just the start. It must be decoded by cipher clerks, read by Baker Street, and then encoded and transmitted back."

"If I get it in under five minutes there's little chance of being caught."

"You've never transmitted before, Josie. Any mistakes in the Morse and you need to start over. Plus, London has hundreds of messages coming in. If yours is not a priority it can take over an hour to get a message back. And you must wait that whole time to know if you've been heard. That's a long time to be vulnerable to their listening vans."

"I'm willing to try," Josie said.

"And now when the Germans hear a radio operator transmitting they turn off the electrical grid, district by district, until the signal stops, so they know the originating area. After that they go door to door until they find the radio operator. We can't risk it."

"Finally you are making sense," I said.

"We'll find another way to send it." Thérèse stood and came to me. "But in the meantime there is one more risk I'm going to ask you to take. You said you are seeing Ernst Weber tonight."

A chill shivered through me. "Yes. What time is it?"

"Almost eight," Thérèse said. "I need you to make sure Weber doesn't leave the café before he has his beer tonight."

I took a step back. "Why?"

"Just sit with him. Make sure he drinks. How simple is that?"

Sit with him while you poison him? I wanted to ask.

"I will have a flower delivery van lined up so you can drive to the country. Tonight if you like."

I sat and placed two hands over my mouth. **How can I agree to this?** "He's not a bad person."

"I will be there with you," Thérèse said. "The café owner is a friend. I will act as hostess."

I stood and walked to the bassinet and watched Willie sleeping. "What if something goes wrong? That place is wall-to-wall Nazis this time of night."

"I will make sure you are fine. I don't have a child. I will not let anything keep you from yours."

I swallowed hard. "I will do it. As long as Josie and I can leave tonight no matter what."

"Understood." Thérèse took my hand, cold in hers. "Don't worry. It will be over quickly."

I CAME ON TIME to the café, just around the corner from my apartment. I tried to dress in a nondescript way, my scarf tied around my hair. It was dark by that time and the whole place was lit up, bathed in amber light, and packed with German officers enjoying a night out.

I stepped in, drawing more than a few glances from the men. There was no place to hide. Surely at least one had seen the wanted poster.

I was happy to see Thérèse meet me as I stepped in.

"Welcome," she said and led me to a table near the door, Ernst already seated there. He stood as I took my seat, and I could barely look at his face, with that eager expression. Just seeing the uniform up close made my stomach hurt. The same one Gunther wore the day he marched off.

"Mind if we speak in German? Then I can tell you exactly how pretty you are without looking up words in a dictionary."

"If it is your preference."

He sat back, taking me in. "How did I get so lucky?"

Tears welled in my eyes. Gunther's very words in the barn so long ago.

"How kind of you," I said.

Ernst leaned in, the candlelight reflected in his glasses, his face smooth. He'd shaved for me.

"No need to look so glum," he said with a smile. "I know it is not a great table, so close to the door, but the hostess suggested we sit here, and I figured I'd better comply. Sometimes I feel like I must repair the reputation of Germans here in France."

"Whatever you like."

The big table of six German officers near the bar erupted in laughter. Was it just a matter of time before one would recognize me?

Ernst leaned closer and waved me to him, brow knit. "You may be surprised to know I'm onto what you and your friend have been doing."

A spasm gripped my throat rendering me unable to speak. "Uh?"

"When were you going to tell me the truth?"

I barely breathed. "I-I . . . what . . ."

"Obviously that is her baby she's always carrying, not some friend's, as you claim." He sends me a knowing look.

I breathed at last. "Oh. Yes. What a good detective you are. You're right, that is not our friend's child."

"I knew I was correct. Make sure you tell her I'll never reveal her secret."

I fanned myself with my menu. "I will."

He squinted at me over the top of his glasses. "You French women and your scarves. Why not take it off while we eat?"

"I don't—"

"For me? It's not fair to keep all that beauty covered up."

I untied the scarf, slipped it off, and kept my face averted from the rest of the room. Ernst smiled. "Did you cut your hair? It looks nice."

I nodded at him and smiled back. The kinder he was to me the worse I felt.

He looked down at his menu. "The duck here is good. And they keep the drinks coming."

"Oh, good," I said and ran one shaking hand through my hair.

From the look of him, a bit red-faced and sweaty around the collar, he'd already had a few drinks before I arrived.

Thérèse approached the table. "What can I get for you? Your waiter is busy in the kitchen."

"Wine, I suppose?" Ernst asked me. "Chablis?"

Thérèse flashed me a look.

"Oh, no," I said. "Actually I'd like beer. Won't you join me?"

He smiled. "A French woman drinking beer? That's a first." He turned to Thérèse. "One beer for the lady. I'll have water."

I leaned in. "You'd make a woman drink alone? How can you call yourself a good German man? Go ahead and have a Weihenstephaner."

Ernst cocked his head to one side. "How did you know that is what I drink?"

I clenched my fists under the table. What a clumsy mistake. No doubt Thérèse was regretting the day she recruited me. "Isn't that what every German likes?"

"Of course." He turned to Thérèse, his eyes trained on me. "Two, please."

He settled back in his chair. "I've been looking forward to this moment. I want to know everything about you."

I sat ramrod straight, my face frozen into some sort of death grimace of fear. Was he processing my mistake?

I looked to the bar. **Hurry, Thérèse.** Was she poisoning his drink as we spoke?

"Not much to tell. I'm from Alsace."

He smiled. "Well, I knew I liked you. I'm from Mannheim."

"So close to where I grew up," I said, trying hard to flirt. "Have a large family?"

"Just my **Mutti** and a brother too young to fight just yet. My only dependents, but I'd like a big family. How about you?"

I tried not to think of his mother and how wrecked she would be by the news her son had died.

Thérèse came, served us each a glass of beer, and left.

I sipped mine, hoping Thérèse had not mixed up the two. "Yes, I'd like a whole houseful of children."

I took another sip to set an example for him to drink as well. "Are you not going to enjoy your drink? Or are you just trying to get me drunk?"

"No need to be nervous. I know this is not natural, being seen here with me, the hated Boche."

An officer from the table of six stood and walked our way, weaving through the crowded tables. I looked for Thérèse at the bar and she met my gaze with a worried look.

Please just pass us by.

The man stepped to Ernst, a bit unsteady, and clapped him on the back. "Bon appétit, my good fellow. See you tomorrow." He glanced at me with a little smile and kept on toward the door.

Ernst bit back a smile. "My colleague at work. Did you see how green with envy he was after seeing I have such a lovely companion?" He tilted his head. "What's wrong?"

"I suppose I'm just eager for you to finish up so we can go somewhere and have fun."

He took a long gulp of his beer as I watched, the horror of it almost too much to take in.

He adopted a look of concern. "Don't feel you need to come home with me. I know you may think, because of some German soldiers' behavior toward French women, that I expect that of you, but I don't. I just want to get to know you."

He hooked one finger into the collar of his uniform shirt. "I'm sorry, but can you excuse me? I'm afraid I may have had too much to drink."

I searched the bar for Thérèse. "Just sit. I will get you some water."

He tried to stand, before he could step away, collapsed onto the café table, bringing them both crashing to the tile floor.

A woman screamed and I stood, unable to move, staring down at him lying there, his face a ghastly shade of purple, foam gathered at his lips. The five remaining officers at the big table stood.

Thérèse came to me. "Go."

I hesitated, transfixed by the sight of Ernst on the floor.

She gave me a little shove. **"Now."**

Trembling as if ice water had been poured down my back, I hurried out of the café and started toward home.

"You there!" two officers called out as they came out of the café.

I would be caught in seconds.

All at once Thérèse came running from the café like a shot, off in the opposite direction, into the night.

"Vive la France!" she called out, and both men turned and ran after her instead.

Soon, both shot at the same time, and she fell.

As the men ran to her fallen there, I tried to move but couldn't. How could I just leave Thérèse there wounded? Or dead.

I forced myself to walk away and hurried back to my apartment.

Leaving my angel there on the pavement.

I MADE SURE I was not tailed and came home to find Josie waiting with Willie in her arms, our suitcases at the door.

"It went terribly wrong," I said, numb to the core. "Ernst died but then Thérèse ran and the Gestapo shot her. It was horrible, Josie. We have to go."

"Are you serious? We can't go now. A Nazi officer has been killed." She paced. "They will have every road out of Paris blocked. Besides, without Thérèse, how are we to find the flower truck? We must wait."

I took Willie from her and held him close, my heart beating against his little chest.

"For now, do you have the transcript of the conversation you never delivered?" Josie asked.

I waved toward my basket on the kitchen table and she removed it from the skirt pocket.

"I have to transmit the message to London."

"No, Josie."

"I can do it in under thirty seconds."

"Ernst is dead. He won't reveal his Calais theory."

"But they need to know there's a spy in their midst who can stop the invasion."

I sat on the sofa, drained. She was right, of course.

"But what about them turning off the electrical grid if they pick up our signal? Thérèse said—" Just saying her name made my insides feel about to implode.

"Thérèse was overly cautious. They won't catch me. I have the whole thing planned out in coded Morse messages. She would want us to get the message through."

I stood. "Well, we'd better hurry up then and do it."

I made a solemn prayer that this would be the last thing the Golden Doves would ever do.

I PUT WILLIE DOWN to sleep, and Josie and I sat side by side at the radio, like two priests at an altar. She put in the tiny quartz crystal that set her frequency, we donned our headphones, and Josie placed her black telegraph key, no bigger than a small mouse-trap, at her right hand.

I counted as the second hand swept around the radium dial of Josie's watch. She had written out her codes. Now we just needed Baker Street to make us a priority and respond quickly.

"Ready?" I waited for the second hand to make it to twelve. "Go."

She flipped a switch to transmit and began dialing in the correct frequency, but turning the crystal she found only static.

Three seconds passed.

All at once a voice came through. "This is London, go ahead."

Without missing a beat, Josie tapped out her coded message. I pictured the rows of young women wearing headphones like ours, pencils poised at a re-ceiving station in Britain picking up the quick chirps of her signals. But it was also all too easy to picture the Germans sitting in a room somewhere in Paris picking up the green dots on their screens.

Josie finished her tapping. I shared the watch face with her. Only two minutes left.

We sat, listening for even the slightest unusual noise.

Were the Germans listening to **us**? Each second we waited for a reply increased the chances the radio vans would pick up the signal and shut down the electrical grid to find us.

I shook my hands to relieve the stress of it all. "Cut the radio, Josie. They will not respond."

"We still have time left."

From the other room I heard Willie fuss.

"Please. We can try again another time."

"Just another minute."

I removed my headphones, stood, and retrieved Willie and brought him back to sit next to Josie.

I checked the watch. "Only forty seconds left. Time to stop."

All at once Josie sat up straighter and grabbed the pencil. I slipped the headphones on and listened to the series of dots and dashes while Josie scribbled words.

Once the line went quiet, she flipped the switch on the transmitter and the radio lights went dark.

I checked the watch. Only ten seconds over the five-minute limit.

We removed our headphones, and I exhaled. "Thank God that's over. What did they say?"

She turned to me and read. "Message received. Thank you, Doves."

A gush of warm spread through my chest. "Thank God."

"We did it," Josie said.

All at once the lights cut out and the whole room went dark.

I barely breathed. They knew where we were.

How long would it take for them to arrive?

CHAPTER 25

ARLETTE

FRENCH GUIANA
1952

THE SWIM MEET IS IN FULL SWING BY THE TIME I arrive at the sugar sand cove the next day, buoy-roped lanes stretching out into the calm water. I stand back near the mangrove trees and observe the boys gathered near the water, laughing and talking with one another. They're a bit far away for me to recognize any of them, but I assume the boys in the red bathing suits are the nine-year-olds. I squint to check their faces, looking for the boy I'd connected with at the soccer practice. **Thomas.** Is it even possible he could be my son? If our blood types match we could be on our way back to Paris soon. The idea is almost too wonderful to consider.

Father Peter startles me from behind. "You're back." He's wearing his black clerical collared shirt and a pair of binoculars hang around his neck by a leather strap.

"Yes, I'll be here until I find my son."

He's quiet for a moment, watching the boys swim, then loops the leather strap off, over his head. "Perhaps these would help."

I accept the glasses. "Yes. Thank you."

They are the same type of Zeiss field glasses my uncle Hans once owned. I lift them to my eyes and see a blur of water.

He comes closer and adjusts the focus, close enough to smell the shave cream on him, and the scene comes into perfect clarity. I look from one boy to the next.

"You must be quick before they start to swim."

"Yes." I find Thomas, standing in line, arms folded across his chest, waiting for his turn to swim, his hair shining in the sunlight. Another boy taps him, a whistle tweets, and he wades into the water.

I hand the binoculars back to Father Peter. "You have boys of all ages here. Orphaned during the war? But some of them are so young. Five or six. The war was over by the time they were born."

"This is an orphanage, Miss LaRue. We turn away no boy who needs a home."

Perhaps he responds best to flattery?

"You've done a good job raising them. It looks like they barely need you."

"I've taught them to be self-sufficient. The older boys supervise. They will all be going out into the world soon as ambassadors, so they need to be able to live independently."

"How soon will they go?"

"We are scheduling it now. In a month I hope."

With any luck I'll be on my way home with my son well before then.

As he bends, I try to check the back of his left arm for a blood-type tattoo. He moves too quickly to get a good look, but I get a better view of his watch, a fine gold tank with an alligator band.

"I think that a boy I met yesterday might be a possible match. How do I request a blood test?"

"The decision to test shouldn't be done on a whim. It isn't an easy process or an inexpensive one."

"Did the Minaus tell you I'm from Alsace?" I ask, hoping some shared interests will make him more cooperative. "Krautergersheim. Famous for sauerkraut but also our stollen."

"I know it well. Alsace. The border has changed there so often it's hard to know what's France and what's Germany."

"And Hans Wietholter was my uncle. He owned a pair of field glasses like those."

"Quite a patriot."

"That was a long time ago. But yes."

"He raised you?" he asks.

"Yes. After he died his wife did." It's out of my mouth before I even realize I've mentioned Auntie. I look toward the path back to Cove House. "I really need to get—"

"Are you still close with your aunt?"

"Yes. I mean I was . . . She passed away. We think. Just disappeared during the war."

Why can I not stop babbling?

He tilts his head. "How unfortunate. Was she—"

"I'm still tired from the flight, Father. Perhaps we can continue this another time?"

"Of course, Miss LaRue," he says, his quick blue eyes searching my face. "I have to get back to the boys."

As he turns and walks back to the practice my legs feel about to give out. What if he finds out what happened with Auntie? It would ruin my chances to take my son home. Not to mention send me to jail.

I fight against the memory of that horrible day, but suddenly I'm back in Paris again, at the apartment. Just before it all went down.

CHAPTER 26

ARLETTE

PARIS, FRANCE
1944

Before.

THE MORNING AFTER JOSIE SENT THE MESSAGE to London, I woke, Willie sleeping on my chest, having fallen asleep on the sofa after the lights went out. Josie slept, head on my shoulder.

We'd spent much of the night quaking with fear the Nazi **Funkabwehr** team would trace the transmission signal to the apartment, but the rap on our door never came. There in the darkness, waiting for dawn, listening to Willie's gentle breathing, I mourned for Thérèse. How terribly I missed her already. Would she receive a proper burial? She had sacrificed herself for me and I had treated her so poorly, resisting everything she asked of me.

In the three months since Thérèse had brought Josie to come to stay with Willie and me, so much had changed for us, starting with the Doves. We had helped the Allied cause, no question. We would have freedom someday, but at such a cost, the Laurents and Thérèse summarily shot and gone. I felt like I was standing on shifting sands, as if the plates of the universe had somehow slipped and would never realign.

It was just a matter of time before they rooted us out.

Josie woke when I stood, and I put Willie down to continue his rest in his bassinet in front of the living room fireplace.

"We need to leave here today," I said, trying to keep the hysterical edge from my voice.

Josie rubbed the sleep from her eyes. "But the roadblocks—"

"We'll have the flower van. We can load the front seat with flowers. I don't know. It's more dangerous to just stay here."

"You're right," Josie said. "But I need coffee first. And I must go tell my mother we're leaving."

"Of course. I'll pack while you're gone. But promise to be—"

Suddenly a **thump, thump, thump** came at the door.

I barely breathed, head cocked, waiting for the sound of the retreating footsteps. **What if I just stayed silent—**

"Who is it?" Josie whispered.

A muffled voice came, a jolt to the heart. "I know you're there, Arlette. And no, I won't just go away."

"My God. **Auntie.** Hide the radio."

Josie hurried into the bedroom and closed the door behind her.

I stepped to the door and again came the **thump, thump.**

Surely, she would attract attention. Possibly the Gestapo. What if she turned me in? What would happen to Willie?

Hands trembling, I opened the door a crack to find Auntie in mid-kick, swinging a suitcase.

"I knew you were here, wicked girl. What happened to your hair?"

"**Quiet.** You'll wake the baby."

She pushed past me into the room, dressed in her old brown coat with the patched elbows, one end of her dirty yellow scarf flapping down her back. "What a dump. You keep it a mess too." She set down her suitcase and stepped to the kitchen. "A pig, like that mother of yours."

"You must leave. I have a child to tend to."

She lit a cigarette. "A child you stole from the Lebensborn home. Property of the Reich. Stupid girl. Do you know how many times they've barged into my house looking for you?"

"Please, Auntie, come back another—"

She headed toward the bassinet. "So, this is the baby?"

I blocked her way. "He's sleeping. When Gunther hears how you've been acting . . ."

"No chance of that happening. He's six feet under by now."

I took a step back. "No."

"Shot the first day he fought. Barely worth the cost of the uniform."

I wrapped my arms around my middle. "No, Auntie. Please tell me it's not true."

"Killed by his own stupidity."

I jabbed my finger toward her. "Your **Hitler** killed Gunther."

"You ungrateful girl. Gunther couldn't cut it as a soldier."

"He was **seventeen.**" I sat on the sofa next to Willie's bassinet, hollowed out.

Auntie came and stood over me. "Go ahead and cry. It's what you do best. I hope you realize you need me more than ever, now that you're a single mother." Auntie looked toward the bedroom door. "Who else is here?"

"Keep your voice **down.** Can't you see the child is sleeping?"

Auntie turned and set the suitcase on the table. "Get your things. We're taking him back to the Lebensborn home."

"This is my home," I said, my whole body trembling. I turned toward the bedroom. "Marmalade, Josie—"

Auntie squinted one eye. "Who are you talking to?"

Willie woke and cried, and I went to him. As I picked him up Auntie lunged for the bedroom door and swung it open.

I held out one arm. "No—"

"**Mon dieu,** what have we here?" She crossed herself in the Catholic way.

Josie stood at the desk, a spool of wire in her hand. At least she'd taken down the aerial. "Who are you?"

"Who are **you**? And what are you doing with that radio?"

She's so loud. Would they hear her at the window next door?

I pulled her by the arm back to the living room. "I'm warning you, Auntie."

She yanked her arm out of my grasp. "You'd rather squat illegally here with some girl with a bad dye job than be with your own blood? You will return that baby to the Reich."

"I'm happy here, Auntie. I'm making art. Money too. I can give you all you want—"

She picked up the brass dove sculpture from the mantel. "You call this art?"

I held out one hand. "Give that back."

Auntie nodded, slowly at first and then faster. "Well, well. I know what's going on here. The radio operating. The short hair. You're the Golden Doves everyone is talking about." She turned, impressed with her own powers of deduction. "Every Gestapo agent in Paris is after you two."

Josie emerged from the bedroom. "I was simply listening to the BBC," she said. "Everyone does it."

Auntie set the dove back onto the mantel and stepped to me. "You'll come now, or I'm telling the police."

"I'll never give up my child."

Auntie hurried back to the bedroom, ripped Josie's radio from the desk in one motion, tucked it under her arm, and came back to me at the fireplace.

Josie followed.

Auntie snatched me by the wrist. "You're coming now. Or I'll march over to that prefecture and tell them what you're doing here, working to sabotage the Reich, with the child you stole from Himmler himself."

I stood my ground and held Willie closer. "No—"

"They'll execute you both, I'll return the baby, get the reward, sell this place, and be set for life. Himmler may just award me a prize."

I yanked my wrist from her grasp. "You wouldn't."

Josie slid bills from her pocket. "If you're caught with that radio, it's you they'll suspect. And if you turn us in, we'll say you're working with us, and they'll execute you as well. If it's money you want . . ."

Auntie waved Josie's thoughts away. "I'm going to the authorities and will return with enough police to shut this all down."

An odd calm came over me and I handed the baby to Josie. "You're not going." I grabbed the brass dove from the mantel, heavy and smooth in my hand, and raised it as a javelin thrower prepares and then took a running start.

She saw it coming and crouched away as I lunged at her and landed a blow to the back of her head, the beak piercing bone with a sickening crunch, like a spike through a terra-cotta pot.

My heart beat wildly as she fell to the floor and moved there, moaning and trying to sit up.

Josie hurried to my side, holding Willie close. "Arlette—"

I raised my weapon again, gathered all my strength, and delivered a harder blow.

With enough force to make sure my aunt would never touch my child again.

CHAPTER 27

JOSIE

EN ROUTE TO LANDSBERG PRISON 1952

"I THINK AUNT BERTHA LIKED YOU," JOHANN SAYS as we drive from Salzburg to Landsberg Prison southwest of Munich. "She offered to host our wedding."

"I'm not eager to revisit Hitler's party castle, thanks."

As he rounds a corner, the leftover soup from the night before, thick with noodles, sloshes in the earthenware bowl in my lap. We'd stayed not only one extra night for Aunt Bertha's little get-together, to which she'd invited half the surrounding town and unbeknownst to us had billed it as our engagement party, but spent the following day touring the castle, Johann unable to say no to her.

Johann takes a deep breath. "Say what you will about Aunt Bertha, she makes great **Hühnersuppe.**"

In the back seat sits half of a roast chicken, brown bread for six, and a white-frosted ring of kringle Aunt Bertha had packed in a brown paper bag and pressed upon us as we left.

I crack the window to rid the car of the scent—of the German food we'd smelled at Ravensbrück so many nights coming from the officers' canteen while we lay in our bunks starving. "I can't stop seeing those home movies. The ones of the German Olympians saluting Hitler."

Johann accelerates on a straightaway. "He was a respectable politician then."

I watch the Alpine countryside roll by, past simple wooden cottages. They're so like the little cardboard chalets my father's mother displayed on her mahogany sideboard at Christmas, buried in plastic snow up to their glittered roofs.

I rub the steamy car window with my coat sleeve for a better view and watch smoke spiral from the chimney of one house. How many committed Nazis live snug in those houses, still quietly supporting Hitler after all he's done? I turn up my collar and set my back to the window to block the view.

"It will be interesting to see Herta," Johann says.

"Not sure she'll tell me much about Snow."

"Looks like, socially, she was right in there with all the Ravensbrück staff, so she knew him for sure."

"Don't expect much. I saw her testify at the

doctors' trial. Ducking her murder rap by playing the misunderstood housewife."

Johann downshifts. "The political climate has changed here. What German prisoners are left are seen more as political prisoners. Demanding pardons."

"But Herta has a twenty-five-year sentence."

Johann shrugs. "She'll probably be out soon. Pardoned by the United States. We need to curry favor with Germany now to make sure they side with us against the Soviet Union, and she knows it. So, you may want to imply you can do it sooner. Karl okayed it."

"Twenty-five years was a light sentence if you ask me. She murdered so many prisoners. Claimed it was mercy killing."

"Did she admit to murder?"

"Yes—in her deposition but not on the stand. But there's prisoner testimony and signed records that show she personally murdered hundreds of innocents, the sociopath."

Johann glances at me as he drives. "True sociopaths are rare. Like your Dr. Snow. **There's** a sociopath. Snow relished the job. Enjoyed the selections and invented new ways of exploiting the prisoners to satisfy his own medical curiosities. To me, that's the real difference."

"Herta was a monster. Killed women with injections to the heart."

"Herta was a rules follower, like most doctors. Probably felt she was just doing her job."

Johann slows the car as a group of kerchiefed

women wearing bright skirts start across the road ahead. "Not excusing her at all, but it's a disturbing psychological fact that participation in mass murder need not require emotions as malicious as one might think. Given the right circumstances it's easy to kill."

He pauses to let that sink in.

"Better when you interview her to think of her as a common criminal instead of some mythical beast. Easier to focus on getting credible information."

Johann stops to allow what looks like a displaced family to cross the road, a mother and two young daughters, each carrying a suitcase.

"So many families are still without homes," I say. "Your aunt could house ten families like these in that castle."

"She'd rather die, I think."

A third girl of about nine years old hurries to catch up with the others, dragging a faded calico sack. I slide bills from the wallet Johann gave me, open the car door, reach into the back seat, pull out the paper bag, and slip the bills into it.

"Hold up there!" I call to the family.

The mother turns and gathers her daughters closer, and I hand them the bag and the soup. The mother accepts the bag, holding it to her chest, the young daughter takes the soup, and all four watch me rush back to the car.

"That was good of you," Johann says as we ease away. "Though I'll miss the kringle, and I'm not sure you can expense that."

“The young daughter there reminds me of a street urchin Arlette and I befriended named Fleur. She was the reason for our arrest.”

“How did it happen?”

“Once the Gestapo identified us as the Golden Doves, they searched all of Paris for us, but Arlette’s apartment was well-hidden behind the Flower and Bird Market.”

“So how did they catch you? I’m sure you were careful.”

“Very. We had Arlette’s little boy, Willie, to think about. But no one could have predicted what happened. It went down in the blink of an eye.”

CHAPTER 28

JOSIE

PARIS, FRANCE
1944

Before.

Arlette and I stayed in her apartment for two days after that horrible thing with Auntie happened, terrified to set foot out the door. We spent hours on our knees scrubbing the blood spot on the wood in front of the fireplace, with floor brushes, bleach, and every soap in the house, but nothing would remove that stain. The scrubbing just seemed to make it larger.

Arlette dropped her brush in the bucket. "We need to leave today, I don't care if we just drive around Paris in that flower van. I'm losing my mind. It's just dumb luck that we haven't been caught. The longer we stay—"

"Of course. I will go see my mother briefly. You get dressed and pack. Try and find something to cover the stain. I'll be back soon."

I hurried to my mother's apartment to say goodbye for now, and to find a button I'd lost, a sterling silver filigreed one from my best blouse that Mimi had given me. Anything to distract myself from replaying that horrible scene and give Arlette some time alone to rest with Willie. We just had to stop the radio work, repair to the country for a while, and stay alert. We would be back.

It was terribly warm in the city and just thinking about our run-in with Auntie sent extra ribbons of sweat down my back. I'd been careful to check for tails in case the authorities had already found the body and traced her back to us.

We had made quick work of disposing of the body. Due to the curfew it was very dangerous to be out, but we had Arlette's pink curfew pass if stopped. We waited until well past midnight, dragged her into a flower seller's pushcart, and took her to the Seine. We had to wait a few minutes under a bridge as a gaggle of rowdy Germans passed, but finally stuffed the brass dove in her left coat pocket to weigh her down, and put an old iron in the other, before we heaved the body over the wall and into the river. There was a soft splash as she hit the water and the Seine gulped her in. We left the cart there and were home within minutes, both dripping with perspiration.

On my way to Mother's, I walked along the river,

casually checking for anything floating in the water, or any disturbance along the banks, but the flower cart was gone and all seemed calm.

I wouldn't tell Mother about it. She had enough on her mind, and my visit had to be a quick one.

The heavenly scent of baking croissants drew me up to Mother's apartment, and I stepped into the kitchen where she stood at the stove, wearing her once navy blue dress, washed so many times it was now a whole shade lighter. A basket sat on the counter, a plume of deep green kale arching out.

"I can't stay long. Any word from Father?"

"I sent him another letter. I'm sure he's working on it." She turned. "Josie, look at what I got with the coupons you brought. Kale. Can you believe it? And half a loaf of bread. Mimi will be so happy when she wakes."

There was something about her too-bright way that made me think she knew I was doing more than writing newspaper stories. Of course she did, but this was not the time to discuss it.

I stepped into the living room, ducking through the sheets hung there to dry, the damp cotton cooling my forearms, and felt beneath the sofa cushion.

"Where is my button?" I came back to the kitchen. "You promised you'd find it. And now I'm late to file my column."

Mother pulled a small basket from the cupboard. "Do I not keep my promises?"

My stomach grumbled. "It's my favorite shirt—one

of my signature pieces—and looks terrible missing a button right in front."

"Calm down, my darling."

"Arlette is so chic. She'll think I'm a slob. You care **nothing** for me."

Mother smoothed one hand down my cheek. "What's wrong, Josie? You're not yourself. Is it the stress of the new job?"

I shifted in my shoes. I yearned to tell her about everything. My real job as a Dove. The Laurents. Thérèse. **Auntie.** She would understand.

"I'm just—" How tempted I was to take her hands and go through every sordid detail. "It's nothing. Just hungry I suppose."

She pulled me closer. "You don't have to tell me everything. But just remember that sometimes it's the most obvious thing that you need to see. And trust yourself."

I nodded, unable to speak for a moment, and she pressed the basket into my hands. "Take these to share with Arlette. I made croissants with the butter you brought me—can you believe it?"

I held the basket to my belly, the contents still warm. "I have to go—"

"Mimi will be delighted. How long has it been since you tasted one?"

I walked toward the door. "Seems like a lifetime. Thank you, Mummy."

"And please tell Arlette they're not my best. The butter is not integrated into the pastry as well as it could have been, not having my good rolling pin anymore, but—"

"Please, Mother. I really need to leave."

"Promise me you'll go directly to Arlette's apartment."

"I've walked that route a thousand times. Give Mimi a kiss for me when she wakes."

Mother gathered me to her and held me tight.

"I'll see you soon," I said.

She reached behind her neck and tried to unlatch her necklace. "Wait, you forgot—"

"Not now. My hands are full. I'll get the necklace next time."

She stepped back. "All right then."

With my new intelligence duties for the resistance it had seemed juvenile to keep up our little necklace exchange game.

"I may have to take a little trip for work, but I'll be back soon. Make sure Mimi keeps the shutters closed."

I blew her a kiss and hurried down the main stairs of the building, the rubber I'd applied to the soles of my wooden shoes silent on the marble steps running down from the Hôtel de Pontalba annex.

I checked the horizon for la tour Eiffel, my touchstone, and found comfort in seeing it so close, rising above the city. I then headed for the usual back streets, twenty-six minutes exactly to the flower market and Arlette's apartment.

As I walked, guilt poked at me for not taking the necklace. Mother had so few things to be happy about. What had she put in there? I would take it next time, for sure.

I entered the flower market and followed the maze of paths to Arlette's apartment door. I rapped our secret knock and she let me in, Willie in her arms. He smiled to see me and flapped his arms, and I smiled back at his sweet face and round little head, an apostrophe of golden hair curling down across his forehead. He had no idea what we'd done to his great-aunt.

Arlette closed the door behind me, her eyes wide. There was something odd about the yellow wool sweater she wore over her green dress.

She ran one hand through her hair. "Where have you **been,** Josie? I burned my shirt with . . . **her** on it. I covered the stain with the bathroom rug. Do you think the sculpture in her pocket was heavy enough to sink her? What if they find the body?"

There was no sign of last night's events. Just the stack of underground newspapers on our dining table, which Thérèse had asked us to deliver.

I stepped to her. "You have to calm down. And your sweater is inside out."

"And then I noticed your **radio** is gone."

"I hid it in that space above the kitchen cabinets. No one will find it there." I handed her the basket. "Croissants from Mother."

She set the basket on the table. "We'll take them with us. I've been bundling the newspapers. We need to get rid of them."

"We'll do it when I get back," I said. "Let's just leave, I will go see about the van. One of the flower sellers will know where it is."

Arlette smiled. "Yes. Thank you. I can't wait to go."

A knock came at the door, and I turned.

"It's me," came a voice.

Fleur.

"Go away," I called to her through the door.

"I need help," she said.

"Not now."

"Please, Josie," she cried most piteously.

I opened the door, and the girl scurried by me.

"What's wrong?" I asked as she hid under the kitchen table.

Only then did I check the walkway outside and see the men pursuing her, calling for her to stop.

One gendarme and three leather-jacketed men.

Gestapo.

"She has my wallet," the lead one called out in German.

I closed the door quickly and slid the bolt. Had they seen her run in here? Fleur had picked the wrong target.

"Hide the papers," I said.

Arlette clutched Willie tighter. "What's wrong?"

My hands shook as I scooped armfuls of newspapers from the table into the kindling basket and covered them with wood.

I could hardly speak. "Gestapo. Following her."

"How could you open the door?" The color drained

from Arlette's face. "Did they see her come in? What if they see the blood?"

"Quiet."

We both stood there barely breathing, hoping no knock would come.

"They'll find the newspapers there for sure," I whispered. "Take them—"

But before Arlette could even move, the dark knock came.

"Police. Ouvrez immédiatement la porte."

"Don't answer," Arlette whispered, a tremor in her voice. "We'll go out the bathroom window."

But before either of us could move, a tremendous bang came at the door. It splintered off the hinges and fell into the living room, and we stood with our hands up.

At long last our luck had run out.

CHAPTER 29

ARLETTE

FRENCH GUIANA
1952

THE MORNING AFTER CHATTING WITH FATHER Peter at the swim meet, I come to breakfast on Cove House terrace, preoccupied with thoughts of the boy Thomas. Upon waking that morning, I'd taken out my grief box and checked Willie's lock of hair, holding it to the sun. How similar the color was to Thomas's, the same golden yellow of mine.

My thoughts keep returning to how quickly I can get back to the camp to see him again and when I can get a blood test to start the official custody process.

I step out onto the terrace wearing white matelassé capri pants of my own design, and my homemade green shoulder bag. I pass Luc's faithful Claudio at the door, where he stands at attention, eyes forward. How bored he must get. Does he ever have a day off? He must go to the beach, swim. Happy to get out of those heavy clothes.

"Arlette?" Luc calls and waves me over to the table he's sharing with his grandmother.

Danae pats the seat next to her. "Sit here, my dear. I don't get much female companionship and I do crave it."

Claudio pulls out the chair for me, and as I sit I catch the scent of woody notes and leather. The bodyguard uses scented soap.

"This view never gets old," I say.

As Luc studies his newspaper, bathed in bright sunlight, I consider him. How old is he? Early forties, maybe? His face is lined here and there, and there's not a strand of silver in that pure black hair. He'd be so much more attractive if he grew his hair longer and used less pomade. For such an eligible man it's a puzzle he's not married.

I look out over the ocean and conjure Gunther, that day in the barn, his gray-blue eyes and sun-kissed skin. Such a beautiful young man he was.

Luc is a fine-enough-looking French man, but the way he wears his expensive clothes is a major part of his appearance, with his blue and white seersucker suit, crisp white shirt, and expensive leather loafers. I imagine Luc in a German uniform like

Gunther's, olive green. Was it the uniform that had made Gunther so attractive? Perhaps the German in me liked the authoritarian feeling of it.

"Arlette?" Luc asks. "Thought we lost you there."

I smile. "Oh. Yes. I was just thinking about your shoes. They're beautiful."

He holds out one foot and examines his shoe. "You have good taste. They were my grandfather's. Kangaroo leather he had made in Hong Kong."

I set my napkin on my lap, glance up, and catch him looking at me.

He leans in. "Forgive me for being so forward, but you look radiant this morning with the sun in your hair. This place is good for you. We should get down to the beach."

Danae waves off his comment. "Don't scare her off, Luc. She's here to find her son, not flirt with you."

Luc sets his mouth in a hard line and returns to his reading.

"I met a boy that might be a possible match. His name is Thomas."

"Oh, Thomas is a **nice** boy," Danae says. "And does favor you, I think."

Just hearing those words makes me smile. "Might I get a blood test to see if we at least match? I know it's not definitive, but . . ."

"It's much too early," Luc says. "We've never done a test this quickly."

"But I have a strong feeling—"

"Wait a few more visits. I will expedite the results when the test's done."

Danae waves Luc's comment away. "We should have it done soon."

Luc closes his paper. "Arlette, if you're going to help us with our PR, you need to really get to know the camp."

"Oh, you've agreed to help us?" Danae asks. "That's exceptional news."

I exhale. I hadn't agreed, of course.

"We've looked long and hard to fill that position," Danae says. "We've had some unfair press lately and really need a hand."

"Unfair how?"

She looks out toward the ocean. "Oh, the usual challenges nonprofit foundations face. People with nothing better to do, making things up."

"I'm just a waitress."

Danae leans in, elbows on the table. "What better qualification could one have than a lifetime spent dealing with the public? We need your beautiful face out front, so to speak. Luc is so busy with meetings and, frankly, I'm not as sharp as I once was."

"I'm only here so briefly. Hoping to leave as soon as I find my son."

Danae smooths the tablecloth. "Much of the job takes place in Paris. You can do it when you return home. And it pays eight thousand francs per month, which might help if you do find your son. It's not inexpensive raising a child these days."

I can barely speak at the thought of that much money hitting my account. How can I say no to her, such a generous woman? If I accept the job, it will mean I'll be over at the camp more often, with an excuse to see the boys. It would also earn me points with the Minaus, essential to fast-tracking official custody. Plus, I could direct the money to help Fleur.

"Can you send the compensation directly to Paris General? I'd like to put it toward a down payment on a spot there for a friend."

Danae sets down her teacup. "How generous of you."

Luc sets down his paper and makes a note in his appointment book. "I'll have my secretary type up a schedule for you. Help keep you on track."

"I don't need a schedule," I say.

He keeps his gaze on his writing. "I'll be traveling quite a bit and it's best to synchronize things."

Danae waves toward Claudio. "And maybe Claudio can take you over to have a nice long visit with Thomas soon?"

"I'd like to visit again tomorrow if I could? I know it's not Saturday, but . . ."

"I don't see why not," Luc says.

Every part of me rejoices at the thought of seeing Thomas again so soon. "I don't need an escort, thank you. And I must ask—is Father Peter always so, well, unfriendly?"

Danae sits back in her chair. "He confessed he was rather inhospitable to you at first and I've asked him to extend an olive branch next time you're over there, so hopefully his manner will change. He can be terribly gruff sometimes."

"Just protective of his boys," Luc says.

Danae sips her tea. "He leaves altogether too many weapons lying around for my taste. There are **children** there. Curious ones."

Luc waves her concern away. "All that war stuff is highly collectible now, and they're always put away. The boys know not to go near them."

Danae turns to me. "He has several knives. And something called a Vampire rifle. Hunts the jungle with it at night. I've told Father Peter that I vigorously oppose it, but I've been overruled on this one, I'm afraid, by my grandson."

Luc shrugs. "It's just a rifle with a night-vision scope. You'd rather have one of the boys mauled by a big cat? He's taken **two** jaguars at night, both near the campgrounds."

"How does it work at night?" I ask.

"Germans debuted it in WWII. First night-vision technology ever."

"It wasn't even a very **good** gun," Danae said.

"The scope gives off a milky glow that gave away a soldier's position. But it terrified those who knew they were being tracked in the darkness by their body heat."

"Monsters," Danae interjects.

"Eventually the Allies figured out that any bright light would temporarily blind the shooter, but not before the Germans killed a lot of unsuspecting men." Luc butters his toast. "Say what you will about the Germans, they were geniuses with weaponry."

Danae waves away a plate of pastries a maid offers. "They should have taken all Hitler's guns and thrown them in the ocean."

"I'm excited to go back to Camp Hope and see the boys," I say, trying to change the subject.

Danae laces her fingers together. "Oh, yes, dear. And perhaps bring your sketch pad? That will help you bond with the boys one-on-one. Luc tells me you like to sketch clothing designs and you're quite good."

"Oh, I don't—"

"You must learn to take a compliment, my dear."

"I do make some of my own things. Made these capri pants from some vintage fabric. This bag from my old dress I wore at the camp."

"I applaud your resourcefulness, but part of what we offer our mothers is a fresh start. And that includes the wardrobe. How would you like to accompany me on a little shopping trip in town soon?"

Luc sets down his paper. "Grandmother's famous for her shopping trips. The entire town of Cayenne celebrates them."

"If you do stay a bit longer, we have the fashion show benefit coming up, and you'll need a proper dress. You could use some resort wear as well. We also need table décor for the show, and you could help me choose that. What do you say?"

"I need to focus on finding my son—"

"Luc has to leave on business anyway, so why don't we girls have our own shopping day? Maybe next week?"

Luc smiles. "She's impossible to say no to."

I turn to Danae. "I'd love to join you."

Suddenly from the direction of the front entrance comes the sound of raised voices.

"Take your hands off me," a woman says in what sounds like an accent of the Caribbean. "No, I will not calm down. You get me the person in charge."

The woman tries to press by Claudio, and he springs after her.

"It's fine, Claudio," Danae says.

The woman breaks through onto the terrace with antelope grace, her hair caught in a neat chignon at her nape. The white of her suit complements her coppery brown skin.

Father Peter follows close behind. "This is a private home."

"I demand to see whoever's in charge here," she says.

Danae stands. "Well, that would be me, I suppose, since this is my home."

"Tell them to back off."

Danae waves toward the empty chair at the table. "Please join us. Coffee?"

"I'm not here for coffee."

"I'm Danae Minau. You're lucky the dogs are penned. They don't react well to . . . unannounced visitors."

"I am—"

"Of course, I know who you are. Dr. Kena Bondi, former ambassador of the Bahamas to the United Nations."

"Here representing the World Health Organization epidemiological task force."

Danae extends one hand. "Terribly nice to meet you. This is my grandson Luc, who runs our Hope Home foundations; Arlette LaRue, our head of public relations; and our program director, Father Peter."

Dr. Bondi ignores Danae's hand and turns to Father Peter. "So, you run the children's camp adjacent to this property? Where Maroon children reside? I don't know what kind of a game you're playing, but I've tried calling you twenty times, with no response."

Father Peter steps away from her. "I don't answer to you."

She follows. "We've had many reports of disease outbreaks in the Maroon villages on the outskirts of Cayenne. As isolated as these tribes are, they've found it necessary to reach out to us with reports of extreme numbers of deaths. I've come from Geneva to check into it. I don't have to tell you how devastating to this population an unchecked virus would be."

"This is the first we've heard of it," Luc says.

"We've also heard that many young Maroon boys have gone missing," Bondi says. "How can I see the camp?"

Father Peter draws himself up to his full six feet or so. "The children are on a schedule and cannot be disturbed. Besides, we are disease free. There's certainly no emergency as far as our facility is concerned."

"I need immediate access."

Father Peter steps closer to her. "That won't be happening."

She folds her arms across her chest. "I'm having the necessary paperwork drawn up to gain entry. You'll be hearing from the Cayenne police."

Danae steps around the table toward her. "Is that really necessary, Dr. Bondi? We're more than happy to show you around. Perhaps at a time that suits all parties involved? Miss LaRue here will set up a day when you can tour. We'll have a lunch."

"I know what's happening here. All of you circling the wagons, with your big house and your security, promising one thing and doing another. All of you banding together to protect whatever this little scheme is."

Luc steps to her. "You need to leave."

"You never make things easy for people who look like me, do you?" She heads for the door, stops, and turns. "But I have one thing you don't. A mandate from the World Health Organization to figure this out, Mrs. Minau. And I'll find out what is going on."

Father Peter escorts Dr. Bondi out, and Danae, Luc, and I sit back down at the table, stunned.

"She was incensed," I say. "I'm not sure I can do this job."

"What?" Luc asks. "First you agree then you waver. It's maddening. We need to count on your word."

"I'll do it, calm down."

"Good. And let's consider this finally done, shall we?"

"Yes. Of course. And what time should I visit Thomas tomorrow?"

"Only Saturdays are visiting days."

"But you said—"

I glance at Danae for support, but she just stirs her tea.

Luc stands. "What do you mean? I said nothing of the sort. Next Saturday—usual visiting hours. I'll be away, but Claudio will escort you."

THE FOLLOWING SATURDAY MORNING Claudio accompanies me along the path to Camp Hope, on my way to see Thomas, a constellation of scarlet birds singing in the canopy above. It's less humid today and the jungle colors seem more vivid, the scent of jasmine and musty earth in the air. Towering ferns arch over the path and meet waxy-leafed trees, woody gray vines slung among them.

Dressed in trousers and a long-sleeved shirt, Claudio holds a leather folder and has insisted on carrying my baby blanket and sketch pad, as well as helping me over every root. Though there's a pleasant breeze today, it's still quite warm, and sweat beads along his brow.

I step off the trail to admire a thicket of ferns as delicate as bobbin lace.

"Mr. Minau has asked me to remind you to stick to the path," Claudio says.

It's a bit suffocating to be accompanied everywhere, though he does have beautiful eyes. He probably gives Luc a detailed report of my everymove.

We walk through a confetti of tangerine-colored rinds falling from the canopy and look up to find a black toucan with his carroty bill ransacking a cluster of papayas.

"You're Brazilian, Claudio?"

"Portuguese and Indian."

We walk on, not speaking, the dull thud of the waves breaking in the distance.

"Does it rain here every day?"

"Pretty much in the wet season, which is now. People don't realize there are many types of rain here. Soft and gentle. Misting. Lots of thunderstorms. And we get the occasional serious tropical storm. There's one on the way right now, actually."

He cups my elbow and helps me over a fat root embedded in the path.

"You know, I'm perfectly capable of finding my way over here alone."

"Mr. Minau has asked me to escort you."

Suddenly, Claudio grabs my arm and pulls me toward him.

A shudder goes through me. "What's wrong?"

He waves toward a mound along the side of the path teeming with red insects. "Fire ants."

He keeps his hand, warm and soft, on my bare upper arm, and then releases me.

"How did I miss them?"

He leans in. "It helps to watch where you're going."

"They look nasty."

"They're just minding their own business. If you're an ant that's the type to be." He flashes me a smile. "Highly respected in the ant world."

Something rustles in the undergrowth near me, and I turn.

"That's just an armadillo," Claudio says as a humped, ebony-shelled creature thrusts out of the underbrush and scuttles across the path. "See the sloth hanging under that lianas vine?"

"Lianas?"

"Woody, aerial roots, really. Here, the vines compete with the trees. They take them down and the tree dies, but the vine survives. The jungle may look calm, but there's a lot happening." He sends me a pointed look. "It's important to pay attention."

A slant of light filters down through the canopy, and he walks on ahead of me through it, the sweat molding his shirt to his back.

I walk along, starting to like having a bodyguard, especially one with such a muscled back, and then marvel at my own ridiculousness. It's pathetic how easily I fall for men. He's not even my type, and he probably has one of the maids waiting for him in his quarters. Or a wife somewhere.

I glance at him. "You must be terribly hot in that uniform."

He takes a sheet of paper from the folder and hands it to me. "Here is the schedule Mr. Minau has provided."

I read. **Wake 7:30. Breakfast 8:00. Write press releases 9:00. Lunch at Camp Hope 12:00. Return Cove House 1:30. Work on commercial shoot logistics 2:00–3:00.**

"Am I not allowed to use the bathroom unless it's scheduled?"

He raises one eyebrow. "I'll ask him to add that if you like."

I ball the paper up and shove it in my pocket.

We head for the dining hut, the largest building there by far, in the center of the camp, its roof peaked like a thatched witch's hat. At the sound of the boys' happy chatter, I pick up my step. The scent of butter and stewed meat fills the air. All I want is a real indication Thomas is mine.

Claudio hands me my blanket and sketch pad. "What time will you like to return?"

"I can make my own way back, Claudio. I'm sure you have better things to do." From what I can tell he also acts as the caretaker, doing odd jobs all over Cove House property.

"Not really." He looks at me with those lovely brown eyes so intently I have to look away.

I send him an awkward little wave. "Fine then."

He walks off leaving me oddly rattled, and I force myself to focus on my mission. I find the boys already waiting at their places at the long refectory tables, white and Maroon seated together. They look handsome dressed in their camp uniforms of shorts and white shirts, each wearing a neckerchief the color of their age level. I search their faces to find Thomas, but don't see him.

I try to avoid Father Peter, who stands at the head of the hut at a steam table, ladling out stew and mashed potatoes onto individual plastic trays. He'd been so defensive with Dr. Bondi. Why not just show her around?

I find Thomas sitting among a cluster of children each wearing a red neckerchief, waiting for their turn to line up for lunch.

I clutch the green blanket at my chest. Will he recognize it? I force myself to be objective. Jumping to conclusions—assuming this boy is Willie—will just make things worse.

I go from child to child, working my way toward Thomas, offering to sketch the boys, and they enjoy seeing their faces on paper.

After a few sketches I take my pad and sit down next to Thomas. "Like to have your portrait done?"

He shrugs. "I suppose." How indifferent he is to me today. Perhaps afraid of being let down?

Not one of the others gives me the tingle of recognition that Thomas does. At close range, his face is so much like Gunther's, the same strong jaw. And he has my golden hair and milky complexion.

I set my pad on the table and stroke the blanket in my lap.

"What's that?" he asks.

My heart thumps my breastbone as I hold out the folded square. "It's somewhat old now. A baby blanket."

He cranes his neck toward the steam table.

"Does it seem familiar at all?" I ask.

"No. Why would it?" He looks at me earnestly.

I exhale. **He was just a baby. Of course, he can't remember.**

"Do you recall anything from when you were little?" I ask.

"Not really. Until I came here."

"No mother or father?"

"No."

"Do you ever wonder about who they are?"

"Sometimes," he says and with two hands pushes his hair back from his forehead, the way Gunther so often did.

I can barely breathe, the similarity is so strong. "My parents both died when I was a bit younger than you are now."

He gives me his full attention. "Do you remember them?"

"Only a little."

"Where did you grow up?" he asks.

"Just over the border from Germany, in France,

with my aunt and uncle once my parents died. But my boyfriend was German. A soldier in the army. Gunther Wagner."

Thomas sits up straighter. "Did he carry a gun?"

"Shall I draw him for you?"

He nods, and I open my pad and sketch the shape of Gunther's face. "He looked very much like you, Thomas. Nice chin. Blond hair. Deep-set blue eyes."

"Did he wear a uniform?"

"Of the German army of course. The First SS Panzer Division." I draw the uniform coat I remember from his photo, with two patch pockets at the breast.

He holds out his hand, palm up. "May I use that, please?"

I hand him the pencil, and he sketches with deft strokes the eagle badge Gunther wore on his upper left sleeve. I marvel at his ability for such a young child, shading the border of the wings for a three-dimensional effect.

"How do you know the badge?"

"Everyone knows about that division," he says as he draws.

"How?"

He shrugs. "History class."

Father Peter's history class.

I sit back as he continues the drawing. What else are they teaching the boys down here?

Thomas finishes. I hold the pad up and consider the sketch. Did they also teach him how that division committed several war crimes in their travels?

How could I tell the boy his father might have been a war criminal? That would have to wait.

"May I keep this?" he asks.

"Of course." I tear off the sheet, he folds it and slides it into his shirt pocket.

"Are you my mother?" He asks with a sudden frankness that catches me off guard.

Everything slows. I nod. "I think so."

He pats his shirt pocket. "And you think he's my father?"

"Yes."

"Would I come live with you?"

"If you'd like and if our blood matches. They will take samples from us both."

"Where is your house?"

"In Paris. An apartment. I work at a café with my friends Bep and Riekie. You'd like them."

He leans in, his expression serious. "You know, I've wished for this every night."

"Me too," I say with a smile.

The other boys gather and Thomas stands. "I have to go get my tray."

"One question before you leave. I was wondering. What's down the path near the dining hut?"

"Just the clinic."

"Can you take me there sometime?"

"It's where the sick ones are."

"Have you been in there?"

"When my belly hurts bad and my head gets hot. Father Peter says it's just amenia."

"Anemia?"

He nods. "And when Obi got sick, he went to the clinic."

"Sick with what, do you know?"

He shrugs. "I can take you there one day when I don't have class."

"I'd like that."

Another boy sets a tray onto the table, and Thomas watches as he digs his fork into the mashed potatoes.

"Looks like you enjoy mashed potatoes?" I ask.

"Oh, very much. That's all I'd eat if Father Peter'd let me."

"Have you always loved them?"

He smiles. "That's a funny question."

I shrug one shoulder. "I'm just curious. I once knew a little boy who liked mashed potatoes more than anything in the world."

CHAPTER 30

ARLETTE

FÜRSTENBERG, GERMANY
RAVENSBRÜCK CONCENTRATION CAMP
1944

Before.

WILLIE CRIED, HIS FACE SWOLLEN SCARLET as we left Pantin station, standing and packed tightly into the last cattle car on the train. We'd been imprisoned in Paris for a week by then and fed next to nothing, so I had little milk to give him. Josie and I still wore the clothes we'd been wearing when arrested at the apartment, a green dress for me and the birthday blouse and trousers I'd sewn for her. Willie wore his undershirt and a diaper, and I'd been lucky to grab Josie's baby blanket before we left, to wrap around him.

Josie took a turn peering out the crack. "My mother will do something."

I wiped the sweat off my upper lip. "What can she do? She'll be lucky not to be on the next train after us."

From the hurt look on Josie's face I knew I'd gone too far. But, after all, she was the one who let Fleur into the apartment. At least the Nazis hadn't discovered we were the Doves; they'd simply arrested us for intent to distribute underground newspapers. And to our knowledge they hadn't discovered the bloodstain on the floor.

I felt Willie's wet diaper and checked his bottom, crimson with diaper rash. How selfish I'd been, thinking I was some sort of daring spy, saving France. Where was France to help us now? Our poor angel Thérèse had been done in by them too. Perhaps she should have left me at that Lebensborn home. At least Willie would be safe.

Fleur appeared and nestled herself in close to me. "My little **draga,**" she said, running one hand down the baby's leg.

Was that something her mother once said to her? I couldn't stay angry with her for long. How could she have known she would get us all sent to God knows where?

Willie turned to her and stopped his fussing.

Fleur leaned close to me and whispered. "A lady gave me this." She slid from her pocket a perfectly lovely teething biscuit.

"Brilliant girl."

She smiled up at me, with her dear, heart-shaped face. **It wasn't her fault. I brought all this bad luck on us by killing Auntie.**

Willie devoured the biscuit and soon slept, mocha-colored flecks speckling his white undershirt.

I sat on the wooden floor and Fleur rested her head in my lap and slept next to Willie. What a sweet-natured girl she was. And maybe ten years old I guessed, though her growth had probably been stunted from being homeless so long. **Does she even have parents?**

It rained for much of the three-day trip, and one evening, after passing through a forest of pines, the train shuddered and stopped. The door rolled open as our eyes adjusted to the light, and guards beat us out and lined us up five abreast in front of metal camp gates. It was still raining, and we lifted our faces to the sky to wet our mouths.

As the guards opened the gates, we stared up at the sign hung above, which read THIS IS YOUR DEATH in German, above a red and yellow painted sign of a hideous fat louse.

Women murmured the word. **Konzentrationslager.**

We walked across a wide gravel **platz,** a yard,

which stretched out as far as the eye could see. The guards hurried us down a crowded road to an open tent where they painted the backs of our clothes with big white **X**s.

From somewhere nearby came the sound of machine gun fire, which caused Willie to cry. We stood at the edge of the tent, and with Josie's and Fleur's help, I desperately tried to soothe him.

I'd seen firsthand the Germans' disregard for life, even the youngest, when they had killed the Laurents' baby boy. Surely, they would simply shoot my screaming child.

"I don't think I can do this, Josie."

"You have no choice. Don't think, just do."

A young woman passing by whispered to me in French with an Italian accent. "French? Don't say a word, just come. And please keep the baby quiet, for God's sake."

I looked at Josie, she nodded, and we followed the woman to a long, low barracks.

"I'm Ariana," she said as we entered the place, which was jammed to the rafters with three-story wooden bunk beds where women lay four or five to a mattress.

We walked by a naked woman hanging her rinsed underpants on a rafter, and I covered Willie's face with one hand as putrid water rained down on us. In the next bunk an emaciated older woman helped a teenage girl vomit into a tin bowl.

Ariana stopped in front of a bunk. "We're up top. Hurry, now."

Josie helped Fleur up and we followed.

Every part of me relaxed to see that bunk, so clean and orderly, an oasis of sanity, with two somewhat clean, blue-striped pillows and a small apothecary chest no bigger than a breadbox leaned against the wall. I liked the woman right away. She seemed better fed than the rest, and was terribly exotic looking, with full lips and short dark hair, and was perhaps ten years older than Josie and me.

She handed me up last. "I saved you all from the shearing; most newcomers are shaved right down to the scalp. Though they're getting more lax about it now."

I lay the baby down on the mattress still wrapped in the blanket.

"Welcome to Block Ten. I'm Ariana. I don't allow just anyone up here, but I saw you have a baby, and you look like good sorts."

Josie sat cross-legged on the mattress. "You're Italian?"

"My father was a diplomat in France," Ariana said.

"Mine, too," Josie said.

I held Willie closer. "I think there's a dead woman in the bunk down there," I said. "Shouldn't someone be called?"

"In the morning the washroom will be full of the dead. Best to go now if you need to. But whatever you do, don't drink the water."

Fleur rested her head against my shoulder.

"How old is the girl?" Ariana asked.

"Around ten, we think." I stroked Willie's head. "And he's twelve months. I'm desperate to get them both some food. Do they feed the children?"

"No, I'm afraid. But we'll have to get creative. Adults get watery soup in the morning and a bread crust. I wash with the coffee. It's good for little else. But at least we all may be out of this hellhole soon. Have you heard? The Allied invasion finally happened. They landed on the beaches of Normandy."

Josie and I exchanged glances. At least our work as Doves had not been in vain.

Ariana slid open one of the little chest drawers and pulled out a waxed paper packet of crackers. "Take these. It's all I have right now."

Willie and Fleur shared the crackers, and soon he fell into deep sleep.

"Lucky you kept your clothes too. They probably ran out of uniforms, finally. Germans must be losing the war. Not usually so lax."

"Why did they paint the white **X** on our backs?" I asked.

"In case you escape. Since you don't wear a uniform it marks you as a prisoner. And makes for a handy target for the SS men if you're running away."

"There are only women prisoners here?" Josie asked.

"The Nazis almost didn't bother to build this place. Thought women were too insignificant to build a whole camp for. But they had so many German prostitutes, homeless women, and political prisoners they made this palace. You will be expected to work every day except Sunday. The prisoners here do all the work. Grow the food. Do the laundry."

"All instructions are given in German?" Josie asked.

"Yes. You both speak it?"

I nodded. "Fleur knows only French, but I've been teaching her."

"This block is a real mix. Hungarians. Italians like me. A good many Dutch girls just came. Some red triangle political prisoners like you."

"And now an American," Josie said.

"You?" Ariana asked with a flirty smile. "I could've sworn you were French. Very nice blouse and trousers."

The color rose in Josie's cheeks. "Arlette sewed them."

Ariana ran one hand down Josie's arm. "Beautifully made."

Josie looked pleased at that and smiled back.

"That makes five Americans here now," Ariana said as she leaned close to Josie and whispered. "And such a pretty one, too."

"I'm afraid I must apologize in advance," I said. "In case Willie cries. He's getting a tooth."

"Try to keep him quiet. If Marcel the **Blockova** hears him crying, she might have him sent off."

I held Willie closer. "Sent off?"

Ariana shrugged. "Children reduce productivity.

But I did hear there is a new policy. A whole block just for mothers and babies."

"Why would they do such a kind thing?"

"This place is one big experiment, so who knows? It may just be another rumor, so get some sleep." She patted her pillow. "Josie, you here with me."

She handed me a second pillow. "And the other three heads at the other end. Tomorrow will be a long day. You must have your wits about you if you want to be among the lucky few to survive."

JOSIE AND I WERE thankful every day we'd met Ariana on our first day. She and Josie became fast friends, and since she was well connected at the camp, she wrangled good jobs for us in the great halls, where we sorted the goods Hitler stole from the countries he'd conquered, and she arranged for the older women in our block who knitted socks for German soldiers all day to care for Willie while we were at work. Ariana even traded her bread for a whole box of farina, which he devoured. But despite our new protector's help, like all of us, Willie grew dangerously thin.

One morning at roll call, as the nasty head wardress Dorothea Binz counted us with the help of our **Blockova,** planes flew low overhead, not an uncommon sight, but these were not German planes.

"RAF," a woman behind us said. "Liberation soon."

Just before we were dismissed the **Blockova**

announced they were moving Willie, Fleur, and me to a new block. Josie and Ariana watched with worried looks as a guard took the three of us to live in the block Ariana had mentioned, a maternity ward of sorts just for mothers and babies, called the **Kinderzimmer.** There, we mothers went out to work and came back at night to our children. We slept in real beds, each with our own eiderdown comforter, a luxury we found strange.

I missed Josie, but I still saw her at work each day, and I made two friends in the new block, Bep and Riekie, both from Holland and with babies about Willie's age, and we looked after one another. Riekie woke me one night, the block bathed in moonlight, when she found a rat nibbling at her son's foot. It was fat as a small cat, with oily, liver-brown fur, and once I bashed it with my shoe it bleated a high-pitched little scream and scuttled off.

We all hoped for more food in that new block, but they fed the ten mothers the same watery soup and bread crusts as the other prisoners and allegedly fed the children while we were out at work. But as winter approached, we knew the children were starving, many near death. Willie's belly had grown distended and his legs so thin I could feel the bones.

We mothers had come to love the other babies as our own and worked as one, begging and stealing, doing everything we could to keep them alive. Ariana did her best, and prisoners from other blocks gave us their crusts of bread. One young guard named Dora, a simple, stocky, dark-haired farm girl from Fürstenberg, snuck the babies much-appreciated extra rice from the officers' dining hall and came to visit the children. I'd picked the lock on Dr. Snow's office storage cabinet and taken some Red Cross packages to feed the children and the mothers as well, but they were running out.

One Sunday, our day of rest, the block was full of happy murmurings as we rocked our babies and chatted with one another. Bep sat on her bed singing to her baby, Thea, who lay wrapped in her arms.

"Your Willie seems to be keeping weight on better than the others," Bep said. "Perhaps Dora feeds him more when we are out working."

"That's not true, Bep," I said, though I suspected she might be right. "He should be rolling over and crawling well by now, but he can barely hold his head up."

Riekie came and sat on my bed. "We can't go on this way, Arlette." She leaned in closer. "The babies can't—"

The door at the end of the block opened and Dorothea Binz stepped in, her German shepherd dog leashed at her side. She walked up the row of beds, admiring the babies. A tall, well-fed blonde wearing a white coat walked beside her, and Dora brought up the rear.

"That's Dr. Oberheuser," Riekie whispered as the pair slowly came our way. "Surely a doctor will understand the children can't survive without more food."

At first glance I mistook Dr. Oberheuser for pretty, with her high cheekbones and hair swept up in a twist. But as she grew nearer, she seemed completely ordinary, with heavy-lidded eyes and a froggy, downturned pout.

The three arrived at the foot of my cot as Binz's dog strained at the leash toward me.

Binz leaned in over the bed and peered at Willie. "This is a fine boy. How old?"

I forced a smile. "Just over twelve months, Madame Wardress."

Binz stepped closer to Willie. "He's a bit quiet."

"All the children are, Madame Wardress. From lack of food. We've found rats coming for the children at night. Some even getting bolder during the day."

Binz tickled one finger under Willie's chin. He smiled up at her and kicked a little jump.

Dr. Oberheuser stood next to Binz.

"Good temperament," Binz said.

"Is he often sick?" Dr. Oberheuser asked. She wore rings on her fingers and bracelets on her wrist. The gold bangles jangled as she held a stethoscope to Willie's chest.

"Not once since he was born," I said in my best German.

She made a note on her pad.

"And look, a new tooth coming," Binz said, like a proud parent.

"Nature's way of saying he needs solid food," I said. "All the children here could use more."

"I was eating sauerbraten by that age," Binz said to Dr. Oberheuser. "With whipped potatoes."

I sat up straighter. "My aunt cooked **Schweinshaxe.** Crispy on the outside, fork tender on the inside."

"And the boy's father?"

"Gunther Wagner. Pure German. A soldier with the First Panzer Division."

"You are a political prisoner? French?"

"I made one bad decision, Madame Wardress."

Binz looked to Herta. "The French. So impulsive."

"Willie was so hungry that I took a job bundling underground newspapers. Now I know how wrong that was. I grew up in Alsace, where I went to BDM class each week."

Binz called over a lady guard and sent her off for something, and soon the woman reappeared with a bowl, which Binz seized and brought to me.

"You have done stupid things, but no child of a German soldier should go without simply because his mother is of inferior birth." She handed me the warm earthenware bowl, and she and the doctor walked off.

I stared at the contents, a dollop of creamy white whipped potatoes, some brown flecks of the skins mixed in, yellow butter melted into the folds.

Binz and Herta headed for the door. My mouth watered as I dipped my spoon tip into the potato and held it to Willie's lips. He moved his arms and opened his mouth for more. How good it was to see him eat that little bit. But how cruel it was to tease him this way. Food one day, nothing the next. The truth was he'd die there in that place if I didn't do something. But if I told them the truth, would they execute me? At least Willie would be out of this place.

My heart beat faster as I stood and hurried after Binz. "Madame Wardress?"

She turned. "What is it?"

I lowered my voice. "I just wanted to tell you my son was born in a Lebensborn home. Promised to a family very high up. I'm sure they would be grateful to you if you got him to them."

"Are you saying you want to give up your child?"

I nodded, tears welling. It would save his life.

"Who was he promised to?" Dr. Oberheuser asked.

How could I say the name Reichman? They would execute me for sure if they knew I was the vanished mother they'd so vigorously pursued. "I don't know the name, but—"

"You are French," she said. "You would not have been allowed at a welfare home. A Norwegian mother, maybe."

"But they told me—"

Binz dismissed me with a wave. "You French are all the same, making up stories to get what you want. Don't bother me with your lies."

"Please, Madame Wardress—"

Binz headed out the door, the doctor in her wake. "I won't hear another word about it."

I stood, barely able to pick up my head and stand straight, having blown Willie's one chance to live.

Once Binz left the block, I joined the other mothers and shared the potatoes, with all except Bep, who refused even a bite and remained on her bed, swaddling Thea in her arms.

"What were you saying to them?" Bep asked.

"Just asking for more food."

Bep rocked her baby. "I heard you kissing up to Binz and Herta. You're working with them on this, aren't you? Providing information on the rest of us, so your child is favored?"

I stood. "I don't know what else you want me to do, Bep. Have I not broken into Dr. Snow's office at great personal risk? Shared the packages with every baby here? If I curry favor with Binz, it will help us all."

Bep rocked her baby. "Just leave us alone."

"We have potatoes. Please let Thea have some."

"No."

I moved to the edge of Bep's bed. "I know you're having a hard time." I reached for the baby. "Let me take Thea for a bit. You rest."

Bep clutched the baby tighter.

I slipped one hand between Bep and the baby. "Come now. You deserve a nap."

"Leave her be."

As I tried to lift the baby, Bep held her back and the blanket fell away, exposing the baby's face.

Riekie gasped. "Oh—"

Sweet Thea lay in the blanket as if sleeping, but dark and wizened, with the purplish-red cast to her skin we'd all seen in the dead there.

Bep sobbed and covered her face with one hand. I gently replaced the blanket, wrapped my arms around them both, and held them close. "I'm so sorry," I whispered.

The rest of the mothers came and encircled Bep and the baby in their arms and stayed there as twilight fell at Ravensbrück, the block silent, except for the sound of ten mothers crying for one of their own.

CHAPTER 31

JOSIE

EN ROUTE TO LANDSBERG PRISON 1952

JOHANN AND I SPEED TOWARD LANDSBERG Prison, near Munich, and the drive seems interminable, knowing Herta Oberheuser is at our destination. Worry about seeing her again consumes me, and I distract myself by reading the roadside billboards.

"Won't be long now," Johann shouts, over the sound of the motor.

"Just want it over with."

The German billboards are a good enough distraction, the West German recovery in evidence in ads for chewing gum and cigars. A blond man with an impossibly white smile grins next to a tube of toothpaste. A dark-haired woman scissors a cigar between index and middle finger.

"Stop the car, Johann."

"What—"

"You need to turn around. Now. I need to see that billboard again."

"But we're already late."

"Please turn around. It will only take a minute."

He does a U-turn and pulls off next to the billboard, the woman's smiling face filling our windshield.

Johann peers up. "She's beautiful. You know her? Or do you just like cigars?"

I can only nod.

I knew her once. Or at least thought I did.

CHAPTER 32

JOSIE

RAVENSBRÜCK
1944

Before.

ARLETTE AND I HAD BEEN AT RAVENSBRÜCK for a few months, her in the **Kinderzimmer** with Willie and Fleur, me in Block Ten, what they called the "Goulash Block," a putrid-smelling mishmash of all nationalities. I missed my mother and Mimi terribly and self-flagellated with the guilt of it all. Why had I not listened to my mother and paid attention to the obvious? I'd known Fleur would get us into trouble. Why had I not been more adamant about keeping her out of our lives?

I felt incredibly lucky I'd met my resourceful, charismatic bunkmate Ariana the first day there, and lived to please her. We became inseparable, sharing most everything, including stories from our pasts. But Arlette and I still kept our secret, that we were the infamous Golden Doves the Gestapo had sought. I'd tucked it away, almost forgotten about it, buried so deep.

In our top bunk, one night in November after lights out, Ariana helped me make a new red triangle badge, USA embroidered in black thread across it. She lit a votive to scent our bunk and I snuck a glance at her as she stitched the A, her face serious in the candlelight. All day I'd looked forward to getting back to that wretched block and our time alone together. With Arlette moved out, Ariana became my everything.

Ariana finished the patch and held it up. "What do you think?" she asked, her brown eyes open wide with just a hint of smile there, lips half parted.

She was famous for those lips. Binz had even given her a nickname. **Kissen lippen.** Pillow lips. I'd seen her kiss other girls at the camp, in a dark alley between the blocks. I once saw her kiss the full-chested **Blockova** named Marcel from our block, feeling Marcel's breast as she did it. But she'd never come close to kissing me. Maybe it was my hideous, red-dyed hair, the roots growing in brown.

"It's perfect," I said.

I lifted my blouse off over my head, leaving me in my undershirt and drawers, and hoped she'd be tempted by my scanty clothes, but she kept her eyes on her work.

"You never talk about your past," I said. "Always change the subject."

She handed me the needle and thread to sew the patch onto my sleeve with. "Too busy living today, I guess."

"How did you get arrested?"

She stared at me for a long second and ran one hand through her short hair. "I've never told anyone here."

"Well?"

"My father was the Italian ambassador to France; my mother was Belgian. I fell in love with Paris. And with a woman."

"And?"

"I'd been trained as a lawyer in Rome, but I became her chauffeur. We entertained everyone. Picasso. Gertrude Stein. Such parties. Then I did one little drop-off for a friend and here I am."

"Well, you certainly know everyone here."

She smiles. "I should, after three years in this charming place."

"Has your friend tried to get you out? She no doubt has influence."

What would I do without Ariana? It was too terrible to consider. At ten years my senior, she looked out for me, and could get anything we needed from her wide network of friends throughout the camp.

"She tried many times, my father through diplomatic channels as well. But nothing has worked. And how about you? You never talk about your time before you were arrested, either."

"Maybe someday," I said, adopting an air of mystery.

She slid a small bottle of Scotch from one of the little drawers in the chest. "But we must drink to our friendship."

"How many bottles do you have in those drawers?"

"Marcel knows Macallan is my favorite Scotch."

"Mine as well," I said, though I'd never tasted Scotch.

Ariana handed me the bottle and I tipped it back. I liked the taste right away, as the warmth ran down my throat.

"You like it?" Ariana asked with a smile.

I took a second, longer pull on the bottle and the Scotch ran around my empty stomach making me feel dizzy and so gloriously free.

"I have things, too, you know."

"Oh, really? Like what?"

"I have a sleeping draught," I said, hoping she'd be impressed.

"Quiet." Ariana sat up straighter. "A sedative? How did you get such a thing?"

I shrugged. "Have a cyanide pill, too."

She smiled and took a drink. "I'm cutting you off."

I held up my hem to show the outlines of the vial and the capsule. "It's true. There's much you don't know about me."

"Oh, yes, you're so mysterious, my little friend."

I took another pull on the bottle. "Arlette and I were actually quite famous. All over Paris."

"Oh, really? Like the Golden Doves?"

"What if we were?"

"But you're so young. They didn't make teenagers spies. Especially half-American ones."

I smiled and leaned in close. "You may be surprised."

Ariana waved that thought away. "They were just a fable made up by the resistance. To taunt the Germans."

"No. It was real. I intercepted radio transmissions." I took another sip from the bottle. "Pleased Churchill himself."

"You, maybe, but Arlette? She's so . . . doesn't seem the type."

"Oh, she's no innocent." I finished the contents of the bottle.

"We should sleep now." She plumped her pillow.

How could she ignore me so easily? "Arlette actually . . ."

"What?"

I paused for effect, the bunk shifting under me. "Killed someone."

Ariana dismissed me with a little wave. "That's ridiculous."

"All true. Her aunt came to our apartment, and I had a radio and . . ."

"What?"

I grew dizzy and set one palm on the mattress to steady myself. "No, I can't say more."

"As I suspected. All a story."

"It happened. I swear."

Ariana sat up straighter, eyes wide. "Her own aunt?"

"We dumped the body in the Seine. Right at Pont Neuf. When we get out of here someday, I'll show you the spot. Now do you believe me?"

"Oh, yes. Such a skilled and daring agent. With a great imagination."

Is she mocking me?

Ariana lifted my hand to her lips and kissed my palm, her eyes trained on me in the candlelight.

I sent her my most sultry look, urging her on, but she just licked her thumb and forefinger, pinched out the flame, turned her back, and settled down to sleep.

Leaving me more than a little drunk, and with a wrench of regret for divulging our past. And more entranced with Ariana than ever.

CHAPTER 33

ARLETTE

FRENCH GUIANA
1952

THE FOLLOWING SATURDAY I ARRIVE AT COVE House for breakfast, ready to visit the camp to see Thomas, and find Luc and Danae already seated, both engrossed in their morning newspapers. It's especially bright out on the terrace, and the wind coming off the ocean stirs whitecaps in the sea in the distance. I glance at Claudio, and he watches me pass. He looks good that morning, his hair a bit tousled. Had he slept poorly?

Luc's suitcase stands at the door. He's leaving on a business trip, and I look forward to having more space, not under his rigid schedule all day.

As I pass Claudio, my bag slides down off my shoulder, taking my shirt with it, exposing my bare shoulder.

"May I help with that?" Claudio asks.

I hand him the bag. "Thank you."

We exchange a look as I pull my shirt back up.

"Good morning," Luc says over the top of his paper. **Had he seen that little exchange?** "Come. Sit."

Is it my imagination or is he starting to talk to me like I'm his dog?

I walk toward them and my eye is drawn to the sun bouncing off something shiny in the middle of the table.

Luc sets down his paper as I approach. "I thought maybe you'd gotten lost this morning."

"Sorry to be late," I say absently as I step closer, my gaze stuck on the metal object on the table.

"Oh, don't listen to him," Danae says. "You sleep as long as you like."

A maid pulls out my chair and I sit, unable to process what I'm seeing.

Danae leans toward me. "What's wrong, dear?"

"It's just that . . . where did that sculpture come from?"

Luc picks up the brass bird. "Oh, this? Father Peter found it in some shop in Paris after the war. Isn't that right, Grandmother?"

Danae wears a puzzled expression. "Did he? I didn't know."

I can't tear my gaze from the golden dove as he turns it in his hands. It has to be the same one. The squat little body. The pointed beak that had—

"Are you listening?" Luc asks. "I asked if you're okay."

"Fine . . ."

Danae sips her tea. "Art can affect one's emotions quite violently, can it not? My first time in Rodin's garden I could barely contain myself—had the sudden urge to strip off my clothes and run about the garden like a mad woman. Remember that, Luc?"

I resist the urge to run from the table as Luc examines the statue closely.

"It's just a little bird." He turns it in his hands. "Not even that well done, actually."

"I think it's quite nicely cast," Danae says.

I grow light-headed and grip the table edge to steady myself.

Luc holds the bird aloft as he talks. "Father Peter told me there's an interesting story attached to the piece. Something about a murder weapon in an unsolved crime. That the person who made it intended it to be a weapon."

My mouth goes dry. I search his face for any trace of awareness of how I'm connected to that bird.

Danae butters her toast. "That's just a story a dealer made up to make a sale."

"He swore it was true. The police had found it in the pocket of a murdered person's coat. In the Seine."

Danae spreads jelly on her toast. "Ninety people a year end their lives jumping into that river."

"Funny thing is, when people try to cover up a murder by throwing the body in the Seine, they don't realize the river has a current. And most of the bodies end up in the same stretch of—"

Danae sets down her knife. "I would like to enjoy my toast without such conversation, if you please."

Luc hands the bird to me.

"No—" The room shifts. How can I touch that again?

"Oh, go ahead."

Is he testing me? How can I refuse without him suspecting something?

I take the thing, heavy in my hand, and feel the need the retch.

"Sounds like a believable story to me. What do you think, Arlette? You're an artist."

My hands shake as if palsied as I set the bird back in the center of the table. Does he see?

I force myself to meet his gaze. "I would imagine the artist made her without malice aforethought. But I suppose people are forced into desperate situations every day."

Luc raises one index finger. "Ah. Self-defense. There's an idea."

I press my moist palms to the napkin in my lap. "Perhaps."

Luc sets his paper next to his plate and stands. "Well, I'm off." He turns to Claudio. "Take care of Grandmother and the place while I'm gone."

"Of course, sir."

"Miss LaRue as well. But not **too** good care, **compreendo**?"

"Of course," Claudio says with a lingering glance back at me as he carries Luc's bag out the front door.

AFTER BREAKFAST DANAE RETREATS to her bedroom to rest and I set out for the kids' camp, the scent of jasmine in the humid air after a morning shower doused the jungle like water on sauna rocks. With Luc off traveling, I have room to think clearly and untangle it all, still shaken from seeing my brass dove again. It's possible Luc's story about the antiques shop is true, but more likely Father Peter is behind it. Some sort of warning to me?

I regroup and focus on seeing Thomas again, my whole reason for being there, after all. The sooner I make my match and leave this place the better.

Thomas checks so many boxes, right down to Gunther's calm temperament and my family's artistic bent. Even the Wietholter eyes. But why is Father Peter so hostile, making it all so hard?

I arrive at the camp and hear Father Peter lecturing in the distance at the main school hut. Classes end on the hour and I would soon catch Thomas as he changed activities. As I pass Father Peter's office, I surveil the area. Maybe that place holds some answers?

I gently push aside the deer hide that hangs at the door, afraid to discover his dogs in the room.

Finding it free of canines, I stop in for a quick look at the remarkably homey little dirt-floored place, with its bamboo desk and glass-fronted gun cabinet, dead animals the main décor. I avoid stepping on the jaguar rug, once a magnificent beast with a lovely spotted coat, the stuffed head in mid-snarl. A glass-encased dead porcupine navigates a branch. And a spotted deer hide upholsters a bench.

I open his pencil drawer. It's meticulously kept, with paperclips, rubber cement, and pens arranged in the compartments of a silverware organizer. I almost miss a clothbound notebook pushed to the back, and slide it out. I page through the intricate pencil sketches on the first several pages, one of twin cow fetuses cross-sectioned, and I'm repulsed by the macabre detail. I riffle the rest of the blank pages and find a black-and-white photo tucked between them. It's like many I'd seen in my uncle Hans's albums, of four men posing in paramilitary uniform, their high black boots shined bright. **Der Stahlhelm.** The Steel Helmet. It's easy to find a much younger Father Peter in the center. Though just a precursor to the SS, it looks like he was marching with his colleagues back then, not studying at divinity school after all.

I slide the photo into my pocket and tap it there with a satisfied little pat. He'll never know who took it. And how could he ask? "Pardon me, but have you seen my **Der Stahlhelm** photo? It's gone missing."

I replace the notebook and move to the gun cabinet. I bend and examine the lock, a simple one, and see through the glass the rifle Danae had talked about, complete with black scope.

The Vampire gun. What would Josie think of that sleek Nazi rifle?

I turn at the sound of footsteps and find Father Peter standing in the doorway.

"Miss LaRue. What a surprise to find you here."

"Is this your office? I was just admiring the animal—"

"I'm curious to know why we have the pleasure of your company here at camp today."

"To see Thomas of course."

"Did no one tell you?"

I pull at the neckline of my shirt. Suddenly the heat is unbearable.

"The boys are studying for exams today. Cannot be disturbed."

"Surely—"

"I'm sure you agree, Miss LaRue, a child's education always takes priority. And now, unless you have some other business here in my office I must ask you to allow these children their study time and find your way back to Cove House."

"The dogs . . ."

"They are penned for now. But I suggest you don't linger if you'd rather not encounter them."

I TAKE THE JEEP to town. I tamp down a sudden wave of missing Josie. She'd help me figure Father Peter out. But in the meantime, in Josie's absence, the former ambassador turned WHO representative seems a perfect partner to lay it all out with. If Dr. Bondi will even talk with me after the way the Minaus treated her at Cove House.

The Cayenne streets are full of people preparing for Carnival parties, sewing costumes of cayenne-pepper red and amethyst satin, and calling out offers of sweet cakes and rice dishes from makeshift storefronts.

I enter the clinic, the dark room a cool respite from the heat. Dr. Bondi stands at a modern treatment table, fitted with the obligatory strip of waxed paper, doling out candies from a bag to the local children crowding around her.

"One at a time now," Bondi says with a laugh.

They line up, all smiles in anticipation of the sweets. What magnificent children they are, a mix of races and colors, but mostly Maroon, with thick-lashed dark eyes and deep bronze skin, simply dressed in woven sandals, linen shorts, and shifts. How like me as a child. Free to roam. They deserve to live without fear.

"Dr. Bondi?"

She glances toward me and continues doling out the sweets.

"Arlette LaRue. We met at Cove House the other day?"

"It's customary to knock, even in this part of town."

"This is quite a nice clinic."

"I assume you're not here to admire the drapes."

"I just wanted to say I'm happy to help you figure out what's going on at Camp Hope."

She lobs the half-full bag to one child, and the group heads out. "And see some sanitized version of what's really going on?"

"Something there doesn't seem right."

She dismisses me with a glance. "Please. You're one of them. Here to report back?"

"I'm trying to find the son I lost a long time ago and I plan on leaving as soon as that happens."

"Of course you'll leave as soon as you have what you want."

"But if something's going on over there it's important to figure it out together."

"Multiple Maroon boys from this area have been kidnapped and brought to that camp. You bring me some info on them and then we can talk."

"I've only been here a few weeks, and from what I can tell the foundation does some good work, but I think it's Father Peter that's the problem. He may not even be a priest. No man of the cloth I know wears such an expensive gold watch. He may be stealing from the foundation."

Bondi flips through a box of charts. "So?"

"One of my sources at the camp says he saw sick Maroon boys in the camp clinic."

She turns and gives me her full attention. "Presenting with what symptoms?"

"Not sure. But it seems like a lot of little things don't add up."

"Genocide has small beginnings, Miss LaRue."

"The boy I think may be my son—his name is

Thomas—is sick as well. Belly pain. Spiking fevers. He's been told it's anemia."

"Fever is not a symptom of anemia."

Bondi stares at me for a long moment and pulls a horn ornament tied on a leather cord from inside the V of her dress. "A Maroon mother brought this to me. Her missing son's necklace. Found it downstream from their village. She was inconsolable." She slides the necklace back into the neck of her dress. "I wear this to remember. What do I tell the parents? Your sons are just disappearing?"

"It's terrible. Surely the police will help."

"I'm sure the Minaus pay them off."

"Think it's some sort of sickness the boys are dying from?"

"One boy escaped the camp and I treated him here, but his family forced me to release him. Poor thing's lungs were ravaged. Doubt he survived."

"If it's infectious, why isn't everyone sick?"

"Not sure, but thanks to that boy, I made a basic vaccine from the disease-causing antigen, and vaccinate who I can. I assume you've had your inoculations?"

"Privately, before I left Paris. So many shots."

"If you're not presenting with symptoms by now, they've vaccinated you to it or you're immune. Not everyone contracts every virus."

"Why not just have WHO backup come down? They could strong-arm their way in."

"They're short-staffed due to a cholera outbreak in Calcutta. I'm here in an unofficial capacity for now.

Fact-finding. My so-called boss has promised more help soon."

"Sounds sticky."

"Prefers his doctors male," she says with a wry smile. "But I'm committed to this. I'd love to get a blood sample from Thomas. Think you could bring him by? That way I could see if the two illnesses are connected. I've brought my microscope and could do a rudimentary comparison."

"I'll do my best. Can you do a maternity blood matching here?"

"I'm afraid I'm not set up for ABO typing. Requires a centrifuge. Most I can do here is examine the samples."

"Let's stay focused on the real problem here of the Maroon kids disappearing. I know what it's like to lose a child. Let's figure it out together."

WHEN I RETURN TO Cove House I park the jeep and walk by Claudio's quarters, just across the way from my cottage, up a set of outdoor stairs above the garage. I resist the temptation to climb the stairs and peer in the window. I haven't seen him today. What was he doing on his day off?

I hear water running and walk toward the back of the building and stop to watch through a tangled thicket of mangrove trees. It's Claudio, standing in the outdoor shower, just a wooden platform, holding his face up to the stream of a silver shower head.

I lose track of time, watching as he rinses his chest. It's hard not to stare at him, sun glistening off his shoulders, lather running down the curve of his back. I'm unable to turn away as he shuts the taps, runs one hand down his torso, shedding water in bright droplets, and then towels off his chest.

He bends to dry his legs and I realize I'm barely breathing.

Could I be more like a schoolgirl? What is my problem, hiding in the bushes ogling Luc's bodyguard on his day off?

He turns to leave the shower and I hurry off to my cottage. The last thing I need is one more problem in my life.

CHAPTER 34

JOSIE

NURENBERG, GERMANY
1952

IT TAKES US ALMOST A WEEK TO MAKE IT TO Munich from Aunt Bertha's castle, forced to seek shelter due to white-out conditions. We arrive at Landsberg Prison, as if in the midst of a snow-globe blizzard, the entry sign bearing the new name the United States had given it, WAR CRIMINAL PRISON NR. 1.

A sudden warmth prickles the back of my neck.

Herta.

These sessions typically run thirty minutes. Half an hour with her, forced to look at that face, would be interminable. She'd do the usual Nazi protesting—the "how unfair it all was" routine. I just want to keep calm and stay in charge.

The windshield wipers fight a losing battle against the snow as we drive through a cluster of Jewish protestors holding anti-German signs. All at once, from the opposite direction, German demonstrators engulf our car, shove placards across the windshield, and pound the windows. American military police in white helmets hold them back as I grab my manila folder and we exit the car.

I look up at the familiar façade, fat copper Romanesque turrets flanking the entrance. The place where Hitler was imprisoned for treason after the Beer Hall Putsch, it feels like home in a way. I'd spent months visiting here after the war, covering the Nuremberg war crimes trials as a journalist, still devastated after my time at Ravensbrück. I'd never interviewed a prisoner there but sat through hours of Nazi testimony and covered the executions of war criminals, the hangings and firing squads.

Just the thought puts a bit of spring in my step.

I note the high wall around the rear courtyard, happy to see barbed wire still being used against at least some Nazis, seven years after the war's end. I turn and survey the crowd, their faces distorted with anger. At least Herta and Fritz Fischer are still imprisoned here. But with this kind of anti–U.S. pressure, for how long?

A protester throws a bottle that just misses Johann, and an MP hurries us in. I'd forgotten how oddly church-like it feels in that place, our steps clacking the beige checkerboard ceramic tiles, the very ones Hitler once trod.

We knock the snow off our shoes and our contact, James Renfro, a baby-faced agent I'd known briefly when he trained at Fort Bliss, hurries to us. "It's FUBAR out there, am I right?"

"Renfro, this is Johann Vitner, my case officer."

Johann offers his hand.

Renfro nods to Johann, ignoring his hand. "You're lucky I could get you in, Captain. Bonn's limiting American interviews with the prisoners."

"Since when is Germany in charge?" I ask.

He flinches as a snowball hits the window. "They're pushing boundaries these days. Rewriting history. Want all these prisoners released. Did you see Princess von Isenburg out there?"

"Didn't have the pleasure."

"She's lobbying hard to get the whole bunch of them out. Cozy with the Vatican."

"Just what we need."

We start down the hallway. "You get fifteen minutes with Oberheuser. Best I can do."

"Where are we doing this?" Johann asks.

Renfro ignores Johann and directs his comments to me. "Waiting area for the prisoner interview room is down that hall. Just so you know, Oberheuser's a heavy lift. Never a straight answer."

"I got this, Renfro."

"Don't let her run out the clock. She's good at it. And don't tell her anything personal. She has a surprising network on the outside, including that princess. And whatever you do, don't reveal your name."

Renfro hurries off but stops and turns, pointing his index fingers at me like guns, thumbs up. "Watch your six, Anderson. And stay frosty. Oh, and tell Tony P. Jimmy sends his best. Miss that guy."

"You bet," I say, though just the mention of Tony P. tanks my mood further.

Johann and I hurry on, and I turn to him.

"You okay? Renfro's a shit. You outrank him by far."

"I'll survive," he says with a sidelong smile.

We pass the cell Hitler had been imprisoned in before the war, for 264 days, the commemorative plaque and shrubberies once placed there by the Germans as a shrine to him now removed by the U.S. Army. I peek into the cell and find it surprisingly homey, with its worn Persian rug and nice view of the surrounding countryside. "Of course Hitler wrote **Mein Kampf** here. Perfect spot."

"**You** okay?" Johann asks.

"Fine. Not looking forward to chatting with Herta. Brings it all back up, you know?"

"Oh, yes, I do. And she may be hard to crack. But you're so good at establishing rapport. She works here in the prison laundry, maybe talk about that. Then you can play the early release card."

A white-helmeted MP comes and escorts me to the prisoner visitation area, a bland, blue-painted room bisected by a glass wall, identical chest-high counters on each side. He guides me toward the end seat, and I sit. This protective custody unit, with its fake houseplants and doctor's office feel, seems too comfortable for the likes of Herta.

From my briefing doc I know she and the others are excluded from excessive forced labor and given the choice of domestic jobs. What is Herta's day like here? According to the sheet, she plays solitaire and writes medical essays. While my mother's silty remains lie at the bottom of Lake Schwendt.

I watch the second hand sweep around the face of the wall clock. We're already two minutes into my fifteen.

The door on the opposite side opens and the horror of it all rushes back as an MP ushers Herta in. I'm disappointed she's not in wrist shackles, just dressed in a beige coverall, a white shirt peeking through at her throat. She must've said something funny to the MP, for he laughs with her as they enter. She seems to be doing just fine here, and a black serpent coils in my chest.

Herta sits and gazes at me, unblinking. **Does she recognize me? Doubtful. At the camp I'd only seen her from afar, always so smug and imperious when the Nazis were riding high. I'd had a closer view of her at the doctors' trial though as she sat with the other accused, pale and drawn like a captured animal.**

The screen above the glass allows us to speak without a telephone.

My fingertips wet on the papers, I sift through my notes, which I've taken from the dossier Karl sent, a refreshingly thick, complete file, marked SECRET.

She looks more contrite these days, somewhere between bored housewife and serial murderer, but surprisingly good for being behind bars for three years. She's somehow prettier, her hair darker and pulled back in a velvet bow. She sits still against the blue-painted backdrop in her glass box, like a zoo animal in a diorama with the plaque: THE NAZI DOCTOR. NATURAL HABITAT. FEMALE. AGE 41. MATELESS.

"Miss Oberheuser—"

"**Doctor** Oberheuser."

"You've waived your right to have counsel present?"

She stares off to one side.

"Don't tell me you're not feeling social today?"

"What good would a lawyer do me now?"

"It's been seven years since the war ended. How is life here? They tell me you work in the prison laundry."

"Is this the part where you establish rapport with me?"

"I need to ask you some questions, and I suggest you answer honestly."

"Or what? I do read the papers in here. Bonn has declared they'll view our Nuremburg sentences as foreign convictions and therefore not part of our criminal records."

I shrug. "You're not going anywhere. But if you speak honestly, I may be able to expedite things for you."

Herta sits up straighter.

I try to fake a natural smile. "I trust they're treating you according to the Geneva Conventions?"

She spreads her hands like Saint Francis of Assisi. "All the **LIFE** magazines I can read. But, of course, I shouldn't even be in here. It's—"

"Many of your colleagues are gone now."

"Hanged two hundred and fifty-nine of them right here in the gymnasium."

I lean in. "Don't forget the twenty-nine by firing squad. You were all found guilty."

She stares me down. "The victor writes the history. But I was not guilty."

"In your pretrial affidavit you admitted you killed 'many prisoners with an injection to the heart.' Why did you lie about that at the trial?"

"You were doing well before that question."

"Maybe you'd rather not get out of here."

She exhales a long sigh. "Such a thing was nothing at all extraordinary. In the Ravensbrück milieu, where thousands of those unfit for work were being culled constantly, a few mercy killings was absolutely nothing that might be particularly noticed. We were told not to make a fuss about it."

"You knew it was wrong."

"I believe in obedience. We simply didn't ask questions. Hitler couldn't have made a mistake." She looks to the ceiling. "It was not my business. But as an outsider one cannot understand this."

"I was at Ravensbrück, Herta."

She regards me with wary, fresh awareness. "You

only have fifteen minutes, four of which are already gone. And they **will** boot you out. They're remarkably punctual for Americans."

"Your boss Dr. Snow was a busy one. Created the **Kinderzimmer.** What was that exactly?"

She pauses. "An experiment of sorts."

"And?"

She looks around the room. "Hitler had ruled that no child could be born at a concentration camp, so those children had to be, well, dealt with, which rendered those prisoners who gave birth unfit for work, from the depression of losing a child. So, the **Kinderzimmer** was created, a block where just the mothers lived, with their children, to see if this made them more productive workers."

"And was this experiment successful?"

"The mothers were happier certainly to see their children when they came back to the block after work. And yes, became more productive."

"And then? You and Dorothea Binz used to visit the children, didn't you? To play with them?"

"I don't remember."

"But the children were given no food."

Herta looks away.

"They started to die, am I right? As a physician, how could you sanction that?"

"The life of Germany took precedence over a crisis of conscience. Food was scarce. Needed for the soldiers."

"There was plenty in the officers' dining hall. Red Cross packages."

"Is this what you came to talk about?"

"And then one day the children just disappeared. To where?"

Herta sighs. "You're just wasting time."

"There was a boy . . . named Willie."

She flashes a glance at me.

"Son of a German soldier. What happened to him?"

She shrugs one shoulder. "Binz took him."

"So, he's alive?" A sweet trill runs through me.

"That's all I know. If you want to eat up your time speculating, be my guest."

She's telling the truth.

I check my notes. "Dr. Snow oversaw experiments, as well. Sulfa, sterilization. Was the final word on selections."

"Snow was a true genius."

I slap a photo against the glass, of the group shot of three men taken from Aunt Bertha's wall.

"Can you identify these people?"

She considers it for a moment. "Hmmm. Let me see."

Outside the window the snow turns to freezing rain, ice crystals pelting the glass.

"Well, the tall one is Fritz Fischer. But you already know that."

"You can't ID the other men?"

She looks away and rubs one ear. "Don't know them."

I take down the photo. "Who else did you report to?"

Herta inhales deeply. "Many people. Dr. Gebhardt among them. Dr. Schreiber. There were over one hundred doctors there at different times, and I reported to many. It was quite lonely there since there were only two other women doctors and the female guards to socialize with. The vast majority were men whom I found vastly disappointing in terms of intellect and family background."

"What did you do to the prisoners in those experiments? My mother was among them."

"I don't remember the subjects—"

"Her name was Lylou."

"Oh. The singer."

"I recently discovered she was very sick from some sort of experiment. Was that true?"

"It was not my job to determine if something was true or not."

"I've checked with my boss and since you had a hand in her death, we'd like to try to extend your sentence. Good news is you get to stay here another, what, ten years?"

Herta glances at the guard. "I know nothing about the viral trials."

"I didn't say anything about viral trials, but since you did, tell me more."

She sits back and examines her hands for a few moments. "I was just their errand girl."

"Do you know about Snow's connection to those experiments? What he planned to do?"

"Perhaps."

"Then we're prepared to offer you a reduced sentence in exchange for that."

"The newspapers say we're being considered for reduced sentences already."

"I'll propose immunity."

She barely moves. "Full?"

I nod, as my stomach contracts. "A release for good behavior. But I want specifics and don't waste my time."

"Five-minute warning," the MP calls out.

"What was Snow doing in those trials?" I ask. "And is he still doing it and where?"

She cocks her head to one side, mouth agape. "Clearly you don't have a top-secret security clearance, or you wouldn't be asking the question that way."

My cheeks burn. "Hurry up."

She evades my gaze. "I don't know what they're doing now if anything. But at Ravensbrück they were studying infectious disease resistance."

"Elaborate."

"We all knew Hitler had tabun and sarin gas. He'd promised a secret weapon he'd use to win the war, and we expected him to use it anytime. Of course, he never did." She inspects her cuticles.

"Herta . . ."

She sighs. "Dr. Blome handled certain viral cultures in his private lab in Poland. As an infectious disease doctor, I could have been more help, but I was needed on the sulfa trials. Dr. Gebhardt shared some details, as he often did with the more interesting experiments."

"Such as?"

She glances at the guard and leans in ever so slightly.

"I know they were looking for particular test subjects among the camp **Häftlings.**"

"Don't use that word."

She sighs. "Very well. **Prisoners.** I helped with the selection of these subjects. There was one group of Hungarian children from a remote area that Snow was very interested in."

Our Fleur.

"Another group was chosen as well, after it was determined they were abnormally healthy organisms."

Tears sting my eyes. "My mother was one of those."

"I believe they then studied disease spread among them, but I was not allowed to participate. Gebhardt said this type of trial had never been done before."

"Hitler wanted to hold the world hostage with some sort of disease?"

"Others had attempted it, and apparently we were almost there but couldn't produce the required vaccines quickly enough. Every German needed to be protected."

"Where's Snow now?"

"They don't write me updates."

"Did Snow operate out of Kurt Blome's lab in Poland?"

She looks puzzled. "No. Poland would be a waste of your time."

"Is Snow still in Germany?"

The freezing rain pelts the window harder.

She locks in on my face. "Clearly you have no idea what you're dealing with. Typical of Americans to run off half-cocked."

"Do you know about him or not?"

She glances at the guard. "I'm not . . ."

I start to rise. "Feel free to protect Snow while he stays out there and you're in here."

Herta hesitates, the sounds of the protestors outside dissipating. She stands, steps to the coffee table behind her, picks up one of the **LIFE** magazines, and flips through it.

"I'm waiting, Herta."

She dog-ears a page and hands it to the guard, who puts it through the drawer to me.

Herta sits. "In this, last December's copy, you will find many amusing stories. Like a profile on a pet woodpecker named Throckmorton and a politician riding an elephant through Oklahoma. Such an intellectually rich country, America. But make sure you don't miss a particularly interesting story about the Vatican. Don't overlook Bishop Hudal."

"How did he help Snow?"

"All I can say is, go visit Saint Mary."

"I don't—"

"In Rome. I expect you will keep the source confidential. If certain people find out I helped—"

"Time's up," the MP calls out.

Herta leans in. "So, when will I be released?"

"Maybe I'll put in a request."

"But I deserve an answer."

I stand. "You didn't get **close** to what you deserve."

The MP steps toward us.

Herta regards me calmly, as she had faced so many prisoner patients. "Relax, Miss Anderson."

I pause. **She knows my name.**

Craving oxygen, I head for the door.

She calls after me. "You'd better watch yourself. Once word gets out you're looking for Snow, you won't be around long enough to care."

JOHANN AND I WAIT in his ice-entombed car, idling in the prison parking lot after the protesters have disbanded in the freezing rain. Our breath fogs the windows as the heater tries to huff warm air. The idea that Herta knows my name hangs around my neck like a weight.

"She figured out my name somehow."

"Josie—"

"I told her Lylou was my mother, and she must've pieced it together. I guess people knew she was married to a diplomat."

"How'd it go otherwise?"

I blow on my hands. "Gotta say, I think she was mostly telling the truth."

"That viral trials info alone was worth the trip."

Johann pages through the **LIFE** magazine Herta supplied, the sun-kissed beach girl on the cover looking strangely at home in the freezing car. "But it's very weird they let the prisoners read American magazines."

"They've been doing it for years. Dr. Gebhardt used a **LIFE** article in his own defense at the doctors' trial."

He opens the magazine to the Vatican article. "So Herta's saying Bishop Hudal is the go-to guy for Snow intel?"

"She said, 'Visit Saint Mary,' whatever that means."

He turns the windshield wipers on, and they scrape against the ice. "Could be a reference to the Santa Maria dell'Anima church in Rome. A haven for German-speaking people there. Hudal's the bishop."

I blow warmth on my knuckles. "Doesn't make sense a priest would support Nazi murderers."

"Hudal's Austrian. They call him the Brown Bishop, a reference to the Nazi brown uniforms. During the war, he tried to cozy up to Hitler. Hates communism and especially Russia. He's going with the home team, I guess."

"Why do I not have his file?"

"Need a top-secret clearance. I know it's frustrating, but Karl wants you to get your own info. Your orders list Poland as your next stop."

"Herta says that's a waste of time."

"You believe her?"

"I do. Think I need to get to Rome."

"Why not check out that Polish lab? I'm tied up the next few days and it's a lot safer than Rome. Half the world's creeps hang out there today. A cesspool of agents and double agents, Italian intelligence, dirty Vatican dignitaries, and former Nazis."

"Fun."

"Herta knows who you are. If she somehow tells that princess pal of hers you're looking for Snow, they'll hunt you down. Not to mention the Russians are tracking us by now. Soviets, NKVD, Cominform. They don't fool around."

"I'll watch my back. Karl will get me in with Hudal."

"It's your show. I'll catch up with you there."

"Where you off to?"

"I have a few things to attend to here—potentially big. I'll tell you when we meet up in Rome. I'll book the Grand Hotel Plaza. Best bathtubs in Rome."

"Wish I liked baths. Showers feel so much cleaner."

"Just to make sure you behave yourself, I'll get us a two-bedroom suite so I can keep an eye on you."

He hands me a film canister. "And this is from our visit to Aunt Bertha. Isolate the frame of Snow's office when you get a minute? In the meantime, wait for me to arrive before you go **anywhere.** Karl has his own reasons for putting you on this, but it's more dangerous than you may realize."

"I have a plan."

"And stay away from temptations that might arise, of the **Aaron** variety. Chances are he'll be there since he can somehow read your mind."

"I'm over all that, Johann."

"He's an experienced agent, Josie. And not necessarily on our side."

"I've got this. You forget I worked in the underground."

"The world has gotten exponentially more

complicated. Lie low until I get there. Trust me, we're playing with fire. And for the love of God, don't be so damned stubborn."

"You're not the first to give me that advice," I say as my mother's face takes shape in front of me and suddenly I'm back at the camp.

CHAPTER 35

JOSIE

RAVENSBRÜCK
1945

Before.

I ALMOST DIDN'T RECOGNIZE MY MOTHER AS SHE arrived at Ravensbrück one morning at dawn. A **Blockova** was hurrying our work crew to the great warehouses we called Canada for another day at the sorting piles, and we stopped to let her group pass by. They marched five abreast, and she was on the end of a row, her hair wet under a gray kerchief tied at the nape of her neck, fresh from the intake showers, a yellow star already sewn on the sleeve of her once navy blue dress. Tears filled my eyes. It was the one she'd worn the last time I saw her in Paris.

Her group stood a stone's throw away, and I stepped out of line toward her.

"Mother, it's me," I called in a loud whisper.

She turned, one hand to her mouth. "Oh, **Josie, ma petite.** You mustn't speak to me."

"Where's Mimi?"

Her group began marching again, and I started after her.

Ariana held me back. "They're on their way to the Jewish barracks. You can't let on that she's your mother. They'll put you there, too."

She didn't have to say what we all knew. Women in the Jewish blocks received the worst treatment, and once they were unable to work Dr. Snow put them first on the transport lists. Most didn't survive long.

The group moved on, and Mother looked back as she walked.

"I'll find you," I mouthed, as they marched on, every part of me ruined.

She shook her head. **"No."**

We marched off in opposite directions.

"I have to see her," I whispered to Ariana.

"She'll be in one of the Jewish blocks. No way you're getting in there."

"I will," I said, glancing back as the guard hurried them off at a running march. "I don't care if it's impossible."

"I suppose nothing is impossible," Ariana said as we marched on. "All we need is a plan."

—

ONE NIGHT ARIANA CAME to me in the bunk with news.

"I spoke with my friend Anna in Commandant Suhren's office. She helps schedule the Jewish work crews."

"Oh, Ariana—"

"It isn't easy though, Josie. She can try to get you assigned to the same work detail as your mother, but it's risky. They change the assignments daily and not all details are mixed Gentile and Jew."

"And the ones that are?"

"You know those jobs are the hardest here? Designed to kill faster?"

"I don't care."

"And you may not even get to talk to her. And if you do, it will be brief."

"I understand."

"So, Anna agreed to try this—one time only. Tomorrow you'll be expected to report to the road work crew. Your mother as well."

I pulled Ariana close and held her. "How can I thank you?"

"Be careful. There's extra scrutiny on the Jewish crews, and punishment's much swifter. You've never seen anything like the bunker. Solitary confinement. Lashings."

"I know, Ariana. Thank you."

I didn't care. Tomorrow I would see my mother.

—

IT WAS STILL DARK when I reported to the road work crew, happier to show up for work than I'd ever been at that place. Searchlights flashed across the camp yard, as our **Blockovas** marched their groups to the work site. The prisoners who'd been there longer wore uniforms; the newcomers wore the clothes they were arrested in or some hybrid of clothes repurposed by the camp staff.

Dorothea Binz stood beside a dirt road along the edge of the camp, dog at her side. A small mountain of gray gravel and the enormous concrete roller I'd seen so many women pull, working to lay down new roads, stood at the foot of the road, almost as tall as me.

The news that sadist Binz was our supervising guard was not the best, but nothing could dull my excitement at seeing my mother. I just wanted to spend the day with her. To hear how she got there. About Mimi. And plot our way out of that place. Just to touch her again.

As we lined up five abreast, I searched the women's faces for Mother, but it was hard to see in the darkness.

Binz announced the usual warning. "No talking. No touching. No resting. The work shy will be punished." She then called out instructions. "Five at a time you will pull the roller when ordered."

She read the numbers and five women stepped to take their places behind the iron bar, my mother the last of them.

Mother. How pale she looked.

This was a terrible change of events. How would I speak with her there?

Binz walked among us. "The rest of you will lay gravel to prepare the road for the roller."

The others, experienced in the procedure, squatted to take handfuls of gravel and scoop them onto the road as Mother and the others raised the iron bar and pressed their weight against it, pulling the roller forward.

I carried handfuls of gravel to the road as Mother and the four others heaved the roller over the sharp stones, embedding them. How I yearned to trade places with Mother, seeing her strain that way, but I kept at my work, hoping for any chance to be near her.

Before long, one of the women pulling the roller fell to the ground.

"Aufhören!" Binz called out, and her assistant dragged the woman to a ditch next to the road. The Germans had no middle ground. If you could work, you were alive. If not, you were dead.

Taking advantage of the distraction and the fact that no one was rushing to take the poor woman's place, I quickly stood next to my mother, hands on the roller handle.

At Binz's command the five of us resumed the task, lifted the iron bar, and pushed with our entire weight. How slowly that roller moved, and mere inches, even with all of our strength behind it.

I leaned in toward Mother. "It's me," I whispered. How I longed to reach out to her.

She glanced left. "Oh, Josie."

Was it my imagination or did a smile play at her lips?

"I had to see you. I've written to Father and—"

Binz passed close by, so I stopped talking until she left.

"I haven't heard back yet, but he will help us."

"You mustn't visit me like this. Why are you so stubborn?"

"How were you arrested? Was it Mimi's radio?"

She nodded. Even in the darkness I could see that her eyes shone with tears.

We pulled the roller in silence, the woman next to her straining, softly moaning.

"Gestapo?" I asked.

"No chance to prepare." She leaned closer. "I have the necklace though. She would be happy."

This was my turn to smile. "How?"

"I'd kept it in the heel of my shoe just in case. Thank goodness they let us keep our clothes."

One of the gravel scoopers fell to her knees. Binz pounced and beat her with her crop, the poor woman creating another welcome diversion.

"How were you arrested?" Mother asked.

"I wanted to tell you for a long time, but I was working in the resistance."

She nodded. Of course, she knew.

"But it was a strange fluke. A young urchin we

knew stole an SS man's wallet and they followed her to Arlette's apartment. They saw some underground newspapers we were bundling and got us on that."

The exhausted gravel scooper lay silent but Binz kept kicking the poor woman's belly.

"So, they don't know you are the Doves?" Mother asked.

I turned to her in the dark. "You knew that was us?"

She nodded and stood a little taller. "I'm proud of you, **ma chère.** The courage—"

"Did Mimi know?"

"She's the one who pieced it together," Mother whispered. "Knew by the description on the radio. She was so very pleased. Of course, claimed you inherited **her** courage."

I leaned closer and touched her hand. "And Mimi—did she—"

All at once my scalp burned, as Binz pulled me by the hair, away from Mother's side.

Binz handed me off to her assistant to take me to the bunker, and as she dragged me, I looked back to see Binz shove another worker into my place.

As I headed off to serve my time in solitary all I could think was, **My mother is so proud of me. And the days in solitary will be good. Plenty of time to figure out how to get her out of here.**

CHAPTER 36

ARLETTE

FRENCH GUIANA
1952

CLAUDIO IS ON AN ERRAND FOR DANAE SO I make my way alone over to the cove at the kids' camp to sketch it for Danae's brochure, walking the sandy path. This time I've had Danae clear my visit with Father Peter so I will be free to roam the camp. I sling my bag across my chest, my grief box, sketch pad, and charcoal knocking about inside it as I walk. All is quiet there, for it is study time. I pass the fenced-off area and look up to judge where I am in relation to Father Peter's watchtower. Is he up there observing all?

I take the long way near the beach, with hopes of seeing Claudio again. Why am I still thinking about it? How ridiculous of me to become reduced to a quivering mess just because I saw a naked man shower. Am I that desperate? It had just been a small moment but a delicious one.

I walk on along an unfamiliar high woven rush fence. The one Luc told me about, which leads to the interior of the peninsula? I find a narrow opening in the rush and consider squeezing through it. If caught I could just claim I wanted new subjects to sketch.

I sidle through the opening in the fence and find the path on the other side is no more than what we called a deer track back in Krautergersheim, badly overgrown. But clearly someone else has been treading this same path for it has not succumbed completely to the woody lianas vines and other jungle vegetation.

A rustle in the underbrush startles me and I'm relieved to find it is only a shaggy anteater hunting the jungle floor. As I walk, I try to stay on one straight path when it forks, to avoid further losing my way, and try not to think too much about jaguars and large snakes.

Just as I'm about to turn back, I sense movement in the distance. I nearly miss it since it blends into the surrounding flora so well, a human form, perhaps an older child, dressed in bland colors except for a slash of crimson. I barely breathe, still as a cat, and watch the figure approach. Soon I see it's a girl, no more than twelve or thirteen, wearing a drab shift and kerchief, her feet bare. She's carrying something—

a stack of folded clothes?— and I wait for her to notice me first so I can observe as long as possible.

She spots me and freezes there on the path.

I reach out one arm. "Don't be afraid. I'm Arlette. Staying at Cove House. The Blue Cottage."

She surveys me for a moment and then drops the clothes onto the path, turns, and runs.

I follow her. "Come back!"

I gather the clothes she left, red shirts like those worn by the boys at the camp. Had she been on her way to deliver them? I walk the path for a bit longer but the vegetation only grows more dense.

"Are you there?" I call out and hear only the sounds of the darkening jungle.

I gather the shirts to my face, breathe in the scent of laundry soap, and then turn and retrace my steps. Even more convinced there's something dreadfully wrong going on down here.

CHAPTER 37

JOSIE

ROME, ITALY
1952

ONCE THE SNOWSTORM SUBSIDES I TAKE THE train to Rome, and it has never looked more beautiful, the Spanish Steps covered in a powdered sugar dusting of snow. Or more **sinistra.** After Johann's cryptic warning to watch my back, I imagine every man in an overcoat, hat brim tipped down, is following me and I take a taxi to the hotel. My instincts are telling me the Herta tip was a good one and I expect a breakthrough from Hudal. I've cabled Karl to get me in with the bishop, and I wait on his response.

Once I make it to the Grand Hotel Palace, it's a relief to be safely home. I enter the lobby, the chandelier shimmering over the hand-painted walls of the lobby just as I remember it.

It's good to revisit this place where Mother first took me for a birthday "girls' trip," both of us reading the Italian newspapers in bed, our breakfast trays heavy with gleaming hotel silver. "This is how every thirteen-year-old should ring in their birthday," Mother said, in her negligee and bed jacket, sipping espresso.

I step to the front desk, excited to use my Italian. "Josie Anderson checking in. A suite with Johann Vitner?"

"Mr. Vitner's not here yet," the clerk says, tapping two envelopes on the desk.

His name is Matteo, if his name badge is to be trusted, and with his dark good looks he's like something out of central casting—the chiseled Italian male, a bit older than most desk clerks, his hair prematurely graying, more salt than pepper.

He hands me a heavy brass room key and the two envelopes. "He is arriving tomorrow, actually. We put you in the presidential suite, his favorite. With the views from the terrace of Saint Peter's dome." He leans in. "Splendid decoration. The lavatory alone is fit for a queen. Ava Gardner's favorite. Last time she stayed for two weeks."

Matteo arranges a telegram to Arlette at Cove House in French Guiana, to share Herta's news about Willie. MET OLD FRIEND OF OURS SAYS WILLIE SURVIVED CAMP.

And then for good measure I scribble a quick hotel postcard to her and drop it in the red-painted iron postbox just off the lobby, the very one my mother and I had used during our stay there. If I'd known Arlette's phone exchange, I would've tried to call her just to hear her voice. The joy of hearing her discover my new evidence that our Willie might truly be alive.

I hurry up the sweeping white marble staircase and run one hand down the mane of Mother's favorite lion statue that guards the steps to the presidential suite, which is even grander than advertised, the dome of Saint Peter's in full view. I step through the thickly carpeted living room, past a carved marble fireplace to a small kitchenette. I check the two bedrooms and move on to the dazzling white-tiled bathroom, complete with bidet and claw-footed soaking tub.

I open the first envelope and find an encrypted cable from Fort Bliss. WHY NO POLAND? NO-GO ON BISHOP HUDAL TOMORROW. STAND BY FOR ORDERS. Karl is pissed I came to Rome instead of Poland. But it was he who said to use my instincts and get my own intel.

In the other envelope is a note from my father, who is requesting I meet him in the hotel bar at eight o'clock.

I chuck the note into the wastebasket. How does he know I'm here? Of course, William Wesley Anderson knows everything. He has one of the top jobs in the CIA, head of European operations, one of the director's right-hand men.

I fish the note out of the wastebasket. If I must endure a conversation with him, maybe I can at least pry out some of that knowledge about Snow.

That evening I step into the hotel bar, one of the loveliest in Rome, with its red velvet banquettes, cherubs and saints painted on the ceiling, and massive oil paintings depicting ancient Rome gallery-lit on the walls. Patrons gather around black cocktail tables, chatting in golden pools of low light, the four-seat walnut bar and the underlit bottles of premium alcohol behind it the focal point of the room. I marvel that even though red is the dominant color used, through some magic of Italian decorating it manages to avoid looking like a house of prostitution and exudes nothing but Old World charm.

Dad sits on a stool at the bar drinking Jim Beam neat, in a haze of cigarette smoke, so thick I can barely see the bartender, the stool closest to the door of course, as every training manual suggests. I consider how to broach the subject of Snow. Best to let him bring it up. And then prepare to endure his overexplaining.

I just have to stay calm.

I approach cautiously since it's been a little tense after our last face-to-face, a two-hour screaming match at my Fort Bliss apartment, which ended in my neighbor calling the police and Dad becoming best friends with half the El Paso force.

His crew cut is shorter, but otherwise he looks remarkably unchanged, in his J. Press blue pinstriped suit and tortoiseshell glasses.

I take the stool next to him. "I see you've found the whiskey."

"Since when are you such a Puritan?" he asks. "Actually, the Puritans brought over more beer than water."

Suddenly I crave Scotch.

He toasts me with his glass. "You should have some. Might make you a more enjoyable companion."

"How'd you know I'm here? Karl?"

"I happen to be concerned about you."

He's a skilled liar so it's hard to know if that's true. "You're ten years too late."

"There's a reason new agents aren't sent out alone."

"I have a case officer."

"Johann Vitner?" He rolls his eyes and downs the rest of his drink. "Hear you wrote a book."

"A pamphlet. Where's Lucinda?"

"Lucretia." He waves toward the door. "Ah, my Juliet."

"Juliet was fourteen, Dad. Forty-year age difference."

Lucretia sways into the bar, displaying more lively cleavage than all the Gabor sisters combined. She sidles up to my father and kisses him on each cheek.

He accepts a rocks glass from the bartender and offers it to her like a boy who's brought home an art project for his mother. "I ordered you gin."

She slides one hand along his thigh. "You take such good care of me."

She's rich, Dad's favorite type, and it shows in her grooming, her nails perfectly buffed, hair color close to natural, as if she spent the war at the Terme Bagno Vignoni spa. Her family is in construction, but the details of her fortune are fuzzy. Perhaps she's wisely less trusting than my mother was when it comes to mixing matters of money and the heart.

Lucretia takes a healthy sip, then turns her attention to me. **"Giuseppina."**

She even smells rich, as she leans toward me.

"So very good to see you," she says, kissing me on both cheeks.

"Is it?"

She resembles my mother so closely it's uncanny. The masses of dark hair worn up in a messy updo and the voluptuous curves. Even down to the red lipstick. Only major difference is her entire personality.

Lucretia sips her gin, slides a golden compact from her bag, and checks her lipstick.

It's hard not to notice the bracelet on her wrist, a diamond bangle set in what looks like platinum.

She snaps the compact closed. "Nice to see you haven't changed, darling."

Closer up, it's clear my father's second wife has aged considerably since we last met two years ago. No doubt she'd found living with William Wesley Anderson less than restful.

"I can't stay long," she says. "Meeting Salvatore for a quick bite. That's Salvatore Rebecchini. The mayor of Rome."

"I figured."

"We're very close. He can barely order without asking me what to choose. Like Billie here." She leans into my father and strokes his hair, causing a little bile to burn my throat.

Light catches the diamond ring on her hand.

"Nice ring," I say.

"Can you believe it? It is the tin anniversary, and Billie finally gives me a diamond."

Lucretia's visit is over blessedly quick, and she weaves her way out of the bar.

"Wow," I say. "She's a gem."

He watches her go. "She's old money."

"Your favorite kind."

Dad drains his second drink. "Your bitterness ages you." He waves to the bartender for another.

"You gave her your grandmother's ring? You didn't even give that to Mother."

"Rumor is Karl has sent you on a big assignment. Must be important. Not that I'd trust his judgment."

"Nice friend."

"Well, he certainly hasn't taught you much." He lights a cigarette. "You haven't once assessed your surroundings. Army training is abysmal. But rumor is they've sent you after a high-value target."

"Are we going to eat something, or do I just watch you assault your liver?"

"If it's Snow, you're in over your head. We're talking about an extensive network. They protect one another, the bastards. All that blood-and-soil crap."

I wave the bartender over to order a glass of Barolo but he ignores me.

Dad adjusts his alligator watchband. "But those high-profile cases do rocket a career. Like mine."

"I'm not you, thank God."

He sets one forearm on the bar and leans in, sending a not-so-terrible wave of Bay Rum aftershave. Mother had loved that scent on him.

"Let's be honest, you got whatever assignment you're on because of me."

"Please." I finally flag down the bartender, and order my Barolo.

"If it **is** Snow you want, you're not alone. Word is he's on Russia's list, to complete their Nazi brain trust. And don't forget the Israelis. Your people, I suppose. Is this a technical collection? Black bag job?"

It's good to have him doing the wondering for a change.

He sits back. "At least tell me how you ended up here?"

"A tip."

"About Bishop Hudal, I bet. Am I right?"

I shrug one shoulder.

"He's a piece of work. And on the U.S. payroll no less."

"You're joking."

"Fifty dollars a month. Did you not get his file? Wait. Do you still not have top-secret clearance? Jesus."

I try to act casual. "Karl wants me to put my own intel together."

"He has you pissing up a rope when half of Rome is probably already tailing you. Do you even know how the ratline works?"

"Mostly by—"

He huddles close. "**One.** The Nazis ski over the Alps and across the border. They all went up there after the war. Hid in the upper mountains since the Brits and Americans looking for them were too lazy to hike up that far. **Two.** They cross the border into Italy. Met by priests and Nazi sympathizers who provide train tickets and a little money."

"And where—"

"**Three.** They arrive here in Rome and Hudal takes it from there."

"And the pope's okay with it?"

"His Holiness holds Hudal at arm's length but hasn't stopped him."

"So, why's Hudal on the U.S. payroll?"

Dad glances about the room. "I can only say that we're in deeper than you might think."

"Did we invent the ratline?"

He raises his eyebrows, impressed for once. "You get your quick thinking from me, I guess. Nice way to make sure we get a gander at what Nazi scientists we want to grab for ourselves, don't you think?"

"And did Hudal help Snow?"

"I can't do all your work for you. But if you do find Snow, don't screw it up by taking him out yourself because of that business at the camp."

A hot flush creeps up my neck. "You mean how he experimented on my mother—your wife, if you recall—and selected her to die, along with thousands of other innocent women at Ravensbrück?"

"You still haven't put all that behind you? You go rogue and kill Snow and you're done, you realize that, right?" He inspects his new drink.

"You'd be fine with all of them walking away free after what they did, wouldn't you? You'd feel differently if they'd killed six million Episcopalians."

He leans closer. "I know how you feel. Like pulling that trigger's the only thing that'll cleanse the stain. But it won't kill what's in your head."

"Thanks for the fatherly advice."

Dad turns back to his drink. "Maybe Karl picked the wrong agent for this."

"Maybe."

He waves his glass in my direction. "But then again, you've never made good decisions."

"Do tell, Dad."

"Turned down Yale for Columbia. Worked as a reporter."

"Liked their engineering program. And I always wanted to be a reporter."

"Good for you. You chose your failings. Didn't just discover them by accident."

I search the Scotch bottles behind the bar and find that beautiful white label. **Macallan Single Malt.**

"Karl hired you because I asked him to, so don't mess this up. You can go all the way if you deliver Snow by the book. Big appointment by the president. What more do you want?"

I look around the bar. "More than this life. Foreign service, maybe. Co-workers I can collaborate with. I want an equal relationship with a life partner who cares about me."

"Male or female?"

He knows about Ariana. I shrug one shoulder, knowing what I'm about to say will poke him. "Why do I have to choose?"

He shakes the ice in his glass. "That'll get you an early leave from the army."

"How do you know about Ariana?" All at once it comes to me. "You surveilled my therapy session? What's wrong with you?"

He shrugs. "Major Vincent and I go way back."

"Bet you do," I say, not sure if I feel more violated by the privacy breach or more touched he took the time to be interested in my welfare.

"I also want forgiveness from my mother," I say.

He drains his glass. "Too late for that. Besides, she got herself into that mess."

"How? By you leaving us in Paris to fight the Nazis by ourselves? Your Jewish wife, her sick mother, and your teenage daughter?"

He winces. "This again? I tried to get you all to leave, but you wouldn't."

"Mimi was sick."

"Mimi was a stubborn old Jew."

"I won't—" I turn to leave.

He grabs my forearm, and it feels oddly good, him touching me, finally caring.

"Josie. Listen to me. I loved your mother like I've never loved anyone. We were inseparable. And when you were born, we were just over the moon."

I swallow hard. "She loved you so much."

"We had the best life in the world, Lylou at her apogee as a singer, me rising fast." He leans in. "A cute-as-hell, loving daughter. Remember when we first got to Paris, the three of us on the Eiffel Tower? Your mother breaking out in song up there? We were on top of the world."

We both pause, lost in the memory of it, and I try not to well up.

He shakes his head. "Until Hitler brought it all down."

"Why did you leave?"

"I missed you both every minute we were parted. Did my damnedest to get you all out."

I pull my arm away. "Did you? Just wrote us a few short letters while we were stuck in Paris."

"I sent **six** detailed letters. It wasn't my fault those bastards kept most of them. But I knew they were monitoring everything. It would have been suicide for me to show up in Paris, and you know it."

"And when we were sent to Ravensbrück, even then you didn't try to get us out. A Gestapo agent had to get your attention."

He flicks that thought away. "I didn't even know you'd been sent to a camp. Your mother, either. They'd reassigned me to research and analysis, here in Rome, and I didn't think to check the transport lists. I figured so close to D-Day we'd be reunited anytime."

"You had no intel about the camps?"

"We knew they existed, but no one understood the magnitude of it, I swear."

"You saw no reconnaissance photos? Please."

"Not one was identified as a death camp. We had no idea the scale of it all."

"What does it matter? You'd already moved on with Lucretia."

"That's bullshit," he says, shifting in his seat.

"Is it? She says you just had your tin anniversary. That's **ten years,** Dad. You were living with her when Mom and I were stuck in Paris."

"I expect better reasoning from you after all those Columbia classes."

I try to breathe. "When we went to Cartier to pawn Mimi's ring, they told us you'd had a diamond bracelet made for someone. Mother knew it wasn't her. Broke her heart."

"Didn't Socrates say, 'Knowledge and belief differ'?"

"Look at you, lousy with deceptive indicators. Just admit you're full of crap. You know **every**one. But you couldn't immediately get the State Department to write a letter to the camp commandant requesting your family be released?"

"You should be grateful I got you and that friend of yours out."

"Just too late for Mom. If you'd acted sooner, she'd be here right now." I look about the room for a moment to compose myself. "Did you know that in Judaism, when someone dies, they sit Shiva and then continue mourning for thirty days? Some say Kaddish every day for eleven months, in remembrance. Not you."

"Since when are you Miss Old Testament? Don't put that on your résumé."

"Maybe it was a convenient solution for you. Got us out of the way so you could live the good life here with her. You'd already squandered Mom's trust fund. And you were never comfortable with the Jewish thing, anyway, were you? Now you could go back to the club."

"You don't know the whole story." He signals for the check. "And be careful with Karl. He's—"

"Karl Crowell is twice the man you are."

He knocks back the rest of his drink. "Hate ages a woman, you know. You should give it up. Try forgiveness."

"That won't be happening." I snatch my wineglass and slide off the stool. "The hate is all I have left."

CHAPTER 38

ARLETTE

FRENCH GUIANA
1952

"ARE YOU READY TO SHOP?" DANAE EMERGES from the bedroom wing of Cove House perfectly coiffed and resplendent in a powder blue caftan.

How do I tell this kind woman who has done so much to help me find my son, "No, I'd rather do anything than wander the stores of Cayenne on this scorching hot day"?

Danae eyes my outfit, the well-worn capris and tunic, my home-sewn bag across my chest, but she keeps her thoughts to herself.

We step out to find Claudio standing near Danae's exquisite black Citroën. He hurries to open the back door closest to us for Danae, and then rounds the back of the car.

"You don't need to open my door," I say, following him.

He opens it and stands aside.

"Let him do his job," Danae says from inside the car.

As I step into the back seat, he rests his hand on the small of my back, causing a lovely little jolt of electricity there.

I sit next to Danae, and she leans toward me releasing her glorious gardenia scent. "People in menial jobs **enjoy** their work. Don't fight it. Besides, you are moving up in the world, Arlette. You are the public relations face of Minau Enterprises. You must embrace your new station in life."

Claudio adjusts the rearview mirror so I can see his eyes. **How humiliating for him to be spoken of in such a way.**

Danae pulls an envelope from her handbag. "This came to your attention."

I pluck the letter from her fingers, perhaps a bit too hastily, and read the return address.

LE JOYEUX OISEAU CAFÉ
ÎLE DE LA CITÉ
PARIS

Marianne. I rip the top of the envelope, slide out a letter, and read the short note. **We all miss you but**

remain envious you are basking in the warmth. It's like medicine just seeing her flowing hand.

A woman came looking for you here today. Said she is your aunt's sister and claims the police would like to know where you are. I didn't tell her anything and had a time of it getting her to leave. Did I do the right thing?

I set the letter down with a shaking hand. True to her word, Auntie's sister won't stop until I'm caught.

What will Thomas do without me if I'm sent to prison?

I pull Danae closer. "It's just intuition, but I continue to think Thomas might be a very strong possible. The more I get to know him the more convinced I am he may be the one."

"I always say the mothers know. He's a special child. One of the youngest in our ambassador program."

"What exactly is that?"

"A very prestigious program. He's going to be a very well-traveled little boy someday. We need you to help us film a commercial about it, actually."

"They'll travel alone?"

"With professional guides, to visit the heads of state in so many countries. You should see the number of passports and visas I had to apply for, each with a made-up last name since their real names were lost. Takes up a whole file drawer in Luc's office. French Guianese visas to Japan. Portugal. The United States."

"France?" I ask. "Thomas will need that to come home with me."

"Those were the first ones I applied for."

"Will there be girls on the trip as well?"

"Only boys for now, I believe."

"I saw a girl. Walking. I was on my way to sketch the beach."

"Sometimes Maroon girls cross through that—"

"This was a white girl. Carrying what looked like laundry."

"Oh, yes. There are girls here at Camp Hope. Not sure how many exactly but Father Peter would know more."

"I have a feeling he wouldn't be particularly open to my questions."

"You're certainly not the first of our mothers to complain about him. But he does mean well."

"I think there may be something he's not telling us. Thomas has been sick."

She turns to me. "How so?"

"Fever and stomachache. Sounds like it's been happening for a while."

"Poor child. I had no idea. But thank you for telling me, dear. I'll have the doctor sent over right away. There's a very experienced one with an office right here in town."

"How do you know Father Peter?"

"He was a friend of my husband's. Helped us grieve when Luc's parents passed unexpectedly."

"So hard for such a young person."

"It took a toll on Luc. You see the evidence of some days in his dismissive behavior. His father was also very hard on him while he was alive. Please keep this confidential, but my son was involved in the Nazi party. Luc is his namesake and heir and doesn't like to speak of it, of course."

"How did his parents die?"

"Diphtheria. Within two days of each other. Luc was sick in the hospital himself when they passed, and Father Peter visited him every day. Was there for him. Not that they always got along, as you can imagine."

"Poor Luc."

"He rarely speaks of it. But our gratitude toward Peter mustn't blind us to his faults. We need to put those children first."

Every part of me relaxes. "Thank you, Danae. And when do you think I could get the blood test to see if Thomas and I match?"

"Oh, did I not tell you?" She reaches into her purse for her appointment book, a deck-of-cards-sized red leather book, the pages stuffed with engraved invitations and calling cards. "I scheduled you next week at the laboratory here in town."

I resist grabbing the book and shaking every card out. "I'm sure it's in there somewhere."

"Oh, yes." She slides out a card. "Here it is. Glad you mentioned it. It's actually today at one o'clock."

I take it, bite back a smile, and smooth my thumb across the time written there. **One o'clock.** Soon I'll know for sure that Thomas is mine, and we'll be returning to Paris. We can go to the country for a while until the police lose interest in me and things cool off.

"And when will he get his blood drawn?"

"Father Peter has already done it." She pats my hand. "I've asked for the results to be sent to my attention just as soon as they are available. I understand you are eager to know, my dear, but have patience and just enjoy paradise."

"Do they process the samples right there at the lab?" I ask. "How many days to receive results? I'd like to get home soon."

"Oh, they send the samples to Rio. I've asked them to expedite yours so they can do the test in a matter of days. Isn't modern medicine awe-inspiring? Though getting the results letter can take longer. Sometimes it feels like it's on the slow boat to China."

AS WE ARRIVE ON the outskirts of town, terrible thoughts plague me. **If I stay here that long, will the police track me down?**

Danae rolls down her window. "We are passing the police station right here on the left."

We glide by a whitewashed stucco two-story building separated from the street by a brick wall. A group of dark-skinned men wearing white uniforms and pith helmets wave to Danae as we pass.

"How efficient are the police here?" I ask. "Do they ever work with Paris?"

"Oh, yes. The captain of the Cayenne force came

here from Paris and the offices communicate often." She returns their waves. "Would you like to stop in?"

"Oh, no." I shield my face as we pass. No need to turn myself in.

She rolls up her window. "Surprisingly hardworking bunch of fellows, the Cayenne police, while everyone else seems to be on island time."

"Do many people come here to hide from their pasts?"

"Many **try.** But just last month a wealthy woman from Biarritz who stole money from her husband came down here with her lover thinking she could evade the authorities. All was fine until these fellows dragged her from her house and extradited her to Paris where she sits in jail with no possibility of parole. People do things thinking they are invincible, but the long arm of the law eventually gets everyone."

Now that I've finally found Thomas, what if I lose him all over again?

I consider asking her about the Golden Dove statue but hold back. **What if she tells Luc how concerned I am about it?**

Claudio lets us out in the center of Cayenne, promising to retrieve us in two hours, and Danae leads me along the sidewalk, leaning on her cane. We edge past people from all countries and walks of life there to celebrate Carnival as luscious scents fill the air, and street vendors hawk cheesy fried doughnuts and pitas filled with pork and beans.

Danae turns. "Keep up, now."

It's both stressful and exhilarating to be on our own in such a chaotic place, where petty thieves roam the crowds and handsome men let their gazes linger, leaving the most tantalizing cologne scents in their wakes.

We come to a tailor shop with **Couture Elégante** painted in script on the plateglass window.

Danae loops her arm in mine and leads me in. "They do fabulous work here."

The shop is a small but surprisingly sophisticated place for Cayenne, with its whitewashed walls, crystal chandelier, and the requisite counter every tailor shop features. A slant of light filters in through the window and lands on a selection of dresses and tops hung on a rack.

"Mostly custom," Danae says. "But they do have some nice ready-to-wear."

Two shopgirls hurry about the place as a trim woman Danae seems to know from her days in Paris meets us at the counter.

"How may I help today, Madame Minau?" the woman asks.

That place brings me back to the Laurents' tailor shop with Magdeleine Laurent and her baby, so happy with her child, and Mr. Laurent the proud grand—

Danae shakes my forearm. "Arlette? Did you hear me? Would you prefer A-line skirts or more of a Dior full skirt?"

"No skirts, thank you. I wear trousers."

"Please show us everything you have in her size."

"I'll never be able to wear it all in the time I'm here," I say.

Danae pulls me close, releasing a wave of her gardenia perfume. "This is all just bribery, my dear. To get you to stay with us forever. And I'd like to see you in some nice dresses for a change."

I consider telling her why I prefer pants, since we are growing closer after all. But that's too much disclosure for a morning shopping outing.

The shopgirls shuttle armloads of couture back to the dressing room, and I follow down the carpeted hallway to try them on.

The dressing room is a lovely little chamber, painted in dove gray, two French chairs upholstered in white linen at one side. A female tailor waits, dressed in black head to toe, her only color a silver pincushion tied to her wrist, bristling with pins, like a bloated little blowfish.

"I'd like to try the clothes on by myself, please," I say.

Danae enters behind me. "Oh, we're all women here, dear."

I run one hand along the silks and cashmeres of the separates and dresses hung on the rack. Clothing made ready-to-wear is a somewhat new thing in the couture world, and it feels unreal to be in the presence of such exquisite pieces.

Danae turns to me, clutches my bag, and tries to lift the strap over my head. "Well, this needs to go."

I recoil as if stung and cross two hands over the bag at my hip. "Get away from me."

She steps back. "My dear—"

I lift the strap over my head and hold the bag to my chest. "I'm sorry. But this bag and its contents are precious to me."

Danae releases a deep sigh. "Of course, Arlette. We all have those pieces we become attached to. I simply thought you'd prefer a new bag."

The tailor waves me to the raised platform in front of the three-way mirror and the shopgirl guides me up onto it.

I set the bag down on a chair and turn to Danae. "I prefer to be alone when trying on clothes."

She steps to me. "Don't be silly. Though I understand your modesty. I once bathed at Corfu naked as a jaybird and that cured me of all shyness."

"It's not that . . ."

"What is it, dear?"

I hesitate for a moment and then unbutton my white pants and step out of them.

The shopgirl drops the clothes in her arms, one fist to her mouth.

The heat rises in my face as I glimpse my leg in the mirror.

The tailor steps back.

"Out!" Danae says to the two women, and they scurry off.

I fixate on my leg, the horror of it tripled in the three-way mirror. It had been easy to minimize the gruesomeness of it all those years, hiding it behind thick socks and trousers, but here under the high-wattage bulbs there's no place to hide, the lights illuminating every inch of my shrunken and withered leg, the scars somewhat faded, but still crimson and jagged, running thigh to ankle.

Danae reaches up and offers her hand. "Come down from there, my dear."

Seeing tears in her eyes brings them to mine as well. I take her hand and step down, and she leads me to sit.

"Is it very painful?" she asks.

"Yes. But times like this hurt the most. The embarrassment of it."

"Is it from your time at the camp?"

I nod, holding my head up so no tears fall. "After they took Willie, I lost my mind. Ran around the camp like a madwoman, and they called the dogs on me. My friend Josie tended me the best she could, but there was no treatment until I got back to Paris. But by then . . ." I look down at my leg. "They saved my life, but the infection had done the damage."

"The unspeakable cruelty of the Nazis."

"Having lost my parents so young, my son was the only family I ever had. Once he was gone, I didn't want to live. But it will not affect my ability to parent in any way. I'm fine now."

"Of course, dear. It just strengthens my resolve to make sure you are reunited with your son." Danae reaches over and takes my hand in hers. "That's why I do this work."

"I'm just so hideous."

"Wear it proudly. It's a sign of your strength and endurance. But don't let the hatred eat you alive. A real woman forgives."

She stands. "But for now I need to get home for a nap."

"I'll stay and walk back after my blood test. I need the air. Plus I want to buy a paper cone for Thomas."

AFTER MY UNEVENTFUL BLOOD draw I shop a nearby store for a paper cone to take home for Thomas, the treat European children love, filled with candies and toys, the common little treasures they adore. It is so nice to be alone, browsing the shops, and I stop by a thatched-roof café on the edge of town, the type seen everywhere in Cayenne, where one can purchase a cool coconut drink and cassava chips.

The sun beats down as I walk toward the line at the takeaway window, change purse in hand, ready to buy a coffee. I step aside to make way for a man returning his tray to the window.

"Excuse me," he says, nudging by.

I stop, incapable of even the slightest movement. I can barely breathe but cannot stop staring. The bulbous head. The Nosferatu look.

Dr. Ebner.

I watch him walk back and join Father Peter at an outdoor table.

Did he see me here? Could Ebner recognize me from years ago at Westwald? I brace myself against a picnic table and watch as the two stand and walk to a nearby building and enter.

How could that terrible man be here, of all places? Was it really him? How had he ended up here instead of wasting away in some prison after what he'd done at Westwald? The nurses there openly admitted he'd euthanized babies, and here he is openly enjoying a meal with his pal.

Of course those two are friends.

Every part of me feels reduced to jelly as I head off in the opposite direction and hail a taxi. Josie had been right about this place. If only she were here to help me untangle it all. I can't go to the police, and Danae is not strong enough to handle all of this. I don't dare confide in Luc for he may be in on it with Father Peter. Bondi seems genuine enough, but she has her own challenges to deal with. And who knows about Claudio?

I will have to figure out a way to take Thomas and leave on my own. I can't trust anyone here.

CHAPTER 39

JOSIE

ROME, ITALY
1952

THE DAY AFTER MEETING WITH MY FATHER, I spend two more days waiting in the suite for Johann, following his order to wait for him before venturing out, but he's a no-show. I don't hear any more from Karl either, so after one more room-service meal alone, I walk to see if I can get an audience with Bishop Hudal at Santa Maria dell'Anima church, the German-speaking parish of Rome. What harm would it do to walk to a church in broad daylight? If Karl won't get me in, I can at least try in person to get some traction on Snow. Meet Hudal in the flesh. Perhaps get a list of those who'd escaped on the ratline?

I check for tails as I leave the hotel, take back streets and hurry through Piazza Navona, following the peal of the bells. I was never a fan of that sound. It reminds me of the hours trapped in the front pew at my grandmother Anderson's church, dressed up for her friends, in baggy cotton tights and too tight Mary Janes, staring, terrified, at the crucifix.

I arrive at the yellow brick façade of the church, frozen through, and step into the nave, the spicy-sweet scent of incense in the air. I stamp my boots to warm my feet and take in the teen choir singing Handel in front of a magnificent altar, a choirmaster dressed in a black cassock conducting.

Drawn down the aisle by one of the soloists singing in Latin with perfect pitch, I take in the stained-glass windows and frescoed saints stretching up the walls to the soaring cross-vaulted turquoise ceiling. Scattered among the pews, women in black coats kneel in prayer. I envy their faith, giving themselves up so trustingly.

A stout priest shuffles toward me, his raised eyebrows like fat caterpillars.

"**Signorina.** Can I help you?"

"I'm here to see Bishop Hudal."

He shakes his head like a horse casting off flies. "He is **not** here."

"I'm with United States Army Intelligence." I flash my badge.

The priest hesitates and then scurries back off toward the choir.

I wait, trying not to look in the niches along the church sides, many bearing a macabre funerary monument, bishops and cardinals recumbent in stone, at final rest upon carved sarcophagi.

The choirmaster stops conducting and rushes up the aisle toward me, the fringed tail of the vermillion sash tied at his waist fluttering behind him. He's fiftyish and blond, with a placid German face and earnest expression. In other circumstances he might be a plumber or a dairy farmer.

I present my badge. "Josie Anderson. Karl Crowell from—"

"Very sorry, Miss Anderson. Bishop Hudal has been reassigned. I am Bishop Becker."

"So, Hudal's just disappeared?"

"Vatican law, Miss Anderson. A diocesan bishop who has completed his seventy-fifth year of age is requested to offer his resignation to the supreme pontiff. I'm afraid I can say no more."

At the altar, the stout priest assumes the job of conductor.

I turn toward the choir. "Is that Handel's **Dixit Dominus,** Your Excellency?"

"Indeed."

"Not sure what illegal substance Handel was on when he wrote it, but the result is magnificent. They sing it well."

He smiles and looks at the stone floor. "Yes. Competing in one week and we are behind schedule." He throws up his hands. "Not to mention we just got word our bus has broken down. I must get back to my work."

"I need information, Your Excellency. Did you not get the message that my boss Karl Crowell arranged for me to meet Bishop Hudal? I'm investigating the whereabouts of a Nazi criminal."

My voice echoes, and a few of the devout turn and look.

"Keep your voice down, please. This is God's house."

He guides me to a side niche where a marble cardinal lies recumbent in stone, at final rest upon a carved sarcophagus.

I shrug. "I can contact the Holy See if you'd rather go that route. I'm interested in information about a specific doctor named Snow. I need to know when he was here and where he may have gone."

He raises his palms. "I am in a delicate position here. I don't agree with what Bishop Hudal did, but there were sins committed on both sides—"

"I was a prisoner in Ravensbrück concentration camp, and I know firsthand the person I'm looking for is definitely on the wrong side. If you want to talk **sin**—"

He leans in. "A Sister of Notre-Dame I knew well was there at Ravensbrück. Alsatian mother, French naval officer father. I have been trying to contact her with no success."

"What did she look like?"

"Very pretty, brown eyes, always with a smile.

She used to cut my hair when I lived in Lyon before the war."

"Could you mean Sister Élise?"

"Yes, Élise Rivet. You knew her?"

"We also knew her as Mother Mary Elisabeth. Her story was a famous one with everyone there. So, you don't know what happened to her?"

"No. She never returned my letters."

"I'm sorry, but she was executed at the camp. Volunteered to change numbers with a young mother and was taken to the shooting wall in her place. Just months before the camp was liberated."

He turns his gaze back to the choir. "I had no idea. She was so young herself."

"I'm sorry, Your Excellency. I understand this puts you in a difficult place, but these criminals cannot just go unpunished."

"It is very hard . . . and many years ago, now . . ."

"Didn't Christ himself say, 'Ye shall know the truth, and the truth shall make you free'? What you tell me will stay classified."

He exhales and runs a hand through his hair. "I can tell you what I know. That is the best I can do. Come with me. We must be quick."

I follow him to the front of the church; he unlocks a door near the altar, which leads to a courtyard where a marble fountain flows. We enter an oak-paneled room with a wall of cabinets and drawers to our left, an open cupboard hung with amethyst, ivory, and emerald green vestments along the right.

"I've never been in a sacristy before," I say. "The word comes from the Latin **sacerdotium,** am I right? Meaning office of a priest?"

He breathes a heavy sigh. "Exactly what information do you seek, **signorina**?"

"I am looking for a person of interest, a Dr. Snow."

The bishop hesitates and we listen to the muffled song of the choir.

I continue. "I believe Bishop Hudal may have assisted him in his journey to South America, or wherever he went."

He paces. "For so long I have been disgusted by this and have prayed for the strength to bear the weight of it. My parents were against Hitler from the beginning. My uncle was sent to Dachau for crimes against the state. He never returned."

"I'm sorry—"

"It has been difficult to watch all this happening, such a stain on the institution, but I am bound to my church. There were many here that risked their lives to save Jews. Father O'Flaherty alone—"

"Yes, of course, Your Excellency, but I need to know what Bishop Hudal was doing."

"Very well." He stops and takes a deep breath. "Bishop Hudal arranged for many to evade capture. Housed some at the seminary across the bridge."

I try to keep the surprise out of my voice. "At the Vatican?"

"Adjacent to it. Limousines bearing diplomatic license plates drove the men there, where they lived as seminarians, protected by local armed youths, until the proper travel documents were procured."

"How did they enter Italy? Were there no Allied troops at the border?"

"That stopped in 1947. So most of those seeking freedom simply came through Austria, over the Alps, crossed the Italian border, and stayed up north around Bolzano. In the final days of the Reich, families of the Nazi elite were already in northern Italy, one of the last strongholds of the regime, and they provided assistance."

"How did Nazis find their way here to Rome?"

"Word spread quickly in the POW camps and elsewhere that Italy was a safe place, and Bishop Hudal arranged lodging for them in a network of monasteries throughout northern Italy. Merano. Bolzano. Many made their way here to Roma and lived quite openly. Around one hundred of them arrived daily. Soon it became common knowledge that the bishop's helpers could supply train tickets. And arranged lodging."

"How long did they stay here before they shipped out?"

"Leaving the country took time. Often months. Required a new passport, one hundred and fifty thousand lire."

"Where did they get the money?"

"That was the hardest part for most of them. They did a lot of odd jobs. Many worked as film extras.

Very lucrative work. A few had speaking roles. One wrote a movie script."

"A bishop helped murderers? Those men killed millions in the concentration camps."

"Hudal's a staunch anti-communist and sees godless Russians as the main enemy of the church. To him, a concentration camp was where the German soldiers were kept after the war. He ministered to Austrian and German soldiers in the Allied POW camps here in Italy."

"He was born in Austria?"

"Yes. And had compassion for those men who'd lost the war, what he felt were anti-communist fighters who tried to save us from the Russians. Many agreed to be baptized Catholic as a precondition to being sent to South America. He supplied batches of passports and requested visas from President Perón for passage. Phoned in his order of berths needed on ships due for South America."

"How do you know all this?"

"The priests talk. And I was assigned here to the bishop's office for a month before he left, assembling his personal effects for the move. Found a letter from Hudal to President Perón requesting Argentine visas. The Swiss provided them, as well."

"Any idea how he paid for it all?"

Suddenly he has trouble meeting my gaze. "The Lord provides."

"Your Excellency, please."

He leans in. "If you must know, the bishop had a charitable fund. Provided by American Catholics, most of them unaware what they were backing. The International Red Cross assisted as well."

Suddenly I crave fresh air. "And you have no record of the Nazis he helped?"

"No, but we've found belongings leading us to determine some identities. A small carton of things left behind. A pair of swim trunks, Zeiss glasses. A few Reich documents. I didn't even like touching their possessions, but it had to be done."

"Mengele? Eichmann?"

He nods. "Among others. Some traveled by boat from Genoa to Argentina, where they fanned out all over South America, or to the Middle East. Some converted to Islam. Worked as arms dealers."

"Didn't they stand out as Aryans?"

He shrugs. "They lived simply, assumed new identities. Some arranged plastic surgery."

"Is there a list of those who escaped?"

"A **list**? No, **signorina.** I don't think you understand the scope of this."

"But do you remember the name Snow? Dr. Snow. From Ravensbrück."

"If you step outside, I will check. But then I really must return to the choir."

I exit the sacristy, stand in the niche at the side of the church, and watch the choir as I take it all in. How could Hudal operate so openly unless he had the pontiff's blessing?

Minutes later Bishop Becker appears with a manila envelope and hands it to me. "This is all we have under the name Snow. Some of the documents are signed by a Dr. Gregor Ebner, if that helps. And don't overlook the pen."

I feel for a weight at the bottom of the envelope and pull out a lovely black fountain pen with a gold filigree overlay. I run my finger down the gold oval, a fancy **S** engraved there.

"May I keep this, Your Excellency?"

He nods. "I don't think anyone will be coming back for it."

I slide out a sheaf of photos, young Roma and Sinti prisoners, all.

"Please be advised some of the photos are quite graphic. Prisoners shackled to metal bedposts, some lying in their own mess. It's hard to imagine God's children treated so."

I flip through the pages of half-starved adults and children lying about the **Revier.** They appear to have been subjected to experiments of some sort, and I come to a girl handcuffed to a **Revier** cot, eyes wild, hair matted.

Fleur.

One hand goes to my chest, and tears sting my eyes.

"I knew this girl. She was arrested with us in Paris and became part of our camp family. She disappeared toward the end of our time there. Had no idea they did this to her."

"I'm terribly sorry to bring you such disturbing

news. I must go now. I hope you get the person you seek."

I stow the envelope in my bag. "One more question, Your Excellency. In the letter, how many visas did Bishop Hudal seek from Perón?"

"In that one letter?"

"Yes."

"Five thousand."

I hold on to the pew. "My God. And how many of those were approved?"

"Not one was declined."

CHAPTER 40

ARLETTE

FRENCH GUIANA
1952

I WAKE THE NEXT MORNING TO THE SOUND OF breathing. I open one eye to find someone in the room, standing in front of the mirror, the slight figure ghostlike and gauzy through the mosquito netting.

I sit up, instantly awake, and gather the bedcovers to my chest.

"Who are you?" I ask.

A hand pushes the netting aside, a face peers in, and I relax. It's the girl from the path. She's as pale as my bedcovers and wears the same oatmeal linen shift and headscarf I'd seen her in before.

"I would like my shirts, if you would please be so kind."

How strangely she speaks, in some sort of archaic mix of French and High German.

I stand and slip on my robe. I want to ask her a dozen questions but hold back, afraid to scare her off. "Good to see you again. What is your name?"

"I'm called Ella."

"Where do you live?"

"Please. I would like to have my shirts? I need to get back."

"Get back to where? Can I help you?"

She wanders back to the mirror and stands transfixed by her own image.

I join her. "You've never seen a mirror?"

"That is vanity, looking at yourself."

"Who told you that? It's not wrong." I step to the bathroom, bring back my compact, and open it. "Take this. It will let you see yourself anytime."

The girl slowly reaches out, takes the compact, and slides it into her shift pocket.

She looks up at me. "Please don't tell."

"I won't."

The girl steps to my armoire and runs one hand down a silk shirt hanging on the knob, one of the many pieces Danae had sent from the tailor shop.

"It's like water," Ella says.

How like me at that age she is, this odd child. Exactly how old is she? Eleven? Twelve?

I step to the dresser and pull out the stack of shirts. "Did you sew these?"

"We all sew."

"They're very well made. Where did you learn such pretty stitches?"

"A woman came and showed us."

"Who brought her?"

She looks up at me. "The doctors." Is that fear in her eyes?

"Do they come to where you live?"

"Sometimes. For an examination. Or with the ink."

"Ink?"

She walks to the door. "I have to go."

Suddenly she doubles over at the waist and clutches her belly.

"Are you in pain?" I ask.

She nods and I guide her to a chair. "Sit while I dress quickly. I know someone who can help."

THE **OPEN** SIGN AT the door of Bondi's clinic is already up by the time we arrive, and I lead my young friend in.

"Who do we have here?" Bondi asks as she walks toward us.

"My friend Ella came to visit this morning and is having some stomach pain."

Bondi waves the girl toward the treatment table, lays her down, and probes her belly.

"Are you one of them?" the girl asks. "The white coats?"

Bondi smiles. "I'm a doctor, yes. How old are you?"

"Oldest of us all, now, thank you."

Bondi helps Ella sit up and applies her fingers to the girl's wrist to take her pulse.

"What is this?" Bondi asks, sliding one finger along the inside of Ella's wrist.

I stand and look at what appears to be a blue number tattooed there: 19.

The girl avoids Bondi's gaze.

Bondi steps back from the table. "Who did this to you?"

Ella hangs her head. "We all have them. It doesn't hurt."

Bondi glances at me and regains her composure. "The cramping you feel is completely normal. You are starting menses and will bleed now every month." Bondi hands her a bag. "That is when you wear these."

Ella takes the bag. "When this happened to Petra two babies started growing in her."

Bondi and I exchange a look.

"Where is Petra now?" Bondi asks.

Ella shrugs, slides down off the table, and heads for the door.

"Can we see you home?" I ask, but the girl keeps walking.

"We need to follow her," I say, but Bondi has already turned her clinic sign over to CLOSED and hurries out after me.

—

"HOW OLD IS SHE, do you think?" I ask Bondi as we walk.

"Can't be more than eleven."

"I think Father Peter must be involved. I wouldn't be surprised if his friend Dr. Ebner—"

"The OB-GYN over near the café? I've seen him."

"Yes. I knew him during the war. He headed up the Lebensborn program, and I wouldn't be surprised if he's involved. I saw him with Father Peter."

We follow the girl through the streets of Cayenne, almost lose her once, but find her again as she scurries up an embankment on the edge of town into the jungle. She's fast and takes a route that's new to me, deep into the **Wald.**

Soon we come to a fork in the path, and Bondi and I stop.

"I think she went right," I say.

Bondi turns to the jungle. "And look what we almost passed without even seeing."

I step down an overgrown walk toward a whitewashed cottage that has been swallowed whole by a tangle of liana vines and climbing bamboo.

A silver padlock catches the light there, the shank looped through a simple door latch. I grasp the lock, warm from the sun. A pretty one. I'm glad it's a padlock, once my specialty in the Doves days.

I take off my bag, set it on the ground, and unpin one of the safety pins from the strap. I bend it straight and plunge the sharp end into the keyhole.

It doesn't give up right away and I wipe a rivulet of

sweat running down the side of my neck. **Maybe I've lost my touch?** I remove the pin, re-enter, double down, and soon feel the pin chambers align. Once the curved shank slips open and the lock surrenders, sweet adrenaline gushes down my arms.

We're in.

I open the door and wave Bondi along.

"I'm assuming you were more than a waitress during the war?" she asks as she passes me.

We both stop and take in the room, filled with what looks like some sort of veterinary equipment.

Bondi walks to a doctor's cabinet. "Hypodermic needles. Epivan, a sedative." She pulls a thin silver tube the length of an umbrella from the cabinet. "And an AI gun."

"AI?" I ask.

"Artificial insemination. For animals. Cows. Pigs."

She returns it to the cabinet as I walk along a treatment table. When I reach the end a glint of silver catches my eye and I lift two stirrups and lock them into place.

"I don't think cows are the only thing being inseminated here."

She pulls a silver tool from a stainless-steel tray. "And it looks like someone's had a forceps delivery."

I wrap my arms across my belly. Just the thought is sickening. Dr. Ebner is involved, of course. With Father Peter. But to what end?

"Can you notify your superiors at WHO that this is happening?"

"I'm afraid we deal with disease. They will consider this too political to take on."

I'm certainly in no position to go to the police about this.

Soon the sound of dogs comes to us in the distance, and we head back the way we came.

As we walk, I plan my escape. I'll just get my son and leave. I still have the money Josie left me, plenty for two economy tickets. I can get him the medical attention he needs and ask Josie to notify the authorities this is going on down here.

All I need is Thomas's passport and we'll be on the next plane to Paris.

CHAPTER 41

JOSIE

ROME, ITALY
1952

After visiting Bishop Becker, it's a chilly walk back to the Grand Hotel Plaza, gulps of fresh air the only cure for the lingering memory of the images of Fleur being so horribly abused, and the thought of thousands of fugitive Nazis running around South America. **Have any made their way to French Guiana?**

Maybe it wasn't so far-fetched after all, my warning Arlette about Luc Minau. Is she at risk down there? I quicken my pace, eager to sit with Johann in our suite, feet up, glasses of Barolo in hand, sorting through it all.

Halfway there, I turn and spot a man in a loden

green jacket following me, so I detour through the crowds in the Piazza Navona to lose the tail, only to find him replaced by another. Russian? Israeli? Could be my father keeping an eye on me.

I duck down a narrow side street, stop, and glance behind me for more tails. I find none, just a few pedestrians and two young women walking arm in arm, deep in conversation.

As I hurry on, I hear the buzz of a motorbike approaching behind me and I move to the narrow sidewalk. The bike passes, hits a hole in the cobblestones, and veers toward me, clipping my hip. I fall to the street, grasping my side in pain.

"Stronzo!" I call after him, but he speeds off without a word.

My hip is on fire as I try to stand.

One of the women hurries to help me up.

"Can you stand?" she asks in Italian. "What a jerk that guy was."

I know the voice right away, and my whole body goes cold.

"You need a hospital," she says, bending over me.

A few passersby gather and her friend, no more than a teenager, stays on the sidewalk.

I wave her off. "**No.** No hospital."

Our eyes meet. She's still just as beautiful. Even more, if I'm completely honest, with her hair grown out and worn long.

She straightens and turns to her young friend on the sidewalk. "We'll need a minute?"

The girl sends a concerned look our way and walks off. Probably used to this type of thing happening.

"Didn't think you'd ever see me again?" I ask.

I fight the pain in my hip and struggle to stand.

Ariana.

She helps me up. "I've felt bad all these years . . ."

The little gathered crowd disperses as I hobble onto the sidewalk and lean against the stucco wall.

"Right." I glance at her retreating friend. "Looks like you feel bad."

I take in her brown eyes and creamy skin. Those lips. **Kissen lippen.** For a woman ten years my senior, she doesn't look it. She has a few new lines, probably caused by some new drama with her little girlfriend.

"It's been seven years since Ravensbrück, Josie." She nods toward the friend. "And that isn't what you think."

Ah, the deftest liar of all. Why can I not avoid her? It's almost as if the universe is trying to force me to confront her. Unless it's not a coincidence she's here.

My hip throbs. "I couldn't care less. That stopped when I came back to the bunk to find you gone. You told them everything, didn't you?"

She watches the girl round the corner and turns back to me.

"They forced me to give information on you and Arlette. Once you'd been arrested in Paris and the intelligence stopped, they suspected the Golden Doves were at one of the camps. All I did was confirm it. I had to."

"You **had** to tell them all the details you got out of me with your fake flirting. You do know Herr Oberg came there to interrogate us?"

She folds her arms across her chest, as she so often did at Ravensbrück. So stubborn, but maybe that's what I liked about her, always so courageous about her convictions. At seventeen I longed for that kind of strength. And her warmth next to me at night. Some days it was all that got me through.

"I'm sorry," she says with convincing concern. "Did you get your mother out, too?"

"Oh, that's right, how would you know since you mysteriously vanished once you ratted us out? We left without my mother; Arlette's son, Willie, too. Your Nazi pals didn't tell you all that?"

Tears shine in her eyes. "I honestly didn't know. I just told them what they asked for, to save someone dear to me. That girl you saw me with? It's my daughter. They had her. Said she would die if I didn't produce information on you and Arlette."

I let that sink in. Another good lie? Hard to tell with her.

"Still an agent?" I ask.

"I—"

"Clearly, this isn't a coincidence, Ariana." I turn to leave.

She grabs my arm. "Don't go." She steps closer and brushes my bangs back, her fingers warm on my cold forehead. "How you've grown up. You've always been beautiful, but now . . ."

I push her hand away. “I forgot. Flattery’s your specialty.”

“I’m telling the truth.”

I brush off my sleeve. “Well, that’s new.”

“You’ve become an incredible woman.”

I turn at the sound of an approaching car. “Anyway, it’s done now. Can’t change things.”

A taxi bumps its way down the little street, and I hail it.

Ariana pulls me back by the arm. “There’s one thing I can change. Something I always wanted to do.” She pulls me to her, one hand cradling the back of my head, and kisses me. Hard and deep. And I don’t pull back.

It’s just how I thought it might be. Sexy and playful and real and I’m happy to go on, but she releases me. Always the first to leave.

“You can’t fake that,” she says, in my ear.

I would have killed for that back at the camp.

She keeps me close and whispers. “Don’t react, Einstein. Anyone could be watching.”

Dread creeps through me. **How does she know my code name?** I try to pull away, but she holds me tight.

“Don’t go back to your hotel. This may give you one more reason to hate me, but I just saved your life.”

My blood runs cold.

“Trust me. It’s not safe there.”

I wrest myself free. “Who are you working for?”

The taxi stops.

She checks up and down the street.

"You have to tell me, Ariana."

She steps back and draws her coat collar up around her throat. "Good to see you, Josie. Please take my advice. I won't be able to help you again."

"I can take care of myself."

"Ciao."

My hip aches as I duck into the taxi, and the driver heads off.

Can I trust her? She's a pathological liar, after all. The tears, the concern, all most likely fake. But why would she lie about the hotel? And how does she know my code name? Johann will help me sort it out.

I run the back of my hand across my lips and force myself not to turn and watch her.

This time it's me leaving her, not looking back.

And that almost feels good.

IT'S A RELIEF TO get back to the hotel lobby. I check the area for anyone vaguely suspicious looking and limp through a mob of Canadian tourists, from Quebec from the sound of them, to the front desk.

"Ah, Miss Anderson. Mr. Vitner has arrived."

"Any mail for me?"

He smiles and hands me a yellow envelope. "Just a telex."

I hurry to the elevator, find it occupied by a British couple arguing about whether to visit the Colosseum tomorrow, let the doors close, and wait for the next one.

I make it to the suite, pull my firearm, and let myself in. The heavy velvet drapes have already been drawn for the evening. I check my bedroom and closets. The bed's turned down, no sign of trouble. I move on to Johann's room and sigh in relief at the sound of running water in his bath.

"Honey, I'm home," I call out. "Got some interesting stuff, I think, from Hudal's replacement."

Mozart plays softly, and I congratulate myself on accepting this job. Tony P. had once complained about staying at the Howard Johnson's Motor Lodge outside Washington, D.C. This is better.

I holster my gun. Johann will help me make sense of all the Ariana craziness, over a couple glasses of wine, with no judgment.

I make my way to the kitchenette, which is stocked with twelve types of wineglasses, set my holster on the counter, open the bottle of Borgogno Barolo Johann left there, and read Karl's message he sent from my telex.

COME HOME. NEW ASSIGNMENT.

I slip off my shoes and sip the Barolo, giving silent thanks to the wine gods, for my hip is already feeling better.

With a glass of red in each hand I wander back toward the bath.

"Karl says I have a new assignment," I say as I rap on the bathroom door. "You decent?"

I nudge the door open with my shoulder. "Johann, you're going to be floating—"

And from the smell alone I know what I will find.

CHAPTER 42

ARLETTE

FRENCH GUIANA
1952

I PRACTICALLY RUN THROUGH THE CAYENNE airport, pulling Thomas by the hand. A plane flies low overhead, and I nearly vibrate at the thought of getting out of here. Thomas seems excited for the trip, buying my story about taking a quick trip to Paris to see a special doctor. Someday I'll tell him the truth about it all.

The airport, which resembles a one-story former stable, with one weedy airstrip, looks decidedly less glamorous than it did when I arrived here, disembarking from president-class and helicoptered to Cove House. I feel for the passports in my bag. How easily I'd managed the lock on Luc's office and found the boy's passport before Danae woke from her nap.

The desk clerk is a French woman with a Parisian accent. I consider telling her the truth and throwing myself on her mercy, and then repeat my new mantra. **Trust no one.**

I hand her the passports.

"No luggage?" she asks, as she holds up our open passports to compare the photos with our faces.

I scan the boarding area as passengers line up. "Just a quick trip today."

"But if you are the boy's mother, why do your last names not match? The boy is Thomas Favreau. You are Arlette LaRue."

A drop of sweat rolls down my back. "He's from my first marriage."

"We're going to Paris," Thomas says. "I'm going to be an ambassador."

She smiles at him. "Of course you are." She leans in toward me. "Well, he's certainly yours, I know that much. So often boys favor their mothers, don't you think?"

Thomas steals a quick look at me, his lips pressed in a sweet smile. "I like her," he whispers behind one hand.

She stamps and closes our passports and hands them back to me. "I don't know why you're standing here talking. They're boarding soon."

I grab our tickets and hurry to join the line at the gate.

"Will I meet Bep and Riekie in Paris?" Thomas asks.

"Everyone. Marianne. You'll be expected to work, though."

He smiles.

We arrive at the gate and stand in line to board, and a bit of guilt pinches me. Danae has been so kind and helpful. But she'll understand our reason for leaving.

I crouch to smooth the lapel of Thomas's jacket. "You must keep our secret, all right? You must say you are my son. We live in Paris, and we're going home now."

"I hope we can say that for real one day."

"Me too, but for now, just play along."

"Like acting in a movie?"

"Yes. And tell me, do you know any of the girls at the camp?"

"Sure. They come to celebrations sometimes."

"From where?"

He shrugs. "Not sure. Father Peter says they deserve our respect. They do the most important job."

I bend to tie Thomas's shoe and an electric eel of fear slides up my spine as I see a familiar man at the boarding door.

"Claudio."

"Yes," Thomas says and starts off toward him. "Can we go say hello?"

I grab his arm. "No, **mon cher.**"

My heart hammers my sternum. **Is Luc getting off that plane? Why else would Claudio be there?**

I look for cover, but Claudio spots us and steps to us.

"Taking a trip?" he asks.

"We—"

He leans in and speaks softly in my ear. "Luc is arriving. If you have other plans leave now."

I set one hand on Claudio's sleeve. "Thank you."

"Come along," I say to Thomas.

We turn to leave just as Luc strides out of the gateway. I step back from the line and pull Thomas to me, hoping Luc will sail by, but he sees us and stops.

"Arlette," he says with a smile. "Tommy. What a happy surprise, to see you two here."

"We—"

"There's nothing a weary traveler likes more than a welcome like this, am I right, Claudio?"

Thomas glances at me.

"I hope you haven't waited long."

"Not at all," I say. **Does he suspect?**

"Let's go home," Luc says, pulling me along with him by the arm, just a little too roughly, toward the exit. "Shall we?"

AS CLAUDIO DRIVES US back, the sound of a plane roaring over us fills the car. **The Paris flight.** We drop a sleepy Thomas off at the camp, and then Claudio drives Luc and me back to Cove House. I try to catch Claudio's eye in the rearview mirror to give silent thanks. He'd almost freed us.

Is it my imagination or is he casting furtive glances at me as we drive? There's an attraction there for sure, as I meet his beautiful brown eyes in the mirror. How close he'd come to helping us go home.

But I have a new plan. Perhaps I'll tell Luc I'm pregnant. Tell him I'm so tired I can't keep my eyes open and feeling unwell. Paris has the best doctors, after all. Maybe then Luc will suggest I just head back to Paris with Thomas, regardless of the blood-test results? It's at least a way to keep his attempts at lovemaking at bay.

Claudio parks the car and I watch as he heads down the path to his quarters over the garage. How nice it would be to follow him, walk up the stairs together to his little apartment, slip off our shoes and—

"Coming?" Luc asks.

He escorts me inside, pours himself a brandy, and looks me over. "If I didn't know better, I might think you and Claudio had something going."

"Please, Luc."

We step out to the terrace, the waves crashing in the darkness.

He runs one hand down my arm "But let's not ruin tonight talking about that. Why don't we re-create that night in Paris? I think about it a lot."

"I don't know, Luc."

"Grandmother's already asleep. My room is far from hers—"

"Luc . . . I'm afraid I have some rather, well, surprising news."

"Must you be coy?" He sips his drink. "I do loathe a guessing game."

"I'm pregnant."

He levels a glance at me. "Are you serious?"

"I'm so sorry, Luc, what are the odds after that one time . . ."

He lifts his glass. "Two actually," he says, eyebrows raised. He knocks back what's left in the glass. "Sure it's mine?"

"Yes, I'm **sure.** What a terrible thing to say. I should probably just go back to Paris."

"No. We'll get you the best care here. Dr. Ebner in town—"

My whole body cringes. "I don't think—"

"And how do you even know for sure?"

I fake a smile. "A woman knows."

He takes my hand. "Well, you need to stay here so I can make an honest woman of you."

I pull my hand away. "But I am an honest woman." **Aside from a little breaking and entering and some petty theft.**

"Just an expression."

"I know your grandmother is religious. She's been so good to me. I'd hate for her to be shocked by all this."

"She doesn't have to know, if we can get a wedding done soon enough."

I step back from him. "**Wedding?** Oh, I don't think—"

"I may not be your ideal man. I work way too hard and I'm not always the most thoughtful person, but I **am** rich. And I can honestly say I've never felt so strongly about any woman."

"But isn't love—"

"Call it love. Call it infatuation. But you make me happy. Say you'll consider it?"

I smile. **Perhaps playing along will get them to speed up the adoption process?** "I suppose. But we barely know each other, Luc. You shouldn't feel obligated. I can take care of myself after this unfortunate—"

"No. This is good news."

"It's better if I just go back to Paris."

"Without finding your match?"

"Under the circumstances, maybe Thomas could come with me while we wait for the results. They have the best doctors in Paris. You could join us there."

Luc leans against the railing and looks out over the dark sea. "Our hands are tied at the foundation on that one. We're required by French law to provide blood-test results before we make the adoption official."

"Certainly you can stall them?"

"And what if you get Thomas home to Paris and it's not a match? The poor little guy is already so desperate for a mom. It would devastate him."

"But—"

"Trust me, Arlette. We'll make this work. How bad would it be to have to stay a little longer? It's freezing in Paris. And Thomas needs a father." He gestures toward the bedroom wing. "Coming?" he asks with a smile. "Last call."

"I need to sleep, Luc. Can we work all that out in the morning?"

"It's up to you." He starts off and turns back. "And by the way, our background check company called."

I barely breathe. "Really?"

"Seems there's been a missing-person claim filed about your aunt. By one Hermione Marchand. Know her?"

I shake my head unable to speak.

"The Paris police would like to talk with you. But I guess we can work that out in the morning, too."

CHAPTER 43

JOSIE

ROME, ITALY
1952

I PRESS THE DOOR OPEN WITH MY SHOULDER AND step into the bathroom, the wineglasses in my hands growing slippery. The tub is filled to the rim and Johann's arm hangs over the edge. I drop both glasses and they shatter on the white tile floor.

Johann.

I stand, huffing breath, open-mouthed, unable to take in the horror, the terrible smell of burnt flesh in the air.

"My God," I say; my voice startles me, echoing off the tile.

The bathtub water is reddish brown and Johann

lies in it up to his clavicle, his head arched back. I step farther into the room, barely feeling the glass shards on my feet, and make myself look. His mouth is agape, tongue swollen, blue eyes bulging wide, soapsuds still matted in his hair. A black starburst is burned onto his skin from the sunken silver wreck of the metal hair dryer resting on his chest. An electrical cord snakes out of the tub, still connected to the outlet above the sink.

I double over.

On the closed toilet seat his khaki trousers and blue cotton shirt sit folded into neat squares, his belt coiled atop them.

I let out a sob and step toward him. But the faint hum of electricity sends me back. I stand frozen, weak in the knees. Who broke in here and did this?

A muffled thud comes from some distant part of the suite, and I can barely breathe.

Are they still here?

I step to the hallway and stand, listening hard, an almost imperceptible disturbance in the air.

I'll be seen if I run to the kitchen for my gun, so I hurry to my bedroom and hide behind the drapes, the thick velvet a strange comfort.

Suddenly the phone on the bedside table rings, startling me. I wait for it to stop; it's so loud. It keeps ringing so I emerge and tread softly to the phone and pick up the receiver, the smoothness of it slippery in my hand. I listen.

"Josie?"

Dad.

"You need to get out of there. Now. Understand?"

He hangs up and the line goes dead.

I hang up the receiver and hurry back behind the curtain.

I wait, my own thumping heart the only sound, as someone approaches. I barely breathe, nose to velvet, and the bedroom floorboards creak, deep beneath the carpet.

With one shaking finger I push the drape aside to find a person in dark trousers and cashmere coat bending over my suitcase.

Aaron Salinger.

I go numb. He's done this.

He straightens and turns toward me. "Josie."

I step out, my whole body shaking. "I know who you are."

"Get your shoes."

I step back. "I'm not going anywhere with you."

"Leave the suitcase. We don't have time—"

"You did that to him."

"No." He tries to take my arm, but I yank it away.

The bathtub. Johann. I suppress a wave of nausea and press shaking fingers to my face. "Get away from me."

He wipes the bedroom doorknob with his handkerchief. "We don't have long. That water will leak into the suite below soon and this place will be crawling with **polizia.**"

I wipe a tear with my sleeve. "I'm not leaving him that way."

He grabs my arm. "If you want to die like he did, be my guest. Otherwise come with me, **now.**"

AARON AND I TAKE the sleeper train from Rome to Paris, where I barely close my eyes, plagued with thoughts of Johann. Waves of despair and revulsion sweep over me, images running through my mind of Johann lying in the tub, self-castigating thoughts playing on a loop. **Why had I not insisted he come to Rome with me?** But perhaps then we'd both be dead. Maybe my father is right. I'm in over my head.

Or maybe I just have to stay calm enough to use it.

We make it to rainy Paris and take a taxi from the station to Aaron's apartment in Le Marais. I breathe deep and consider him as he watches darkened Paris go by. Why should I trust him? Johann didn't. I need to contact Karl and fill him in, but how do I know he's not involved in Johann's death? Could Ariana have done this? My own father? I just need to stay centered and sane and sort it all out.

How will I continue the mission without Johann? What would he advise? I feel my backpack for the photos Bishop Becker gave me. Poor Fleur. She'd remember Snow. Maybe even help me put together a composite drawing. Why hadn't I thought of that lead before?

"Drop me at my friend's apartment. Île de la Cité."

We speak in low tones, so the driver doesn't hear.

Aaron's eyes flash in the dark taxi. "It's safer for you at my place in Le Marais."

"I decide what's safer for me."

"You dying doesn't help me much. Come to my apartment and regroup. Then do what you want."

He returns his gaze out the window, staring through the raindrops collected there.

"One night," I say. "Then I'm gone."

We make it to his apartment, a one-bedroom, on the small side, the air inside stale. It's furnished with a white slipcovered sofa and Persian carpets worn to the knots. Decorated by his ex-wife? He'd been married, according to Johann's dossier.

Johann.

We rush about the room feeling along the frames of mirrors and prints for listening devices. Once we've checked everything, I step toward him and slide off my wet backpack and jacket.

"I know what you **do,** Aaron, or whatever your name really is. And just so you know, if I disappear, my unit chief will be looking for me."

"Noted."

We stand there in the dark.

"It's too bad," he says. "We could've partnered to get Snow."

Of course, he knows my mission goal.

"Like we partnered at the Ritz?"

He looks at me without blinking. "It's just part of the job, and you know it."

Hard to tell if he's lying.

"Did he carry a briefcase?" Aaron asks.

"Johann? I don't know. Sometimes." I step to the window and lift the sash, letting in the sounds of cars on wet pavement. "You say you didn't kill Johann, but why were you there in the suite?"

He pushes me away from the window, shuts it, and sweeps the drapes closed. "I followed you from the church. Along with half of Moscow."

"Did you see that—"

"Motorcycle? Yes. You're lucky you're not in traction."

"You saw me enter the suite?"

He nods. "Pretty hard not to know you were in there, seeing your firearm lying on the kitchen counter. Did you get any training?"

"What do you want from me?"

He grips my shoulders. "I want you to go home."

My hip aches as I bend to grab my backpack. "To **Texas**? That's not happening."

"This isn't some sort of game, Anderson. You're in deep and now I am, too. If they have his briefcase, they must know you're involved. You flew under the radar before, but chances are there's now a **spetsnaz** commando assigned to you."

"No one tailed us here."

"Tell me you're joking. They're paid to take you down. Five hundred rubles. Know what that buys in

Moscow? A house. And they're competing. You don't think they'll figure out where you are? Me too, now."

"You should've left me in Rome."

He heads off down the hallway. "Starting to agree."

I sling my backpack over my shoulder and follow him to the bedroom. It's a snug jewel box of a room, with a good-sized bed by Parisian standards and a love seat tucked under the window.

"You can sleep here," he says.

I set my backpack on the bed, removing what few possessions I have left. My wallet. Compact developing kit. Johann's last canister of film.

Aaron steps to the dresser. "My ex-wife stays here when I'm gone—keeps a drawer here. Not sure if these'll fit you." He pulls out a pair of cotton pajamas.

I sit on the edge of the bed, numb. "I don't wear those."

"Oh." He looks away. "Right." He tosses them back into the drawer. "I'll take the sofa."

"Fine. I'll be gone by morning."

"You can't do this alone, Anderson. We'll get Snow if we join forces." He pauses, and I listen to the rain pattering the window. "I know you and your friend Arlette were the Golden Doves."

Of course, he'd seen my dossier.

"You two gave the Germans a run for their money."

I sit up straighter. "Perhaps you should show me more respect."

"The world has changed a lot since then. But I think we could do good work together."

I stand and step to the window and close the Venetian blinds. "Hard to trust someone who sleeps with a person just to find out her next move. Especially with your résumé."

"I know what the dossier on me probably said, but I'm with a more . . . restrained division now."

"And how'd you know I'd be in Rome? Some restrained pawing through my belongings?"

"You shouldn't write things down. That's pretty basic."

I look away, hollowed out. "I'm willing to consider sharing resources, but . . ."

"What?"

"I don't know. I want ground rules."

"Such as?"

"How about honesty?"

He shrugs.

"And no . . . **us.**" I wave that thought away. "Whatever that is."

"You got it."

"What happened at the Ritz was just stupid on my part. So, going forward, no more . . . that."

"Fine."

"Say we do share what we know. Tell me who killed Johann?"

"Not sure, but probably Russians. He may have gotten too close to someone's truth. Stepped in it big time, obviously. Think you came close to the same fate. I scared someone off from the room while you were in there."

A shiver goes up my back.

"Have any leads on Snow?" he asks.

"No," I say, keeping my Fleur lead to myself.

"You went to see Hudal?"

"Dead end. But right before I came back to the hotel, I saw an old friend."

"Looked like you two were friendly."

I breathe deep and exhale as I sit back on the bed. "I knew her from Ravensbrück. Think she had that motorbike run me down. Warned me not to come back to the hotel. Used my code name."

"May be a Russian double agent."

He's so earnest, with his furrowed brow and concerned expression. Or just another skilled liar? I seem to attract them.

"Say we do team up. What if I'm the one to get Snow first?"

Aaron leans against the dresser. "Then the choice is yours. You decide if he goes back to Texas, or with me to Israel where he'll face actual justice."

"Not one war criminal has been executed in Israel."

"Well, that'll change if we get Snow. And light a fire under our war crimes division."

"Karl would have a stroke if I gave Snow to you."

Aaron shrugs. "The main objective is just to get him, and we can do that better together. In the meantime, you're way too recognizable on the street. You need to cut your hair. Dye it, maybe."

He sits next to me on the bed and rubs my cheek

with his thumb. "And no makeup—attractive women stand out."

"I don't wear makeup."

He meets my gaze, starts to say something, and then abruptly stands.

"For now, stay inside. I have to go away tomorrow, just overnight, but I'll be back. The kitchen is well stocked. So don't leave. I won't be here to babysit you."

"This alliance is already going well."

He walks to the door. "Get some rest. No one's breaking in here on my watch." He turns back. "And, by the way, I didn't sleep with you just to find out your next move."

He walks out, sends me one last annoyingly attractive sulky look, and gently shuts the door. Why does everything with him have to be so difficult?

I pull back the covers and climb into the bed with my firearm. As I turn out the light, I replay seeing Johann in the tub, and I cry there in the dark for my friend. How stupid I'd been to not see it coming and fend it off somehow. What a good man he was. Did he suffer? I try to force that image away. What lead had he been following? Could I have saved him if I'd been there?

I try to think of anything but that bathroom, and sink back into the down pillow. It smells like Aaron.

Aaron. Has he turned over a new leaf as he claims? He's still killed people, done the same types of things I'm going after Snow for. Just on a different team.

I turn and inhale some sort of delicious cedar-pine man-soap. He smelled of it that night at the Ritz. A twinge of guilt nips at me for not being transparent with Aaron, but I must stay focused on the prize and my one lead.

As soon as he leaves in the morning, I'll go to see Fleur.

CHAPTER 44

ARLETTE

FRENCH GUIANA
1952

THE NEXT DAY LUC AND I STAND ON A BLUFF out on the Cove House peninsula, overlooking Camp Hope, and watch as a German film crew shoots the tenth take of the final scene in our commercial. Thomas stands with six of his fellow youth ambassadors posed behind him, each dressed in the uniform I designed, which all the boys long to wear: gray shorts and a matching jacket with burgundy trim and cap. Thomas waits between takes, his face as gray as his outfit, in stark contrast to the other boys' healthy appearances.

At least I snuck Thomas over to Bondi's clinic for

a blood draw of my own this morning. We would know more about his health situation soon.

Luc has promised me that Thomas and I can have a sleepover this week, and I hope tonight's the night. We've gone two hours over schedule due to a brief squall, and we're well over budget. But at least I've been able to see my son an extra day this week. It's been a grueling shoot and has strained one of my most important abilities as a French woman: to make everything look as effortless and graceful as possible.

Luc runs his fingers through his hair. "I wish I'd known we were over budget."

I turn to him. "I never said I'd be good at this."

He holds my upper arm with a firm grasp. "Father Peter says he heard you took Thomas out of camp today without permission. I wish I'd known you were doing that. Is the schedule not working for you? Claudio says he had no idea you'd left."

Thanks for having my back, Claudio.

I yank my arm away. "What, am I some sort of prisoner? I'm here to get my son and go home, Luc. Not to ask your bodyguard for permission every time I have to **pee.**"

My raised voice earns glances from the film crew.

"Calm down." He wraps one arm around my shoulders and with the other rubs my belly. "It's not good for the baby."

I step away from him. "Please don't do that."

Luc is suddenly so attentive to me since I shared my fictitious baby news, and I try to be solicitous back, knowing all it would take is one call to the background check company and my son will be lost to me. But there's something creepy about men who stroke their pregnant wives' bellies. Not that I'm his wife.

"Have you thought about my proposal?" he asks. "I know women prefer a declaration of love on bended knee, but that's all so dramatic, don't you agree?"

I consider the worst-case scenario if we go through with a hasty marriage: I officially get Thomas, depart for Paris, and get an annulment. I could even end up richer for it.

"Of course, Luc."

As we wait for shooting to resume, I take up Luc's field glasses and scan the surrounding area. The bluff provides an incredible bird's-eye view of Cove House and the guest cottages, and I find Claudio's quarters above the garage. He stands at the top of his stairs talking to one of the maids, her arms full of bedsheets, probably mine. A spike of jealousy stabs me. Does he like her? **Just more schoolgirl stuff.**

"What are you looking at?" Luc asks.

Does he have to monitor my every move?

"Just making sure Claudio is delivering my press releases as I asked."

I move the binoculars to the heart of the peninsula jungle and search for the creepy little hut Bondi and I found. I see a bit of the roof peeking through the vines and move on to search the interior for any sign of a house where my new friend Ella might live. A short way from the hut I find what looks like some sort of high wall. I toggle the focus to get a better—

Luc takes the binoculars. "Let's pay attention to the commercial?"

"Of course," I say.

"Just so you know, my grandmother told me that Father Peter continues to give you problems. I've asked our search team to find a replacement for him immediately. They're lining up some candidates to look at this week for training. As soon as they're up to speed, Father Peter has agreed to join a parish he's done some work with near a diamond mine we're part owners of in Brazil."

"How did he take it?"

"Not well. But I explained that we cannot have the head of the program acting so hostile to our adoptive parents. He says he'll go wherever God calls him."

Every part of me relaxes. Finally, some progress.

"Quiet on set," the director calls.

Thomas poses for the camera, hands on hips. What a sweet boy.

"Welcome a Hope Home ambassador to your town," Thomas says with a smile. "Let's bring the world together."

"One more time," the director shouts.

Thomas looks at the ground, one hand pressed to his belly.

I set out toward him. "No," I call to the director. "That's it. We have plenty of good takes."

"Way to take control," Luc says.

The director wraps the set and Thomas hurries to me. "Did I perform well? I'm afraid I'm not feeling good. May I stay with you tonight? I drew you a book about Paris."

Luc smooths his back. "Not tonight, Tommy. You've had a long day."

I step to Luc. "You said Thomas could spend one night this week—"

"I said no such thing."

"Yes, you **did,**" I say, but Luc just leads Thomas off.

Take care of him. Don't let anything go wrong before I can get him back to Paris.

"By the way," Luc calls back to me. "We heard back from the lab in Rio."

I clap one hand to my chest. "About the blood-match results?"

"Sorry to report Thomas's sample was corrupted. They have to redo the test."

"Oh, no, Luc."

"But they tested your sample. You're right. You're type O."

Every part of me deflates. "I can't believe we're back to square one."

"We'll get a sample tonight and I'll expedite it this time."

"But Danae said she expedited it last time."

He adopts a puzzled expression. "No. It costs a king's ransom, but we'll get it done."

As Luc and Thomas walk off, a wave of longing for Josie washes over me. She'd be able to sort out what's going on down here. The reversals. Constant lies. Was he even telling the truth about Thomas's sample being corrupted?

That afternoon, since Claudio is busy fixing the storm shutters on the main house, ahead of a rainy forecast, I walk into town to Hotel Lotus and after much conversation about the telegraph machine not working, finally send a telegram to Josie in care of the address she gave me in Vienna.

> DEEP SUSPICIONS ABOUT WHAT'S GOING
> ON HERE. FOUND WILLIE. COME DOWN
> TO CAYENNE. DR. BONDI WORLD HEALTH
> SUSPECTS SOME SORT EPIDEMIC. GOOD
> STORY FOR YOU.
> YOUR FAVORITE FEMALE

CHAPTER 45

JOSIE

PARIS, FRANCE
1952

I WAKE TO FIND THE SUNLIGHT-FILLED APARTMENT quiet and Aaron gone. I step through the living room to the kitchen to make coffee, and notice the flat is curiously devoid of photographs and intimate objects. Did they own it together before the divorce?

On my way to see Fleur this morning, I plan on calling Karl to find out what he knows about Johann's murder, but the thought of stepping out in broad daylight makes my hands shake. I need to disguise myself well and be extra vigilant about checking for tails.

I take my coffee to the bedroom and slide open the top dresser drawer in search of something nondescript to wear. I paw through more satin lingerie than street clothes, wondering if Aaron and his wife are really as estranged as he claims.

She's a similar size to me, and I slip on a satin camisole and a gauzy blue blouse. I pull out an alligator clutch and snap open the clasp to find a silver compact and a pack of Gauloises cigarettes, relatively fresh. Before I snap the clutch closed, I see a ridge behind the silk lining, feel behind it, and slide out a passport, the green leatherette cover printed with the imperial eagle, DIPLOMATIC PASSPORT lettered in gold along the bottom.

I sit on the love seat. Aaron's wife is a Russian diplomat? Was this left here for my benefit? I open the cover and find a black-and-white photo of a serious young woman, perhaps a year or two older than me, dark hair. Wide-set eyes. Lips slightly parted as if about to ask a question. I check the passport date, 1949. Why wouldn't Aaron tell me his wife was a Russian diplomat? I guess our new alliance only goes so far.

I replace the passport and clutch, slide on the sunglasses, grab her Hermés scarf to tie under my chin, and pocket a black cashmere wrap.

I choose the long way to the Metro to avoid tails. As I wait for a train, I read the headline on the Paris newspaper of the man across from me on the platform: VATICAN BISHOP KILLED IN FREAK BUS ACCIDENT.

Bishop Becker? My knees feel about to give out. Someone must have seen me talking with him.

When I reach my stop, I duck into a café, buy a phone token, and make a call with reverse charges. It's Saturday, and I pray for Karl to answer the phone himself.

Debbine answers, half-asleep. "Crowell residence."

"Mrs. Crowell, it's Captain Anderson."

I check my surroundings, so exposed.

"Josie? Are you in France? I can hear the people talking in the background. Such a pretty language, but they speak so **quickly**—"

"Debbine, may I talk to Karl?"

"He's down in his new study, has insomnia these days, barely sleeps a—"

Someone picks up the extension.

"Hang up, Deb," Karl says, and she clicks off.

"Anderson? This is not a secure line."

"I don't give a shit, Karl." Hot tears prick my eyes. "What happened to Johann?"

He pauses a long second. "We need to talk. How's the weather there?"

"Hurry up," a man behind me says, startling me.

"**Hot,** Karl. I'm out here without a net."

"You need to come home."

"The bishop I saw in Rome is dead suddenly? An agent there knew my code name. What the hell is going on?"

"Where are you? You need to get back here stat."

He's trying to keep me on the line for a trace.

"I need the **truth,** Karl."

"We'll talk about it when you get back. Come home today, and that's an order—"

I slam the receiver down, blood pounding in my ears, and leave the phone to the man behind me.

I exit the café, checking my surroundings. One thing's for sure. I won't be heading back to Texas before I figure out what's going on.

I HURRY TOWARD THE Metropolitan Women's Hospital in Nanterre. As far as I can tell, I'm not tailed as I arrive at a dingy brick building on the outskirts of Paris, the kind of place where the perfectly sane enter and emerge feeling mentally ill. I want to contact Fleur and let her know Arlette and I are on her case. And any info she can provide about Snow will be a godsend.

I follow a man carrying a medical bag through a door with a sign above it that reads PHYSICIANS ONLY. The distant screams from the bowels of the old place send a chill up my back as the man ahead of me flashes his identification card and the head matron admits him. I show the identification card I borrowed during my therapy visit, and she waves me toward a logbook.

"Welcome, Dr. Vincent. You know where you're going?"

"Of course," I say and follow the doctor to an

anteroom, where he exchanges his overcoat for a white jacket.

I do the same and emerge into the hallway as a nurse hurries by.

"Excuse me, Nurse. I'm trying to find a patient of mine. A Hungarian girl. I think she's been moved."

"The schizo?"

"She's around twenty years old or so."

"They haven't moved her. You doctors are so forgetful. She's still in solitary, but they let her have Art Studio Two on Ward Ten these days."

"Thank you."

"Next time ask at the desk; don't bother the nurses. We have our own work to do and don't need all yours as well."

I make a note not to get my medical degree and work here anytime soon, and then head to Ward Ten. On the way, I pass a tiled shower room where a gaggle of naked female patients huddle while a young male attendant sprays them with what looks like a fire hose. He seems to be enjoying his work, aiming the water at their breasts and groins, causing them to cry out piteously.

"You there," I say, stepping into the room. "Stop that."

The man lowers his hose. "Sorry, Doctor. It won't happen again."

"See that it doesn't," I say and move on, enjoying my doctor role.

I find the art studio and start to enter through the metal door.

A man who appears to be an orderly, missing a few teeth and showing at least three days' beard stubble, stops me. "What business do you have in there?"

"I'm here to see a patient. They tell me she's here in the studio."

"Only person in there's a half-wit Gypsy girl."

"I am Dr. Vincent. I need to consult with her physician."

"I'm he. Dr. Tremblay. Don't look so high and mighty. You may be the first outside doctor that's ever come to see her." He leans down and scrutinizes my identification badge. "Affiliated with the American Hospital? Didn't I meet you at the Mental Health Symposium in Vienna?"

I gasp a quick breath. **That's all I need, him calling Dr. Vincent to report me.**

He jabs at my badge. "The Dr. Vincent I met was at least fifty."

I step back. "You're crowding me, Doctor. How's this patient's treatment going?"

"Treatment? Hopeless case if I've ever seen one."

"When was she admitted?"

"Been a ward of the state since I've been here. In the notes it says a Nazi doctor dropped her here. She said the girl had been experimented on by some Nazi doctor."

"May I see the notes? Was the doctor named?"

"No, but something must have triggered some

sort of mood disorder. Delusions. Hyperactivity. Diagnosed schizophrenia as a result of idiopathic trauma. We keep her isolated from other patients since she's inclined to fits of rage. Requires extra staff just to hold her down."

"I need to examine her."

"Well, she doesn't talk. Not one word."

"Would you let me in?"

The man rolls his eyes and fans out the cluster of keys at his waist. "Come along, then. Fair warning, it smells like a latrine in there."

We enter the high-ceilinged room, light streaming in from greenhouse windows above. As the door opens, it lets in a breeze and the pastel drawings taped to the wall wave in greeting.

"There she is," the man says.

I step to the desk, take one look, and wrap my arms across my belly.

"My God, Fleur, what have they done to you?"

"You knew her before she got this way? Where was she?"

"A terrible place, monsieur. A place no child should ever see."

CHAPTER 46

JOSIE

RAVENSBRÜCK
1945

Before.

TWO WEEKS AFTER I CAME BACK FROM THE BUNKER, Arlette and I launched a plan to see my mother again. The bunker had indeed been hellish and worse than Ariana had described. The beatings. The isolation. The icebox-cold cell was the size of my grandmother's actual walk-in icebox back home in Virginia. The cold didn't stop the cockroaches from gathering there in great numbers, especially at "meal" time, finding their way into my watery soup. But it had all been worth it to see my mother for three glorious minutes, and the time off from work allowed me time to think.

My new plan was to smuggle Mother back to our

block, get her a new prisoner number, and have her assigned to our work detail. All I needed was for Ariana to come through with a new job.

Every day that Mother was left in her block was risky, since women were selected for transports so randomly and more frequently from the Jewish blocks. Just seeing her again would be a balm.

Though she'd resisted involvement, claiming she didn't want to participate in any more stunts that could get me thrown in the bunker again, Ariana succumbed to my badgering and wrangled Arlette and me a plum job, delivering the dinner soup. It was tiring work, finding the assigned blocks in the darkness, carrying the heavy metal pots full of tepid soup, and doling it out to ravenous prisoners. But that job meant extra soup and larger crusts of bread for us, and a few extras Arlette could sneak to Willie and the other babies. The plan was to deliver to my mother's block, claiming we'd gotten mixed up, and I could visit my mother again. That evening, Fleur would slip my sleeping draught into the **Blockova** Trudi's afternoon coffee so Mother and I could speak undisturbed.

We struggled with the heavy metal pot across the gravel of the **Platz,** as Fleur walked ahead. For such a young girl she knew the camp inside out and expertly navigated the alleys and shortcuts.

"This way," she called, waving us toward the Jewish blocks.

She led us to a unit that stood cordoned off with

barbed wire. The searchlights from the guard towers washed over the side of it, showing most of the windowpanes to be missing. A young SS man stood at the entrance, a machine gun on a strap slung over his shoulder. Seeing we had the soup boiler, he waved us in, and the women crowded inside made a small space for us.

The Jewish block was arranged with the same tiers of bunks as other blocks and the latrine off to one side, but the women here were even more emaciated. As crowded as our quarters were, with three hundred or more in a space built for two hundred, this one was worse. There were many more women jammed together there, some simply standing, no bunks to be had.

Arlette and I exchanged glances. My mother was there somewhere.

"Where is the **Blockova**?" I asked no one in particular.

Someone in the shadows of a bunk called out. "She's sleeping."

Only one woman approached the boiler, four tin cups in hand. How different this was from the other blocks, where hungry women mobbed us the moment we entered.

"Why are you not coming to get your soup?" Arlette asked.

"We make sure the sick are fed first," the woman said.

I looked for my mother, along the rows of bunks where women waited, dented tin cups in their hands.

How tenderly they cared for one another, friends holding up friends in line. Did Arlette and I look this thin?

I thought of Mimi and blinked away the tears. Thank goodness she was not here. But where had they taken her?

A slight woman with a distinguished air approached. She wore her hair tied back in a dirty white kerchief and held one cup in each hand.

"Is the second cup for another person?" I asked. "Otherwise, I cannot give you two."

"It is for a sick compatriot. But if you cannot break the rules, I will take only one for her and come back."

"It's fine," I said, and ladled soup into both cups.

"Thank you. And Lylou thanks you, too."

I dropped my ladle into the soup. "Lylou?"

"Yes. A woman dear to us. A famous singer, in fact."

"Take me to her."

Arlette leaned closer to me. "Go ahead. I'll take over. But please be fast. Trudi may wake any moment. And we must get the boiler back before too long."

The woman turned as she walked to the back of the block. "I am Natalie. Dr. Dresch. Chief of pediatrics at Berlin General once upon a time. Prisoner doctor now. Assistant in the **Revier.** Do you mind if I ask how you know our Lylou?"

"She's my mother."

"But . . ."

"I don't wear the star, no. She wanted me to have—"

Natalie drew me closer. "No need to explain. She speaks of you often. Josie, is it?"

I could only nod.

"Please do not show your shock upon seeing her, Josie. It has been very difficult for her. She contracted a lung ailment somehow; we think in a clinical trial of some kind led by the medical staff here, and her condition has deteriorated rapidly."

Dr. Dresch walked me toward the back of the barracks, through women standing three and four deep waiting for the soup. We came to a bottom bunk, where Mother slept. She wore her old navy blue dress, curled up on her side, so terribly thin.

I knelt next to the bed. "Mother. It's me." I stroked her cheek.

She turned to me. "I told you not to come, **ma petite.**"

"I'm going to get you out of here, Mother."

"No . . ."

"Where is Mimi? Can you tell me now?"

She brushed away a tear. "French police took us both. Sent us on separate trains. I tried to stay with . . ." She closed her eyes.

I touched her arm. "Mother—"

Dr. Dresch knelt next to me. "It's hard for her to talk about her mother. She goes in and out. She's had some sort of injections."

"Just her?"

"A few from here were taken as well. All we know is they screened for healthy prisoners."

"She's never been sick a day in her life."

"It was some sort of experiment. The doctors here do many. Sulfa experiments. Sterility trials. Infected half this block with various things. They do whatever they please."

"I want to take her to my block."

"I'm afraid I can't let you do that. It's far too dangerous. If they find her missing at roll call this whole block will be punished. Plus, she's too ill to be moved."

Fleur hurried to my side. "Arlette says please come."

I held my hand to Mother's cheek. "She's burning up."

Mother reached for my hand. "The necklace."

"You had it. In your heel?"

"They took it. I told them my father made that."

"Who has it, Mother?"

"The doctor. Snow. I saw . . ."

Dr. Dresch felt Mother's forehead. "Dr. Snow is the worst sort here. Apparently headed up the experiment."

I smoothed the hair back off Mother's forehead. "What did they do to you?"

Fleur crouched next to me. "Please come now, Josie. Trudi is awake and not happy."

I kissed Mother's cheek. "I'll be back."

She attempted a faint smile. "Don't tell anyone we're related, Josie. Promise."

I nodded, gave her one last embrace, and hurried back to Arlette, guilt gnawing at me for my cowardice. **How could I just leave my own mother that way?**

I met Arlette near the block door.

"She can't be moved," I said. "I'm staying here."

Arlette grabbed my arm and pulled me close. "Are you insane?"

"She's sick. Barely able to—"

"Stay here and you'll get you **and** your mother killed. And what about the rest of us? Fleur, me, possibly Ariana, plus this whole block will be sent off in a transport for conspiracy."

"You'd do it for your mother."

She paused, pulled me closer, and spoke softly. "Do what your mother has **asked,** Josie. We can come back again. With medicine."

After one last look back toward Mother's bunk, I grabbed the boiler handle and we headed out into the darkness, past the guard, young Fleur at our heels.

I looked back at the block as we walked. "The doctors have done some sort of experiment on her. Took her necklace."

"I'm so sorry," Arlette says.

"I like your mother, Josie," Fleur said, her face so serious. "I can get that necklace back for her."

CHAPTER 47

ARLETTE

FRENCH GUIANA
1952

I LIE IN MY COTTAGE BATHTUB LISTENING TO AN American jazz song, as the wind picks up. I've lit three candles that give the white-tiled bath an amber glow, floating in the cool water a welcome relief from the stormy, humid air. Since Luc told me the maternal-match blood test has to be redone, the air has gone out of my world here. It will now be at least another week before I can take Thomas home, and with Dr. Ebner down here possibly joining forces with Father Peter I need an immediate solution.

If there weren't so many disturbing things going on down here, I might just enjoy Cayenne, here in my own guest cottage with this luxe bathroom, a fresh, long, white pique robe waiting on the hook behind the bathroom door each day.

A high-pitched tone comes on the radio. **Alert. Hurricane winds approaching the coast. This is not a test.**

I think of Thomas and the boys. Will Father Peter make sure they are protected from the storm? And about the girl living somewhere out in the heart of the jungle. Will she have shelter? My next thought surprises me. It's about Claudio and if he's safe in his quarters. I sit up, push the bathroom curtain aside, and see his light is on above the garage. Will he come to close my storm shutters?

I lie back in the cool water. What would Claudio think of my little tryst with his boss? Would he even care?

What is it about Luc's bodyguard that makes him so intriguing? He's not my usual type. But there's something about the way he reacts when I catch him looking at me. He doesn't turn away and feign disinterest as men often do. He just looks deeper. How old is he? Maybe thirty to my twenty-six? Probably an accomplished kisser.

I'm startled to see the door to his apartment opens and Claudio hurries down the steps, putting up the hood of his rain slicker. I hear him close the shutters on the front of my cottage.

I towel off, slip on my robe, and step to the bedroom. Outside, the shutters close over the windows with a series of thumps as Claudio goes around closing the rest of them.

Before long a knock comes at the door. "Miss LaRue?"

I open it to find him standing there as the rain blows sideways behind him and the palms bend in the wind.

He steps in and closes the door behind him. "I'm afraid you're about to lose power."

"Sorry to bring you out in this."

He's shirtless under the rain slicker and wears pajama pants, the bottoms tucked into tall rain boots. He'd been preparing for bed.

"I closed your shutters."

"Thank you." I smile. How nice it would be to just crawl into my bed with him. But he works for Luc.

Claudio looks around the room. "I shouldn't be in here."

Rain pelts the roof and I step closer to him. "May I ask you a favor?"

"I'm not big on favors."

"I need your help getting out of Cayenne."

He's silent for a long moment. "Why me? You know I work for Monsieur Minau."

"I just thought you might help."

"Why do you need to leave so badly?"

I search his face. Can I trust him?

"I just do."

"Have any rum?" he asks.

I step to the wet bar, pour us each a glass, and return. My robe opens as I walk back and he stares openly at the glimpse of exposed skin.

He takes the glass I offer, and I tie my robe closed. "And what's in it for me?"

I sip my rum. "I can get you money."

He knocks back his drink. "I don't know. This is going to complicate my life. And I don't do anything for less than four thousand francs."

"I can arrange that. I just want to take the jeep and leave with Thomas. Can you cover for us?"

"I could. But that won't work."

"Why?"

"They'd find you within the hour. Even if they didn't, it's not like there are petrol stations at reliable intervals along the way."

"You could chopper us out."

"And be reported and lose my license? Besides, the helicopter's in for repair."

I shrug one shoulder. "I'm sorry I brought it up."

We both stand there and listen to the rain tapping the roof.

"I can get an advance on my salary. At least two thousand. The rest later."

He stares at me. "The mail guy does a run each week. I can ask him to let you and Thomas tag along. Get off at the next stop, Tobago."

"Would you?" Just the thought of soaring away from here lifts my spirits.

"Have to check his schedule, but he always leaves at five."

I step closer to him. He smells so good, of that soap he uses. "But they'll know you helped me."

"I can take care of myself. But my offer comes with conditions."

Of course he wants something in return. Sex, of course. Though, after being close enough to reach out and touch that beautiful chest of his, I'm already warming to the idea.

"What conditions?"

"Lie low for a while in Tobago. Don't go back to Paris. They know you committed a crime. Heard Father Peter say something about a dove."

Is he just trying to get information from me?

He steps closer. "Not that sending you away helps me." He brushes my hair back off my forehead. "May be the stupidest thing I've done in a long time."

How light his touch is. "You barely know me."

The bedside lamps flicker.

He runs one finger down my cheek. "I know more than you think."

"Are you working for someone besides Luc?"

"The less you know the better. What I do can be dangerous."

"I see."

Suddenly the whole cottage goes dark, and we stand in silence, the only light in the room coming from the amber glow of the bathroom candles.

"I'll go," he says.

I nod.

He stays. And draws two warm fingers along my lips.

I gently slide the raincoat down off his shoulders and it falls to the floor. How good it would be to run my hand down that chest, but I hold back.

I huff a little gasp as he sweeps his fingers down the V of my robe, so smooth, hardly the hands of a laborer.

A shutter bangs somewhere as he steps closer and bends in to kiss my mouth, his lips soft against mine.

"I've been wanting to do this," he says in my ear, "since the first day I saw you."

I pull the tie of his pajama pants and he trails kisses down my neck with new urgency, the stubble of his beard grazing my skin.

A knock comes at the door startling us both.

"Arlette?"

Claudio steps away from me. **"Jesus."**

Luc.

I retie my robe and stand motionless in the dark.

Claudio turns and pulls his coat from the floor.

"One minute!" I call out.

Claudio steps to the door and, with one look back at me, opens it to Luc and Father Peter standing there, rain pelting their shared umbrella.

"Monsieur Minau." Claudio stands aside. "We lost power and I came down to help Mademoiselle LaRue put up her shutters."

Luc steps past him. "Inside?"

"Just checking to make sure they're secure."

Father Peter follows, carrying a black doctor's bag.

"Then keep to it," Luc says. "The shutters won't lock themselves."

I step between Luc and Claudio. "Claudio's been invaluable. We were lighting candles when you came. Is Danae all right?"

"Fine." Luc runs his hand through his hair. "But Thomas is not."

I wrap my arms across my belly. "What's wrong?"

Father Peter sets his bag on the bed. "Just the anemia. He had a fainting spell—"

"My God—"

"It's not life-threatening," Luc says.

Father Peter removes his coat. "He's resting comfortably for now, but a blood donation will put him right—if you wouldn't mind? Luc tells me you are a universal donor?"

"Yes, I am. And of course I'm happy to help him—or any of the boys."

I sit in the desk chair, and Father Peter swabs the crook of my arm with alcohol.

Luc steps to my side and runs one finger down the side of my neck. "What have you done to yourself?"

"Where?"

"Looks like a scrape along here."

I feel the abrasion from Claudio's beard. "Oh, it's nothing."

Father Peter opens his case and pulls out a rubber

bag connected to tubing. "Should take only a few minutes. We just need one pint."

Claudio steps from window to window, locking the shutters and glancing at me now and then. It's comforting to have him there as Father Peter gently presses my skin to find a vein.

"Just a pinch," Father Peter says as he inserts the needle.

I prepare for the sting, but the procedure is close to pain-free.

"Where is Thomas now?" I ask as I watch blood flow down the tubing into the bag.

Father Peter calmly tapes the needle in place at my arm. In the candlelight, his face almost seems kind.

"We moved the boys to the clinic to shelter them from the storm. He's safe there with the others. This is just a precaution. Got to keep our ambassador spokesperson healthy, don't you agree?"

"Can I be with him when you do the transfusion?" I ask.

"It's better you stay here for now," Luc says. He turns to Father Peter. "She's pregnant, Father."

An awkward silence settles over the room.

Father Peter seems taken aback and then recovers. "Oh really? Congratulations, Mademoiselle LaRue."

Is it my imagination or did he emphasize the "Mademoiselle" in a judgmental way? Not that long ago, good Germans celebrated babies born to unmarried women. Not that I'm actually pregnant.

I sneak a peek at Claudio. How did he react to my pregnancy lie? His face is stoic as always.

"You're so good at this, Father Peter," I say. "I didn't know you're a physician."

He smiles. "I'm not. Just years of practice at the camp."

Which camp?

"You do lots of medical procedures for the boys? Perhaps hire a nurse."

"Why waste the money when I am perfectly capable, Miss LaRue? Just sit back and relax. You're giving a great gift to this boy."

As Claudio walks past, Luc strokes my hair. For his bodyguard's benefit? Marking his territory?

Luc steps behind me and rubs my shoulders. "With any luck, Thomas will be well enough for the big surprise we have for you at Grandmother's fundraiser." He bends and murmurs in my ear. "Something our friend Claudio will be very interested to see as well."

CHAPTER 48

JOSIE

NANTERRE, FRANCE
1952

I STEP CLOSER TO THE TABLE WHERE FLEUR SITS, gently rocking, her head bowed, hair shaved to the scalp, face covered in plum-colored welts and scratches. She wears a dirty brown canvas straitjacket, the arms buckled across her chest in a gruesome hug, with more straps and buckles attached to the collar to form a leather cage around her head. My heart breaks for her as I run through ways to get her to describe Dr. Snow.

"Is the straitjacket really necessary?"

"The restraint suit? For starters, she bites. And when she isn't drawing, she's whirling around like a mad cat. Comes direct from solitary to here.

Defecates in that bucket. Scared all the other patients away to the other art room."

"It's inhumane."

"Almost put out one orderly's eye."

"Is she medicated?"

"Yes, but it doesn't help much. Electroshock's been considered, but that's expensive."

"It's freezing in here."

"Can't expect the hospital to heat the whole room for one patient."

"And she's been beaten."

"Sometimes the staff gets a little handsy. But mostly she tears herself up. Take away her colored pencils and she's a beast."

I step to the wall of drawings. "Art must be how she communicates. How terrible to be trapped in there. Please remove the jacket."

An orderly looks at Dr. Tremblay, who nods to him.

Once the buckles are undone and the jacket is flopped over a nearby chair, Fleur stands at her drawing table, the back of her hospital gown open.

"Can you not afford underthings? A sweater even?"

"She doesn't feel the cold."

"What is she on now?"

"Just started her on Benzedrine. Keeps her focused at least."

I examine the drawings on the wall. "They're beautiful."

"She often does this many in one **day.** All

nonsensical. We've spent a small fortune on paper and colored pencils, since it's one of the few things that calms the wretched thing."

Dr. Tremblay stands next to me and puts on his glasses. "Won't write many words, just this one phrase." He reads from one of the drawings: "**Fert aurum industria.** Latin, maybe Greek."

"Yes. It means 'Work creates abundance.' "

I step to Fleur, as she sits at the table and hunches over her paper, drawing.

"Fleur." My eyes grow moist.

The last time I'd seen her was when she went off to get the necklace back for my mother and she never returned. I unwind my black scarf from around my neck, still warm from my body heat, and wrap it around her shoulders.

"Arlette's been looking for you. What's happened to you, dear girl?"

She turns and searches my face, and then stands to embrace me.

I hug her in return, and she's so thin I can feel her backbone. I push back the tangle of hair from her sweet face. She's so grown up now, her eyebrows more pronounced, but she's still so thin.

"Can you tell me what happened with Dr. Snow?"

Fleur leads me back to the table. Her cold hands are crosshatched with scratches, and I take them in mine and warm them.

She slaps down a fresh sheet of white paper like a butcher getting ready to wrap a ham and then bends over her work. She sketches quickly, and holds up a golden castle, the crenellations along the parapet like notched teeth.

How devoted Fleur had been at the camp, Arlette's little helper with the babies. Once Arl taught her to draw, there was no stopping her, and she acquired colored pencils and paper from places in the camp only she knew, the offices of the doctors and nurses her favorite targets.

I take the paper from her. "What castle is that, Fleur?"

Dr. Tremblay stands nearby, his arms folded across his chest. "I told you she won't answer. God knows what's going on in that head."

I rub Fleur's shoulder, flashing back to the photos from Rome. "She's been through a lot."

Fleur casts aside the castle and sketches a shallow boat filled with gold coins. Then a shaggy beast with a long snout.

"Calm down, Fleur. Are you trying to tell me something?"

The doctor walks the length of the drawings along the wall. "None of these make any sense. No people, just mythical beasts and fairy-tale things."

Fleur frowns and holds up another drawing, of three fleurs-de-lis on a cobalt field, and thrusts it toward my face.

"She's becoming agitated," the doctor says. "I think it's best you return another day."

"Fleur, can you draw Dr. Snow?"

She pushes the pictures toward me, slapping her palms down on them.

The doctor snatches the straitjacket and steps toward the table. "I'm afraid it's time."

Fleur lunges toward me and flings her arms around my neck.

I hold her tight. How satisfying it would be to just walk out of there with her.

"It will all be fine. I'll return soon. I'm going to get you out of here."

The orderlies tear her from me, and Fleur breaks away and runs to the wall, pounding her forehead against the plaster.

"My God," the doctor calls out. "Stop her."

The orderlies pin her to the ground.

I rush to them. **"Careful."**

Fleur continues to flail as they stuff a rubber gag in her mouth, wrap her in the jacket, and secure the leather straps about her head.

I step to the doctor. "You call yourself a doctor."

"She's a ward of the state. This is more than most get."

"I'm having her transferred to Paris General. I'll take her with me now."

"And have me stripped of my right to practice? You can't just walk out with her. You know how much paperwork transfers require."

As the orderlies pull her toward the door, Fleur looks back with a glint of tears in her eye.

"I'll be back soon, Fleur," I call to her. "Arlette, too."

The doctor turns to me. "You need to leave now."

I gather the drawings from the table. "I'm taking these."

The doctor shrugs. "As you wish, but you must go."

"Start the paperwork for her transfer to Paris General." I hand the doctor a business card. "Send the bill to this man."

He takes the card and reads. "Karl Crowell, U.S. Army? As you wish. But nothing can help that girl."

I gather up Fleur's drawings and hurry off, back to Aaron's apartment, my heart breaking for our poor Fleur, and my last lead now gone.

CHAPTER 49

ARLETTE

FRENCH GUIANA
1952

A FEW DAYS LATER I WAKE TO FIND ONE WHITE sock pinned to the line, gently blowing in the breeze. It's the signal Claudio and I have set up to say the mission is a go. It will be a good day to fly.

Claudio has offered to bring Thomas to the air-strip to meet me that evening and I cannot believe my good luck. He's the only thing I'll miss about French Guiana. Hopefully he can be trusted.

I spend most of the day at the kids' camp pretending to sketch various locations while trying to catch a glimpse of my son. Soon I won't have to wait for Saturdays to see my own child.

I set up and sketch Father Peter's watchtower and

catch a glimpse of Thomas walking with a group of boys. He waves and I wave back. What a delicious secret it is, that he'll be with me tonight winging our way to Tobago.

I know I shouldn't break the rules and talk to him, but he is my own son after all.

"What is your schedule today?" I ask as he passes.

"Just geography class and dinner," he says. "Will you join us? I can ask Father Peter."

"Oh, no. Please don't mention it. I'm just curious."

I get back to my cottage and pack a few pairs of underwear and my toothbrush in my green bag. No need to lug a heavy suitcase to the airstrip. We can find whatever we need in Tobago.

IT MUST BE ONE hundred degrees when I arrive at the airstrip, just a field of burned-out grass and a small, whitewashed hut surrounded by a chain-link fence.

A cluster of skinny goats graze on the field and the scene shimmers in the heat. I keep to the cool edge of the jungle, look for Father Peter's watchtower, and find it in the distance. It's so exposed here. But by the time we're in the air he won't be able to touch us.

Twilight begins to fall and soon a plane circles above. He's early.

At first, I'm wary of a setup and step carefully to the little hut but find only a small canvas mailbag.

I stay under the canopy of trees near the gate and watch the biplane make a wobbly landing. Is the pilot already getting ready for happy hour? The plane looks like a wooden bathtub with wings. With mail leaving like this twice monthly it's a wonder any mail gets through.

The pilot, a stocky man wearing a denim coverall, his white hair loose and flowing, removes himself from the cockpit, jumps to the ground, and heads into the little hut.

"If you're my passenger we leave in five," he says in French.

"But we need to wait for—"

"I'm not waiting. You try flying this thing in the dark."

"But they're on their way."

"You're not in that plane when I'm ready then you don't go."

As the pilot carries the canvas bag to the plane the sound of a car comes in the distance. **Claudio.**

"Here he comes," I say.

Claudio will have to stay under the cover of the canopy to avoid Father Peter's gaze.

The car rounds the bend in the distance, Claudio driving, and I hurry to meet them. I try to tamp down the joy. I must keep my wits about me, for within minutes we'll be airborne.

CHAPTER 50

JOSIE

PARIS, FRANCE
1952

THE NEXT DAY, BACK AT AARON'S APARTMENT, I spend hours adrift, sitting on his sofa drinking his best pinot nero. How hard it had been to leave Fleur there at the asylum. That place is a hellhole but I'll stay on my new doctor friend to follow through and transfer her. How can I possibly continue without Johann, all leads gone? Surely Karl will find me somehow and demand I come home. After I drain most of the bottle I think of the canister Johann gave me and asked me to develop. At least it's something concrete to do.

As twilight falls I stand in Aaron's bathroom in the near dark and develop the last of Johann's film. The red light bulb I placed in the socket over the medicine chest gives the room an eerie glow as I pull the film from the developing bath. I wait for the negatives to dry and try hard not to look at the bathtub, the events in Rome still seared deep.

It's haunting, seeing Johann's last photos, and my eyes well, missing him.

Icy snow pummels the windows as I hold my jeweler's loupe to the shot Johann took of the photo on his aunt's wall, the jolly bunch of Ravensbrück workers in Snow's office. It's a typical camp office, with a heavy oak desk and chair. There's a travel poster thumbtacked to the wall, with palm trees leaning, the ocean beyond, **Viens et joue! Come and play!,** written in script across the top and a wooden armoire at the far end of the room.

I lob Fleur's drawings onto the bathroom floor and sift through them. Nothing really stands out, but what is she so desperately trying to tell me?

There's the long-snouted beast. A fairy-tale castle, a white flower. A water lily? Actually, she has drawn the same flower Odysseus came upon on his return. A lotus.

I grab the jeweler's loupe again and hold it to the negative of Snow's office, to the travel poster. There's a coat of arms in the bottom corner, **Fert Aurum Industria** written across the top of it.

All at once it comes to me. How could I not have seen?

CHAPTER 51

ARLETTE

FRENCH GUIANA
1952

CLAUDIO COMES, DRIVING DANAE'S LIMOUSINE, and brakes with a screech.

I hurry to the car and find the front seat next to him empty.

A claw of despair rakes my chest. "Where is he?"

Claudio steps out of the car. "I looked everywhere but no Thomas. Think maybe they got wind of this?"

The disappointment crashes down and I can barely speak.

"I'm so sorry. I know this must be hard."

Was this all a setup?

I walk away from the car. "You never intended to bring him, did you?"

He follows. "Why would I set all this up for nothing?"

"I don't know."

Out on the airstrip the pilot starts his engine and the propeller whirls.

"You should get on that plane and just go," he says. "It isn't safe here."

"I can't leave Thomas."

"I can't say any more but you need to go. You're in way over your head here."

"You better drive back without me—I'll walk. But I'm not leaving. Not without my son."

I WAIT ON THE terrace for Danae on Saturday morning, trying to unravel it all, Claudio's cryptic warning, Thomas's sudden disappearance. I'm frantic to know how he's doing after the transfusion. It would have been nice to just fly off into the sunset, but how could I leave without my child?

Had they kept him from me on purpose or was he lying sick somewhere? Surely Father Peter had seen me meeting Claudio at the airstrip. Perhaps Danae's attitude will tell me something.

Luc has gone off to the office early and I survey the damage the storm did, the wreck of a small fishing boat overturned on the beach below. **What's the big surprise Luc has waiting for me at Danae's fundraiser?** I'm not a big fan of surprises after surviving Ravensbrück, where so many unanticipated events were not exactly positive, so I'm not looking forward to what Luc has in store. But as long as he brings Thomas so I can make sure he's okay, I'll be happy.

I'm feeling overdressed in my baby blue linen tunic, white pants, and faux pearls, one of many lovely outfits Danae had bought for me. I watch the white-capped sea as I consider Luc's proposal. If I loved him, it would certainly solve a lot of problems for me.

"Arlette!" Danae calls from the bedroom wing. "There you are."

Danae walks toward me, leaning on her cane, dressed in an airy ensemble of creams and light pinks.

I rush to her. "Have you heard anything about Thomas?"

"After the transfusion? I hear he's feeling much better." I help her sit, a wave of her lovely gardenia perfume wafting up.

As I sit, she raises her water glass. "Here's to that." She leans in. "Perhaps you shall see him at the fundraiser."

"I would love that." I place my napkin in my lap. "Your hair looks especially well done today, Danae."

"I've always said either dye your hair your natural color or go all gray. Keep salt and pepper for the table."

I smile. "And your skin—" What a handsome woman she is, her silver hair coiffed, the radiant skin French women are so famous for, hers the result of great care, expensive creams, and treatments, no doubt.

She leans toward me. "I'll share with you my secret: a gin martini straight up. Take one daily."

"Have you checked the mail today? I'm waiting for those new blood-test results."

"I haven't made it through the mountain of envelopes in my office yet. But I will check. It's a bit overwhelming, what with the fundraiser and all those letters to answer. I really should hire a secretary."

"I'm happy to help."

"Oh, I wouldn't wish that on my worst enemy. You have enough on your plate."

I smile. "Champagne for breakfast?"

Danae toasts me. "Here's to a successful fundraiser today **and** to the hope that Thomas is your match."

"Thanks to you and Luc. It's like I'm dreaming."

"Just splendid." She leans in. "And I hope you don't mind that Luc told me you might consider his proposal."

How to explain to this lovely woman that, although I'm flattered, and her grandson would improve my net worth substantially, I could never marry someone I didn't love and would much prefer his bodyguard? But if I reject Luc, will he and his grandmother be less eager to help me bring Thomas home?

"I'm truly flattered, but it's all happened so quickly. I have a child to consider now."

"Yes, a proposal should be done properly. And the boy should be consulted."

"I'm not sure Luc and I are right for each other."

Danae sips her champagne. "I understand. When I married my husband, it wasn't what you'd call a love match. But two people can grow together."

"Not sure what he sees in me."

"A stunningly beautiful woman, who could be the face of Balmain, who isn't after him for his fortune? To be honest, most of the girls in his past would have proposed to **him** by this point. Once they realize they'd inherit this place, our apartment on Avenue Montaigne, and ninety million francs they suddenly find they're in love."

Not to mention a diamond mine.

"It's a lot to think about, Danae. Having my son back. A proposal. You'll understand if I need time to digest it all? And getting my son formalized is my priority."

She pats my hand. "You have good instincts. But if we **did** have the wedding soon, there are many of our friends here for Carnival. We'd have quite a guest list."

"Let's take it slowly."

"Of course, dear. An official engagement would have to come first. But now we must go to Hotel Lotus for the luncheon. Quite a nice affair. One even Luc will tear himself away from his work to attend. And, trust me, this is one event you do not want to be late for."

—

THE SWEET SCENT OF gardenia greets us as Danae and I enter the hotel ballroom, a massive crystal chandelier shimmering above, the tables set with centerpieces of white flowers and forced cherry blossoms. Every table is full, the room humming with conversation, and the chamber orchestra plays a waltz. The stage is decorated with a painted canvas backdrop of the Eiffel Tower, and someone has set up a catwalk through the middle of the round tables.

"Like it?" Danae asks. "We sold out the place. At fifty dollars a ticket I'd say we reached our goal." She waves to guests here and there as we walk through the tables. "Oh, look—Antonio Caggiano is here. Argentine bishop. A friend of Father Peter's. Women have flown in from all over, quite a few from Rio."

All heads turn as Danae slowly makes her way toward the stage. A waiter escorts me to a table close to the catwalk with a perfect view of it all.

Danae steps up onto the stage, assumes the podium, and taps the microphone.

"Hello, everyone. Thank you for joining us for the third annual Hope Home fundraising event. Your special gifts will help us reach our goal."

Luc slides into the chair next to me. "Have you figured out what this is all about yet?" He waves toward the stage. "It's all for you."

Danae continues. "This year we have a fashion show for you, and I know you'll like it. Sit back and enjoy . . . as we ask the question, why is it just April in Paris? What about Paris in June?"

A model starts down the runway, dressed in a blue chiffon cocktail dress, the fabric billowing out behind her as she walks.

"What a beautiful dress," I say.

"Isn't it?" Luc asks. "Look familiar?"

On closer inspection it's identical to one from my sketchbook.

A woman at the next table gasps. "Lovely."

Danae adjusts her glasses. "Who doesn't love blue chiffon, layer upon layer of it for a night at **l'opéra**?"

Luc places his arm around my shoulders. "Do you like it?"

"I don't understand."

"Keep watching."

Another model walks down the catwalk and removes her jacket. "A yellow Dior-inspired day dress and bolero jacket for an afternoon lunch in Le Marais."

All the designs are mine. And, even from where I sit, I can see the workmanship is exquisite, down to the beige satinet lining of the little jacket, which is just as delicately fashioned as the exterior.

Luc leans in and murmurs in my ear. "Danae's been planning a fashion show for months, but when she saw your sketches, she was inspired."

"How did she see them?"

"I took the liberty of borrowing them."

I grab the edge of the table, light-headed. "You took them from my room?"

"We wanted it to be a surprise."

I shake my head, regaining equilibrium. "She did it all so quickly."

"Thanks to that tailor shop she likes."

"Couture Elégante?"

"Stitched day and night, apparently."

My designs keep coming.

Danae's voice rings out across the ballroom. "Get ready for the approaching revolution in clothes. The caftan has arrived."

My pearl-gray caftan moves in the way I hoped it would, and my lavender sunsuit is next. **Why are they doing this?**

Danae leans into the microphone. "And now for the pièce de résistance. Everyone loves a wedding. Am I right?"

Bridesmaids start down the catwalk dressed in my apricot chiffon designs, gardenia bouquets in hand.

"And the bridal suit," Danae calls out. "Who says it has to be snow white—**or** even a dress for that matter? Ecru is **au courant.**"

Dread rises in me. The wedding suit is my design, nipped in at the waist in the style of Dior, layered over pencil-thin silk trousers.

"May I ask the models to please do a final turn?"

The applause rolls over me, and I consider what's coming with panic.

Danae waves to the crowd to quiet. "Thanks to your generosity we've raised over five thousand dollars today alone for Hope Home and had some fun, too, I daresay. I'd like to call my grandson Luc to the stage and our friend and the designer of today's fashions, Arlette LaRue."

Luc takes me by the hand and pulls me onto the stage, and the applause swells.

"Arlette is one of our match moms from the foundation," Danae continues. "When we learned she's a crack designer, we wanted to showcase that talent. All the pieces are available by silent bid. One more way to give. And now, my grandson Luc. Please say a few words?"

Luc steps to the podium, and Danae stands next to me onstage.

He adjusts the microphone higher. "Thank you for coming. I think Arlette's story of survival and persistence is an inspiring one. All these years after her son went missing, she never lost hope. Always said 'Yes, I can.' But I'm hoping she'll say yes to another question today."

Luc comes to me and my stomach lurches.

"What are you doing?" I whisper.

He kneels on one knee, and a collective gasp rises from the audience.

"Arlette, from the moment I met you, I knew this was right. We mustn't auction off that last ensemble, am I right? Will you marry me?"

I feel disconnected from my body and look out over the audience, so many of them cheering and clapping. I want to stop the whole thing and explain, but I'm immobile.

All at once the crowd erupts in a chorus of "aahs."

I turn to find Thomas dressed in a pale gray suit, walking toward me holding a satin pillow, a ring tied to it. He smiles at me, steps to Luc, and presents his gift. An emerald-cut diamond the size of Devil's Island, set in . . . platinum?

My eye catches something in the crowd and I find Claudio standing at the back of the room, his arms folded across his chest, watching, a concerned look on his face. I want to call out to him, "I'm just doing this to get my son."

Thomas looks up at me. "Please say yes?"

I take in his hopeful expression, the bruise-purple smudges under his eyes. He's been through so much in his nine years. Will they take him from me if I say no?

I smile, numb to it all, and wish Josie was here. Has she even received my telegram? I'm falling out of a plane with no parachute but can always walk away once I have Thomas secured.

I hold Thomas close, still reeling from the proposal. Luc on one knee. The incredible kindness of Danae, having my designs made. The wedding suit. The lights play in the diamond on Thomas's little pillow. **Engaged.** Something I've always wanted but not like this, certainly.

Danae assumes the podium once again. "Well, Arlette? The world is waiting."

CHAPTER 52

JOSIE

PARIS, FRANCE
1952

I KNEEL ON THE BATHROOM FLOOR AND REARRANGE Fleur's drawings into the parts of the crest. The lotus. The golden castle. The Latin motto. Two anteaters.

It's brilliant. Fleur has drawn the elements of the crest in Snow's office. Trying to tell me where he is.

I don't recognize the crest. To what country does it belong?

I run the glass over the poster and find more writing along the bottom.

"My God," I say and sit back.

Cayenne, French Guiana.

If Fleur is right, Snow is there somewhere.

I flash to Arlette there with Luc Minau, unaware

of the threat. Why did I not listen to my instincts and insist she wait before flying down there?

I have to help her, but am I crazy to head off to French Guiana right now? Karl will think I've gone rogue, disobeying his direct order to come home. I could hop an army transport back to Fort Bliss, grab a posse, and go down there ready. Karl was wrong to send me on this mission unprepared to begin with. My father had said it. Johann, too.

Johann. If they got him, an experienced agent, I would be an easier target alone in South America.

But if I go back to Texas, will Karl even let me out in the field again? Doubtful. He'll send Tony P. and friends, and they'll bring Snow back in time for bowling night. Or botch it and we'll all die at the hands of the Russians for sure. Who's better to find Snow down there, since I'll have Arlette to work with again? No one else will care about her safety like I will. I'm only one person, but Arlette and I can do anything together.

I compose a cable to send her at Cove House, with details of my arrival.

And a warning.

It's time for toast with marmalade.

CHAPTER 53

JOSIE

FRENCH GUIANA
1952

When we land in French Guiana it seems a miracle we've finally arrived, more than a week late, after an emergency landing in Lisbon for lengthy repairs. We descend over a lush rain forest, as if into a prehistoric world, a flock of enormous black birds skimming the palmtops below. The green expanse stretches out for miles inland. No wonder Nazis come down here to hide. Thousands of meters of impenetrable jungle. Good news is, it's an easy place to dispose of a body.

Customs takes forever, and I finally exit the one-room terminal to a wall of green jungle, the scent on the light breeze so like my grandmother's greenhouse back in Alexandria, of decomposing plants and wet moss. I undo the top button of the shirt I borrowed from Aaron's ex-wife, cuff the linen pants I also borrowed, and try to ignore the idea we wear the same size.

I'm eager to see Arlette. Knowing Snow's down here, I just want to have eyes on her to know she's okay. Maybe she'll have some insight into his whereabouts. I feel for the filigreed pen in my knapsack and I find it there, cool and heavy. If it really is his, he may recognize it.

It's late afternoon and must be one hundred degrees by the time I taxi to Hotel Lotus, the largest hotel in Cayenne, the capital. The streets are full of Carnival revelers, and soon I arrive at a soaring white grand dame of a building, recently renovated, according to the lobby brochure, but clearly in need of another face-lift. At least the tiled lobby is coolish, and ceiling fans are stirring the muggy air. The sound of waves crashing somewhere, hopefully along a sandy beach, is a bright spot.

I head to the front desk counter, my backpack slung over my shoulder, and the young clerk smiles as I approach.

"Checking in," I say, plucking at my linen shirt, soaked through. "The name is Anderson. I'd like to send a telegram."

"So sorry, Miss Anderson, our lines are down after the storm. But I do have a letter for you." He hands me a white envelope, **Josie Anderson** written there in Arlette's flowery script.

I open it.

WELCOME TO FRENCH GUIANA,
MY DARLING! EAGER TO SEE YOU AT
COVE HOUSE. PLEASE RING WHEN YOU
ARRIVE, AND WE WILL SEND A CAR.

"A lovely gardenia plant accompanied the letter. Should I have it sent up to your room?"

"Yes, thank you. And may I use your phone? I wish to call a taxi."

"Our phone is out, so you must hail a street taxi if you can find one, but most drivers go home this time of day to sleep. Too hot. Or I can have someone take you in the hotel jeep. It's right out front."

"I'll drive the jeep."

"You, madame? Alone? That is highly unusual."

I slide a twenty-franc note across the desk and he hands me the key.

"May I have a bellman take your bags—"

"I have no bags. How do I get to Cove House?"

"Go north on Coast Road quite a way until you see pillars on the left."

I grab the key, hurry outside, and start up what they call a jeep, more an open platform with seats, which makes me yearn for my old jeep at Fort Bliss.

As I drive along the narrow dirt road, which winds

along the oceanfront cliffs, the views of the ocean and Devil's Island in the distance are breathtaking. After almost veering off into the ocean at one or two precarious spots along the way, I remind myself to keep my eyes on the road. It will be like medicine to see Arlette.

I suppose I've officially gone rogue, after hanging up on Karl, and then not telling him I was going to French Guiana. On my own now. Could I even get a status update to him from here if I wanted to?

Just as I note I'd not seen another car the whole drive, I hear an engine behind me and slow for them to pass. It's a service truck of some kind, as wide as the road, and as it passes by, it swerves and scrapes the side of the jeep, bumping me toward the cliff edge.

I lean on my horn, but no sound comes out. "Hey—"

The driver, up high so I cannot see them, bumps me again and I skid off the road. My whole body goes cold as the jeep heads for the cliff edge. I brake hard, skid, and go airborne.

I AWAKEN ON THE ground as twilight is falling to find the hotel jeep impaled on the stump of a severed palm tree. I stand and take a few steps, walk into a puddle, and sink ankle-deep in mud, marveling that I managed to avoid the fifty-foot drop.

A chill goes through me, there in the warm air.

Who knows I'm here? Russians? Arlette, of course. The Minaus, clearly. Who else?

I walk the rest of the way to the Cove House pillars. As darkness falls, two uniformed sentries eye my muddy trousers, check their list for my name, and then escort me by jeep to the main house.

Soon the compound comes into view. Knowing the connection to a children's camp, I had pictured Cove House as more rustic, but it's an ultrasophisticated one-story villa. Perfectly situated in the cliffside, the low-slung, modern main house is a great example of sleek Bauhaus style, designed without interior walls.

My stomach growls as we approach the villa. The meals on the flight seem eons ago. Inside, a few people move about in the amber light. A tall man who may be Luc fixes drinks. An elegant, silver-haired woman sits on the sofa. Luc's grandmother? I inhale a quick breath as Arlette walks past the window.

The guard knocks on the door. The front light comes on and Arlette and the man emerge, the older woman close behind, leaning on a cane.

One guard steps forward. "This is the guest of Miss LaRue?"

Arlette embraces me. "My goodness, Josie! What's happened to you?"

I brush off my sleeve. "Just a little accident. Drove the hotel jeep. Not used to the roads."

"Did you get my note? Danae's gardenia? We're just thrilled you're here."

"Emergency landing in Portugal took forever. Sorry, this is all so last-minute. But I've been assigned a story here."

The man steps toward me, and Arlette introduces us. "Josie, this is Luc. Luc, Josie. My favorite female."

He squints one eye. "I'm sorry. 'Favorite female'? Is that an American expression?"

"Just something an old friend of Arlette's called her once upon a time."

Luc leans in and kisses me on both cheeks. "What a happy coincidence you've been assigned here. When did your flight arrive?"

Though he looks quite taken with Arlette, Luc Minau seems all wrong for her. While he'd be considered by some to be attractive in a bland way, he's almost fifteen years older than she is, with all the charisma of a clam. Without his excellent shoes and lovely linen shirt, he'd be a brush salesman or grocer.

I smile. "Just a while ago."

The elegant woman hurries to me, leaning on her cane. I assume this is Luc's grandmother Arlette spoke of.

"Come in, please. We would have sent a car. You must be tired from your trip. By the time one gets to the Azores it seems the trip should be finished, don't you agree? And it's barely half over by then."

Arlette slides one arm around the older woman's shoulders. "Josie, this is Luc's grandmother, Danae Minau."

"Let's get you cleaned up," Danae says, reaching

down to brush off my trousers. "And we'll contact the hotel to come pick up their car."

A truly elegant woman, Danae seems to have gotten all the charm and compassion in the family.

Arlette looks to Danae with a smile. "The Minaus have asked me to do some public relations work. So, I'd love it if you could do a story on Hope Home—their foundation—while you're here."

"What a good idea," Danae says.

Arlette looks to Luc, half teasing, half scornful. "Would be great for fundraising, don't you think, Luc?"

Luc looks at me. "Of course."

"**Would** you, Josie?" Danae asks. "We'd be terribly grateful."

"But it's better if you stay at the hotel," Luc says. "Our guest cottages were damaged in the storm."

"I couldn't impose," I say. "And besides, I must file my stories with the hotel telex. I'm on deadline for the **New York Journal American.** Based out of New York City."

"The lines are down from the storm," Danae says. "But they'll be repaired soon. Maybe just stay here one night? So you two can catch up?"

Arlette takes my hand. "Yes, please stay. I really should get you to the cottage to change."

Danae smiles. "It's settled, then. Just hold off on taking Josie over to Camp Hope."

Arlette turns to her. "But I thought—"

"We'll get her over there soon enough for the story, but give them a chance to clean up. There are palm fronds everywhere. Don't want a mess like that ending up in the paper."

"Of course," Arlette says.

She leads me outside and along a path toward a thatched-roof cottage in the distance. We enter a well-appointed room, the bed already turned down. Our steps echo on the wide Spanish tile floor, and I run one hand down what look like Italian sheets on the mosquito-netted bed.

"Check for bugs?" I mouth.

"First thing I did when I got here," she says with a smile. "And every morning. Old Dove habits die hard. You must be starving, Jos. I took my tray in the room tonight, trying to get some sketching done. Help yourself to it."

I sit next to the dinner tray Arlette hasn't touched, which holds a piece of bread alongside a sweating butter pat, some tea sandwiches, and a bowl of chopped papaya.

Arlette turns on a bedside light. "I've missed you so much. Did you get my telegram?"

"No. Things have been . . . busy."

"I got yours, though."

"Just one?" I ask.

"Yes, the one about toast with marmalade. What's wrong?"

"It's a long story, but I think a doctor from Ravensbrück may be here in French Guiana. Snow."

Arlette steps back. "How do you know?"

I pause.

"Are you back spying again?" she asks.

"I—"

"You **are.** I knew it."

I take a stale tea sandwich from the tray. "U.S. Army Intelligence. I've agreed to track down Dr. Snow."

"No, Josie."

"I've wanted to tell you, but I didn't want you to know too much. It's dangerous here, Arlette. I was deliberately forced off the road on my way over from the hotel. Russians, maybe. Not sure."

"Russians? What makes you think Snow's here?"

"Of all people, Fleur."

Arlette leans in, eyes wide. "You saw her?"

"She's in a terrible way, Arlette. Can't even speak."

"Yes, I saw her before I left—from afar."

"But when I asked about Snow, she drew the crest of French Guiana."

"Fleur did?"

"It was on the poster in Snow's office, I realized. So, unless he's already moved on, there's a good possibility he's here somewhere."

Arlette leans back. "My God. I think I may know who it might be. Father Peter, a priest who helps the Minaus run this place."

"German?"

"Says he's Swiss, from Jungfraujoch, but it doesn't track. I've been told he's being reassigned, but he's still quite powerful here. Needs to sign off on my getting my son."

I pull the filigreed pen from my knapsack. "This supposedly belongs to Snow. We can see if he recognizes it."

"Perfect. And did you get my letter about finding Willie?"

"No." I clap my hands together. "It's true? How wonderful, Arl."

"A boy named Thomas. He's my son, Jos, I'm sure of it. Just waiting for the blood-test confirmation. I knew it first time I saw him. So much like Gunther."

"I interviewed Herta at Landsberg. She said Binz took Willie."

"What?"

"You didn't get my cable? Sent a postcard too."

"No."

"So, it's entirely possible it's your boy."

Arlette comes to sit next to me on the bed, new hope in her eyes. "It all seems so unreal."

"Does this boy Thomas remember you at all? How did he get here?"

"He doesn't remember much from his babyhood. Ended up in an orphanage after the war—Binz must have saved him after the **Kinderzimmer** and then someone brought him there. He's been sick though. I need to get him back to Paris, but Father Peter's blocking it."

"The one you think might be Snow?"

"Yes. An older gentleman. Odd sort. Very secretive. Has a watchtower at the kids' camp that he climbs and uses his field glasses to follow everyone's comings and goings."

"Probably saw me arrive, then."

"He has a creepy gun collection. One with a scope that he hunts at night with."

"A **Vampire**? Never seen one in person."

Arlette pulls a photo from her green bag. "And I found this." Four men smile there, swastikas bound to the upper sleeves of their uniforms.

"Doing information collections again?" I ask with a smile. "Just like the old days."

"Look. There he is in the middle. In **Der Stahlhelm.**"

"Many ex-servicemen joined that group. It's not like it was SS."

"Strange for a priest to belong though, isn't it? **And** he claims he's not a doctor, but he drew my blood to transfuse Thomas, and he was **very** good at it. And I saw a weird notebook of his, with cross sections of twin cow fetuses—"

"I hate to say I told you so, but I warned you about coming here."

Arlette levels her best cool look at me. "Please don't say that to me."

"You have to admit—"

"And he has made an enemy of a doctor here, Kena Bondi."

"From World Health? She's famous."

"And Thomas told me Father Peter has some of the local kids in the camp clinic sick."

"Do we really need to stay away from the camp tomorrow? I want to meet Thomas. And Father Peter. He could easily be Snow."

"Agreed. But I don't recognize him from Ravensbrück."

"There were over one hundred doctors there at different times. We never saw them all. The smart ones hid their identities."

"I can sneak you over there and deal with Danae later. We should go to town and see Dr. Bondi, too. And in other news . . ." Arlette walks to the closet and returns with a diamond ring on her palm, a massive, brilliant-cut stone. "I had to take it off when I was sketching, but I'm engaged."

"I'm sorry, what did you say?"

"To Luc."

"**Arl.** You've only been here five weeks."

"I had to say yes. I doubt he'd support my adopting Thomas if I didn't return his affection. I started doing PR work for them, and before you knew it Luc proposed in front of the whole world, and I just couldn't say no. Danae is planning a whole rehearsal luncheon soon, where Father Peter is introducing us . . ."

"Slow down. And when's the wedding?"

"They want to do it the next **day.**"

"Why the rush?"

"I may have told him I'm pregnant."

"Tell me you're joking."

"Don't worry, I'm not. But things did get a little,

well, intimate back in Paris and I thought leveraging that might get him to send me back to Paris with Thomas, but no dice. Now Luc just keeps implying the wedding is part of me getting my son. He's become so controlling. Prince Charming to the rest of the world, but so rigid when we're alone. He has a **schedule** for me to follow. He may just be trying to keep me here. And worst of all . . . I think they know about Auntie somehow."

"Calm down, Arl."

"Calm down? The brass dove I made for you? It's **here.**"

A chill runs through me. "It can't be the same one."

"It certainly is. I checked."

"That's not good."

"**Yes.** And Dr. Ebner's here. From the Lebensborn home."

"I think he came here through Rome."

"He and Father Peter are definitely working on something creepy. Maybe inseminating girls."

"Oh, Arl—"

"They say there are no girls here but I saw a wall out in the jungle—could be a whole separate camp for girls. This place is beyond creepy. Can you just call your boss and get us out of here? That is bigger than anything we can handle."

"Hold on. If this Father Peter is Snow, I need to take him, and you could be a huge help."

"Let me guess. Stay here at Cove House and gather intel for you?"

"Together like the old days. You'll be my inside agent."

"No, Josie. I can't."

"Admit it. You miss the Dove days. There's something thrilling about—"

"Yes, but now that I have Thomas, I can't risk losing him. Besides, I'm not sure Luc's in on it."

"If this Father Peter is Snow, then Luc's probably at least complicit."

"The thought has occurred to me. But a Nazi? Luc's French."

"Lots of French men fought for the Reich. Many with the Charlemagne Division. Recruited by Hitler when his master race ran low. Help me figure it out."

"Thomas has been exhausted and has fevers that come and go. They say it's anemia, but—"

"It's only a few extra days. Just play along with the whole wedding thing, say I'll be your maid of honor. You're a wonderful actress."

"This is hard."

"If Father Peter's Snow, I can take him, maybe right from that rehearsal luncheon, and then you're out of here, courtesy of the U.S. government. If I can contact Karl. What's that shack on the hill with the big antenna?"

"Ham radio. Think it's Father Peter's. No way he'd let us use it." Arlette looks out the window. "It's all so overwhelming."

"Let's get some sleep."

Arlette steps to the tray, picks up a piece of bread,

and hands it to me. "Remember the night at the camp when you saved your bread for me? Seems like a million years ago."

I take the bread, and Arlette and I slip into bed and rest there, me spooning against her. It takes me back to that night in the Ravensbrück barracks when we slept in just the same way in a narrow bunk. Icy rain pelted the windows as I held her, and she cried for her lost child, an infection already raging in her from the dog bite. I'd bandaged her the best I could, gave her my crust I'd saved from dinner, and matched my breathing with hers as she slept.

My thoughts float back to the present. **Can I really deliver as promised, get Arlette and Thomas out of here? Should I try to contact Karl? Will he find out I'm here and intervene?**

It's a lot more complicated than I'd imagined but it's good to be reunited.

The Doves can do anything together.

CHAPTER 54

ARLETTE

FRENCH GUIANA
1952

THE NEXT MORNING, WE SKIP BREAKFAST AND I walk Josie to Camp Hope. It's already terribly hot, the light so harsh and hazy. Despite the heat, my hands are cold as we hurry along the path, the rhythmic crash and lull of the waves in the distance. What will Josie think of Father Peter? Thomas? But it's comforting to know we now have the U.S. Army on our side. I just want Josie to arrest Father Peter and get us back to Paris.

We make it to camp in the middle of the daily Catholic mass held at the dining hut. All the boys sit at the long tables, led by Father Peter, dressed in his black clerical uniform of short-sleeved black shirt and belted trousers.

"Agnus Dei peccata vestra ut auferat," he says as he holds the host aloft.

His dogs, lulled by the drone of Latin, lie outside the hut sleeping in the shade.

"That's Father Peter?" Josie whispers.

"Ever see him at Ravensbrück?"

She shakes her head.

The mass ends, sending the campers in every direction. I catch Thomas's eye and wave, and he hurries over and hugs me, arms around my waist.

"You're looking well," I say. "I'd like you to meet an old friend, Josie Anderson."

Josie extends one hand and Thomas shakes it, terribly serious. "Very nice to meet you."

She bends to speak to him. "I knew you very well once upon a time. Held you as a baby. In Paris."

The tears in Josie's eyes make me well up.

Thomas leans against me, and I hold his hand in mine. "I'm going to visit Paris soon. Other places, too. I've been chosen to be a Hope Home ambassador."

"Sounds like a very big honor," Josie says.

He turns to me. "Have you found out if our blood matches yet?"

"Not yet. Soon though."

"And when will we have our sleepover? I've asked Father Peter, and he doesn't answer me."

"I will set it up." I keep his warm hand in mine until the last second.

An older camper calls to Thomas.

"That's my block leader," Thomas says. "I must go or get a demerit."

He gives us each one more embrace and then hurries off.

Father Peter makes a beeline for me.

"Who is this?" he asks, his gaze fixed on Josie.

"My friend Josie Anderson, a reporter. She's here to see the camp."

Josie offers her hand. "Pleased—"

He waves her hand away. "You were told not to come here today."

Josie steps closer to him. "Mind if I take a photo for the paper?"

The blood rises in his face. "You must leave immediately."

"Arlette tells me you are from Switzerland." She takes a pad of paper and a filigreed pen from her pocket and holds it poised above her pad. "Which town?"

He stares at the pen in her hand, the color draining from his face. "I will not be included in any story." Surely it is his pen.

"Didn't you say you come from Jungfraujoch, Father?" I ask.

Josie writes. "Oh, in the Alps."

She hands him the pen and pad. "Can you write the name of that town for me? We Americans aren't used to such unique spellings."

He cannot tear his eyes from the pen.

Josie forges on. "Arlette was telling me about your

shortwave radio. Would you consider allowing me access? I need to send a story back to the States."

"The radio is not working," he says, regaining his composure. "And this camp is **not** a public place one can just waltz into. You both need to leave immediately."

He turns and whistles for his dogs.

As he turns, it's hard not to see the blue mark there on the paper-white flesh of the back of his left arm.

Father Peter's dogs lope to him in a pack, and Josie and I step back from them.

"Fine," I say. "We'll go."

Josie links her arm in mine as we hurry back toward Cove House. "My God, I think it really might be Willie," she says once we're out of earshot. "He looks so much like you, Arl. Even has the Wietholter eyes."

"Isn't it incredible? He isn't the only one here with pale blue eyes, but he's so like Willie. You should see him draw. Better than me by far."

"It seems like a dream, doesn't it?" She squeezes my hand. "I'm sorry I tried to wave you off this trip. What's the holdup with taking him home?"

"Luc says they're required by law to have a maternal blood test, which matches, and it's taking forever. And I think Father Peter disapproves of me."

Josie turns and checks the path behind us. "The whole place is so like Ravensbrück. The blocks with the bunks."

"And Father Peter built the whole thing."

"And they give the boys demerits. What's next, the bunker?"

"I suppose. But all sleepaway camps are—"

"The older campers are like the **Blockovas.** And those uniforms . . ."

"All campers wear uniforms."

"You may not see it since you grew up around Nazis—"

"What does **that** mean?"

"Those boys look like Hitler Youth, Arl. Your boyfriend dressed like this, right?"

"I suppose."

"And Father Peter's not Swiss. He does a good job covering it, but the Bavarian accent is definitely there. And he displayed ten deceptive markers in that one conversation. **And** you saw the blood-type tattoo on the back of his left arm? Plus, that Latin he was reciting at mass made no sense. So definitely not a priest."

I shiver despite the muggy air. "Such an elaborate cover."

"He's hiding from something. He's probably lying about the radio being broken, too."

"I need to get Thomas out of here."

"Have you told Luc about your suspicions?"

"I told Danae. She says they go way back. His father and Peter were friends."

"Don't say anything more to Luc or his grandmother. Let's check out that girls' camp. We need hard evidence, but I think we may have found our Dr. Snow."

Josie and I take the jeep to town, park it on a side street, and walk to the jungle path Bondi and I took to follow my young friend Ella. This time, without her to follow, it seems to take longer. I wear my green bag across my chest and my grief box inside it bumps against my thigh with every step.

Josie's right. There is something thrilling about being back Doving again with her by my side and soon we pass the odd little white hut. She takes a quick look inside and I lead as we move on and follow the left fork in the path.

"I think it's this way," I say.

Josie swats a circling bug away. "What exactly did you see out here?"

"I only got a glance, but it looked like high walls, an encampment maybe? In this direction for sure."

Suddenly Josie stops and holds out one arm. "Wait," she whispers.

Up ahead in the thick of the jungle comes a movement. A man in a white jacket and carrying a black doctor's bag comes sidling out of a narrow opening in a tall rush fence.

Dr. Ebner.

Josie ducks behind a cluster of palms and I follow.

I hold my breath as he walks to the path. He sets down his bag, removes his coat, picks up his bag, and strides by us.

We wait for him to make it far down the path and then hurry to the same part of the fence where he emerged. Josie pulls the fence aside for me, I squeeze past the woven rush fence and emerge into an open camp. At the center is a wide, graveled courtyard and small wooden outbuildings stand around it. An A-frame hut stands off to one side and seems to be the focus of activity, and a series of low wooden barracks stands at the far end next to a wide garden.

Young women, barely teens, and some children mill about, engaged in various tasks. The older girls are in the garden intent on their work with hoes and shovels. Somewhere a baby cries and the scent of cabbage wafts to us, mixed with the smell of starch. Sheets hung on a clothesline next to the blocks billow in the breeze and the little ones duck in and out of them.

Josie slips through the fence and joins me. "My God."

I check for Father Peter's watchtower and don't see it above. At least he can't track our every move here.

I step out onto the courtyard, gravel crunching beneath my feet, and Josie follows. As we approach, a child carrying a watering can sees us, drops the can, and steps back.

I reach out one hand. "Don't worry. We won't hurt you. We're here to see Ella."

The child turns and runs off to the A-frame and returns with Ella.

She comes to us with a grave expression. "You can't be here."

"This is my friend Josie. We won't stay long."

Ella glances at Josie. "They won't be happy if they find you here."

"We just want to admire the garden," Josie says.

"We won't tell anyone," I say.

Ella takes my hand. "Very well."

As Ella leads us across the **platz,** from every part of the camp come girls of all ages, all wearing shifts, homemade sandals, and kerchiefs identical to Ella's. A girl barely ten years old carries a toddler at one hip.

Slowly they gather around Josie and me. A toddler girl raises her arms to me, and tears sting my eyes. I lift her up and she rests her head on my shoulder. Where are their mothers?

"Hello, sweet thing." She holds out her palm, a blossom resting on it.

My gaze rests on the blue number tattooed on the inside of her wrist, **39.**

I look into that perfect face. How can anyone harm such innocents? I'm careful to hold back the tears.

"Thank you." I tuck the flower behind one ear.

I crouch down and they surround me, run their hands down my hair and caress my cheek. They pull Josie low and stroke her hair and hands. She seems just as overcome by it all as I am.

"Who takes care of you?" I ask.

"We help one another," Ella says.

"But someone taught you to garden."

"They tell me I came here when I was four. My earliest memory is of the doctors bringing a woman who taught us to sew and plant things. Now we teach the little ones."

Soon I realize with a start that the girls are all, in many variations of tone, blond-haired and blue-eyed and the older ones among them wear their hair to their waists. Has no one ever cut it?

A child runs one hand down my bag and I pull out my copy of **Puss and Boots** and hand it to her. She hesitates.

"Go ahead. You can read it."

"What is it?" Ella asks.

"A book," I say.

The girl turns the cloth pages and the others gather to marvel at the pictures.

"You may keep it."

The girl looks to Ella, who nods, and then holds it to her chest.

Josie and I exchange a look. Such a lovely group of children. How can we leave them?

"That doctor who just left," I ask Ella. "Does he help you?"

"He brings us cloth. Gives us examinations."

"How did you get here?" Josie asks. "Where are your mothers?"

Ella smiles. "We are here to do a very important job."

"Take care of the boys," another girl says. "We grow food—"

"Yes," Ella says in a patient tone. "But an even more important job as well."

Josie looks at me wide-eyed. It's inescapable how like Ravensbrück this place is.

"May we see the rest of the camp?" Josie asks.

We pass the well-kept garden where jade green plumes of kale sway in the breeze.

"You must eat well."

"This is for the boys," Ella says.

"They come and harvest it?"

"I deliver it. That is the job of the eldest. We all have our assignments."

"This is where you sleep?" Josie asks.

I step into the closest barrack. It's cool and dark inside with only narrow windows at the tops of the walls, and wooden bunk beds lined up in rows.

At a table near the door the girls have assembled a shrine of sorts. A deck of playing cards. The compact I gave Ella. A pristine 1946 calendar with all of its pages intact hangs above it.

A baby cries not far off and Josie and I turn in the direction of the A-frame hut.

I step to Ella. "I do love babies."

Ella smiles. "We have a new one."

"Any chance we can see? I haven't held a newborn in so long."

"Yes, but then you must go."

We step into the A-frame hut, and as my eyes adjust to the low light it takes me a second to understand what I'm seeing. There in the shadows are rows of bassinets, at least ten, each holding a child. The older girls walk between them bringing bottles and changing diapers. An older girl carries a set of year-old twins, one on each hip.

Josie wraps her arms around herself. "So many babies."

"May I hold one?" I ask.

"Here. This is Maria. We named her after her mother."

"Where is Maria?"

"Father Peter said she had to go away."

I lift the newborn from the bassinet closest to me and hold her warm little body to me. The blanket falls away and reveals her hand is red and inflamed where a number has been inked on her wrist, **72.**

I look about the room, blackness coiling in my chest, and it's all I can do not to scoop up every child there and head for the exit. Bring them to Bondi. But we must pick our moment. Otherwise Father Peter will certainly make sure Josie and I don't live to speak of this horrific crime.

I set Maria back down, knowing she will soon be free of this terrible place.

"You really must go now," Ella says. "Thank you for the book but you mustn't return. The doctors will be angry at me for allowing it."

"When will they return?" I ask.

"I don't know. But the doctor says I'm next to have a child. He's coming back soon to help me."

CHAPTER 55

JOSIE

FRENCH GUIANA
1952

ARLETTE AND I LEAVE THE GIRLS' CAMP, shaken to the core.

"What's going on in there?" she asks as we retrace our steps along the jungle path we took to get there.

"I'm not sure but it's so similar to Ravensbrück. The gravel courtyard just like the **platz** at the camp. Though we were never tattooed—"

Arlette stomps along the path in front of me. "My God, this is so upsetting."

"The nursery was odd—"

"**Odd?** Please. They're inseminating these children. Some have multiple births and don't seem to survive, poor things. The ultimate sacrifice for the master race. I just know it's Father Peter behind it all. He built this whole place."

"More proof he's Snow. At Ravensbrück Dr. Snow worked as a gynecologist."

"He and Ebner are in this together. But why?"

"Let's get into Ebner's office tonight and take a look."

"I'm in. Let's hope he keeps good records. But first you need to meet Dr. Bondi. She'll help us figure this out."

WE PARK THE JEEP down the street from Dr. Bondi's clinic.

I link arms with Arlette as we walk to the clinic. "I agree Father Peter's the most troubling, but Luc and Danae. Are they in with him? They employ the man."

"Who knows? They're always too busy with the foundation to see the day-to-day. All I know is, Father Peter's the first step."

We enter the dirt-floored infirmary, one room, which contains only the padded treatment table and two chairs. The doctor is examining an older Maroon man who sits on the table.

"Dr. Bondi," Arl says. "This is my friend Josie Anderson. A reporter with the **New York Journal American.**"

The doctor helps the man down off the table, hands him a bottle of tablets, and he leaves.

I step to Bondi and extend my hand. "A pleasure to meet you, Dr. Bondi. Or should I call you Your Excellency? Are former ambassadors not entitled to that honorific permanently?"

Bondi smiles. "Kena Bondi. World Health."

"Your reputation precedes you, Doctor. Didn't you head up that group fighting leprosy in northern India? Saw it in **National Geographic.**"

"We had an incredible team. How can I help you two today?"

"We found where Ella lives," Arlette says. "A girls' camp in the center of the peninsula."

Bondi leans against the treatment table. "How did you find it?"

"We saw Dr. Ebner coming from there. It's an entire complex, ringed by a high fence."

"We saw a whole nursery of babies," I add. "They all have numbers tattooed, like Ella."

"How old are the babies?"

"All ages," I say. "One newborn. Several pairs of twins."

"Well, we saw the equipment in the hut," Bondi says. "Clearly, they're breeding the girls."

Arlette paces. "My God, this is horrible."

"Father Peter and Ebner are somehow impregnating them once they get old enough."

"Josef Mengele did extensive research on twins," I say. "Good way to bolster the master race."

"Though where do the babies go?" Bondi asks.

"Probably once they're old enough the boy

babies go to the boys' camp," Arlette says. "The girls stay there."

"And the cycle continues," Bondi says. "I have a feeling I know whose sperm they're using."

I swallow hard at that unsavory thought. "How is this all connected to the bigger picture?"

Arlette paces. "I don't know but Thomas is always sick. After I gave him blood—"

"They asked you to transfuse him?" Bondi asks.

"He seems to get better and then relapse."

Bondi turns to me. "As I told Arlette, I think there's something very serious happening with that organization. The native Maroon tribes here have filed a complaint with Geneva. Some sort of viral infection's hit them hard. It's highly unusual since they have little contact with the outside world and like it that way."

I sit on one of the chairs. "The Maroon people are descended from fugitives who escaped from the slave ships on their way to the Caribbean, if I remember my history?"

"Yes—isolated, independent tribes. But somehow this Father Peter has Maroon kids living at his camp."

"How does he get them if they live in isolated villages?" I ask.

"I'm just figuring it out now. I've seen the boys come to town to sell rubber and Brazil nuts. Seems they hear about things like soccer and want to be a part of it all."

"So, Father Peter kidnaps them?" I ask.

"Last week I visited a village, and they told me one of their boys said that one night in town a white-haired man had offered him a ride in a car and a hot meal. Smart boy ran back to the village."

"What does Father Peter get out of all of this?" I ask.

Bondi shakes her head. "Claims having Maroon kids at the camp is some sort of goodwill olive branch between the races, but I don't buy it. I think somehow the infections are originating there. But the tribal elders aren't much help, blaming spirits for the disease."

"What disease exactly?" I ask. "You must have a guess as to what's happening here."

She smooths her hair back with one hand. "I think it's some sort of experiment."

"**Experiment?"** Arlette asks. "My God."

"Why the Maroon kids?" I ask.

Bondi shrugs. "Perhaps they're brought to the camp to be vectors. They have little immunity to any disease."

"Perfect to test on," I say. "A Nazi source told me they were working on a similar project during the war. Maybe they're still at it down here."

Arlette sits on the treatment table. "This all sounds so . . . far-fetched."

"Not at all, actually," Bondi says.

"So, they just put the Maroon kids in close contact and then wait for them to contract it and die? It's inhumane."

Suddenly I can barely breathe. I step to the window and open it, hoping for a breeze.

Bondi nods. "That would explain the patient I had with the respiratory distress. He didn't stay long, but I got enough material to make my own vaccine. Enough to inoculate myself and my patients. We believe Arlette was inoculated, but, Josie, if you'd like—"

"Is it safe?" I ask.

"Gave it to myself and many others. It will just take a second."

I roll up my sleeve. "If you don't mind."

Bondi prepares an injection.

"So where does that leave us?" Arlette asks. "Have you had a chance to look at Thomas's blood sample?"

"Not yet. I have everything I need except a chemical cross-linker like formaldehyde to fix the slides. There's not a bottle to be had in all of Cayenne."

"Maybe they'll have some at Dr. Ebner's office?" I ask. "We're planning a little collection mission there."

"He'll probably have bottles of it in his storeroom; it's commonly used as a disinfectant. Hate to ask you to steal."

I exchange a glance with Arlette. "Oh, that's not a problem, Doctor. In our previous life in the resistance we did a lot of that."

Bondi rubs cold alcohol on my arm, and I wince at the needle stick. "We were known as the Golden Doves once upon a time."

Bondi sets down the syringe. "I read about that.

You were the ones the Nazis were searching all of Paris for?"

"There's always room for another," I say.

Bondi smiles and checks her clipboard. "Bring me formaldehyde and I can tell you more about the samples."

"We'll keep you updated on what we find," I say.

"Good." Bondi walks us to the door. "Once this spreads to the general population, well . . . most of those not vaccinated won't be around long."

WE HAVE A FABULOUS dinner of rice and beans with Bondi and it's growing dark by the time Arlette walks me to the building she had seen Dr. Ebner entering.

After hearing Bondi's take on all this, Father Peter looks sure to be our Snow. Nazi friends like Ebner. Gynecology background. Obvious nationalism. And at his age he'll be an easy catch. With over one hundred million acres of jungle and mangrove swamps in this country, Arlette and I won't have trouble hiding the body. I'll show him my mother's photo before I do it, just to make sure he remembers.

We just need some primary evidence for Karl, in order to make the grab.

Arlette and I wait across the street from the place and watch. There are no streetlamps in this part of town, just a slip of a moon for light. It's the perfect hiding spot for a doctor trying to leave a dirty past behind, a nondescript colonial façade with a porch overhang, like every other in town. It's dark inside, shuttered up tight.

We step across the street onto the porch, the brass of the sign next to the door glows in the moonlight. OBSTÉTRIQUE ET DE GYNÉCOLOGIE. After all, why use his name? He may as well advertise: Nazi doctor who escaped justice looking for gynecological work. How brazen of him to operate here in broad daylight, with no fear of being caught and sent back to Germany.

In less than a minute Arlette gets us in and I follow her through a waiting room, down a short hallway to two opposing doors. Arl steps into one, a typical exam room, with treatment table and a set of upper and lower cabinets, possibly containing formaldehyde.

I enter the opposite door into Ebner's darkened office. It's somewhat Spartan for a Nazi doctor. Certainly a comedown in prestige. But there is a mahogany partners desk, as big as a Metropolitan Museum sarcophagus, in the middle of the room, and a leather chair sits across from it.

I stop and examine a painting. It looks familiar. I step closer. It's **Langlois Bridge at Arles.** Göring's stolen Van Gogh right here on Ebner's office wall.

There's a whole desk drawer of treatment files. I set three on the floor and document them. I'm too busy flipping pages and photographing to read details, but there are penciled initials on the patients' paperwork: P.V., J.E., and others.

Arlette hurries in. "Got the formaldehyde."

Far off, a door closes with a thud. The entry?

The phone on the desk rings, startling us, and we crouch and hide in the well of the desk, both of us frozen there.

Someone pads in, turns on the desk lamp, and lifts the receiver. "Ebner."

A muffled male voice speaks on the other end, too faint for me to hear properly.

"Of course, I'm here. I left dinner to come talk about this?"

Arlette takes my hand, her fingers cold.

". . . No. A charter flight. I told you. Yes, it's all set . . ."

Ebner listens.

"Of course, he has the cultures. Why are you so worried? Our Fort Bliss friend will take care of it."

I barely breathe. **Fort Bliss.**

". . . I see. Fine. But don't call me again. I'm going to bed."

He hangs up the phone and leaves the room, closing the door behind him.

I pause in the silence of the room, the words still hanging in the air. **Our Fort Bliss friend.**

Arl and I are still as we listen to his footsteps on the stairs. "He lives upstairs," she whispers.

When all is quiet I help Arlette out of our hiding place, return the files to the drawer, and slide the camera into my pocket.

As we slip out into the night, I link arms with Arlette. "Think you can get some info on the ham hut? I need to warn Karl there's a mole at Fort Bliss."

"I can try," Arlette says. "I'm supposed to go somewhere with Luc tomorrow. He says he has a surprise. I can probe a bit."

"Good. In the meantime, drop the formaldehyde at Bondi's, and not a word to the Minaus about any of this Ebner stuff. I'll develop this film and we're on our way. Surely we have enough to take Snow."

CHAPTER 56

ARLETTE

FRENCH GUIANA
1952

THE NEXT MORNING, BACK AT COVE HOUSE, after an early breakfast, Luc leads me to the jeep. It's hard not to scrutinize every word he says, thinking he may be partnering with Father Peter in his terrible work. But I do my best to play my part and wait it out. If Josie's right, it will all be over soon.

"Excited for the rehearsal luncheon Monday?" Luc asks. "Just two more days. Fifty RSVPs, all yeses. Everyone Danae knows is coming. Most are staying for the wedding the next day." I want to ask if Claudio will be invited but hold back. I haven't seen him in days.

"Terribly excited, Luc."

He guides me into the front seat. **How much longer will I need to keep up this pretense?**

We set off and soon the misty sea breeze whips my hair around my head. I try to hold it back.

He waves toward the glove box. "Grandmother keeps a scarf in there if you need one."

I pull out one of Danae's Hermès scarves, scented with her gardenia perfume, and tie my hair back with it.

"I need a hint about the destination," I call to him over the sound of the motor.

He downshifts. "Well, it's the site of something taking place a few days from now. On the highest point in French Guiana."

I force a smile. "The wedding." Not that it will actually happen, if Josie comes through.

"Thought I'd give you a little preview. I'm not a big wedding expert, but what Grandmother's done with that place is remarkable. You'll barely recognize it."

"Can't wait."

As we start our ascent up to the helipad, I look back at the other peninsula, at the shack there, the antenna rising through the clouds.

"I've also been researching honeymoon destinations," Luc says. "What about Bali? We'll bring Thomas, of course."

"Blood-type match results back yet?"

"Any day now I'm sure," he says with a smile.

I take a deep breath of salt air. "Can't wait." I grasp for anything else to talk about. "How's the search for Father Peter's replacement going?"

"Good. One candidate we're excited about."

"What will you do with that giant antenna when he's gone? Just take it down?"

"Lots of men in the area have started using it. I wouldn't go in there if I were you. I've never seen so many girlie magazine photos tacked up in one place. Grandmother would have the place burned down if she knew."

"What kind of radio do they use in there?"

"Shortwave. It's rather crude."

"My uncle loved his. Could talk to Bora-Bora."

"Peter stays up half the night speaking to the strangest places. But let's not talk about that. I'm taking you to see something spectacular."

The jeep strains against the incline as we climb through the thick jungle to the helipad and he glances at me as he drives. "How about we have a fabulous party when we're back in Paris? You can invite whoever you wish, and Danae can ask half of Paris. Or we can keep it small. Whatever makes you happy."

Suddenly, Luc stops the jeep, unties my scarf, folds it, and reties it as a blindfold around my eyes.

"I want to reveal this sight to you."

He resumes driving, and I try not to worry. What if he's bringing me up there to push me off the cliff? My heart thumps against my breastbone. Wouldn't be surprising given all the crazy things happening around here.

Soon I feel the terrain leveling off and we park.

"No peeking," Luc says as he exits the car. He comes around and ushers me out.

"Almost there."

Blindfolded, my other senses dip in the warm bath of that place—the wild cries of seabirds, Luc's arm around my waist guiding me, the scent of the ocean as waves crash below.

He leaves me alone for a moment and I reach out. "Luc?"

I feel fingers undo the knot of the scarf.

"Are you ready?"

Luc fumbles with the scarf knot.

"Just one more second—"

The silk slips away and I take in the scene, the flat, cliffside area near the helipad transformed into a lush wedding venue. Someone has covered the area in emerald sod and arranged white folding chairs in rows in front of a wooden platform. Atop the platform an arch of white flowers stands, the lilies and gardenias swaying in the gentle breeze. Three Maroon women stand at the arch weaving in more calla lilies, freesia, and white roses.

"Well?" Luc asks, with a wide grin.

"It's—"

"Grandmother had the sod flown in from the United States. It's Kentucky bluegrass. And the roses and lilies are from Holland."

"It's . . ."

Such a waste of flowers.

"There are no words, Luc. I can't thank Danae enough."

"Thomas will bear the rings, ahead of you down the aisle. He'll hand them to Bishop Caggiano, who will officiate."

"Not Father Peter?"

"We asked him to introduce you at the rehearsal luncheon. That's enough for him." He pulls me close and locks his fingers at the small of my back. "This is about celebrating the four of us, you, me, Thomas . . ." He rubs my belly. "And this one, too. I've drawn up the adoption papers to make Thomas official no matter what the blood test says. After the wedding we'll go straight to Paris."

I force a smile. "They'll love Thomas at the café."

"You won't need to work at that place anymore."

Of course, none of this will happen.

He takes my hand. "All I know is I want to dedicate my life to caring for you all. Make sure you never have to do another day of work."

I release his hand. "For now, I better get back and start preparing for the rehearsal luncheon."

"So, you're happy with all this?" he asks, so earnest, real concern in his eyes.

"Of course."

"I have something I need to tell you."

I brace for the Nazi confession.

"We got the background check back on you."

I step back from him. "Luc . . ."

He pauses.

"I know about your aunt, Arlette."

I clasp my hands together to stop them from shaking. "How?"

"It isn't hard to put two and two together. The missing-person claim. Paris police say they suspect foul play. What exactly happened to her? And please be honest with me."

"Yes, I . . . ended her life. I had to. It was during the war, and she was going to turn me in to the police with some made-up story. She wanted my parents' apartment. I should have told you. I just thought it would ruin my chances to get Thomas."

"To be honest, I'm stunned."

"I'm so sorry, Luc—"

He brushes a stray lock of hair from my cheek. "I suppose we've all done things we aren't proud of."

"She was a horrible woman."

"How old were you?"

"Seventeen."

"To think that you lived with her all those years." He looks out to sea and then turns his attention back to me. "But please don't worry about it, my darling."

I breathe out a long sigh.

He shrugs. "Who needs a piece of paper? You are my family."

I freeze there. **Should I tell him it's probably in a pile of mail in Danae's office? What if it turns out it's not a match after all?**

"Does this mean Thomas can finally come and

stay with me at my cottage? He has his heart set on a sleepover."

"Of course, my darling. Whatever makes you both happy."

Just the thought of my son coming to spend the night sweeps away all my other cares. "He'll be thrilled."

He wraps one arm around my shoulders and kisses me. "I'm so glad we can finally make you and Thomas official."

I kiss him back, trying to make it feel genuine. "Me too."

CHAPTER 57

JOSIE

FRENCH GUIANA
1952

BACK AT HOTEL LOTUS, SOAKED WITH perspiration, I close the bathroom door, develop the film, and hang it over the shower rod to dry so images can emerge.

I try to sleep, but my monkey brain takes charge. That mission had gone well, just like the old days of the Doves. How lucky we'd been that Ebner didn't see us. But this is so much bigger than just taking out Snow. Karl has a traitor in his ranks of scientists, and I need to warn him. Then there's the virus. As much as I hate to admit it, I can't do it alone.

I draw the shades, fall deeply asleep, and wake at late morning to the sound of footsteps in the room.

I grab my firearm from the bedside table and train it on the dark figure as it approaches until I recognize the face and every part of me relaxes.

He looks good standing there in the darkness, his broad shoulders silhouetted against the dim window light.

I set down my weapon. "Really, Aaron. I could've killed you."

He steps to the end of the bed, and I prop myself up on one forearm, holding the sheet to my chest. "Can you hand me the robe on the chair there?"

"Sleeping in? Sorry to wake you. Figured you'd be up by now."

"Can we do this later?" I dredge my mind for how I left it with Arlette. **What time is she coming over? After Luc shows her his surprise?**

"I would've visited you sooner, but in Paris I had to figure out where you'd gone and then hitch a flight to São Paulo on a Hungarian cargo plane. It was no Paris Ritz, as you can imagine. And then a Russian gentleman who'd followed you here to the hotel last night had to be taken care of."

I rub the sleep from my eyes. "You've been busy."

"You're welcome. Did you miss the 'losing the tail' part of basic training? And I thought we had an arrangement that we'd work together."

"That was before I found your Russian wife's passport."

He pauses. "Didn't know that was in the apartment. Former wife. And it's not what you think."

All at once my head aches. “I need coffee.”

“What’s happening with Snow? If you have him, it’s your responsibility as a Jew to give him to Israel.”

I massage my temples. “What time is it?”

He takes the hotel robe from the chair and lays it at the foot of the bed.

“Almost eleven. Will you at least tell me before you take Snow? Or just do the right thing and hand him over to me.”

Can I trust him?

I sit up. “Hey, did you see that hut with the big antenna?”

“Why?”

“Think there’s a radio in there? I need to get word to someone.”

He looks at me for a long second. “I wouldn’t—”

A knock comes at the door.

“It’s me.”

Arlette.

I throw back the covers and slip into the hotel robe. “It’s a friend.”

Aaron turns, steps into the bathroom, and closes the door.

I wait a few seconds to open the room door and wave Arlette in.

She presents two coffee cups and a brown paper bag of something that smells delicious. “Good news. Luc has approved my adoption of Thomas.”

“**Arlette.** Wonderful.”

“I’ll believe it when I see it, but at least it’s

progress." She sets the coffees on the table. "Did you get good pics yesterday? I dropped off the formaldehyde last night. Told Bondi we'd come by if you got anything good."

I take a deep breath.

"What's wrong? Did you develop the film?"

I glance toward the bathroom. "Yes. And we'll need Bondi's help with it."

"Let's have a look . . ."

I stand between her and the door. "No—"

"What is it?" she asks, voice low. "Where's your gun?"

"It's fine. No. It's just . . ."

Aaron emerges from the bathroom and nods to Arlette.

Arlette looks from Aaron to me. "I can come back later."

Aaron moves toward the door. "I need to be going." He steps out the door and, with a glance back at me, closes it softly behind him.

Arlette comes to me. "You can't just pretend that didn't happen. I need details. Has he broken your never-been-kissed-since-Tommy-Kennefick streak?"

I smooth my hair back, aware it's a deception indicator. "Maybe."

"Are you two serious?" Arlette asks. "Hope you brought some decent lingerie. But it's better if he buys it for you."

I wave that thought away. "I'm not like you. The kind of woman men want to do things for."

"Co-worker?"

Arlette hands me a coffee and I drink. "Nowadays career-minded women don't get involved with co-workers."

"When they look like that they do."

"We met in Paris. At the Ritz, actually."

"My God, Josie. So you've slept together?"

"Okay, maybe we've . . ."

"How was it?" Arlette asks.

"Let's just say it was fine."

Arlette folds her arms across her chest. "You have that rash on your neck you get when you're rattled."

"Okay, slightly better than fine. Let's get over to Bondi's. I can share what I found on the film. From what I can tell, Father Peter's involved. Ebner. Maybe Luc."

"It's so stressful keeping up this pretense," Arlette says.

"Ever wonder why Luc even came looking for you in the first place? Why the sudden need to marry you?"

"He says he's trying to arrange a wedding before the baby shows."

"Maybe Thomas is helping them somehow, and they want to make sure he stays alive? Keep you here for him? Hard to say. Let's see what Bondi has. If it points to Father Peter, I may take him at the rehearsal luncheon on Monday. Ebner too if I can."

"So public? If Luc sees you do it, he may not certify the adoption."

"Don't worry. It'll all work out."

Arlette sets one hand on my forearm. "No matter

what, you'll be there at that luncheon? They think you're my maid of honor, after all."

I cover her hand with mine. "Of course. I wouldn't miss it for the world."

ARLETTE AND I STEP along the street toward Bondi's clinic and as we approach it's clear the place has been ransacked. We hurry inside and see the treatment table is overturned, with papers strewn about the dirt floor as if a great wind has blown in the door. Bondi steps to us through the debris.

"What happened?" I ask.

"What does it look like? I've been attacked. Along with two mothers who just lost their sons. Whoever broke in abducted two sick patients."

Arlette brushes Bondi's hair back from her forehead where a nasty-looking lump is forming. "You're hurt."

She pushes Arl's hand away.

"Who did this?" I ask.

"Maybe you tell me. I trust no one anymore."

I hold out my film. "Brought you photos from Ebner's office. Could be some good info."

"How does that help those mothers?"

I step to her. "Full disclosure, I'm Army Intelligence. Here to find a person of interest."

"Show me some ID."

I pull out my badge and she reads. "U.S. Army captain. So you've known this is going on for days and you haven't called for an evacuation?"

I slide my ID in my pocket. "I have my orders."

"Who does that sound like?"

"My mission is—"

"Why are sick kids never a priority?"

"We think the Minaus' friend Father Peter may be a Nazi doctor named Snow. A virologist from Ravensbrück."

"So, it's okay to let children die and a virus to spread while you follow him around?"

"I'm taking the asset at the rehearsal luncheon. Day after tomorrow."

Bondi pauses and breathes deep. "Thank God. Why didn't you say so?"

"It would help to do this together. Have you had a chance to look at Thomas's blood work?"

Bondi nods and looks around the room, as if gathering strength to relive the break-in. "I surprised them just before dawn when I came to open up. One of them got me with some sort of bat. Woke up on the floor."

We follow her to a smaller room, which is lit by one bare hanging light bulb and walk around the desk.

"Did they get much?" I ask.

Arlette pulls a first aid kit from a heap of papers on the floor.

"They tried to take my microscope, but I'd bolted it to the desk. And they got some patient charts and papers. They must know I'm getting close. Was up half the night sorting it out."

Bondi bends to pick up papers from the floor

and slaps one page onto the desk. "World Health wrote—they want me to continue to keep this virus under wraps for now."

"We may not need WHO." I pull the negative strips from my bag. "I got a lot from Ebner's office." I hold one to the light and set the jeweler's loupe to it. "First thing I noticed is every woman's chart is initialed. P.V. or G.E."

" 'PV' means **per vaginal** to physicians," Bondi says. "Or **polycythemia vera.** A cancer."

"Or Peter Vogel," Arlette says. "That's Father Peter."

Bondi sits back. "And G.E.?"

"Gregor Ebner, maybe?" I ask.

"Let me see." Bondi takes the loupe from me and looks for herself, one eye shut. "It's as I thought. They're using their own semen to inseminate women. Why else would they brand their patients like that?"

Arlette leans against the desk. "A baby factory?"

We pause at the sound of Carnival revelers shooting fireworks somewhere far off.

"To grow the master race," I say.

Bondi hands me the film. "Not a particularly efficient way to do it, one old guy's semen at a time. Slow swimmers."

I hand Bondi a different film section. "Also looks like Father Peter, or someone, has been keeping old Ravensbrück records about viral trials, too."

"So, they **are** experiments," Arlette says.

"From what I can tell, much of the paperwork is

stamped with the Ravensbrück seal. Mostly records of injections."

Bondi sets the loupe to the file and reads. "Freeze-dried viral cultures." She sits back. "**Totale Lungenzerstorung.** Total lung destruction. It's consistent with the blood work."

She peers into the eyepiece of her microscope. "I compared Thomas's sample to the boy who came in presenting with total lung destruction. Thomas's lymphocytes are cleaning up, overactive, while the Maroon lymphocytes are inactive. It makes sense their lungs are failing."

"So, Thomas isn't anemic?" Arlette asks.

"Far from it. He's depleted of white blood cells, not red, and at the same time has an ultra-functioning immune response."

"What are they doing to him?" Arlette asks.

"It seems they're harvesting antibodies from his blood," Bondi says.

Arlette folds her arms across her belly. "My God, they're killing him."

"Oh, no. At least not intentionally. It would be in their interest to keep him alive since he's the source of their whole system. Without the antibodies he generates, none of this would be possible. But he is at risk of renal failure if they harvest too aggressively."

Arlette folds her arms across her belly. "How can they be so cruel?"

"What's the purpose of it all?" I ask.

Bondi glances up at me. "I believe they're developing a germ bomb."

Arlette grabs the side of the desk. "Tell me you're joking."

"But how do they get it out into the world?" I ask. "If they want to use it as a weapon, they need to spread it."

Bondi shakes her head. "That's the only part I don't know."

Arlette steps to me. "You have to stop this **now,** Josie. Take Father Peter—Ebner, too—and get us out of here."

"I need access to that radio to send word to Karl—to tell him one of his scientists at Fort Bliss is working with Snow, and request backup. Can you get us in tonight?"

"That site is so exposed. We'll need to go after dark. But what if we're caught there?"

Bondi stands. "Don't they think you're a journalist, Josie? Have Arlette carry one of your stories, and she can say you were there trying to send it."

Arlette nods.

"Both of you, just hang in there until I contact Karl, and I promise I'll take Snow the second I can. After that, I'll activate a CASEVAC. All the kids will be out of here to a hospital. And you, Arlette, will be on your way home to Paris with your son."

CHAPTER 58

ARLETTE

FRENCH GUIANA
1952

JOSIE AND I HIDE THE JEEP OFF A SIDE ROAD AND walk up the hill to the radio hut, my linen shirt soaked through from the muggy air. The jasmine-scented wind changes direction, and a bad feeling sets in as soon as twilight falls. Had we used up all our luck with yesterday's escape from Ebner?

We wait, dressed in dark colors, in a nearby grove of trees, surrounded by what sounds like a thousand croaking frogs. We swat mosquitos and watch the quiet two-story hut on the hill, with its tall exterior staircase and antenna rising through the clouds, a slip of a moon glowing through.

The wind picks up. There's rain coming. I feel my

pocket for Josie's decoy newspaper story. At least we have an alibi if caught.

We just need to get in, send a message, and get out.

"Please tell me you'll be quick," I whisper.

Josie answers in my ear. "Shouldn't be long. I know Karl's call sign."

"Can't believe you can talk to Texas from here."

"Though it's not secure, obviously."

Satisfied the hut is unoccupied, we start toward the place but are surprised when the door at the top of the staircase opens and Father Peter steps out. I hold Josie back with one arm as he turns and locks the door with a little jangle of his keys and hurries down the stairs.

I finally breathe again as he staggers unsteadily down the hill away from us, toward Cove House. Has he been drinking? Was he talking to someone in there?

Josie and I hurry up the steep wooden stairs. At the top, I work the pin-and-tumbler lock with my wrench, but it's not turning over.

"What's the issue?" Josie whispers, peering over my shoulder.

"The issue is give me some space to work here. It's a new one." **They care about what's in here, whoever chose it. No one spends extra money on a lock if they're not protecting something precious.**

The lock finally concedes, and I push open the door. It's pitch-black in there. We keep the lights off as we assess the room like we once did as Doves. I turn on my flashlight, filter it through the cotton of my shirt, and run the beam across the walls of the sloped-ceilinged room, past a black-handled electricity kill switch and along photos of naked women, mostly from German magazines. My light avoids the only two windows, one at the far end of the room, the other near us, next to the radio. I open the closest window and look out over the rolling countryside to the jungle beyond; it's too high up for an easy escape.

I train my light along the desk, on two standard boxlike transmitters, a microphone, and headphones. Josie flips a switch on the radio, and the red lights give our faces an eerie glow.

"Someone will see," I say.

"Relax," Josie says. "I'll be quick."

"For your convenience," Josie reads from the label on the transmitter, written in German, "the principal shortwave stations of the world have been clearly marked on the dial."

I read them. Singapore, Cairo, London, Havana.

Josie sits at the desk, puts the headphones on, and gets to work, so like our days as Doves, dialing the knobs like a safecracker. "Hello. This is FG-Cayenne calling. Go ahead, please, El Paso."

She doesn't have much luck, just some static and an enthusiast from Albuquerque asking about the weather.

Hovering over her doesn't make it go any faster, so I step to the far window and take in the expansive view below, in the direction Father Peter had walked, across the peninsula to Cove House. The lights are just coming on in the main house's bedrooms. I find my cottage; the maids are probably there turning down the bed. A string of lights glows along the Cove House terrace railing, which juts out over the ocean, and fireflies hover in the air. Is Danae there in her bedroom office? I itch to get in there to see if she has the blood-type letter from the lab. How can one letter take this long to arrive? Or is it better not to know the contents of it?

My gaze drifts to Claudio's quarters above the garage, windows dark. It's been days since I've seen him. Where has he gone?

Beyond Cove House, a bonfire burns at Camp Hope, and beyond the camp, another steep-cliffed peninsula juts out, the helipad and wedding venue there atop it.

The wedding venue. A shiver tickles the nape of my neck. Hopefully I'll be gone well before that fiasco happens. Once Josie takes Father Peter and Ebner, Thomas and I will be on our way back to Paris no matter what Luc says, hopefully courtesy of the U.S. Army.

I turn back to Josie. "How's it going?"

"Not well. Can't get the frequency. Karl may not have his radio turned on."

"Maybe try the other transmitter?"

Josie switches to the second machine, and all at once she smiles with recognition at a voice.

"This is El Paso. Go ahead, French Guiana."

A bit of that male voice escapes through the headphones. She glances at me and smiles wider. Must be Karl.

I exhale. Finally. How incredible we're talking to someone over six thousand kilometers away. How odd it is to hear that voice, after Josie spoke of him so often. A kind voice. Reassuring. The first real sign of hope this will all be over soon.

All at once it seems too quiet in that room. Complete silence, no more cacophony of frogs.

I return to the far window and watch with growing dread as a figure approaches, the milky glow of a beam bouncing as someone lurches up the path.

CHAPTER 59

JOSIE

FRENCH GUIANA
1952

"WEE-EL PASO," HE SAYS LOUD AND CLEAR in my headphones.

I smile for the first time in so long.

Karl.

"Signal's coming in fine, El Paso," I say. They're three hours behind us, so it's still Saturday afternoon there. "This is Cayenne-212."

"Come in, Cayenne."

Just hearing his voice makes me teary. "I don't have long."

"What's the weather like there?" he asks.

"**Hot,** actually. Need some relief. Heard a weatherman talking about the rain in your area."

In the silence the static on the line amplifies. There's a football game on in the background.

"Still there, El Paso?"

"An embedded storm?"

I feel a hand on my arm, and Arlette leans down. "Josie. Someone's coming."

I raise one hand and gesture for her to hold on. "Yes," I confirm to Karl. "Thought you'd like to know."

"What's the forecast for this week?"

Arlette leans down again, eyes wide. "We need to go. Now."

I stand and nod to her. "Would help to have some rain gear. All you can spare. Got some sick kids here."

"Do the best I can, Cayenne."

Karl signs off, but before I can remove my headphones another voice comes on the line.

Some part of me recognizes it. He's speaking Russian, and I strain to listen. I know only a few words. He's extending some sort of invitation. It takes me a moment, but the voice is so familiar. And then it hits me.

Of course.

It's Aaron.

CHAPTER 60

ARLETTE

FRENCH GUIANA
1952

After Josie pushes me away the second time, I pull the main kill switch. The radio dies and we're left in darkness. Rain starts to patter the roof.

I glance out the window and the shadowy figure rounds the corner of the hut, carrying a rifle.

Josie yanks off her headphones. "Why did you—"

"Someone's coming," I whisper. "Think it's Father Peter." **With that Vampire gun.**

Footfalls thump the wooden stairs outside.

We both freeze. The metal flashlight grows slippery in my hand.

"Stand back." I see a glint of metal as she slips the gun from her holster.

"You can't kill him **here,**" I whisper.

"Why not?"

"It's too dangerous. Even if you take him by surprise you can't match that firepower." Not to mention the police would certainly be called and might make the connection that I killed Auntie.

Josie holsters her gun. "You can't run fast enough. I won't leave you here."

"I have a plan. Trust me." I push her toward the window. "When I say jump, you go."

The footsteps keep coming, vibrating the whole hut. They stop for a moment, and we barely breathe.

"Go," I whisper to Josie.

The rain falls harder on the roof and the door opens.

The milky glow of the rifle's scope shines like a cloudy opal in the darkness. The figure scans the room, the glow slowly coming our way, and I wait for the scope to find me, my heart pounding. One . . . two . . .

Just as it reaches me, I flip on my flashlight and shine the beam directly at the scope and the gunman recoils.

"Shit," he says in German.

"Go," I say to Josie again, and she jumps out the window and lands with a soft thud below.

I watch her run across the scorched field toward the jungle. A lightning flash illuminates her, rain soaked and limping a bit. Hurt from the fall? I silently urge her faster. The rifle could still reach her at that distance.

The gunman pulls up the kill switch, and the lights and radio come back to life. Father Peter stands there, rain soaked through his black shirt and trousers, his white hair splayed down his forehead.

Eyes squinting in the light, he aims his rifle at me.

I start to shake.

"Father Peter. Thank goodness it's you. The lights went off and I couldn't find my way out of—"

"Stand over there." He jabs the rifle toward the middle of the room.

He steps to the open window, aims his rifle at Josie as she runs, and fires.

"No—" I say and push him, two hands on his back.

He turns and trains the rifle on me. "I knew it was you," he says and nods toward the door. "Get going. Now we'll finally be rid of you."

I SIT SLUMPED ON the Cove House living room sofa, doors open to the terrace, and Luc looms over me, his face flushed.

"I didn't need to be brought here at gunpoint, Luc."

He jabs an index finger at me. "You have thirty seconds to tell me what's going on here, Arlette."

I unfold the paper from my pocket and offer it. "Josie needed to file her story and I thought I'd help."

He bats the paper away. "Was she with you?"

"Josie? No."

He runs his fingers through his hair. "Father Peter says someone was with you. They ran."

I sit up straighter. "Where's Thomas?"

"Not available right now."

I try to stand. "Please don't keep him from me."

He pushes me back down. "You **sit.**"

"We're having our first sleepover and he's terribly—"

"You can forget that for now."

Father Peter lurches in from the vestibule. "I found this." He holds up the silver Himmler cup in one hand, my grief box in the other.

"How could you let him search my room?"

Luc takes the cup and shakes it at me. "So, you **did** steal from me that night. From the safe."

"That cup was meant for Willie."

Luc takes the cup. "I thought I could trust you—"

Father Peter steps to Luc. "I told you she's not a suitable parent. She should at least go to jail, stealing from the Hope Home safe. My personal effects. We need to reconsider all of this."

Luc turns to him. "Leave us, Father. I can handle this."

Father Peter heads for the door and calls out over his shoulder. "Send her home on the next flight. Alone."

Luc stands over me.

"Don't punish Thomas for my—"

"I've sent Claudio away."

I sit up straighter, my heart thumping my chest. "Away where?"

"Don't worry about it."

I swallow hard. "You've killed him, haven't you?"

"Don't be ridiculous."

"How dare you violate my privacy? Let Father Peter paw through my things?"

"You're ruining everything, Arlette. Why didn't you just ask me if Josie could send her story?"

"Please don't take Thomas from me."

"How do you even know how to use a shortwave radio?"

"I don't really. Just saw my uncle use his. Please let me see Thomas."

Luc paces, manic. "This is extremely disappointing. You broke into the radio hut?"

"What about the wedding, Luc? I hope this doesn't change your feelings about me."

"I don't like getting angry, but you've made this hard on **yourself,** Arlette. Do you have a shred of feelings for me? You don't even wear your ring."

"I left it in my safe in the cottage. It's hard to sketch while I'm wearing it. But of course I have feelings for you." I force a smile. "It was just a stupid mistake. Being pregnant and all . . . I find myself doing the oddest things sometimes."

He leans against the railing, arms folded across his chest. "I need to think about it all."

I step toward him. "I wish I hadn't listened to Josie."

"I suppose we might be able to take this as an aberration." He looks out to sea. "Just trying to help a friend. Egged on by her?"

"Yes. That's right. It's true. Josie did suggest I break in."

"I don't know, Arlette. So many things don't add up. Do you even want to go ahead with the wedding rehearsal luncheon? Tell me now, and we'll call it off."

If I ask to call it off, will I be sent home without my boy?

"Of course I do," I say. "What was I thinking, possibly jeopardizing the happiest day of my life?"

"This is a big commitment on my part, too, you know. We need to have marital trust." He steps to the door. "Grandmother and I will discuss it."

"Please, Luc. I'll do anything to keep my son. You don't know what it was like to lose him once."

CHAPTER 61

ARLETTE

RAVENSBRÜCK
1945

Before.

AFTER CHRISTMAS, JOSIE AND I FORGED INTO the new year at Ravensbrück. There was cautious optimism up and down Camp Road since it felt like we were nearing the end. Rumors sprang up of liberation. The Russians. The Americans. The Swedes were on their way with buses to save us.

But the selections continued, the black vans coming to blocks day and night to take women to the nearby Youth Camp. Everyone knew what came after that, since only the clothes came back, reeking of gas. Would we make it to liberation?

We mothers in the **Kinderzimmer** had lost all our body fat, but the wasting away of our own bodies was much easier to take than watching the children growing so thin, some unable to hold their heads up. Starving to death with a child is an exquisite sort of torture. And succumbing first is not an option. Who would lay him on the pile with the same care? The mother must say the prayer.

It grew dark as I ran back to the **Kinderzimmer,** hungry to see the children after work at the warehouses. Our horrible Christmas still lingered in my mind, Willie's too, since he woke at night crying about the dog in the puppet show. I stepped faster, eager to hold Willie, feeling the rubber ring in my apron pocket. Ariana had found a pink rubber teething ring in the course of our work sorting clothes for the Reich and slipped it to me.

"For Willie," she whispered.

I entered the block to find young Dora sweeping the floor, the beds stripped to their blue and white ticking.

"Where are the children?" I asked.

"You are to report back to your old block for **Appell,**" she said, without looking up. "I'm to tell you punishment will be swift if you do not comply." She stopped sweeping and leaned on her broom. "The bunker."

I smiled. "Come now, Dora. You mustn't joke about something like this."

"Get out or I'll call Binz. And I got rid of what's left of those Red Cross packages under your bed. You're lucky. I could've turned you in."

I held the doorjamb. "I don't understand. Are they not at the play yard?" I began to shake all over. "Dora. Who took them?"

"How should I know?"

The light caught a glint of a tear in her eye.

I touched her arm. "Dora, you know how precious—"

Dora yanked herself away. "Don't touch me. I am a wardress of the Reich."

The room tilted. "You have to help us."

"Talk to Dr. Snow about it. Maybe you two could have tea together."

Blood thumping in my ears, I rushed to the barren patch of dirt near the **Revier** they called the play yard. Only the rusted washing machine lay there toppled on its side.

Where were they?

I bent at the waist, breathless. Why could I not think? Where could Willie be? I hurried on to the **Revier.** Perhaps the children had been taken there for checkups? I stepped in and was met with the usual mass of sickness and despair, the prisoner nurse Clara from Copenhagen at the front desk. Always a beacon of goodwill in that terrible place, doing endless numbers of good deeds, Clara had once slipped me a headache powder for Riekie, a dangerous act of kindness.

"Have you seen the children from the **Kinderzimmer**?" I asked.

She came to me with a grave expression. "You should not be here, Arlette."

I choked back a sob. "But they must be somewhere." I pounded on the door to the back offices. "Dr. Snow!"

Clara pulled me away by the arm. "Are you **insane**? You cannot just call for Dr. Snow that way. You'll be punished."

"The children are gone." Were the words even making sense?

Clara pulled me close. "They were taken this morning when you all went off to work." Her eyes shone with unshed tears.

"No!" I clutched her forearm. "Where are they?"

"A van came here to pick up the sick, and the children were on it." She evaded my gaze. "I will find out more, but you have to calm down."

"I can't live without my son."

Clara shook me by the shoulders. "Quiet. You'll be no use to him dead. Roll call has already begun, so hurry back. I have a friend in Commandant Suhren's office. She'll know what happened. But you must go now, or you'll be thrown in the bunker."

I ran out of the **Revier** to a pelting rain and accosted whichever prisoners I found walking on Camp Road. "Have you seen the children?" I grabbed their arms, shouted at them, and they recoiled.

I stumbled across the gravel **Platz** toward the camp front gates, my clogs filled with water. I would appeal to them at the guardhouse—ask to visit the administration building. They would know where the children were.

As I approached the gate, the light from the guard tower above bathed me in a bright pool. I wrapped my hands around the iron bars and called to the guards in their little house. "They've taken our children. I must see the commandant. I can get you money. Whatever you want. Please just help me find my boy. His father is a German soldier. Fighting right now."

Behind me, a male guard called out. **"Achtung!"**

I did not even hear the dog run to me, but first heard the growl and felt the deep sting of teeth clenching my right leg. Whipping his head back and forth, the dog set his teeth deeper and brought me to the ground.

I tried to get up, but he dragged me across the gravel as I called out, "Please. They've taken my boy."

"Stop struggling," the SS man called out, "or I will shoot."

I kept trying to stand, the dog sinking his teeth deeper. **Please shoot,** I thought. **Just shoot.**

CHAPTER 62

JOSIE

FRENCH GUIANA
1952

I WAKE IN MY HOTEL ROOM THE MORNING AFTER our ham hut adventure and replay my escape from the radio hut after leaving Arlette alone. After I ran from the hut in the rain, I barely evaded a rifle shot, waited in the jungle, and then followed from a safe distance as Father Peter walked her back toward Cove House at gunpoint. I watched through the window as Luc interrogated her and it seemed they ended up on friendly terms at least.

How happy Arlette will be when I tell her the details of my radio chat with Karl, and I can finally take Father Peter at the rehearsal luncheon tomorrow. Will Karl come himself with backup?

He'll probably send someone else. Hopefully not Bobby Flynn.

Or, worse, Tony P.

I spend the day reviewing the mass of evidence I've acquired: Johann's film, the Ravensbrück file photos, Bondi's virus feedback. The only thing missing is how they plan on spreading this virus they've acquired. But Dr. Snow can tell us that on the plane back to Fort Bliss. As darkness falls I call down for room service. I'm suddenly starving for a steak, and my best friend at the front desk promises it soon. I imagine how good it would be to take Snow myself as he stands onstage at the rehearsal dinner. But that won't happen with Karl sending backup. It'll be a group affair. Snow will probably be delighted to go to the United States but will put up a phony fight. I turn on the television and watch the Carnival parade.

After what feels like an eternity, a knock comes at the door and I answer it, service weapon in hand in my robe pocket. A white-jacketed waiter arrives and pushes his wheeled cart past me into the room. There's a silver domed plate on the cart, a metal ice bucket, a full water glass, and two crystal decanters, dark liquid sloshing at the bottom of each.

I wave him farther into the room. "Set up over there, please."

He pushes the cart to the sofa and straightens.

It takes me a second to register who it is.

CHAPTER 63

ARLETTE

FRENCH GUIANA
1952

THE MORNING AFTER BREAKING INTO THE HAM hut, it's clear I'm under house arrest. Claudio's uniformed replacement now walks the grounds, a slender older man. **What has Luc done to Claudio?** Luc has told me my meals will be sent in for the time being, and he's punishing me by withholding access to Thomas. The thought of the blood-test results letter sitting in a mail pile somewhere in Danae's office pricks at me. **Do I even want to know the results? At least we'll be one step closer to resolving all this when Josie takes Father Peter and Ebner at the rehearsal luncheon tomorrow.**

Danae comes to the cottage early, knocks, and

walks in, leaning on her cane. "It's terribly out of character for you to do something like this, my dear."

I guide her to the table near the window. "Josie and I have been through a lot together. I was just trying to get her story filed for her, with the hotel telegraph lines down after the storm."

"I know you were just trying to help a friend, Arlette. You must forgive Luc. He's been on edge lately, searching for a new head of Camp Hope. Trying to keep this place together."

Perhaps she's seen the test results. Knows whether Thomas is my son or not. It itches at me like camel hair on bare skin.

I sit next to her. "It's just that Thomas is the one to suffer. He's been eager to know if the test results have come back. And now Luc says we can't have our sleepover."

"Oh, my dear, I hope you won't be cross with me, but I think I may have seen a lab letter in the mail a few days ago. I'll check. And I'll talk to Luc and make sure you two have your sleepover. Men. It's asinine to punish a child that way."

"You're an angel, Danae."

"Luc and I have to go to a Hope Home board meeting this afternoon, but you can expect Thomas after dinner tonight."

I see Danae off as she totters back toward Cove House. Once I hear Luc's car motor out of the drive, I head for her bedroom office.

With plenty of time to find the blood-test results letter.

IT'S LATE AFTERNOON BY the time I get into Danae's bedroom, having been delayed by the maids cleaning in there. It's a lovely room, with light ash-paneled walls and a bamboo canopy bed swathed in mosquito netting, a gardenia-scented candle flickering on a windowsill, the radio playing soft classical music. I step through the far doorway opening into her office, ready to tell the truth if caught. I'm just there looking for the blood-test results.

It feels too easy, since I walk right in, the door not even locked. I step to the bamboo desk and take in its beige ostrich desk set and blotter, a silver-framed photo of Danae and what must be Luc's grandfather in their younger days. A second desk nearby is heaped with envelopes. I pick up a stack—mostly what looks like bills from local companies. Gas. Electricity. None of them opened. How can they live this way? I'd heard the rumors that the rich never pay their bills, but this is proof. Or maybe she's just declining more rapidly than Luc realized.

I sift through the envelopes, having to stop several times upon hearing the maids in the hallway.

I dig deeper and come to a letter with the blue return address of **Rio Biologique.**

My hands start to shake. **Please let the results be a match.**

I rip it open to find blue letterhead, heart pounding, and run one finger down the page.

MATERNAL BLOOD TYPE: O
JUVENILE BLOOD TYPE: B
MATERNAL MATCH: INCONCLUSIVE

I slump against the side of the desk, the bamboo edge bruising my hip bone.

It's not a match.

I read it again. **Inconclusive.**

The heft of it weighs me down like an anvil.

Thomas is coming to my cottage any minute. I try to pull myself together, slip the letter into my pocket, and head back to my cottage for the sleepover.

I RETURN TO MY cottage minutes before Danae brings Thomas to my door, still rehearsing how to tell him about the blood types not matching. How had I been so stupid to come down here? To get my hopes raised and the hopes of this poor child? Of course, it had all been some sort of ruse. By Luc? Father Peter? Both? Josie was right as usual.

Thomas steps in, already wearing cotton pajamas, his stuffed rabbit under one arm, and Willie's blanket and a hand-bound book under the other.

I can barely meet his gaze he looks so expectant, his blond hair still wet from the bath and parted to one side. I want to wrap my arms around him and pull him close but hold back. What if he isn't my child?

"Enjoy this special night, you two," Danae says with a smile and shuffles off.

"May I sit on the bed?" he asks. "Isn't that what we do at a sleepover?"

"Of course."

I pull the covers back, he hops up onto the bed and smooths Willie's blanket next to him with care. "I brought you the book I made."

I can barely look at his sweet, upturned face, the purple smudges under his eyes. "This is the book I made you." He hands it to me, **Our Good Paris Trip** beautifully lettered on the cover, across a detailed pencil drawing of the Arc de Triomphe. What a fool I'd been to assume he was my son simply because he can draw and likes mashed potatoes.

"Can we read it?" he asks.

I sit next to him and open the book to the picture of Le Joyeux Oiseau Café. I'd spoken of it so often he's drawn it accurately. The tile floor, the marble-topped tables.

I turn to a drawing of the candy shop I'd told him about. He sets his hand on the page next to mine, and I'm transfixed by it; our skin colors are an exact match.

"Can we go soon?" he asks. "Even if you haven't got the results of the blood test?"

I swallow hard. "But I do know the results, Thomas."

"You do?" he asks, eyes wide.

Hot tears slowly come. "When I saw them, I knew I had to tell you right away."

He sets one hand on mine.

"It isn't definitive, Thomas. Tests can be wrong . . ."

He turns his gaze up to mine, so expectant. "Is it you?"

I wrap my arms around him and pull him close, his scent of soap and talcum powder wafting up, the little boy I'd wanted for so long.

"Just as we knew all along, my darling. Yes, it's me."

CHAPTER 64

JOSIE

FRENCH GUIANA
1952

"Jesus, Tony."

Tony P. lifts the silver dome on the room service cart and reveals what appears to be a plane ticket on the white plate.

"Hey, Einstein. I got you president-class."

"What are you doing here?"

"Established an aerial port just south. Did an air land. Pretty cool. Karl sent me."

"But I just spoke to him."

"Got the deployment order four days ago. Karl was pissed you're not sending full status reports. Thought you went rogue on him."

"I'm not rogue, Tony."

"Told him I'd handle things. I've listed you as isolated personnel. Simply separated from your unit."

"Big of you."

Tony steps about the room sweeping for bugs.

"Don't bother. I already checked."

He runs his fingers along the frame of the mirror above the sofa. "Already checked?" He pulls out a metal box the size of a matchbox. "Homemade. A good one."

Aaron.

Tony steps to the room service cart, drops the bug into the water glass, pulls the stopper from a decanter. "Surprisingly good stock of brown goods here. Scotch. Bourbon." He helps himself to the lighter of the two. "I'm a bourbon guy, as you know. Want some?"

It takes every bit of my willpower to decline. "No."

"Lobby's crawling with Germans. It's like old home week at Camp Nazi." He settles in on the sofa, legs spread, arms stretched along the back of the cushions. "Mid-flight Karl radioed to say you found Snow."

"This is **my** asset."

"He told me you'd say that. Like it or not, he wants me to head this up. That's why he sent me with six highly motivated colleagues who are excited to assist me, Lieutenant."

"Captain, asshole." I stare at the plane ticket and review my options, none of them good.

"I could send you back today. But if you make

nice and share, I'll consider us partners. Do you even have a target asset?"

I breathe deep. "Former Nazi posing as a priest."

"In custody?"

"Well—"

"Why not?"

"I wanted to be sure."

He rolls his eyes. "Asset visibility?"

"Lives at the kids' camp here. Runs it. Goes by Father Peter. Says he's not a doctor but he did an expert blood draw so that doesn't add up."

"Any of this primary evidence, or is it all just women's intuition?"

"He has a blood-type tattoo on his left arm. And I got into the locked files of his partner, a Dr. Ebner. Both came over on the ratline, I learned from a credible source. Ebner's a party member and former Lebensborn home head. I've documented a systematic plan to multiply German births. Also, info about a virus they've been testing on the native kids here."

Tony sips his drink, ice clacking. "Impressive."

"Dr. Kena Bondi from the WHO is here investigating an outbreak in the Maroon community, and she confirms my findings."

"Wow. What a shit show. I got here just in time."

I breathe deeply to try to stay calm.

Tony P. stirs his drink. "Just remember, you better play ball on Snow. The boys placed ten-to-one odds you're in cahoots with the Israelis, and Karl is inclined to agree. I know you're part Jewish, but just in case, you know how important this is as an American, right? To keep Snow for us?"

"You can be Jewish and American, Tony. But Snow's an actual sociopath and shouldn't just retire in Texas with the rest of Team Hitler."

"I get the personal vendetta. But call me crazy, the idea of dying from some cockamamie plague while the Russkies dance on our graves is not so great. Word is, some of their best agents are here."

"Yeah. Think one drove me off the road."

"Bottom line is, either you cooperate enthusiastically, or I send you home to Texas bound and gagged." He gives me his horny look. "And don't think I wouldn't enjoy seeing that."

I step to the window and scan the pool below for operatives.

"So, when do we engage?" Tony asks.

I watch a white dinghy bobbing in the azure sea beyond. "There's a rehearsal luncheon here in the ballroom tomorrow at noon. Father Peter will be there. He's going to introduce the happy couple. I want to take him there."

"Here's the deal. I'm fine with this being your show. Once you secure the guy, we'll be there as support. But then we fly him out while you stay behind to mop up. Everybody's happy."

"Including Snow. He probably **wants** to go. But I can't just let him off the hook. He basically killed my mother."

"I get it. Just don't go trigger happy on me here."

He leans in. "When you come back to El Paso, once all this has died down and we all get the credit for the collar, I'll make sure you can do what you want with him."

I stare him down. "Give me your word?"

He shrugs. "It's a big desert. Hard to find bodies around there sometimes."

"I can live with that. After you take him, we'll need a CASEVAC for all the kids here."

"You got it." He toasts me with his glass, then downs the rest of his bourbon. "This'll make our careers, little lady." He sets the glass on the room service cart. "I've got your back," he says, stepping toward the door. "And, hey, Anderson?"

"Yeah?"

He smiles. "Admit it. You've always kinda dug me."

I open the door. "Just go, Tony. Noon tomorrow. Make sure you're on time."

ONCE TONY P. LEAVES, I try to sleep, but the street revelers in town are reaching a fevered pitch and my mind races.

Should I just give Snow to Tony and get it over with? My mother will not be avenged if Snow goes to America and parties at the pool, but I can rectify that later. If Tony keeps his word. Aaron wants him, too, but after hearing him speak Russian on the shortwave, how can I trust him? When confronted, he'll simply deny it. Was he posing as a Russian operative?

Am I betraying him, and Israel, by bringing Snow home to Texas? Aaron seems sincere about bringing Snow to justice. And you can't fake what we had at the Ritz that night.

I wonder what my mother would do. Probably see the best in everyone.

I drift off to sleep, and my mother's there, as always. I'm so happy to see her, just like before. It's not the camp at first, just a field somewhere, but I feel the rumble of a truck in the distance.

"Hear that?" I ask.

She reaches out to me.

"No, **run,**" I say.

Now it's Camp Road at Ravensbrück. She's in line, and Dr. Winkelman, one of the most feared men at Ravensbrück, is approaching with his long white selection stick. She reaches out to me, and I try to run to her.

Arlette holds me back.

I try but can't take one step toward the truck, and I wake, heart pounding. I sit up in bed, relieved.

At least I didn't get to the worst part.

I step toward the bathroom, hoping a drink of water will help me get back to sleep, and pass the room service cart.

What harm would one Scotch do? I grab the last of the melting cubes out of the silver bucket, fill a rocks glass, and take the decanter back to bed.

Three glasses later I'm fast asleep. And back at Ravensbrück.

CHAPTER 65

JOSIE

RAVENSBRÜCK
1945

Before.

THE MORNING AFTER ARLETTE'S DOG ATTACK, I dozed standing up at roll call, stomach rumbling, and dreamed of liberation. Would my father somehow figure out we're here and free us all?

Suddenly Marcel the **Blockova** grabbed my arm and yanked me from line.

"You're to report to Binz right away."

It was the summons we all dreaded, to appear **nach Vorne.** In front of camp command.

The women around me stood wide-eyed and watched me go as I flipped through the possible reasons for the summons. Were we being released? A wave of dread washed over me. Or had they discovered the connection to my Jewish mother? Sent her on a transport, with me to follow? I searched for Lylou in the ranks of prisoners as they marched off to various work details. Ariana had heard she'd recovered enough to go back out to work.

An SS man, machine gun slung over his shoulder, hurried me to Binz's office, in the front of a building close to the **Revier,** just off Camp Road. It smelled of real coffee and pastries, and my stomach growled as he presented me. Binz sat at her desk, a portrait of Hitler behind her, two wooden chairs opposite the desk. It was hushed and quiet in there. Warm. I'd almost forgotten how a well-heated room felt.

"Come in," she said, like we were old friends.

I glanced at the chart on her wall, THE NUREMBERG RACE LAWS written across the top. Through various grids it showed what ancestry qualified one to be pure Aryan or Jewish and listed the marriages allowed.

Binz leaned back in her chair.

"It has come to my attention that you're an American."

"Yes, Madame Wardress."

"You know there are a few others here as well. We call you **Weissbrot Fressers.**"

White bread eaters?

"For eating that white bread you all love so much. Even Jews know better than to put that in their bodies."

A movement outside the window caught my eye. It was a group of women wearing yellow stars, struggling to carry heavy wooden crates down Camp Road. I searched the group for my mother.

Binz stood and joined me at the window. "See anything familiar?"

A spike of fear shot through me. "No. Nothing, madame."

"I mean in my hairstyle." She turned her head to the side. "Hedy Lamarr?"

"Oh, of course, Madame Wardress. Very similar."

I glanced again at the chart.

"Who gave you permission to read that?"

"I'm sorry, Madame Wardress. I thought I might learn something important."

"It **is** important. It tells who under Reich law is a Jew. See? Here is the pure Aryan. And this is what we call a **Mischling.** Mixed blood. If you have one Jewish grandparent, you might qualify as **Mischling** One."

"And what if, say, a person's mother was Jewish?"

"**Mischling** One for certain. There are many in the Jewish barracks."

"Even Americans?"

"It makes no difference. Mayor LaGuardia's sister is here, just **married** to a Jew. She's not budging from the bunker. It's Hitler's law."

"Are Jews ever released?"

Binz stepped back and frowned. "Of course not. Why do you ask such a thing?"

"Just curious, Madame Wardress."

She stepped back behind the desk. "Just remember, I expect a good word from you when all this is over. About my mercy and compassion for prisoners such as yourself. But for now, we expect a visitor. A very important one. And here he comes now."

Out on Camp Road a man greeted Commandant Suhren and showed his disc.

Gestapo.

Only secret police presented a warrant disc in lieu of photo identification.

Suhren escorted the man into the building. He looked like any typical German civilian man one might see in the street, dressed in wool overcoat and fedora.

My whole body went cold. I checked the road for Arlette. At least they hadn't called her in.

"Nothing for you to worry about, White Bread," Binz said. "He just wants to ask some questions."

The office door opened and Commandant Suhren, a tall, ruddy-faced man I'd only seen from afar, ushered the agent into the room. "May I present Chief Wardress Dorothea Binz? She has brought the prisoner you requested."

Binz performed her best German salute. "It is a **pleasure,** Herr Oberg."

Oberg paused a moment. What a careless slip to mention a Gestapo agent's name in front of a prisoner.

He recovered nicely and removed his hat to reveal a ridge of dark hair. "Thank you. If you could leave us now?" He left his overcoat on and sat in Binz's desk chair.

My heart pounded as Suhren and Binz left the room and Herr Oberg waved toward one of the wooden chairs. "Please, you must be tired."

The name Oberg was well known. He was Himmler's longtime friend who ran the Gestapo in Paris. In the underground we used his name as a verb. To "Oberg" was to feign kindness while torturing a suspect with no mercy.

Outside the window Ariana hurried by and glanced in, a concerned expression on her face. Why was she not at work at the warehouse?

I sat, relieved my knees hadn't given way, and raced through the possibilities. Did he know I was a Dove? I'd die before I gave up Arlette. I made a mental note of where my cyanide pill was in my hem.

Herr Oberg glanced out the window. "I hope you don't mind if we wait a moment? I've asked someone else to join us."

"I'm not required to answer under the Geneva Conventions."

He removed a bottle from his coat pocket, poured some liquid into the water glass, and slid it toward me. "Care for a drink? Twenty-five years old, this Scotch. Macallan."

I looked at my clasped hands.

"As you wish." He leaned back in the chair. "Are they treating you well here?"

I felt my hem for my cyanide pill.

"You may be candid with me, Miss . . . uh, Porter.

And I wouldn't resort to that cyanide pill just yet. You owe it to yourself to hear me out."

The door opened and Arlette limped in, her face gray and drawn, and every part of me crumpled.

Herr Oberg stood. "Ah. Do sit. They tell me you had a bit of a run-in with the famously well-trained Ravensbrück guard dogs? Very sorry to hear about that."

Arlette said nothing, just sat on the edge of the chair and met my glance, hands clasped in her lap.

"So, ladies, let us get right to it. I've brought something you might be interested in."

Herr Oberg reached into his pocket and pulled out a pale blue handkerchief wrapped around a fist-sized orb.

"It isn't every day one sees such a lovely object."

He set it on the desk and let the handkerchief fall away to reveal our golden dove, the window light shining off the brass. "Quite a nice little . . . pigeon?"

He stroked one finger up the bird's tail.

"I actually believe it's a dove, isn't it? And the funny thing is, while doves are the symbol of peace, this one had been used for some sort of dark purpose." He lifted the bird and inspected its bottom. "Such a coincidence this golden dove was found with the body of an unidentified woman. And, funny, Miss LaRue, your aunt just happens to be missing."

Arlette grew whiter still.

"Let's stick to business, Miss Anderson." Herr

Oberg leaned back in his chair. "And get to the heart of it, shall we? I know you're not a French Gentile named Porter. I know everything. About your diplomat father and your mother who is also here—in a Jewish block, I believe . . . You worked as a radio operator, intercepting signals from our headquarters on the Île de la Cité. Am I correct?"

I looked away.

"You, Miss LaRue, deprived the Reich of a healthy child born at a Lebensborn home in Chantilly. And my condolences, by the way, regarding your aunt's unfortunate demise."

Arlette and I exchanged a glance, and a wave of nausea traveled through me.

Ariana. She'd told him everything.

How had I betrayed Arlette so stupidly?

Oberg shook a cigarette from Binz's pack, lit it, and then lifted the dove from the desk. "I assume you know the Golden Doves carry substantial bounties on their heads. You caused me a great deal of embarrassment last year, uncovering our secrets. But then, curiously, it all just stopped. Not that I was interested in others knowing how stupid we were not to know you were right here under our noses."

He leaned back.

"So that brings us to today. Here you sit. Probably very much in need of some clean bathwater and a piece of soap. I'm prepared to offer you that and more. Miss Anderson, what you may not realize is that your father now resides in Rome."

He pulled a sheet of unlined paper from the middle drawer of the desk and slid it toward me on the desktop.

"I'd like you to write him a letter explaining how well you've been treated here and how I, in particular, have enhanced your stay and as a result should receive an immigration visa to the United States immediately and full immunity postwar."

"He'll never do it."

"I would not be too quick to assume that, Miss Anderson. Our records indicate your father wrote six letters addressed to your mother at the diplomatic housing in Paris. Each detailing the lengths he would go to to assist in your removal from Paris. He never came in person as we hoped, but I think you'll agree there's a strong possibility he would come through for you this time. Once he wires me the necessary paperwork and I'm confident it's legitimate, you two and your mother will be free to go, all of this unseemly business forgotten."

Arlette sat up straighter. "My son came here with me. I need to find him."

"Willie LaRue," I said. "He should come with us and my mother, too."

"I'll do the best I can for you ladies, but the sooner Mr. Anderson arranges that visa, the sooner we can all have those things we want. Of course, there are many ways your story could end here at Ravensbrück. Some greedy guard could figure out you've been in our midst all along, and we'd be forced to administer punishment."

He pulled a pen from his breast pocket and offered it to me.

I hesitated. It was certainly the hope we'd wished for. But Herr Oberg would go free without punishment. And could he even be trusted?

An image of my mother out on a work detail fighting for her life flashed before me, and I took the pen.

Herr Oberg smiled. "Smart girl. Let's hope we hear from Papa soon."

CHAPTER 66

ARLETTE

FRENCH GUIANA
1952

THE MORNING OF THE REHEARSAL LUNCHEON, A few minutes before noon, Luc and I enter the Hotel Lotus ballroom, the glorious scent of gardenias in the air. Thomas walks at my side and slips his hand into mine. Our sleepover was a great success, and I'm at peace with the lie I told him. I'll come clean someday, but for now I'm not going to break a young boy's heart. Or my own. Besides, once U.S. Army backup arrives, I'll have more power to do what I please and take the boy back to Paris regardless of blood types.

Danae has transformed the room into a fairy-tale palace, festooned with yards of mosquito netting and tiny white lights, a tall vase of cut gardenias at each table.

I check the crowd for Josie. **Why is she not here yet to take Father Peter?** He is already onstage, adjusting the microphone, wearing his usual black shirt, trousers, and clerical collar. The tables are mostly filled, with friends of the family, I assume, and Luc takes me around to meet some of them. I scan the crowd for Dr. Ebner but there's no sign of him.

Danae approaches, leaning on her cane, a vision in ballet pink cashmere and satin. "Hurry now. We need to get onstage to welcome everyone."

Danae leads us up onto the stage to join Father Peter and takes her place at the microphone.

I recheck the crowd for Josie. **She'll be here soon.**

"Can we stall?" I whisper to Luc. "Josie's not here yet."

He squeezes my hand. "I'll draw out my remarks a bit, sure."

Danae taps the microphone. "Hello, everyone. Thank you for being with us on this very exciting and memorable day, for the celebration of the union tomorrow between my grandson Luc and our beloved Arlette LaRue."

I crane my neck to check the crowd for Josie, table by table, but don't see her. My palms sweat. Has she been hurt somehow?

All at once, the ballroom doors burst open and armed men rush into the room and head for us on the stage. Americans, it looks like. The crowd reacts with great gasps and shock, and Father Peter pulls me close, at first I think to protect me, but then he locks one arm across my throat, cutting off my breath. Armed men surround the stage, their guns pointed at us, and I start to shake.

"Get back," Father Peter calls out.

Luc steps to us. "Peter, my God—let her go."

The armed men approach. "Let her go," a tall one with pompadoured black hair calls out.

Danae comes closer. "Take me, Peter. Not the girl."

Guests scream and cry out and run for the exits, as Peter tightens his grip.

The last thing I remember is that as the men storm the stage, Peter throws me to the floor, and I fall into blessed darkness.

CHAPTER 67

JOSIE

FRENCH GUIANA
1952

I WAKE, HEAD POUNDING.

A knock comes at the door. **"Bonjour. Service de ménage."**

I sit up and throw the covers back. What time is it? Light streams in through the hotel drapes I never closed. Kids are laughing, down at the pool.

Shit. The rehearsal.

I run for my watch. Twelve fifteen. **How did I sleep so long?**

I can still make it. Did Tony take Snow without me? I strap on my holster and throw on trousers and a wrinkled button-down shirt. On my way out I pass the room service cart, the Scotch decanter empty. Even with three glasses of it, how did I sleep so long?

I rush past the maids, run down the stairs to the lobby, and race to the ballroom. Guests are streaming out, visibly shaken.

"What happened?" I ask.

A woman stops and replies in French. "It was terrible. American officers came to arrest the **priest.** But he held the bride-to-be hostage as the men stormed the stage. It was awful for the poor girl."

I hurry into the ballroom and push through the crowd huddled around Arlette just as two male nurses ease her onto a stretcher.

I make it to Arlette and kneel beside her as Luc and Danae hover above us. Arlette's face is ashen, and a purple goose egg of a bruise swells on her forehead.

I squeeze her shoulder. "I'm so sorry."

"Where **were** you?" Her eyes well with tears.

"I'll tell you later."

"I needed you."

"I'm so sorry—"

Luc smooths Arlette's hair back from her forehead. "American agents came out of nowhere and stormed the stage. Father Peter panicked and held her hostage."

Danae bends and straightens Arlette's blanket. "She fell and hit her head. She's in shock, poor girl. And in her condition . . ."

I lean in and murmur to Arlette, "Pretty sure I was drugged. And we need to talk."

She whispers back, "Get me out of this."

"Some maid of honor you are, showing up late," Luc says.

"Where is Thomas?" Arlette asks.

Danae leans closer to Arlette. "He's been taken back to Cove House but saw it all. Quite shaken up, poor thing."

The nurses take up the stretcher and move Arlette toward the ballroom entrance, Luc and Danae by her side.

I try to follow but get squeezed out by the crowd. "I'm so sorry, Arlette," I call after her. "I'll make it up to you."

Luc turns to me. "I think you've done enough, thank you. We'll take it from here."

IT'S MIDAFTERNOON BY THE time I hurry back to my room, badly in need of aspirin and coffee, and consider how badly I've screwed things up. I catch sight of myself in the lobby mirror, with my porcupine hair and bloodshot eyes. Clearly Tony P. drugged the Scotch to ensure I wouldn't interfere with his show. I run one hand down my holster. I hadn't gotten the chance to take Snow out, but at least he's in custody.

No doubt he and Karl are overjoyed that Snow is winging his way back to Texas to live in luxury. Will Tony even come through with that CASEVAC as promised?

How could Karl do this to me? I've let Arlette down, and she's in deeper than ever.

Do I just barge into Cove House and say Arlette and Thomas are coming with me? Keep trying to send telegrams to Karl via the hotel? Revisit the ham hut to speak with him again? The next commercial flight is almost a week away. Plus, the Minaus have legal custody of Thomas. And do we just leave Luc here and free? He's no doubt as guilty as Snow. Plus Ebner's still at large. And what's going on with Aaron, Mr. Russian-speaking double agent? Is he still here in Cayenne or has he already moved on since Snow's gone?

I pass the front desk.

"Is the dining room still serving?" I ask the desk clerk. "I need coffee."

He gives me a cursory look. "Yes, you certainly do. But I'm afraid not. Perhaps in town . . ."

My temple throbs. "Can I send a telegram?"

"Wires still down. So sorry." He waves a letter. "But a **most** attractive gentleman dropped this off."

He slides the envelope across the counter to me.

I lift the flap. **Meet me at the barn** is written there in black pen. What barn? The only one I know is the big one on the outskirts of town. It's the first time I've seen Aaron's handwriting, and it's bold yet oddly childish. Is it a trap? After hearing him speak Russian on the radio, it's hard to know what to think.

I head out of the hotel, hurrying through town. The costumed Carnival revelers are already in high gear, clogging the main street and sidewalks. **Why do they have this festival in the hottest months in the Southern Hemisphere?**

I dive into the crowd and it's even hotter in that scrum as I push past the stiff fabric of cheap costumes, the smell of sweat and grilled shrimp in the air. A firecracker explodes close by and I bump into one man who's dressed as a zombie, covered in molasses, and it sticks to the length of my bare arm. I force myself to think past the headache and consider my options. Going back to Fort Bliss is not an appealing one. I'd be back in my spider hole in the basement—although maybe I could finally take care of Snow. But will Karl even help us get out of this place?

Finally, I leave the crowds behind and keep walking to the outskirts of town, a weathered barn in the distance, a great wall of jungle beyond.

A wave of dread passes through me, and I shake it off. **Aaron.**

Maybe he just wants to say goodbye. Or to rail at me for not handing over Snow earlier. Or maybe he has orders. To get rid of me? He could easily be a Russian operative. Johann had warned me.

I pull my gun and step into the barn. It's dark in there, lit only by the afternoon sun slanting in through the louvered windows. Cardboard boxes and a silver grinder stand on a long sorting table, and an enormous mountain of ground cayenne pepper stands on a tarp mid-room, ground as fine as the sand of the gypsum fields of El Paso. I breathe in the earthy-spiced scent of chili pepper and moist dirt floor.

A voice comes from the far side of the room. "Hey, Anderson."

Aaron. He steps toward me.

I tighten my grip on the gun. "Stay right there."

He looks tired, dressed in green cargo pants and a gray T-shirt clinging to his chest with sweat, his dark hair tucked behind his ears. Probably has his gun stashed in his back waistband.

He raises his hands. "Whatever you say."

I want to get right to the part about him being a Russian agent, but just step closer, keeping my eyes on his hands and scanning the site in case he brought friends.

I barely breathe. "Here alone?"

He lowers his hands. "Of course."

I steel myself to the firehose of attraction that scrambles my ability to tell if he's lying. "I'm sure you know everything. My colleague took Snow."

"Perhaps."

"I heard you on the ham radio."

His eyes blink in the near darkness.

"So, you're working for them?" My hand grows slippery on the gun handle.

"It's complicated."

"Right."

"You do know that wasn't the real Snow they got?" Aaron asks. "That priest was just a decoy."

I huff a breath. Just the thought of Tony P. getting the wrong guy sends a warm gush through me.

"You sure?"

"Positive."

"Then who's Snow?"

"I've actually been talking to the real Snow. Except he thinks I'm a Russian agent."

"You have a radio here?"

"Yes."

"So, you've been posing as a Russian agent in order to get Snow?"

He nods.

I exhale.

Aaron steps closer. "And I need your help. The real Snow is coming to the wedding venue tomorrow at eleven."

"Next to the helipad?"

He nods. "I've told him I've arranged transport for him to Moscow."

"How do I know you're being straight with me?"

He stares at me for a long moment. "You'll just have to take my word, but trust me, I wouldn't do anything to hurt you."

I shift my gaze away. Why can I not stop thinking of our time at the Ritz, his warm skin on mine?

He steps within arm's length. "I've kept an eye on what the Minaus are doing—and your friend Arlette."

I holster my gun but stay ready to grab it. "Hard to know who to trust these days."

He runs one hand down the stubble of his beard.

"Surprised you didn't take me out earlier after hearing me and my bad Russian."

"You could've told me sooner."

"Let's hope my mark doesn't suspect." Aaron folds his arms across his chest. "For now, the real Snow thinks he's choppering to a landing strip to meet a cargo plane to Moscow. I suspect it might be Luc."

"Nice. You know about their whole virus operation?"

He nods. "And I could use your help on the ground. Maybe both of you Doves? Lure him out of the car."

"So, whoever gets out of that car is Snow? Why do you think it's Luc?"

"I don't. Sounds like him, but I can't ID him by voice."

"Could be Dr. Ebner, a gynecologist in town."

"He's on my radar."

"Any other leads?" I ask.

"This place is crawling with Nazis. Could be any one of them."

"I should at least warn Karl."

"I wouldn't."

"Why?"

He pauses. "Let's just say Karl doesn't have your best interests in mind."

I step back. "What do you mean?"

"You may've gotten too close to the truth."

"That makes no sense."

"Think about it. Maybe that's why Karl sent you

on this wild-goose chase to begin with. You may have unwittingly been onto him from the start."

Karl had been so interested in my office. The map. My tracking of Snow.

"You mean he's in on this whole thing? The virus . . . everything?"

"That's what my sources tell me from chatter they picked up. He'll do anything to keep Snow on his side. Probably offering him at least a million to come to the States. But the fake deal I offered Snow to come to Russia is much sweeter."

"But why did Tony P. take Father Peter then?"

"Not sure. But the less Karl knows, the better. Let's just let him think his relationship with Snow is on track."

"There's another piece to all this. Like how Snow plans on spreading their virus."

"No doubt it runs much deeper. But we need to grab the real Snow now, and he can tell us from the comfort of his cell in Tel Aviv. Think Arlette will be in?"

"She can't wait to get out of here with her son."

"If it's Luc, he may bring her with him tomorrow. Think she's capable of disarming him?"

"Most definitely."

"Then loop her in."

We stand there for a long moment in silence.

"I need to get back."

Aaron turns to me. "Hey, sorry it ended up this

way. I know you wanted to get Snow yourself. But trust me. He'll see justice."

"Where are you staying?"

He nods toward the jungle. "Out there."

"You can use my shower if you like."

He smiles. "Is that an invitation? But how would Tommy Kennefick feel about that?"

"Wait."

"Yes, I bugged your room."

"You heard our whole—"

"What was it you said about our night at the Ritz? Oh, right. 'Slightly better than fine.' Funny, I seem to remember someone that night begging me not to stop."

It's growing darker in the barn, and he steps so close I can smell the musky scent of sweat and cigar smoke on him.

I steel myself to it, still not all in on Aaron.

"How about you come see my campsite?" he asks. "You'll be safe there. And I make edible beans and rice."

He's so serious.

If I go, no doubt it will end with some sort of physical intimacy. Something glorious and entirely satisfying. But how do I know he's being completely honest with me?

I nod toward the door. "Gonna turn in early. Tomorrow's a big day."

Is that a flash of disappointment on his face?

"I get it." He runs his fingers through my bangs. "I'll tail you back to the hotel just to be safe."

What if I just kiss him, standing there? It might be my last chance. After tomorrow we both go our separate ways.

"See you at eleven tomorrow, then?" I ask.

He attempts a smile. "I'll be the one in the unmarked helicopter. With plenty of backup."

I start off toward the barn door. "See you there."

"And for the record, Anderson, Tommy Kennefick was a fool not to wrap you up in eighth grade."

With one last look back at him, I slip out the door.

On my way back to the hotel I avoid the partying crowds. As I walk, a word Mimi often used bubbles up. **Schicksal.** Fate. Would Mimi say Aaron just wasn't my fate?

More likely she'd say, "Are you crazy? Run back to him."

It's growing darker, what the army calls End Evening Civil Twilight, EECT, one of Karl's favorite acronyms, when the sun has dropped six degrees below the horizon—no longer able to see objects with the naked eye. **Karl.** How did I misread that one? How stupid I'd been, thinking of him like a father.

As I near the hotel, my holstered gun heavy at my chest, I consider who the real Snow is. Luc, no doubt, though he doesn't seem the doctor type. What if I try to take him out myself? Or bring him back to Texas? But screw Karl. He's no doubt got me on a hit list, as well. Nice guy. And it feels good to have Aaron trust me after all I've done to double-cross him. That is, if Aaron's being straight with me.

I'll fill Arlette in tomorrow morning before the wedding. Hopefully I'm still allowed on Cove House property after our ham-hut adventure. If Aaron's right about Luc, it'll be an impressive grab. Arlette and Thomas will be free to go back to Paris.

And the real Snow will finally see justice.

CHAPTER 68

ARLETTE

FRENCH GUIANA
1952

THUNDER WAKES ME THE MORNING OF THE wedding as I dream of Claudio. We're riding burros up to the wedding venue, and he stops on the way and kisses me. I'm happy to see him, with his dark eyes and quiet way.

My head pounds as I sit up and shake off the dream. Poor Claudio has run into the Luc buzz saw—the dark side of whatever is going on around here. Just more proof I'm not meant to be happy with a man.

I throw back the covers and stand, a bit dizzy. I slip on my robe, touch the bruise at my forehead, step to the glass-topped vanity table, and bend to look in the round mirror. The swelling has gone down a bit, but it's turned a deep shade of lavender.

When will they let me see Thomas today? What's Josie's plan C?

I take the wedding ensemble from the closet, hang it on the hook on the back of the door, and run one hand down the satin. Hopefully all this will be wrapped up before I actually have to walk down the aisle.

Father Peter's gone, and there may still be some loose ends, but I'm looking forward to having the day over with, so we can get back to Paris. Six new, fully packed white Samsonite suitcases sit near the door.

A chill shivers through me. It will still be cold back in Paris, but how good it will be to see everyone at the café again. They'll love Thomas.

As I sit at the vanity table, my window slides up and Josie scrambles over the sill and into the room.

"You can use the door," I say.

"Didn't want to risk them throwing me out. How are you feeling?"

I run a silver-backed hairbrush through my hair. "Like a caged animal. But well enough to get on a plane bound for home. Which will be when, by the way? Now they've got Snow, it's time to end this charade. What's your plan?"

"I'm working on it."

"Just like your plan for the rehearsal luncheon?"

Josie steps closer. "Let's not fight. Looks like you're ready to go."

"To my supposed honeymoon. Took three maids two days to pack. Hope I get to keep the clothes."

Josie sits opposite me in a slipper chair. "Sorry to tell you this, but Aaron thinks they got the wrong guy."

I turn to her. "**What?** Please tell me you're joking."

"Luc may be Snow."

"Luc? Then who was Father Peter? Just some random Nazi down here experimenting on kids?"

"Not sure. Maybe a decoy for a bigger thing."

"But Luc is Dr. Snow? I just don't think so."

"You're not softening on him, are you?" Josie asks.

"What are you suggesting?"

"You did grow up in that world. Willie's father was a Nazi, for God's sake."

"Gunther was just a brainwashed Wehrmacht soldier. Of course I'm not softening. I want to figure this out as much as you do. I just need to go home." Tears pool in my eyes. "And, besides, I don't think Thomas is my son after all."

Josie pulls her chair closer. "What makes you think that?"

"Found the letter from the testing lab."

"And?"

"I'm O and he's B."

"So?"

"They need to match."

"Did Luc tell you that? It's not necessarily true. If mother-child blood types match it's a good indication you're related, but an exact match isn't required.

The only true indicator is the father's blood type. In this case, Gunther would have to be type B for you to be the parents of a B-type child. That would be definitive."

Every part of me relaxes. "Oh, Josie, I thought it was over."

"Thomas is yours, I just know it. The minute we get back to Paris we'll redo the test and write to Gunther's parents to find his type. But for now, don't listen to Luc. He's a good liar."

"What is he even doing down here? Can we just leave?"

"I don't understand a key piece of it yet. But I do think it's some sort of play for global power. And we know it revolves around Thomas somehow. He may be a critical asset for them. So we have to be careful."

"Every minute we do nothing they're making him sicker. Let's just leave. We can come to your hotel. Sort out the adoption later."

"I know this is a big thing to ask, but can you hold out a bit longer?"

I stand and toss my hairbrush onto the glass vanity top; it lands with a clatter. "You're asking me, and my sick child, to stay here to help you get Luc? They're drugging him, he told me. He's a sick **child.**"

"I'm so—"

"Can't you just call Karl to send another plane and end this?"

"It's just a few more hours."

"It's not you that has to do this. Living here,

pretending you like Luc Minau. I know you want revenge for your mother's death, but she's **gone,** Josie. Thomas is still here. For now."

Josie looks down at her hands. Something in me lifts, happy she's feeling my pain.

"It's not about revenge," she says.

"Then get us **out** of here. I've spent weeks acting out this charade, and I just can't do it anymore. Thomas is in trouble, and all I hear from you is you need more time."

"If you'd—"

I wave her away. "You've been given everything your whole life. It's all about what you want."

"We need to have each other's backs—"

"Like you had mine at Ravensbrück? By telling Ariana I killed my aunt?"

"You know I'll never forgive myself for—"

"Do you even have a plan?"

"I do. Aaron has been talking to Snow, under a Russian MO. He's arranged to chopper him off from the helipad to a ship bound for Moscow, today at eleven o'clock."

I step back and let that sink in. "And you want me to play along to see if it's Luc?"

"Yes. It'll all be over before noon. Just act naturally. As if the wedding is a go, the honeymoon, everything. And if he brings you to the helipad today, make sure he can't use his gun on me."

"What if he forces Thomas and me to go with him?"

"I'm a good shot."

"I'm scared, Josie."

She runs one hand down my back. "I won't let you down."

"You need to promise this is it. No more delays. You'll get us out of here?"

"Promise." Josie steps to the window. "You'll be back in Paris tomorrow."

ONCE JOSIE LEAVES, I sit and finish my toilette as best I can, smoothing on lipstick, fingers shaking. All at once my forehead aches, my old leg wound, too, and I yearn to see Thomas. A fresh worry sprouts. **Will Luc take him and leave me behind?**

Danae knocks and enters, wearing a fabulous gray silk dress with a knife-pleated skirt, leaning on her cane. How much has Luc shared with her?

"How's the patient? Sure you're still up for this wedding, my dear? We can easily postpone."

"I'm fine, really."

If she's in on it, she's a very good actor.

Danae sets a pair of pearl stud earrings on my vanity table. "I want you to have these. They were my mother's."

"Oh, no. You mustn't."

"You're the closest thing I'll ever have to a daughter. Please wear them knowing you are a valued part of our family. I don't have much time left on this earth, and I'm grateful I lived to see this day." She pulls a hankie from the cuff of her sleeve. "I must say, seeing you injured that way . . ."

"I'm sorry about Father Peter. You need to find a new leader for the camp."

"Oh, we've already been looking, so that won't be hard. Thank goodness that man's been expunged from our good foundation."

She turns to go, and the light catches the gold necklace around her neck. I lean closer and see it's a perfect replica of the one Josie and her mother so often traded, back in Paris before the war.

Everything quickens.

"What a lovely necklace. Mind if I ask where you found it?"

"Oh, my little acorn? Given to me by Luc of course. A birthday gift."

"I know someone who used to wear a similar one. Any idea where he got it?"

"Oh, he just said he picked it up during the war. The oak is a symbol of strength, so this acorn reminds me to keep calm and carry on, as the Brits say."

Danae hurries off to oversee wedding preparations, and before I can even regroup, Luc appears at my door. He rushes in, dressed in the same rumpled shirt and trousers from the day before. Thomas slowly follows, wearing his fashion show suit, and steps toward me, Luc's new bodyguard close behind.

Thomas wraps his arms about my neck. "They said I couldn't see you, but I don't feel good at all."

Luc walks to the window and peers out. "I was trying to give you some time to get ready."

I gather Thomas to me and feel his forehead. "Another fever."

"My arms and legs hurt again this morning. My stomach again, too."

A cloud of dread descends. "Like before?"

He nods. "Can I stay with you?"

"Of course—"

Luc yanks Thomas by the hand and leads him to the bodyguard. "Keep him out of here."

Thomas turns back for me. "Please—"

"He's sick again, Luc. Just let me keep him with me."

The bodyguard leads Thomas out.

"What's really going on, Luc?"

He meets my gaze and swallows hard. "There's been a change of plans."

"Why aren't you dressed? Shouldn't you shave?"

He thinks he's taking us to Russia.

He crouches next to me. "There won't be a wedding today, Arlette."

"I don't—"

"I'm sorry. You've really been looking forward to it. I don't know how much you've put together, but before I fill you in, just know that I really do love you."

"I know that Father Peter isn't Dr. Snow. And about the virus."

He's genuinely surprised. "Really?"

"You've been experimenting on the kids this whole

time. Using Thomas as your antibody cow to make your germ bomb."

He takes my hands in his. "It's not as bad as it sounds. I've wanted to tell you many times, but I couldn't endanger the mission."

"I need details, Luc." **I'm almost afraid to hear them.**

"It's all so exciting, Arlette. We've created perhaps the most valuable thing of this century. It's something everyone in the world wants right now." He pauses and leans in. "Something Truman, Stalin, and every head of state is desperate for, and you and I have it. I'll explain it all on the plane."

"You were experimenting on the kids at the camp. Thomas. That's why the Maroon kids got so sick."

"The Maroon children were necessary casualties, I'm afraid. They're easily infected, having been completely isolated for so long."

"And what about the girls' camp?"

"What a good sleuth you are. Well, as our boys age we need new youngsters to feed into the program. Peter and Dr. Ebner couldn't have been more willing partners in this repopulation of true Germans, in their own likenesses."

Just the thought makes me nauseous.

"You three couldn't have done this alone."

"I've had a powerful partner—been working all along with the Americans. They brought us from Italy early on. Cut a deal with someone high up in U.S. Army Intelligence. They wanted this project badly."

Karl.

"He funded our trip, worked with a Vatican bishop, provided this house."

Clearly, Karl never told Josie any of this.

"At the rehearsal luncheon, the Americans made a great show of taking Peter, allowing me to operate freely. It was all arranged."

"And Thomas?"

"He's a very special boy. Key to our mission. Of course, he'll come with us."

"So why bring me here? I saw the blood-test results. Inconclusive."

"We needed a mother for the boy—he was despondent without one. If we lost him, we'd lose the whole project."

"But why me?"

"It wasn't that hard, really. You left a paper trail looking for your son. We had your ex's photo and realized he resembles Thomas. You fit the promising profile. Single. Low on funds. Still holding out hope you'd find your son."

Something splinters in me. **Such a cruel thing to do to a person.**

"Please don't be cross with me. For all we know he could be yours. I promise to love him like our own."

I wipe the tears away. "Danae's in on this?"

"She helped us find you, but she hasn't a clue about the master plan. She thinks you and I will be honeymooning in Leningrad."

"Now what?"

He takes my hands in his. "Here's the fantastic part. I'm selling our masterpiece to the highest bidder."

"The Americans."

"Before, yes. But now the Russians have made a spectacular offer. Why sit on an army base in Texas with one million dollars when we can live in a villa on the Volga with ten times that? We'll be rich beyond our dreams."

"I need to know what this project is."

"Your life will be wonderful—far better than working in some dreary café. Servants, summers in a villa on the Black Sea. Living like royalty with Thomas and our own child. Diamonds from the czar's vault. Your own clothing line." He pats my knee. "Those Russian ladies need you, Arlette."

"So, you want to kill everyone in the world except Germans and Russians?"

"Not at all. We'll simply have the leverage to get the world powers to do what we want. We'll be in Moscow before the Americans know we're gone."

If I stay behind, I'll never see Thomas again, and Luc will have someone finish me off for sure. Josie, too. I have no choice but to play along and hope Josie comes through.

I attempt a smile. "Sounds incredible."

He leans in. "I know this isn't perfect, that you'd prefer Paris, but we'll go back there someday. I'm terribly fond of you, Arlette. Yes, this all started for the wrong reasons, but I've grown to love you. Think you can feel the same way someday?"

I squeeze his hand. "Just wish you'd told me sooner."

He stands. "We need to go. Thomas is on his way to the car. The helicopter's waiting."

I stand and force a smile. "Off to a new adventure."

CHAPTER 69

JOSIE

FRENCH GUIANA
1952

BACK AT THE HOTEL AFTER SEEING ARLETTE I wonder who will show up at the helipad today. Luc? Dr. Ebner? A mystery guest? If it's Luc, will he bring Arlette as well? Clearly there will be no wedding.

What would my mother say about Snow's plan if she were here? **Sometimes it's the most obvious thing that you need to see.**

I turn on the television and watch the local news. The newscaster reports that the first group of Hope Home ambassador kids are flying out today on a chartered plane, first stop, New York City, to see the Statue of Liberty, the new United Nations, and Coney Island. Otherwise, the big news is Carnival, the crush of people filling the streets, which I can hear loud and clear from my hotel room.

I shower, dress, and strap on my service weapon, ready for the hilltop face-off. There's a familiar voice on the television and I sit at the end of the bed as I brush my teeth. It's Arlette's Hope Home commercial, starring Thomas dressed in a gray uniform, with other boys standing behind him. It's a good ad, too, with her caring voiceover. If I didn't know better, I'd write a check and send it off.

Thomas smiles and delivers his lines well for a nine-year-old. **Welcome a Hope Home ambassador to your town. Let's bring the world together.**

I stop mid-brush. All at once I see.

I hurry to the sink and rinse my mouth. I was right.

It really is ridiculously simple.

I TAKE THE HOTEL jeep to pick up Bondi, and we speed directly to the airport to stop the plane of little ambassadors from leaving, both of us flashing our IDs to the pilot. I disable his radio, return to the jeep, and we head for the helipad doing at least sixty on the rocky road, straight uphill.

It's almost eleven by the time we arrive. Aaron's unmarked helicopter already waits at the helipad, adjacent to the wedding venue, blades at rest. He's in there, waiting for the right moment to spring the trap.

I exhale. No Snow yet.

I park, and Bondi and I walk in silence to the circle of emerald sod at the cliff's edge, the white folding chairs arranged there in rows.

"Watch the cliff," I say as Bondi surveys the vista.

I step to the arched arbor of white flowers set up on the platform stage, lilies and gardenias ruffling in the humid breeze.

Someone's dream wedding. Just not Arlette's.

A few minutes after eleven, Danae's Citroën limo, with its dark-tinted windows and whitewall tires, creeps up the road, and stops just yards from us.

"Keep back," I tell Bondi and center myself, blood pounding in my ears, eyes trained on the car doors. Whoever steps out is our guy.

The door opens, a man unfolds himself from the car, and I curl my fingers around the handle of my weapon.

CHAPTER 70

ARLETTE

FRENCH GUIANA
1952

LUC DRIVES US TO THE HELIPAD IN THE limousine, the rest of us seated in the back. Thomas sits next to me, quiet, his head resting on my shoulder. I can feel the heat from his face through my shirtsleeve. **Why had I waited so long? I should have insisted he be sent to a proper hospital**

Danae brushes something off her skirt.

How can she just go along with Luc on all this?

Despite the somber mood, I can't help but smile a bit, thinking about the little theft I'd made and how Luc will react when he discovers it. My plan upon arrival is to take Thomas and go to Josie at my first chance. If he's not too sick to make it.

We arrive at the wedding venue, the white flowers of the arch blowing in the breeze as the helicopter waits at the helipad nearby. I steal a glance at Danae. Is she thinking about all her hard work on the ceremony gone to waste?

Josie and Bondi are already there, standing by the hotel jeep, about two car lengths away from us.

"Shit," Luc says. "Just what we need."

Luc exits the limo first, Danae next.

I help Thomas out of the car.

"What are you doing here?" Luc calls over to Josie and Bondi.

"Just wanted to see our friend off," Josie shouts back.

"Arlette has nothing to say to you," he says.

He turns to rush us off down the path toward the chopper, but I hold Thomas back.

"I'm not going," I say.

Luc grabs me by the arm and goes for his holster.

"I wouldn't try that," Josie says, drawing her gun. "Trust me, I'm happy to shoot."

"Plus, a gun's not much good without these." I hold out my palm to show him the bullets and then pitch them over the side of the cliff.

Luc turns to me. "After all we've done for you? We're taking the boy."

Panic rises in me. "No."

Danae pulls Luc by the arm. "Perhaps it's time we left, dear."

"Going to Russia?" Josie calls out.

Luc turns to me. "Come with us. I love you." He beckons to Thomas. "Come along now, Tommy. We're going in a helicopter."

Thomas sags against me, and I place my arm around his shoulders. "No, we're not."

Luc's eyes darken. "We'll just take the boy. He's coming with us, or I'll tell the authorities you killed your aunt."

Once, just hearing those words out loud would have turned my knees to jelly. But now I don't care. "Go ahead. I'll fight it. Once I'm back in Paris with Thomas getting him actual medical care."

"He's not even your real son," Luc calls out. "Let him go with us and I'll tell you where your Willie is."

Suddenly the world slows. They've known where Willie is this whole time? My entire body vibrates.

Thomas looks up at me, lips parted, his eyes two pools of hurt.

"You've known all this time?" I ask Luc.

"Just hand him over and I'll tell you where to find Willie."

"He's lying," Josie calls out.

"Won't you always wonder?" Luc beckons to Thomas again. "Come along, boy. You know you need to do this for Germany."

Thomas releases my hand and steps toward Luc. "I'll go."

"No." I hold him back by the shoulder.

He looks up at me, tears welling. "So you can have your real son."

"No, Thomas." I draw him to me, so close I feel his heart beating against my chest. "I already have my real son."

CHAPTER 71

JOSIE

FRENCH GUIANA
1952

I KEEP THE GUN TRAINED ON LUC AS ARLETTE hurries Thomas over to Bondi and me.

"I just figured it out this morning, Arl," I call to her. "When I saw your commercial. This whole youth ambassador program was designed to send their little disease carriers out into an unsuspecting world to trigger global death. First stop the United Nations to infect world leaders, or at least hold them hostage to it."

"Don't listen to her," Luc shouts.

"You were at Ravensbrück, weren't you?" Arlette calls over to Luc. "You're Snow."

Once at the helipad, the chopper stairs fold down.

"How did I ever think I loved you?" Luc shouts at Arlette.

"Come, dear," Danae says, pulling Luc toward the helicopter.

As Luc and Danae approach the chopper, Israeli agents dash down the steps.

Luc and Danae turn back toward us.

"Mossad, Arlette?" Luc calls out.

Aaron comes to the helicopter doorway with a tall, dark-skinned man.

"Claudio—" Arlette says.

The agents step toward us along the path, pushing Luc and Danae toward the cliff.

"Time to go," Claudio shouts.

Luc shifts his attention to me. "We can be of great service to the United States. Just call Karl Crowell. He'll tell you . . ."

Karl.

The Israeli agents close in and hold their ground.

"Come, my dear." Danae links her arm in Luc's, and a gold chain swings free of her jacket and sparks a yellow glint in the sun. She brushes back her silver hair with one hand. Suddenly time slows.

"It's you," I say.

Danae steps toward me. "Of all the people to get me, White Bread."

"What did you say?"

She inches closer. "It took you a while."

I barely breathe, unable to take it all in. "I don't—"

"That's the first time I've seen you speechless. I hear you have my pen, by the way. Would like that back."

"You're Snow."

"Is it really that surprising a woman could achieve so much?"

I train the gun on her. **How had I not seen?** "It was you at the camp. Drew up prisoner lists for transport."

She shrugs. "A doctor's necessary task. To euthanize those unfit for life."

"How do you remember me? I was one of thousands."

"The only American with a father who could save us all? Binz heard your whole conversation with Oberg. Was convinced your father could help her too."

The memory nudges me, and I tamp it down. "Not another word, or I'll shoot you right here."

"Binz was obsessed with you two. The **Doves.** Please. Suhren would have gladly hung you if Oberg had allowed it."

I feel my pocket for Mother's picture. It would be just like I'd planned. Show Snow the photo and then blow her off the cliff.

"Not to mention that touching final scene with your mother. The famous Jewish Nightingale. We watched from the **Revier,** you wailing like a stuck sow."

"I'm warning you."

Danae rolls her eyes. "The whole camp was subjected to it."

All at once I'm back at Ravensbrück with Arlette, on Camp Road one frigid Sunday, as the wind whips off Lake Schwendt. I help her walk, her leg bandaged the best we could manage, the infected wound making every step painful. Prisoners roam the camp dressed in rags and scavenged clothes and most of the block windows are broken and covered with paper or rags, as bands of motherless children play their rough games. The crematoria now operate day and night, burning the bodies from the makeshift gas chamber, huffing a thick, yellowish blanket of smoke over the camp.

Two bus lengths away from us, SS men holding revolvers have emptied out the typhus block again, with the unruffled movements of people performing everyday tasks. In front of that wretched block, rows of women stand at attention, stripped to their underthings.

It's that most solemn of occasions, one hard to look away from.

A selection.

"Don't watch that," Arlette says, watching as intently as I.

I step closer. Fat Dr. Winkelman wanders down the rows, tapping unfortunates on the shoulder with a long white stick. "I hope you do well," he shouts to the women. "Move your arms and legs to pass the test."

The women wait, heads bowed. Upon feeling the dreaded tap upon the shoulder, some crumple, dragged by an arm to the waiting truck. Others walk, as straight up as kings, to join the doomed.

"I'm not sick," one woman cries out as the guards escort her to the truck.

"Dr. Snow thinks otherwise," Winkelman calls back to her.

After long months at that place, we've all seen worse. I force pity for them from somewhere, but I'm just happy it isn't the Jewish block.

A woman, blue from the cold and unable to walk on her own, presents a macabre sideshow. She escapes the group and drags herself along the ground toward another block, only to be picked up, hauled back by her arms and legs, and swung up into the truck.

Circling closer, we watch more of the chosen take their walks. I feel nothing, my humanity lost, witnessing the parade, their bodies alike, sunken chests and knobby legs, their pantalettes puffed out.

Winkelman stops at one who accepts her tap, turns to bid silent adieu to her compatriots, and steps toward the truck. This one has a way of walking that I know, that my body recognizes before my brain does, and I flush despite the cold.

"Mother."

Arlette is just one second behind me and locks her arm tighter in mine.

My mother.

I free myself and walk toward her.

"No—" Arlette calls after me.

I don't care anymore who sees me.

"Mother," I call out.

She turns toward my voice.

I smile, as if she'd know me from the other skeletons. "It's me."

She steps to me. A moment of joy. **"Ma petite."**

"Stop!" a guard behind her shouts.

Her joy fades, replaced with a sort of vexation. The look she'd give me if I burned the morning toast. "No, Josie."

I wave to the guards. "Please," I say in German. "I'm American. This is my mother."

"Turn back!" a guard shouts at her.

As if she doesn't care there is a gun trained on her, Mother steps to me.

I call to the guards. "Please. My father's a diplomat. Getting us released any day."

The truck starts up, and Mother shuffles faster toward me.

I wave her to me. "Yes. Hurry."

She comes, one arm outstretched.

I offer my hand, desperate for her touch. "Quickly."

One guard raises his arm, aiming his revolver at her.

I wave to him. "Don't shoot! Ask Herr Oberg . . ."

I hear slow footsteps behind me. It's Arlette. "Josie, please—"

The air fills with exhaust as Mother steps faster to me, stumbling a bit. **"Je t'aime."**

I walk faster. **I just need to hold her. When I explain to Suhren—**

I'm almost to her when a shot rings out, and I freeze.

The bullet passes straight through Mother's chest, and she falls like a deer I'd seen shot on a television show my father and I had watched, the wounded doe stunned, standing for a moment, motionless, before dropping.

"No—" I start off toward her with a sob, when something metal thumps me between the shoulder blades, knocking me to the ground. Arlette limps to me, tosses away the gas can she'd hit me with to the ground, and bends best she can to embrace me, shoulders heaving, crying herself.

I try to follow my mother but Arlette holds me back and I watch from the ground, wailing as if possessed, and Arlette rocks me in her arms as the men drag Lylou to the waiting truck.

A VOICE COMES FROM somewhere and Arlette squeezes my arm. "Josie, are you all right?"

"Fine," I say, breathing deep, the tide receding.

I'm drained but swept out. Lighter. The world's brighter, in better focus.

I step closer to Danae. "You killed my mother. Selected her to die."

"Don't say anything, Danae," Luc calls out.

She leans back and looks over the side of the cliff, the golden acorn swinging at her chest.

Arlette pulls me closer. "Your mother's necklace."

Danae grabs the chain and raises an eyebrow. "Your mother was a clever Jew, wasn't she, hiding this so skillfully in the heel of her shoe? I almost hated taking it from her."

I control my breath. "Give it to me."

Danae holds the acorn and examines it. "You call off your patrol and tell your boss you're the true hero here. Stopped us from going to Russia. He'll have us on our way to Texas in no time." She lifts the chain over her head and dangles it over the edge of the cliff. "Then I may be more inclined to let you have this back."

What if I just pull the trigger? It's the moment I've waited for, but the gun grows heavy in my hand.

"The U.S. and Germany can partner. And I'm happy to share part of that million dollars with you. I didn't relish the idea of Moscow anyway."

"It's over," I say.

"Karl Crowell wants what we have—and it's better than being carted off to Israel with the Jews."

I slide my gun back in the holster. "You're so filled with hate."

"And you're not?"

I step back. "I'm not like you."

Aaron hurries toward us. "Let's go."

Arlette steps to Danae.

"Give her the necklace."

Danae turns to Arlette with a smile. "Ah, the long-suffering Arlette."

"It was you on the phone when I called for references, wasn't it? How could you do all this? Sicken those poor Maroon boys. Use Thomas for your experiments." Arlette steps closer to Danae. "You created that horrible **Kinderzimmer.** Watched all those children starve."

Danae inches backward. "Those children would have died anyway."

"But you kept Willie."

Danae shrugs. "It was Binz's idea to keep the boy. And Willie'd no doubt love to be reunited with his dear mummy."

She steps closer to Arlette and switches effortlessly to charm mode. "Convince your friend here to take us to America, and I'm happy to tell you where he is."

Arlette leans in. "They'll hang you in Israel."

Danae smiles. "Like you're above it all, Fraulein Krautergersheim. You're just as German as I am, and yet you sabotaged your own people during the war. How many good German boys were you responsible for killing?"

"Germany raped France."

"Do you know how sickened I was to play mother-in-law to you all these weeks? And to see Luc falling for you—a thief and a murderer."

"Who are the real Minaus?" Arlette asked. "Did you murder them, too?"

"Your uncle Hans would be disgusted by you." She looks about, cornered. "How can you just hand me to these people?"

I wave Aaron toward Danae. "Take her."

Danae looks behind her, over the cliff.

Aaron's agents approach and I grasp Arlette by the arm. "Stay back."

Danae looks in the distance to Luc and offers a silent farewell, and in that one second, I see her plan.

"Grab her," I call to the agents, but they're too late. Danae falls back like a believer baptized in a river, skirt sent up around her gartered stockings, Mother's necklace swinging in her hand.

"No—" Luc wails.

Arlette and I step closer to the cliff edge and watch her plummet, twisting as she falls.

Aaron hurries to us with Claudio, as Danae splashes through the white breakers, sending up a geyser-like white plume of ocean water.

Silence blankets the air, the waves lapping the shore below the only sound.

Aaron turns to Claudio. "Scramble a dive team. Retrieve the body."

I peer over the edge. No sign of anything floating in the churning waters. A sense of great calm spreads through me. "She did the world a favor."

Bondi and Thomas join us.

Aaron turns to me, and his eyes say it all. **Sorry you didn't get the chance to get her, that it was her**

choice not yours. It takes all the restraint I've got not to take his hand in mine.

"Will send word when we get Luc secured," he says. "There'll be a trial."

He heads off toward the chopper and then turns. "Thank you." He walks backward for a few steps. "See you. At the Ritz maybe?"

I smile for the first time in days as he hurries down the path to the chopper, and he and Claudio shove Luc up the stairs.

After we look once more over the cliff edge, Arlette takes Thomas by the hand and she, Bondi, and I link arms.

"Let's go home," Arlette says.

The chopper takes off, straight up, and flies over us. The whirl of the blades rips up tufts of emerald sod and whips the flowers on the arbor, swirling them around us like smooth, white confetti.

We watch the chopper bank out over the ocean as we walk Thomas back to the jeep.

And the Golden Doves head back to Paris.

CHAPTER 72

ARLETTE

PARIS, FRANCE
1952

It's a busy spring day at Le Joyeux Oiseau Café, door flung open wide, the scent of lilacs wafting in. The flower sellers sit at the marble tables and play whist and drink cherry brandy, the cool light of Paris filtering through the shutters. Raphael and I stand at the ancient porcelain sink up to our elbows in warm dishwater, my Thomas perched atop a high stool, dish towel outstretched like a hammock, waiting to dry cups and plates.

Bondi was right about my son. He was Luc and Danae's prized antibody cow and "Father Peter," aka Peter Vogel, enabled them, along with Dr. Ebner. Once we made it back to Paris and met with a treatment team of the best doctors, Thomas's mysterious ailments cleared up, and he thrives here.

His hair has darkened a bit, he's already grown taller, and the walls of our apartment are filled with his watercolors, so like those my parents painted. He's gotten over his nightmares, and someday, if Thomas wants it, we can redo the maternal-match blood test and know for sure, but it really doesn't matter.

I already know he's mine.

Our orange cat, Saffron, has been a big part of Thomas's healing, for although she can have a temper, she seems to understand he needs her, and she sleeps alongside him each night, his hand resting on her sleek back.

Life isn't perfect, but I'm the boss now, since Marianne has retired and I own the café, which has its pluses and minuses.

I auctioned most of my couture clothes, and my diamond ring sold for a nice sum, allowing me to buy the café, make some updates, and start a nest egg. I couldn't wait to sell that ring, for every look at it reminded me of Luc and Danae and their plan to send their germ-spreading ambassadors out into the unsuspecting world. Had they even thought twice about all those Maroon boys they hurt?

Detectives told us Josie's boss Karl had stolen Luc's and Danae's new identities from a wealthy French couple, who were arrested by the Nazis during the war for underground activity. The whole extended Minau family had died at various camps, so there was no one to call them out down in French Guiana, and they just took over Cove House, a winter home the real Minaus seldom used. Luc had dyed his graying hair to look younger, and Danae did a good job of appearing frail and older than her fifty-nine years. Originally from Berlin, she didn't have a drop of French blood in her, but having grown up in Alsace she spoke near perfect French. Those two met at Ravensbrück and were just bound by greed.

I pat the letter in my apron pocket. It bears Claudio's return address: **Cove House, French Guiana.** Turns out I was right about his smooth hands. He had become a freelance agent working for Aaron and disappeared when Luc started suspecting him. He stayed behind to work with Bondi to return the Maroon boys to their families and turn Cove House into a hospital for the people of Cayenne. We share the job of making sure Ella and the children at the girls' camp are reintroduced into society and find loving homes, along with the boys at Camp Hope.

Claudio had promised news of his impending trip to Paris to arrange it all, and I hope this letter has details. Thomas will be happy to see him.

Me too.

I had dreaded confronting my aunt's missing-person claim when I came back to Paris, but it turned out Luc exaggerated the French police's eagerness to find me. Once I returned to Paris and revealed my identity as one of the famous Golden Doves, the police visited to congratulate me, did a cursory search of the apartment, and closed Auntie's file.

I consider my staff as I swish cups in soapy water, Saffron rubbing her silky body against my calves. Sweet Bep works the outside tables delivering the French presses while Riekie takes orders inside, her six-month-old daughter asleep in the corner in Willie's old bassinet. I've passed along Willie's diapers and the last of his clothes, and it feels good to see her baby in Willie's white cotton shirt with the Peter Pan collar I'd made so long ago.

I've even given up my grief box. One night when Josie came through Paris, we placed the dove statue inside it, along with a small boulder from the garden, taped it up, and the two of us took it to Pont Neuf and dropped it into the Seine. This time it will stay, current or no current. It was Aaron who'd found out how Luc got his hands on the little statue. His good friend Oberg had given it to him at Ravensbrück, along with the whole story of us being the Doves.

Bep comes and stands at the cash register, coffee cup in one hand. "The drawer's stuck again, Arlette. Should Raphael fix it?"

I dry my hands. "I'll do it." I bang it with the heel of my hand in just the right spot, and the drawer opens.

Marianne, still very much a fixture here, helps Fleur bring me a vase. It holds red and white striped parrot tulips arching out, no white flowers or gardenias allowed.

"Perfect, my darling," I say.

Fleur has gotten better each day since Josie and I finally got her out of Metropolitan Women's Hospital and she's come to live with Thomas and me. Well into her teen years, she's still small for her age but finally filling out a bit. After only a few weeks at her new school and at-home therapy, she finally spoke. Just one phrase, but when she said those words, the whole café became silent, and then we all burst into applause and hugged her, and she became quite overwhelmed.

I brush her hair back from her forehead. **"Je t'aime."**

"Je t'aime," she replies. Her beautiful words.

I cannot stop smiling, for there's a secret hidden in the back room—a gift for all of them.

"Everyone gather," I call out to the whole café. "I have a surprise."

Raphael and Marianne go to the back room and carry out our new Italian cappuccino machine, a copper monstrosity like something out of a Jules Verne story.

Bep steps back to allow them to pass. "**Three** espresso ports?"

Riekie hurries over. "We can make café crème? We'll never sleep."

I get the machine up and running, and Bep and Riekie can barely deliver the cafés crèmes and espressos quickly enough. The word and aroma spread quickly, and soon there's a line at the counter.

Raphael and I watch it all, elbows deep in suds.

He hands me a cup to rinse. “I told you that guy was shifty, did I not?”

I smile. **Shifty.** One of the people behind a plan to blackmail the world with a germ bomb.

“Very shifty, yes.”

“You should be married to me, you know,” Raphael says.

My old self might have considered his offer, but I’ve left my old self in French Guiana.

I shake my head. “Oh, no. A girl should be only two things. Who and what she wants. And I’m already both.”

He smiles at that, happy just to be in my orbit. And I watch the sun shine in on that imperfect little place, happy to be home.

With my family at last.

CHAPTER 73

JOSIE

PARIS, FRANCE
1952

I TURN ON THE TELEVISION TO KEEP ME COMPANY and think about those German kids at Fort Bliss, so long ago, watching **Winner Take All,** and hope they're adjusting well to America. I lie back on the most comfortable bed in Paris and sink into the down pillows. It seems like I've lost the weight of ten anvils off my chest, knowing Dr. Snow and her bizarre plan are over and done with.

It's lovely being back at the Ritz, every detail perfect, down to the vase of yellow roses at my bedside table, which Arlette had sent that morning. I've even booked the penthouse room with a view of **la tour Eiffel** and have flung the windows wide to let in the warm spring air. But I miss Aaron. After he choppered out with Luc and Claudio, WHO sent in a medical team for all the kids at the camp, and Bondi finally got the backup she needed to assist the Maroon families.

Father Peter is going back to Germany to stand trial. Turns out he was a doctor at Majdanek concentration camp with a dirty résumé of his own, had escaped justice, and came to South America with Dr. Anna Snow, "Luc," aka Lucas Brandsberg, and Ebner, via Bishop Hudal's ratline. Plans are in the works to send Dr. Ebner back to Germany for trial as well, on charges of crimes against humanity. Since word from Washington is I'll be getting Karl's job, I'll make sure those charges stick.

Karl admits to aiding Luc and the others to come to French Guiana, but claims he was just following orders to acquire Snow and her program at any cost. My father has used his connections to open an investigation with the Army Criminal Investigation Division into Karl's actions. Not without a lengthy "I told you so" from Dad, but I appreciate the help.

The tube warms up and the local news channel is carrying the trial, live from Jerusalem. I climb back into bed and finish my omelet while I watch. It's hard to tear myself away, Luc standing there in the bulletproof glass box, dressed in an ill-fitting suit and tie, listening intently to what's being said in his translating earphones.

A female voice reads. "Attorney general against

Lucas Brandsberg, aged forty-five, French national. You are accused before this court of twelve counts of crimes against humanity against Jews and non-Jews."

The seven hundred spectators listen as the charges are presented, outlining his work with Dr. Snow at Ravensbrück. The viral experiments. The thousands of prisoners sent to their deaths on transports.

Luc dodges a question from the judges.

"I had to obey the rules of war and my flag," he says.

Stripped of his couture clothes and luxury estate, Luc's lost the bravado he had on the helipad that day. Without the fake identities that he and Danae stole from honest French citizens, he's smaller somehow, an empty hot water bottle, flaccid and slack, his backdrop now two Israeli officers standing at attention.

The prosecution shows photos of Luc in uniform at Ravensbrück and references the selections he supervised there with his colleague Dr. Snow. No mention of Karl and his backing.

I sit up straighter as Kena Bondi takes the witness stand.

"Tell us how you know the defendant," a judge says.

"From 1945 until very recently, the accused had been running a front of a children's camp in French Guiana, experimenting with a lethal virus. I came as a scout for the WHO. We'd had reports of an outbreak in the tribal Maroon community. Male children were disappearing."

"The connection to the Reich?"

"It was a continuation of Hitler's work. Documents recovered by my colleagues indicate the groundwork for this was laid at Ravensbrück by Rapportfuhrer Lucas Brandsberg, formerly of the Charlemagne Division, and Dr. Anna Snow, now deceased. Both are responsible for the deaths of many Ravensbrück prisoners by these experiments and myriad others, and for the deaths of children in the Ravensbrück **Kinderzimmer.**"

"Can you describe this virus for the layman, Doctor?"

"It is my medical opinion they were continuing the Reich's quest for a viable germ bomb. Toward the end of the war, Adolf Hitler had acquired the medical expertise to discharge one but could not scale the vaccines necessary to keep his own people safe. Dr. Snow's project made millions of vaccines possible and was just days from activation."

"And how does this virus work exactly?"

"We're not sure how the Russians planned on activating it in the young ambassadors, but the virus, once unleashed and contracted by the unvaccinated, liquefies the lungs."

The courtroom erupts with chatter, and a shiver runs down my legs.

The shower turns off and the bathroom door opens.

"I missed you," I say.

Aaron steps out of the bathroom with a white towel wrapped around his waist, running a comb through his hair. "I was only in the shower five minutes."

He snaps off the television and comes to stand near me. “Old Luc’s not long for this world.”

It’s dangerous gazing up at Aaron, at that beautiful smooth chest, those lips, with him looking down at me. I have work to do but it will have to wait, for that towel won’t stay on for long.

“I brought you something.” He tosses a white box onto my lap.

“Why?”

“Because you’re the kind of woman men want to do things for.”

I smile at that and pick up the box and shake it next to my ear. “What is it?”

“It’s a surprise. Why would I tell you?”

I pull off the top of the box and it takes me a moment to fully understand what I see. **“Aaron.”** I grasp the edge of the bed for support.

“Thought you might like it.”

I lift the gold-link chain from the cotton, the golden acorn swinging there. “So, you found her body?” It’s as if my insides are melting.

“No, just this.”

I run one finger down the break in the gold links.

“The chain must’ve snapped in the fall,” he says. “Not surprising from that height.”

“It can be fixed.” I cup the acorn in my hands. “You don’t even know the story. My mother wanted to give it to me the day I was arrested, but I was in a hurry. My grandfather made it. It has a secret spring lock if you press it just so.”

"It opens?"

I shake it, next to my ear. "Not sure there's anything in here. But if there is, it's the last message from my mother. I want to savor it."

How good it is to remember her, standing in the kitchen of our Paris apartment, her sheets drying, a lavender scent in the breeze.

"Well?" Aaron folds his arms across his chest. "I can't stand the suspense."

I take a deep breath and press the tiny oak leaf atop the acorn, and the cap flips open.

"Oh my." My belly contracts with a sob.

"What is it?" Aaron asks.

Inside the little golden cavity is a silver filigree button wedged in tight, and I pull it out.

I hold it up, the silver catching the light. She'd found it after all.

"What is it?" Aaron asks.

"The morning of the day I was arrested I looked everywhere for a button I'd lost. I accused Mother of not caring about me, since she wouldn't help me find it. But it looks like she'd already found it. Wanted to surprise me."

I look at Aaron through a blur of tears.

He sits on the bed and takes my hand. "I'm sorry."

I shake my head and wipe my cheek. "Don't be. It's like I got to be with her one last time."

A rustling sound comes at the open window.

"A pigeon," Aaron says as he stands. "I'll get rid of it."

I throw back the duvet. “No.”

I step to the window and watch her there, crimson feet clenched around the black balcony railing, puffing her emerald throat, one tangerine eye taking me in.

I hold out one hand, and she takes off and flies over the rooftops of Paris, beautiful and strong. I watch until she’s just a dark speck in the sky, and look back at Aaron with a smile.

“She’s a dove.”

EPILOGUE

JOSIE

FORT BLISS, TEXAS
1953

MOVING BACK TO FORT BLISS AND GETTING Karl's job isn't what I thought it would be.

It's better.

With Tony P. and the gang reporting to me I can finally get things done my way. I've amended our intake of Operation Paperclip scientists to include a strict protocol of clean résumés only. I hired two new women to vet them and promoted Anna Paganini from the cafeteria to head of Tony P.'s unit.

The lunches suffered but it was more important that Tony P. did as well.

Aaron recently has visited me here, shrouded in secrecy of course, and we holed up at the Glenwood

Motel for a long weekend, hiking the gypsum fields and staying abed for as much of the time as possible. He wants me to come meet his daughter at boarding school but I just want to take it slow.

It's a little strange taking over Karl's office, with him living right there in El Paso with Debbine while the army reviews his case. He has influential friends, so I don't take anything for granted and use each day to send true believers back to the Fatherland. Every contract revoked I sign with Snow's gold filigreed pen.

First thing I did was move my bulletin board with the yarn tracers to the wall of my new office. Second thing I did was terminate all intramural teams for the scientists. Johann would have loved that I canceled Tuesday night Nazi bowling league.

I'm working late one night, taking a break from vetting a portfolio of new scientist candidates, eating Chinese takeout, and talking to Arlette long distance.

"I miss us," she says. "Think we'll ever do another mission?"

"You can come work with me here. Though Tony P. might be reduced to a blathering mess. He's in love with you, you know."

My assistant, a recent Vassar grad from the typing pool who I'll soon promote to take Bobby Flynn's job, knocks and enters.

"Major, this came for you." She steps to my desk holding out a cellophane-wrapped florist's basket.

"Hold on a second, Arl. Some flowers just came."

"Aaron?" she asks.

I tear off the cellophane and from the scent alone know what they are before I see them.

Gardenias.

"Josie?" Arlette asks through the phone. "You still there?"

"I—"

"What is it? Oh, wait. Flowers just arrived here for me as well."

My assistant waits. "Shall I read the card?"

I nod, not sure I want to hear what it says.

She clears her throat. "It says, 'Watch your back, White Bread.' "

"My God," Arlette says.

I stand. "See you soon, Arlette."

"I'll be waiting."

It's time for toast with marmalade.

AUTHOR'S NOTE

Meeting Irene Zisblatt in 2016 changed me.

I'd come to the David Posnack Jewish Community Center in Davie, Florida, on my book tour for **Lilac Girls,** and Irene gave my introduction that night. I met her after my talk, and loved her right away, with her big smile and incredibly positive way.

"What a pretty pin," I said, leaning in for a closer look at the silver Hebrew letters on her lapel.

"It means 'Always remember.' " She undid the pin and stepped to me and pinned it on the collar of my dress.

That night Irene and her daughter offered to drop me at my hotel, and we ended up talking for hours in her car. I listened as Irene told the details of her arrest in Hungary by the Nazis in 1944. How she and her family were deported to Auschwitz-Birkenau death camp and she was chosen upon arrival by

Dr. Josef Mengele for medical experiments. As she stood with her family holding her little sister's hand, Mengele smashed their joined hands with his baton, separating Irene from her family. She never saw them again and is the only survivor from her big Hungarian family.

"Getting through a day at that place was a miracle," she told me.

There in the dark, hearing how Mengele experimented on thirteen-year-old Irene in her own words, so matter of fact, I felt honored she would trust me with the details of such a horrific time. The idea that Mengele and so many other Nazis had escaped justice seemed unfathomable. And I knew someday I would do what I could to shine light on the horror of it.

And always remember.

When it came time to write my fourth book, I dove back into that world of WWII.

In corresponding with my friend Dr. Stafford Cohen, a cardiologist from Boston I'd met in the course of my **Lilac Girls** research, he sent me a newspaper article that featured a woman named Janina Iwanska, whom I had based the Polish character Kasia Kuzmerick on in **Lilac Girls.**

I was stunned by it.

It told how Janina, after being released from Ravensbrück where she and her friends were the victims of experimental operations, came to the United States at the invitation of philanthropist Caroline

Ferriday. While undergoing treatment at Beth Israel, Janina learned that Dr. Walter Schreiber, who had supervised those experiments, was free and living in Texas. He'd come here through the U.S. Army's Operation Paperclip, the secret intelligence program that brought Nazi scientists to America after the war.

The article described how, with the help of Caroline Ferriday's friend and colleague Dr. Leo Alexander, Janina went to the FBI and told them Schreiber had headed up the experiments at Ravensbrück and, backed by the doctors at Beth Israel, demanded this "former Nazi" be expelled from the program and sent back to Germany for trial.

The scenes in **The Golden Doves** that feature Nina and Schreiber are based on fact. Once the FBI obtained Nina's absolute ID of Schreiber, the U.S. Army expelled him from the program and sent him to Argentina where he lived comfortably with his family, applied to the West German government to add the prefix "von" to his name to connote baron status (it was approved), and lived in a home he named "Without a Care." All while those victims of the experiments lived desperate lives back in Poland with little access to healthcare.

That propelled me to dig into the number of other Nazi war criminals that had been brought here to the United States to work in secret government programs. I'd known that many men were allowed to escape justice and take refuge here and found it outrageous, but when I started looking deeper and read

Operation Paperclip by Annie Jacobsen that outrage grew. Jacobsen's superbly written book is a fascinating look into the secret intelligence program that brought these Nazi scientists to the United States, much of the information based on documents declassified in the 1980s.

The more I researched the ratlines, the gateways to South America and other friendly havens for fugitive Nazis, it became clear that this had been a coordinated effort, abetted by the International Committee of the Red Cross, civilian Nazi sympathizers, and members of the Vatican. While many Catholics such as Father Hugh O'Flaherty, known as the Scarlett Pimpernel of the Vatican, saved thousands of Allied soldiers and Jews (my own uncle, shot down during the war over Messina, Italy, was rescued and nursed back to health by Catholic nuns), postwar there was another group at work there, operating a well-managed series of Nazi escape routes. After the war Rome became a center for Nazis escaping justice from the Allies. They would come down through Austria, many via the Brenner Pass, and once in northern Italy in towns such as Merano and Bolzano were contacted by nationalistic sympathizers such as Helene Elisabeth, Princess von Isenburg, and Gundrun Himmler, who worked with Stille Hilfe, an organization that aided the escape of hunted fugitive Nazis.

I traveled to northern Italy to see for myself the place where the Nazis came across the Alps and into freedom, escaping Allied justice, abetted by Vatican envoys like Bishop Hudal and others. To the monasteries and inns, still standing today, where the fugitives slept while awaiting their forged travel documents. In Rome, I visited the Santa Maria dell'Anima church where Bishop Hudal served as rector while harboring the men the Allies sought for crimes against humanity and the Collegio Teutonico (German College), one of the Pontifical Colleges of Rome, which abuts the Vatican, where Nazi fugitives hid while they waited for their documents. Today Bishop Hudal is interred at the Teutonic Cemetery adjacent to St. Peter's Basilica in Vatican City, under the Good Samaritan Station of the Cross, a testament to his good standing in the church even after harboring and abetting so many criminals.

In Rome, some fugitive Nazis even worked openly in the Italian film industry, wrote screenplays, and can be seen acting in films of that era. There has been much written on this subject, including Harvard professor Kevin J. Madigan's "How the Catholic Church Sheltered Nazi War Criminals." And for those seeking primary evidence a simple search on CIA.gov turns up myriad unclassified documents about the subject. Philippe Sands's fascinating book **The Ratline: The Exalted Life and Mysterious Death of a Nazi Fugitive** provides a great inside look at that world.

Something else I wanted to bring to light in **The Golden Doves** was the treatment of children at Ravensbrück, Hitler's only major all-female concentration camp. It's impossible to forget a dusty leather-bound ledger I saw while researching at the Ravensbrück Memorial in which a camp staffer had written in perfect script the name of every child born at the camp, their mother's name and nationality, and a simple black **X** next to every infant's name.

Many prisoners arrived at the camp with infants and toddlers and in varying stages of pregnancy. During the six years the camp operated, the Nazi policy concerning the children born there changed. At first, Ravensbrück staff followed Hitler's rule that no child could be born at a camp, and the children were quickly killed by medical personnel, including former midwife Gerda Quernheim, a prisoner nurse.

I had my Arlette LaRue and her son, Willie, arrive at Ravensbrück to shed light on a horrific place there known as the **Kinderzimmer.** Later in the camp life, Commandant Suhren established this maternity block where prisoners lived with their babies in better conditions, with down comforters on the beds. The babies were looked after while the women went off to work. The Nazis performed this sad experiment to attempt to solve their problem of new mothers who became unable to work productively once they bore children at the camp. Many spiraled into depression when their children were murdered per Hitler's orders. The experiment failed when the camp staff did not feed the children and in months the babies had all perished from lack of food.

Finally, as Germany lost the war and the camp descended into chaos, more children and infants arrived, too numerous to manage, and to this day there are many adults who were born or raised at Ravensbrück, saved by that chaos.

As I shaped the characters of **The Golden Doves,** I knew I wanted to set the women's early years in occupied Paris and have them be a part of the underground working there. While researching **Lilac Girls** I had discovered the fascinating world of the SOE British intelligence after learning about the French-British spy Violette Szabo, who was imprisoned at Ravensbrück and executed there. I've always wanted to explore that world and gave Josie and Arlette past lives as SOE spies.

A great help in this was reading **A Woman of No Importance** by Sonia Purnell, the story of Virginia Hall, an American spy who worked in France for the British underground. It is a great companion book to **The Golden Doves** for it brings to life the true story of what it was like to be a woman working covertly to bring down the Nazis in France, and it was the perfect inspiration for Josie and Arlette. Selma van de Perre's remarkable memoir, **My Name Is Selma,** in which she shares her life as a resistance fighter and a prisoner at Ravensbrück, was also very inspiring and a great companion book as well.

Readers may be surprised, as I was, to learn that there were several American citizens imprisoned at Ravensbrück. I'd long known about Mrs. Aka Chojnacka, who had been arrested and sent to Ravensbrück where she befriended the Polish

"Rabbits," and later hosted the women when they came to California on their American tour. Aka was released early from the camp due to tremendous efforts by the United States, and she informed the authorities about the criminal medical experiments carried out in the camp. But I found there were many other Americans at Ravensbrück, from the famous sister of Mayor Fiorella La Guardia, Gemma La Guardia Gluck to lesser-known Elsie Ragusin, who escaped Ravensbrück as a child and made her own U.S.A. patch, which she wore at the camp.

Readers of **Lilac Girls** might have noticed some recurring characters in **The Golden Doves,** Dorothea Binz, the cruel female Ravensbrück guard, Commandant Suhren, and Dr. Herta Oberheuser. I based Danae Minau, aka Dr. Snow, in part, on a second German female doctor I discovered at Ravensbüuck, Dr. Erika Jantzen, who served willingly as a Reich camp doctor and then disappeared just before the camp was liberated.

Dr. Gregor Ebner was a real person as well and the medical leader of the Lebensborn program, an SS-initiated, state-supported, registered association in Nazi Germany that ran maternity homes. According to the Jewish Virtual Library, at the Steinhoering Lebensborn house alone, "Ebner presided over the birth of some three thousand illegitimate children and performed reproduction experiments on women." According to **Master Race: The Lebensborn Experiment in Nazi Germany** by

Catrine Clay and Michael Leapman, Dr. Ebner was a university friend of Heinrich Himmler and "an important influence on Himmler's thinking about heredity." Ebner helped shape the program, the goal of which was to raise the birth rate of Aryan children of people classified as "racially pure" and "healthy" based on Nazi racial hygiene ideology and to incorporate stolen children from eastern European countries with Aryan characteristics. Children who did not meet Ebner's standards for Aryan looks or who displayed any kind of handicap or any personality trait deemed unacceptable were euthanized or sent to concentration camps.

The Lebensborn homes were personally outfitted by Himmler with furniture and upholstery obtained from Jewish residences and institutions, which were unloaded at the homes by concentration camp prisoners. The homes were often sited in what had once been Jewish-run clinics or sanatoriums in order to offer a "beautiful landscaped environment" to the expectant mothers.

I had first researched the Lebensborn program back when I wrote about Herta Oberheuser's time at a Lebensborn-style camp in **Lilac Girls** and have always wanted to write about the program and expose the bizarre nature of the maternity homes. I set Arlette's delivery of Willie at Westwald, the only French Lebensborn home, located in the Château Menier in Lamorlaye, near Chantilly.

Dr. Ebner was eventually tried, served two years

and eight months and was released to continue a medical practice.

Not all Nazi criminals were apprehended and tried, of course, with Dr. Josef Mengele being the most famous of those who escaped justice. I based my camera-shy Father Peter, with his watchtower and pack of dogs, on Mengele to bring attention to the fact that he lived quite openly in South America once he escaped on the ratline. **Mengele the Complete Story,** by Gerald L. Posner and John Ware, tells the unputdownable true story in chilling detail.

When I looked for inspiration for my Dr. Bondi, I knew I wanted her to be a strong woman with experience in medicine and the World Health Organization and found it in Keva Bain, permanent representative of the Bahamas to the United Nations office at Geneva and recently elected president of the World Health Assembly. I hope the character of Dr. Bondi celebrates all those dedicated to working to protect underrepresented people worldwide.

Thank you to all my readers who have reached out to me through the years to share your own stories. You continue to be my inspiration and my oxygen. Like Irene Zisblatt's they all need to be shared.

I met with Irene on Zoom last week and she is just as vibrant as ever, swimming regularly and playing mahjong. She seems to be reverse aging, at ninety-three still so sharp and curious about everything.

We talked about my book and her book and everything under the sun. How Steven Spielberg's

The Last Days, which she appears in, had just come to Netflix. I told her I thought her mother would be proud of her for living such a purposeful life. And for speaking the week before at a U.S. Army gathering, introducing a five-star general. And she told me she feels she's racing against time to help stop the spread of antisemitism.

I showed her the pin at my collar.

"I remembered," I said.

She smiled. "Now you must give it away. Do a mitzvah. And make sure someone else remembers, too."

ACKNOWLEDGMENTS

MANY THANKS TO THOSE WHO MADE WRITING **The Golden Doves** such a joy:

To my husband, Michael Kelly, who happily read every draft, brainstormed plot with me, and cooked amazing dinners. I'm grateful every day for the Bango Safari that fall day in Chicago. You are the source of all the best things in my life.

To my daughter Mary Elizabeth Kelly for cheerfully reading countless numbers of drafts at the drop of a hat, for her brilliant editorial insights, and unflagging love and support.

To my daughter Katherine for her supreme Moishe wisdom, for keeping me sane and laughing during the pandemic and always knowing the best shows to watch on Showtime.

To my son, Michael, for answering endless questions about science and disease spread while holed up with us during COVID and for helping me create Claudio.

To Kara Cesare at Ballantine Bantam Dell, the most caring, talented editor a person could wish for, who makes every book a joy to work on.

To Jesse Shuman and the whole team at Ballantine Bantam Dell for their seamless collaboration and enthusiasm: Debbie Aroff and Corina Diez for marketing, Jennifer Garza and Allyson Lord for publicity, Jennifer Hershey, Kim Hovey, Kara Welsh in the publisher's office, Dennis Ambrose in production editorial, copy editor Michelle Daniel, and Elena Giavaldi and Laura Klynstra for cover design.

To Irene Zisblatt, who so generously shared her story. It was a constant touchstone throughout the writing of this book, especially in the girls' camp chapters, for it gave me insight into what it was like to be a child caught in the grip of Nazi experiments. Her wonderful, heartbreaking memoir about her experience, **The Fifth Diamond,** is a testament to the triumph of the human spirit.

To my amazing agent, Alexandra Machinist, who plucked me from the slush pile ten years ago and continues to be the best North Star.

To my sisters, Polly Simpkins for her wisdom, generosity, and unconditional love, and Sally Hatcher, a model big sister.

To my sister-in-law author Mary Pat Kelly, who long ago at a Florida restaurant said, "Just do it."

And to sister-in-law Randy Strapazon, who encouraged me early on to write this story.

To Dr. Stafford L. Cohen, M.D., who so generously shared his research about Nina Iwanska (staffordcohenmd.com).

To Robin Homonoff, who is perfectly named to be a godmother to this book so filled with birds, of **Reading with Robin** fame (www.robinkall.com/reading-with-robin), for helping me name Josie, and for being a great first reader and my go-to for all things Jewish.

To Christophe Belkacemi of the John Frieda Salon for helping me name Arlette and for the best hair and advice on all things French a person could want.

To Melissa Minds VandeBurgt, Head of University Archives and Special Collections at Florida Gulf Coast University, for telling me about Elsie Ragusin and the U.S.A. patch she wore at Ravensbrück and for her untiring work spreading the word about the Ravensbrück Rabbits.

To Peg Shimer, site administrator of the Bellamy-Ferriday House and Gardens, Connecticut Landmarks, for her continuing support and friendship.

To the wonderful Susan McBeth of Adventures by the Book for her unflagging support and for all the sounds of rain.

To Jan Klein for so readily sharing so much information on Jewish mourning.

To Richard Furniss for so generously sharing his knowledge of firearms with me.

ing to state-of-the-art [illegible] with this story.

13. [illegible]

14. [illegible] with [illegible] Jewish.

16. Christopher [illegible] of the Jewish [illegible], for helping me [illegible] and advice on all things [illegible].

17. [illegible] Kings [illegible] about [illegible]

20. [illegible]

21. [illegible]

22. [illegible] Jewish [illegible]

[illegible] so generously [illegible]

ABOUT THE AUTHOR

MARTHA HALL KELLY is the **New York Times** bestselling author of **Lilac Girls, Lost Roses, Sunflower Sisters,** and **The Golden Doves.** She lives in Connecticut and New York City.

marthahallkelly.com

Facebook.com/marthahallkelly

Twitter: @marthahallkelly

Instagram: @marthahallkelly1

LIKE WHAT YOU'VE READ?

Try these titles by Martha Hall Kelly,
also available in large print:

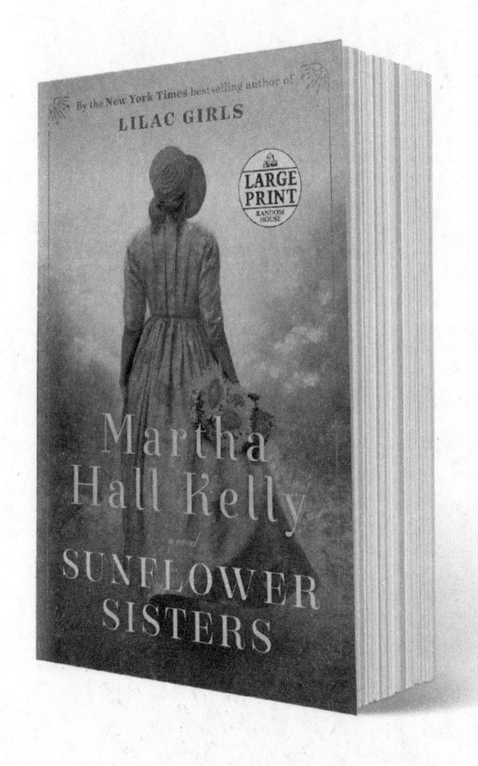

Sunflower Sisters
ISBN 978-0-593-39868-5

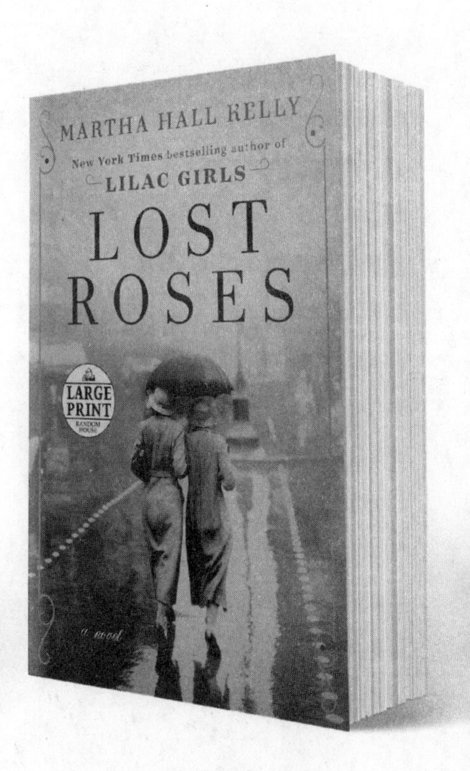

Lost Roses
ISBN 978-1-9848-8621-7

For more information on large print titles, visit
www.penguinrandomhouse.com/large-print-format-books